▶ on target	TIME SCULLEY with PETER GILBERT
	a novel

PROWLER BOOKS

On Target by Tim Sculley with Peter Gilbert

First printing March 2000. Printed in Finland by WS Bookwell.
Cover photography © 2000 MIllivres Prowler Group

web-site: prowler.co.uk
• ISBN 1-902644-32-8

British Library Cataloguing in Publication Data.
A catalogue record for this book is available from the British Library.

contents

CHAPTER ONE

"His greatest asset hangs between his legs. Very appetising," said Adam. "Brown bread or white for your sandwiches?"

"Oh...er... I don't mind. Either/or. I really don't mind. It all tastes the same to me." My mind was still reeling.

"It certainly doesn't. I see I shall have to teach you to be a bit more discriminating. I remember one thing that you enjoyed tasting. Beef or prawns?"

"Beef, please. That was a long time ago, and best forgotten. Actually, I think I ought to get going after the sandwiches. I've got a lot to do and I ought to get a letter written before the last post."

"Balls! Speaking of which, I think you'll be impressed by Steve's. I think I'll give him beef sandwiches too. He likes a bit of meat, does our Steve, as you'll see."

"I really think I ought to go, Adam. Some things are best done in private."

"A quaintly old-fashioned notion. Hang around — I might let you show me how you've advanced since those days."

Those days, as far as I was concerned ,were in the past and long since dead and buried. I can honestly say that I wanted the floor to give way and send me crashing down through ten storeys.

It was a Friday and I had gone to the Taj Mahal for lunch. The firm's canteen always does shepherd's pie on Fridays, and it's no secret that they use up the remains of the previous week's meat.

I was in a happy, self-contented sort of mood in the restaurant. I'd been with Nimrod Systems Ltd. for over a year. It was the job I had always wanted. I had a nice little flat. Just a sitting room, a small bedroom, a tiny little kitchen and an even tinier bathroom, but it suited me. Life was treating me well — at last.

"Good God! Tim Scully!" The familiar voice smashed my happy little world like a hammer on a goldfish bowl. It was Adam Saunders.

I guess that everybody has someone he never wants to see again; a sort of skeleton lurking in a dark cupboard that you never talk about and try to forget. Adam Saunders was my skeleton.

***

We first met at school. I was about sixteen at the time. That would have made Adam seventeen. I knew about myself, of course, but nobody else did. I made sure of that. When you're the son of a serving naval Captain, you don't come out. You didn't at school, either — for, despite what you may have read and heard about boarding schools, just about the quickest way to become an absolute outcast is to admit to being gay. It was at our school, anyway. Sure, we wanked — when we had a chance — but even that wasn't easy with two other boys in the same room, and if we were found out, we told lie after lie about the girl at home.

Adam was the chief among the leading characters of my masturbation fantasies. He was incredibly good-looking. He was tall. He had a really pleasant face and long legs. I don't know how many times I stopped on the drive to do up my shoelaces when he and his cronies were chatting — just so that I could imagine what his cock looked like. I never spoke to him, of course. You didn't. All I knew about him was that he was a pretty good athlete. I made a few very discreet enquiries about him. He wasn't so hot academically but he made up for his lack of brains by over-using his tongue. There was nothing, according to Adam, that he hadn't done — and done well — and there was nothing that he wasn't capable of doing.

One afternoon, I was standing on the steps of the squash court watching the departing figure of my opponent, Ashley Duarte-Dyson, vanishing down the drive. If I am to be honest with you, the sight of his long legs and neat little behind was provoking some very pleasant thoughts. I was suddenly aware of a person standing next to me. It was Adam Saunders.

"Nice," he said.

"Beg pardon?"

"Nice, attractive curve to his backside. Make a good fuck. Bit tight at first, I think, but once he got used to it…"

I couldn't believe my ears. I thought I must have misheard. I'd been thinking exactly the same thing, but for some reason that I have never fathomed out, I was so revolted that I felt physically sick.

My first instinct was to say "Sod off!" I didn't. I just stood still.

"I might have a go at that one day," he said. "Fancy another game?"

I'd recovered some of my composure by that time. "What sort of game do you have in mind?" I asked. My heart had started to pound. I'd never seen Adam Saunders in squash kit before. That had a lot to do with it. The blond hairs on his legs, I noticed, were exactly the colour of his hair. I wondered about the hair elsewhere on his body.

"Squash, of course. What do you think I am?" I began to think that the earlier conversation must have been some sort of daydream.

So we played squash and I got well and truly beaten. I knew I would be. I wasn't really concentrating on the game. Those long honey-coloured legs and tiny shorts got most of my attention and when, halfway through the game, he peeled off his sweat shirt, it was all I could do to hold the racquet, let alone get the ball in the right places. I wondered if he was going to suggest taking a shower together. There were showers in the squash courts, but hardly anybody used them. For a start, they weren't kept very clean, and the supply of hot water was always problematic.

He didn't. We finished the game. He said something about playing again some time. I nodded agreement and we went our separate ways. He had some work to do and I was desperate to relieve built-up tension. Fortunately, my two room-mates weren't in.

I really can't remember how the walks round the sports field started. I guess we must have met there accidentally and one of us — it could easily have been me — suggested taking a stroll. Soon they became a daily event. I was surprised that Adam could afford the time. He was due to take his A levels in a matter of weeks. Every afternoon, when lessons ended, we set out from the pavilion and circumnavigated the entire sports area — sometimes twice. Any onlookers — you never did anything in that school without being seen — seeing each of us in such unusual company possibly thought we were revising. How wrong can you be?

In fairness, I have to say that I usually came up with the subject for discussion and then let Adam take over. Little frissons of excitement ran up and down my spine as he elaborated on the theme of the day. There was a Canadian boy who had just joined the school and had been put into my class. Ralph something. He kept Adam going for days on end. If wishes had been turned into reality, Ralph would have died of exhaustion.

Then came one afternoon in the middle of the A levels. I remember that Adam said the paper he'd done that morning was a piece of cake. We were just approaching a cricket sight-screen and I was enthusing about someone. I can't remember who it was. All I can remember is that I had seen him in the showers. Adam wanted to know all the details.

"It's enormous! Thick, too," I said.

"Suckable. Suitably suckable," said Adam and, once again, it was if he was reading my mind. I said nothing but he was beginning to worry me. Nonetheless, I altered my schedule on the next day so that I was in the showers when the boy concerned came down. I had to sit for ages on the bench which ran round the room after he had gone upstairs again, and wait till the lump in my towel had subsided sufficiently for me to stand up.

"You know what you said yesterday about cocks?" I said that afternoon. Adam at that moment wasn't discoursing about cocks, although they were his favourite anatomical feature. Adam could rhapsodise about penises for ninety-seven minutes — that was two slow circuits of the sports field.

"Oh yes. The guy you saw in the showers. How is he — or should I say 'it'?"

"Both fine as far as I know." I wasn't going to let on. In fact, I could have described it in the finest detail, right down the faint line of hair which connected it to the boy's navel.

"Going to go for it, are you?"

"In this place? You must be joking!"

"It's easy enough to find a place if you look carefully enough."

"Like where, for instance?"

"The New House boiler-room. Eminently suitable. Central heating on hand for those cold winter afternoons, and the only person who ever goes in there is the caretaker — and he's a part-timer."

"Have you been in there, then?" Curiosity was overcoming caution.

"Many times."

"Oh yes! Who with?"

"Mark Lester, Harry Walton, Robert Cosford, Matt McBrine...."

He had to be lying. I didn't know the first three very well, but Matt McBrine was a close friend. His father was a naval officer too, and we'd been at prep school together. I was determined to call Adam's bluff as he related how he'd got a finger right into Harry Walton's backside and how Robert Cosford had wriggled with pleasure at what Adam had done to him. It was all nonsense, of course. I realised that. I may not have known the other three very well, but I did know Matt. What would Matt say if I asked if his balls had really been in Adam's mouth? I knew very well what he would say, and I had a good idea of what he would do. I'd have an aching jaw for weeks. Adam's description of him might well have been accurate for all I knew. His cock was uncircumcised. I knew that, but then, so were ninety-nine percent of the others in the school. Whether or not it was about six and a half inches long when aroused I had no idea. I had only caught very brief glimpses of it. The only thing I could pick him up on was the boiler-room.

"Show me," I said, expecting him to find at least three good reasons why it was impossible on that particular afternoon. Instead, to my surprise, he agreed.

Following his lead, I pushed through a hedge and slunk round the windowless building. The doors were steel and, although there was a clasp, there was no lock. Adam pulled one of them open. We slipped inside. "There you are," he said, turning on the lights. "How about that?"

The railing between the boiler and the concrete walkway were exactly as he had described. There was no doubt that he had been in there before. I still had strong doubts about the stories, but the most extraordinary thing was happening to me. School trips to the Tower of London had evoked the occasional excited shudder when I came face to face with an axe which had gone through several people's necks. That railing had a similar effect. An axe did nothing to my penis, but the thought of Matt McBrine hanging on to that rail, writhing in a paroxysm of lust whilst Adam's fingers and tongue worked on him, brought my cock to attention in seconds. Unfortunately, Adam noticed. He reached down and felt it through my trousers. I did the same to him. He wasn't exactly unmoved, either. He whispered something. I nodded. I couldn't speak for excitement.

We undressed. I didn't want to, but Adam insisted. He leaned back over the railing with his arms behind it and I knelt on the hard concrete floor in front of him. That was the first time I had ever touched somebody else's cock and the first time I had ever had one in my mouth. I didn't do very well. I let it slip out of my mouth at the last moment and ended up with his spunk dribbling down my chest from my shoulder. I didn't need any help. Mine splattered over the floor. There was a pile of old rags in the corner. We used those to clean up, and slunk out again.

That was the first time. After that it became a daily occurrence until we were caught. We were so lucky.

We'd taken to wearing track suits for our walks — which got shorter and shorter as our sessions in the boiler-room got longer. Track suits are much more convenient for what we both had in mind. Once inside, the tops and bottoms were off in seconds. I slipped off my boxers. Adam at that time wore those athletic things. They came off easily enough. It sprang up eagerly enough. I was always a bit nervous — at least at first — but once I'd got it in my mouth, and his balls in my hand, I was in a world of my own: a world which seemed timeless until the moment Adam's thighs tightened and he lunged forward.

After that it was my turn. Adam liked me to bend over the railing. He'd press up close behind me and put his hand round my waist and toss me off in that position. The railing was uncomfortable so I padded it with my tracksuit.

I suppose we'd been doing it every afternoon for about six weeks when we were caught. It happened to be a very wet day, so we cut the walk and the talk down to a few minutes. We pulled off our track suits and hung them on the railing, where they soon began to steam. They weren't the only things steaming that afternoon. He'd brought some special stuff with him. In the last few days he had tickled my ass. Once he'd even licked it. That felt pleasant enough, but I didn't view the prospect as eagerly as he hoped I might.

"You'll go wild once you've got a finger in there," he said. "They all ...."

At that moment the door opened and Mr. Bailey, the Housemaster, stood framed in the doorway.

"I thought I heard something," he said. "What the hell do you think you're doing in here?"

I don't know what made me think of it. God, I imagine. I explained that we'd got soaked and had decided to dry our clothes in the boiler-room. He believed me. My cock was pointing stiffly towards him, tenting my boxers. Adam's had actually found a gap between cotton and thigh and was pushing eagerly through. Amazingly, Mr. Bailey didn't seem to notice. He told us to get dressed. We promised never to go into the boiler-house again and that was the end of the matter.

The new padlock on the boiler-house door wasn't the only thing that closed my sex life at school. The McAlpine scandal hit the newspapers soon after I got home. I imagine that, like most people, you just read the headlines and turned to something more interesting. Unfortunately, my dad worked in the Ministry of Defence and knew the people involved. For most of that holiday, it was the sole subject of dinner-time conversation.

Malcolm McAlpine was a civil servant in the Ministry. He was the man who awarded armaments contracts to the various suppliers of what they call 'military hardware'. It turned out that McAlpine was gay, and that many directors of the companies involved were gay, too. Apparently the investigators went in and uncovered all sorts of oddities. There was a Rear Admiral who enjoyed spanking teenage boys' bottoms. A senior civil servant and the contracts manager of a firm which made radar equipment ran a Boy Scout group together, and had orgies round the camp fire. Some new aspect of the McAlpine scandal broke into the papers almost every day.

"I'd horsewhip the buggers and then put 'em in prison and throw away the key," said my dad one evening. The managing director of the firm which supplied torpedoes had admitted that he was homosexual.

"Do the torpedoes work all right, dear?" my mother asked.

"Of course they work. We wouldn't have bought them if they didn't."

"Then I can't see what all the fuss is about." Nor, come to that, could I, but my comments were never welcome.

"Corruption like that spreads. One rotten apple contaminates all the rest. It wouldn't have happened in your dad's day. They didn't have fairies in those days."

"Don't talk nonsense. Of course they did. It's just that in those days things weren't so open as they are now. Do you remember Mr. Bullimore, the works manager?"

"Can't say I do. It was a long time ago," said my dad.

"You met him several times when we were courting. Collected china dolls and grew orchids..."

"No." Even I could see that dad wanted to change the subject.

"He fancied you. I could see that right from the start. You must remember him. He invited us round to his place often enough, but you never wanted to go."

"Well, there won't be any more fairies in the Ministry or the industry from now on. They're going to screen everyone from the First Lord right down to the lowest tea-boy."

"Mr. Bullimore must have retired," said my mum. "I wonder if there are any more up there. I must tell mum. She'll be interested."

"Don't you dare. Investigations like this are secret," said dad.

At this point I had better let you in on something else that I keep to myself. My grandfather — that's my mum's dad — founded Weaver's, one of the biggest privately owned armaments firms in the world. Some of the things which came out of their factory in Yorkshire did a lot to help us win the Second World

War and, of course, they're still going.

Grandad died when I was little. I loved visiting the factory with him. Possibly that's where I got the notion of going into the industry myself. I could utilise my enthusiasm for computers in an industry that never seems to experience slumps. Gran was still very much alive and she plays a very important part in this story, as you will see. But back to that dinner-table conversation.

"How can they possibly find out about people?" I asked. "If a man says he's not gay and if he doesn't get caught doing anything, how can you tell that he is?"

"Oh, they have their ways," said my dad. "They find out who his friends were and are and they ask them. They find out who he was at school with and make a few enquiries there."

I actually felt myself going pale. The future I'd envisaged for myself, doing research on computer guided missile systems, seemed about to evaporate. For all I knew, Adam could at that very moment be with some friend in his home town, sounding his mouth off. Knowing his gift for wild imaginings, I had a pretty good idea what he was saying. "There's this chap at school. Tim Scully is his name. God! He can't get enough of it. Of course he finds it difficult to take it all in."

At least, I thought miserably, he might do me the favour of exaggerating the size of mine when they came to interview him. I was never very happy with the size of my cock.

"So just make sure you use it for its proper purpose. Don't do anything daft," said my dad.

"I wouldn't." I tried to look him in the eye.

"Of course he wouldn't! What a thing to say to your own son!" said my mum indignantly, and dad shut up.

When I got back to school in September I was shattered to find Adam in the same form as me. Not, thank goodness, in the same house. He'd failed his A levels badly and was going to have another go. I think he was similarly shattered. It can't have been easy for him after all his bullshit about Oxford and Cambridge fighting each other for the privilege of having him.

He was still the same old Adam in other respects. We still went for the occasional walk, but nothing else. According to him, he was having it off with one of his room-mates; a boy called Miles Merton. I was happy enough to listen to highly unlikely accounts of the delight Miles experienced when impaled on

Adam's cock and of Miles' insatiable appetite for Adam's spunk. He showed me the condoms he'd bought especially for use with (or in) Miles. We'd part at the pavilion and I'd go back to my house, have a solitary wank and then get back to my studies — a routine which paid off. I passed my A levels reasonably well and the University of Brighton accepted me for a Bachelor of Science course in Computer Studies. I celebrated my eighteenth birthday at home with my parents. They wanted me to ask some friends from school, but I didn't. All in all, that was a pleasant summer; mostly because Adam was in the past. There were several nights when I wanked to memories of being with Adam. I remember thinking, as I wiped it dry, what a good thing it was that I would never see him again.

CHAPTER TWO

University was an eye-opener. They had told us it would be. I was prepared to work alone without close supervision. It was great to be able to hand in an assignment slightly late and not get put down by sarcastic remarks. I actually enjoyed digging out information for myself in the library. At times I felt a bit like I'd had some sort of metamorphosis and woken up in a strange environment but, generally speaking, I managed to cope with the change. There were shocks. The first was discovering that there was a gay club. I was tempted several times to pay a visit. They met in a pub in the town on Tuesday evenings. I didn't go. I was far too anxious to get a job with Nimrod and both my dad and my tutor had warned that the security people would be checking up on me. The Tim Scully who went to Brighton University was much the same as Tim Scully the schoolboy. I worked hard. I went out with the lads about once a week for a drink and laughed with them about "queers" and "arse-bandits". I told them about Susan at home and showed them her picture. Susan was actually my cousin, which enabled me to describe her home life and hobbies without having to wonder what lies I had told about her on previous occasions.

And then I went back to my digs, did a bit of studying, turned in for the night and then, just as I had at school, I could let my imagination run riot. My consumption of tissues must have made Mrs Higgs, my landlady, think I suffered from perpetual catarrh. Mrs Higgs lived in Hove, which is the "upper class" end of Brighton. My father had found her. She was the widow of a Royal Navy Commander. She had a huge photograph of him saluting and staring down through hooded eyes at the old-fashioned but expensive furniture in her lounge.

Mrs Higgs graded everybody into classes. There were "a nice class of people", amongst whom, I am glad to say, I was included, by virtue of dad's job. Then there were the others. There were "rather common people" and "common people", with whom she had nothing to do and for whom she had nothing but contempt. Common people, according to her, bought their food from the Co-op and had massive hire purchase debts. They also sent their sons and daughters to university.

"In a few years time there won't be a manual worker to be found and there'll be queues of graduates looking for soft jobs. I'm just glad I shan't be around to see it," she said — often.

But Mrs Higgs didn't worry me. In fact, Mrs Higgs spoilt me. She was an excellent cook. I hardly ate anything for breakfast, but it was nice to come home for a huge evening meal. I offered to wash up, but she wouldn't hear of it. "You've got more important things to do," she said. "Run upstairs now and buckle down to it."

I did, but not to my studies. I developed a technique which was infinitely better than the furtive wanks I'd enjoyed at school. My bed at Mrs Higgs' house was a large one and the two pillows were supported on a long bolster. Thinking hard about the person of my choice — and there was no shortage of potential candidates — I'd get undressed and feel it around for a bit to get it really stone-hard. After that, I arranged the bolster lengthways in the bed, padded it at the appropriate place with a wad of tissues and then, hugging it for all I was worth, I fucked it.

Chief amongst the potential replacements for a latex-stuffed, cotton-covered item of bed furniture was Bob Haywood. Bob was in my group and that's really all I knew about him. He was so shy that it was almost impossible to get a word out of him. If a lecturer spoke to him, Bob's face went red and he stammered so badly that the lecturer soon gave up and diverted the question to somebody else. I don't honestly know why I was so attracted to Bob. He was quite good-looking, I suppose. He was tall, a little on the plump side, and he had short, black, shiny hair. I think it was his smile. He didn't smile very often, but when he did my heart started to race. It was a pathetic little smile; the sort that says "I'm smiling despite the awful tragedy of my life". It made you want to rush over and hug him. It made me want to, anyway.

That's as far as it went. I had made an absolute and irrevocable decision to lead a totally chaste life. If Catholic priests could do it, so could I. I cursed Adam time and time again - usually in the middle of the night when my fantasies about Bob Haywood had got the better of me and I ended up with a clump of soggy tissue. But there was to be no more actual sex. On that point I was adamant.... for four months and seventeen days.

Tim Scully with Peter Gilbert

I was in Boots, the Chemists. I was due to go home that weekend with the usual pile of washing. My mum has a neurosis about the condition of my toothbrushes so I thought I'd forestall her and get a new one. I'd just about got to the display rack when I thought I heard a familiar voice. I looked over the top of the rack. There was no doubt as to who it was. Even at weekends at school, Adam never seemed to wear old jeans. They always looked brand new. It was him. Pale blue jeans with sharp creases forming an inverted V on his backside together with what I would describe as a tank-top, save that it had obviously not come from the same sort of shop I used. He was over at the pharmaceutical counter talking to the assistant. I just heard the words "I'd better take two tubes then.".

I panicked. There's no other word for it. I grabbed the nearest toothbrush, rushed to the cashiers by the door, paid for it and was outside on the pavement within minutes. Then common sense took over again. "So?" it asked. "You've just seen Adam. What of it? You don't have to speak to him. You're your own boss." Distractedly, I reached into the plastic bag in my hand and pulled out the brush I'd just bought. "DENTURE BRUSH' was printed in large letters on the wrapping. I was still staring at it, wondering whether to go back and change it or sling it into a rubbish bin, when he came out.

He didn't seem in the least surprised to see me. He made no attempt even to shake hands. "I wondered when we'd run into each other," he said.

"And you?" I said. "What happened to Oxford and Cambridge?"

"Brighton's much better for business studies. Besides which, it has certain other advantages, as I guess you've found out."

I knew what he was talking about, of course. You can't be in Brighton for more than a few weeks without finding out that the town has a considerable gay population.

I agreed that Brighton wasn't bad. He asked if I had time for a drink and I, like a mesmerised rabbit, said I had. It would have been so easy to invent an excuse but I didn't. We ended up in the bar of the King and Queen, a mock olde worlde pub not far from the seafront. I'd left my car at Mrs Higgs' that day and gone into town by bus, so we drove to the King and Queen in Adam's bright red Mazda MX 5. The car, I thought, was typical of Adam. He always had to have something better than anyone else. At that time I was driving a second-hand Metro, and finding it hard going to keep it on the road.

"So what do you do with yourself when you're not working?" he asked as I took my first sip of John Smith's.

I had a sudden vision of a bolster and of the matching curtains and bedspread in my room. "Nothing much. You?" I replied.

"Ha! Three guesses. What a place, eh? A bit different from school. I had it off every night last week. A different one every time. God! They come out of the woodwork for you."

I didn't believe him, of course. I looked round the bar. Fortunately there was nobody within hearing distance. "Oh yes?" I said, trying hard to sound uninterested.

"Just been to Boots to re-stock on essentials," he continued. "Would you believe it, they don't have the giant size K Y. I know they make one. Our vet's got a tub in his surgery. These tubes don't last long in a place like this." His eye fell on the Boots bag sticking out of my pocket. "Looks like you've been doing the same thing," he said. I explained that I had bought a toothbrush on behalf of my landlady.

"Landlady, eh? Doesn't sound much fun," he said, and that gave me the chance I was waiting for. There was no way I was going to have Adam Saunders pestering me. I told him that Mrs Higgs rarely went out and even when she did, she invariably returned hours earlier than the time she'd told me. I told him about her insatiable nosiness: how she often barged into my room without warning — all of which was a pack of lies, but I finished off with the truth: that she knew my dad and that my parents occasionally came down to Brighton for a weekend.

"Bugger that!" said Adam. "I've got a flat."

"A flat?" I asked.

"Sure. Dad pays the rent. Usual thing. Kitchen, bathroom, lounge, two bedrooms. One for studying and the other for you know what."

"Where is it?" I asked.

"Just outside the town. Not far. I'll tell you what. Why don't you come out and have a look?"

"Could do, I suppose." What in heaven's name made me say that? I knew when I said it that it was a crazy idea. Again, I could have got out of it so easily — but I didn't. We drank up and set off.

I had a mental picture of a block of luxury flats. That image dispersed as we drove. The surroundings became seedier and seedier. Betting shops, video shops and various charity shops selling second-hand clothing appeared on both sides of the road. It was typical of Adam, I thought. I half expected the 'flat' to turn out to be a bed-sit. In fact, 2A Mersham Parade was above a fish and chip shop. To enter, you had to go into a small yard and then up a cast iron staircase. Steam, stinking of fish and chips, blew from a ventilator under the staircase.

"Here we are," said Adam, producing the key and unlocking the door. "Welcome to the knocking shop. This is where it all hangs out."

He showed me the lounge, which I thought rather too large for comfort. The furniture was nice. I like that bent beech-wood stuff. He showed me his work room. (His study, he called it.) Now I may be a bit dumb in some respects, as you have found out by now, but I do know something about computers. That one of his eclipsed mine. There was no reason whatsoever for a business studies student to have a thing like that, no matter how many programs he'd installed. It was typical of Adam. Then he showed me the bedroom. The bed was no exception to the Adam rule. It was huge and he'd made no attempt to tidy up. The duvet was half on the bed and half on the floor and the corner of a pillow peeped from underneath it. I wondered for a moment if his tale of nightly sex had been true, and then dismissed the idea.

Back in the lounge he made coffee. We talked about school. Not about sex or about us. Just school. That was reassuring. Silly little incidents but they brought back happy memories. Mr. Barker's strange habit of scratching his left ear by putting his right hand over the top of his head. Mr Bourton's pronouncements. "In Switzerland the milk comes down wires" and "India is much bigger than this map". We laughed at them all. Then Adam brought up the subject of Mr. Goodchild, somebody I didn't want to remember. Everybody at the school save, apparently, the Headmaster knew about Mr. Goodchild's penchant for the bottoms of very small boys. Thank God I was never in the prep department, having come from another school, but I suffered his attentions during my first year there.

"He was an evil sod," I said. To my amazement, Adam disagreed.

"He was okay. He knew what he liked. He got it, too. None of us minded. That's why he's still there."

"None of us? You mean you….?"

"Sure."

The thought of Adam, who was just beginning to come across as not a bad bloke after all, being subjected even to the minor attentions I had received was nauseating. I hadn't drunk too much but my mouth tasted of vomit. I swallowed it back.

"If it hadn't been for him, we would never have met," said Adam.

"How do you mean?"

"He reckoned you had it in you. You just needed to be brought out. That's what he said. I used to go to tea with him on Sunday afternoons — not for sex, of course. That had finished long ago, but he gave me some good tips. You would have been what when we first met? Sixteen?"

"That's right."

"Always watch out for the loners. That's what he said. That Scully boy now. He spends far too much time on his own. A boy like that needs a helping hand."

"What else did he say about me?"

"Nothing much." I could see that he was holding something back, so I persisted.

"Come on. Tell me."

"Just about one incident. He said you had a lovely bottom when you were thirteen."

At that point there was nothing for it. I made a dash for the toilet and got rid of two pints of John Smith's, together with what was left of my lunch. I sat on the lavatory seat for some minutes getting my thoughts together and wondering why I couldn't leave the flat and Adam and why I couldn't banish all memories of Adam and Mr. Goodchild for ever. My life seemed blighted. I'd never be able to escape from the past. They'd both see to that.

"You won't tell anybody, will you sir?"

"Of course not, Tim. This will be our little secret."

"I meant the cigarette."

"That's forgotten already. You were a silly boy to smoke right outside my window, though. I couldn't see who it was but I saw the smoke. You must promise me never to do that again."

"I promise."

"Good. My word! You have got a lovely bottom, haven't you? What a shame that your parents sent you to Mill House Prep and not here. Come and lie across my lap."

"You're not going to smack me, are you sir?"

"Certainly not. Bottoms like yours are for feeling and kissing. Not smacking."

I had to stand up again. I only just had time to open the loo-seat before I was sick again. I cleaned up at the wash basin and went, unsteadily, back into the lounge.

"You don't look too good," said Adam. I made some excuse about my not being used to South Coast beer and cigarette smoke.

"Yet another thing you need to get used to," said Adam. "Have a brandy. That might do you good."

I started on a long-winded excuse about having to get back to Mrs Higgs. He didn't stop to listen. The brandy appeared. I sipped it. It did make me feel a bit better.

"Old Bailey wasn't a bad bloke," said Adam. "Lucky he didn't come into the boiler-house a few minutes later," he added. A shiver ran down my spine. Why did he have to keep on about sex?

"I wonder if he realised but decided to say nothing," he continued. I'd been wondering the same thing for nearly a year. If he had, there might still be a possibility that my coveted job with Nimrod might come to nothing.

"No. He'd have gone ballistic if he had," I said.

"He must have been as short-sighted as hell. I had a hard-on. You did, too."

"Well, he didn't seem to notice. Let's leave it at that," I said. I was wasting my breath. Adam leaned back on the sofa. "Those were good times," he said. "Pity they locked the boiler-house."

I was glad. If we hadn't been discovered and they hadn't sealed it off, we would have been in there every afternoon. I knew myself well enough to realise that. In fact, just being in the same room as Adam was beginning to have a slight physical effect. It was time I went — but I didn't.

"It was good fun though, eh?" he said.

That remark annoyed me. I didn't see myself as a fun object for anybody. "For you, maybe," I said.

"Oh come off it, old boy. You enjoyed it. Slobbering on it like a kid with his first ice cream, you were, and now that we've met up at last...." He stood up and walked over to where I was sitting. The creases in his jeans had been augmented by a large bulge. There was nothing for it but to explain my position. I told him about the McAlpine scandal's effect on the industry and about my dad. He said dad was exaggerating. I said I wasn't prepared to take the risk.

"But who would know?" he asked. There's only me and you. No hidden cameras and no recorders."

I wasn't falling for that. "You. You're the risk," I said. "You just can't help bragging. It'd be all over Brighton within days. You know damn well it would."

I quite thought then that he'd admit that his so-called 'conquests' had been a pack of lies, but he didn't. "You don't understand, do you?" he said, sitting down in the chair next to me. "The others are good fun, I admit. You're different. I like you and we were at school together. Chaps like us never rat on each other. I wouldn't say a word. I thought you realised."

I hadn't. It would be true to say that Adam never exhibited the slightest indication of affection at school. I didn't know what to say. 'Prove it' would have had disastrous results.

"I wanted to write in August. I rang the school but they wouldn't give me your address," he said. "Then I read in the yearbook that you were going to Brighton so I decided to come here. I went to the computer studies people and all they would tell me was that you were here but they wouldn't give me an address or phone number."

"What's wrong with sticking a note in my pigeonhole?" I asked.

"Never gave it a thought, to be honest. I knew we were bound to meet up sooner or later."

"And here we are," I said. My voice sounded strange. My mouth had gone dry and my throat felt constricted; the same feeling that I get when the dental nurse opens the door and calls my name.

"And here we are," Adam echoed. He looked at his watch. "Ten past five," he said. "Does the dragon do you an evening meal?"

"Mrs Higgs? Yes. I'd better be off soon. I've got some work to do as well."

"Couldn't you ring her?"

"What for?"

"Tell her you're staying the night. We can get fish and chips from downstairs."

"No way! Sorry, Adam. Definitely not," I said. "I'll be off." I drank the last drop of brandy, put the glass back and stood up.

"I'll run you back," he said. I said there was no need. Buses ran every ten minutes along the main road. He stayed sitting in his chair. I went to shake hands. He grinned, grasped my hand and pulled me towards him. I lost my balance and before I knew where I was, I found myself sitting on his lap. The guys at school who'd known him had all said that he was incredibly strong. He really was. He put both arms round my chest and there was no way that I could struggle out of that grip.

"And here we are," he said again, whispering the words into my ear. I struggled again and he pressed against my chest so hard that I couldn't breathe. I stopped struggling and he relaxed his grip.

"What time is the evening meal at the dragon's lair?" he asked.

"Eight o'clock."

"And how much work have you got to do before then?"

"Not a lot." My resistance had evaporated. I knew why. So did Adam. He reached down and touched it through my jeans.

"I've missed this," he said. If the truth is to be told, there was something I had missed too. I could feel it against my backside. It was like sitting on a broom handle.

"Stand up," he whispered. I did so. So did he. For a few seconds we just stood there looking at each other. Our faces were only inches apart. I wondered if he was going to kiss me. In the state I was in, I wouldn't have minded but he didn't. I felt his hands on my waist. He started to undo the buckle on my jeans. I did the same to him. He undid the top button and pulled down the zip. So did I. I was wearing a tee shirt. His had buttons. I opened them, starting from the top, and, when I had finished, raised my arms. He pulled off my tee shirt. Getting shoes and socks off wasn't easy. We were breathing like a couple of walruses and sitting down when you've got an erection can be pretty uncomfortable but we managed it. We stood up again. My jeans were the first to come off. Then his.

They were the same legs and the same golden hairs. His belly was as flat as I had remembered it and he still had the huge brown circles round his tits. The only thing that had changed was his taste in underwear. This time Adam was in boxers, as I was, and what I really wanted to feel and taste was making its presence very clear indeed. He slid mine down first. I stepped out of them and, putting my fingers in the waist band, I slid his down. His cock popped out and cannoned against my thigh. It felt strangely cool.

Adam reached down and took mine in his fingers. I looked up at his face. He smiled. I took hold of his. I'd forgotten what it felt like to have that huge, silky cock in my hand. I ran my fingers up and down its surface. Adam grinned. "You want it, don't you?" he said.

Up to that moment something in my brain had been telling me what an idiot I was and urging me to get out of that flat as soon as I could. It shut up. Adam let go of my cock and put his hands on my shoulders, pressing down on them. I got the message. I lay on the floor. For a moment it was like being under some sort of colossus. The hairs on the lower part of his legs stood out clearly. The rest of him was slightly out of focus — except for that gigantic cock sticking out from a patch of hair as thick as a piece of coconut matting. Then he got down on his knees somewhere behind my head and it swayed enticingly a few inches from my eyes. He leaned forward over me. It touched my forehead, then my nose and brushed against my lips. The familiar odour brought back memories of school. Names flashed through my mind. Walton, Cosford, McBrine, They had all been in Adam's imagination, but this was real. I opened my mouth and took his cock in. I felt Adam licking in my pubes and then my cock, too, was engulfed. I felt his lips sliding up and down the shaft. I didn't need to move my head. Adam was doing all the work. His cock reached the back of my mouth. I think I choked slightly. It moved back a bit and then went down again. Instinctively, I brought up my knees and felt Adam's head against my thighs. His massive member was suffocating me. I pushed up against his hip bones. He got the message and lifted his body. I coughed, took a couple of deep breaths and then let my tongue flick over his cock head. He did the same to mine.

I don't know how long it lasted. I don't even know who came first. It was almost as if I'd fainted. I remember choking slightly as his spunk pumped into my mouth, but not a drop was lost that time. I made sure of that. I wanted as much of Adam as I could get and I swallowed every drop. So did he. There wasn't even a fleck on either of us or on his beige carpet.

"Christ! That was something else!" said Adam when we were standing up again. "Do you know something?"

"No. What?" I asked, still gazing at that beautiful swaying cock.

"You're as good as ever!" he said. It was the first compliment he'd ever paid me. I blushed and muttered something similar about him.

"Let's make it a regular thing, eh?" he said.

"Could do, I guess," I replied, pulling my boxers up over my still half-hard cock.

He gave me his phone number and the number of his mobile phone when we were in the car. He insisted on driving me to Mrs Higgs' house. I wasn't keen. Hove and Mrs Higgs' house were one part of my life and sex and Adam were another. It felt wrong for his car even to be in my territory.

"Give me a call," he said as I opened the car door.

"Sure," I replied. I stood on the pavement as the car swept away and then went indoors.

"Who was that, Tim?" Mrs Higgs must have been watching through the lace curtains.

"Oh, an old school friend. He's at college here too."

"You must invite him round. What does his father do?"

"I don't actually know. I think he's some sort of property developer. Something like that."

Mrs Higgs frowned. "Hmm. Not exactly the cream of society."

"Oh I don't know, Mrs Higgs. Just a different sort of cream, really," I replied and I licked my lips as I went upstairs.

CHAPTER THREE

"It's someone for you, Tim dear," said Mrs Higgs. "A young man, by the sound of his voice."

I took the receiver from her. As always, she hovered near the phone.

"Hello," I said.

"Hi. It's me. Adam. Long time no see. Why not get that delectable little ass of yours over here?"

Four weeks had elapsed since that disastrous night. Four weeks of misery. I had broken my firm resolution never to have sex. I felt dirty and guilty. Adam must have realised that I never wanted to see him again. I said something about having far too much to do. He didn't sound in the least disappointed. He just said something like "Oh, okay then," and put the phone down.

"One of your student friends?" Mrs Higgs asked. I said it was and went upstairs again.

"You can always ask your friends to tea, Tim," she called after me. "It's not good for a young man to be alone as much as you are." No truer words had ever been spoken, but the idea of Adam eating cream cakes in Mrs Higgs' house did not appeal.

I lay on the bed. That was a silly thing to do. I tried to think about other things; the family and Ben, my dog who had cut his paw when dad had taken him for a walk; college work — but Adam kept intruding. The were several matters I wanted to clear up. I wanted to tell Adam that I never wanted to see him again. The trouble was that I knew very well that if I did see him, I wouldn't be able to say it. And there was something else...

Two days after that incident I was sitting with Mary Grimshaw and Alec Maine in the 'Agadir' — a coffee bar much frequented by students — when Bob Haywood came in. Amazingly, he made a bee-line for our table. I'd never seen him in there before. Bob didn't mix. He sat himself down. Alec and Mary continued to talk about some disco they'd been to. He listened without saying anything and then, turning to me, he said, "Did I see you in Adam Saunders' car the other morning?"

I hope the other two didn't notice my reaction.

"No. Who's Adam Saunders?" I said.

"I could have sworn it was you. I was at the bus stop and you went straight past me."

"Where was this?" I asked, beginning to get my composure back.

"Out on the Ditchling Road."

"Well, it couldn't have been me, could it? I live in Hove."

Alec and Mary made the usual daft remarks about the residents of Hove. 'A nice hice with a lovely lynge, my dear!'

"You've got a double, then," said Bob and that brought even more witticisms from Alec and Mary. For some days after that I was worried. How the hell did a shy, retiring person like Bob Haywood come to know a big mouth like Adam Saunders? More important, as he obviously did know him, was he going to ask Adam the same question?

As the days turned into weeks it appeared that he hadn't. Bob never mentioned the subject again, and I found myself getting more and more interested in him. He was undeniably very good-looking. There was something in that shy smile of his that began to appeal to me. I knew that quite a few of the girls were barmy about him. They didn't get very far, and neither did I. He rarely, if ever, spoke, and when lectures were over for the day he just vanished. You never saw Bob at any social functions or in pubs.

Something Mrs Higgs said stuck in my mind. She was entertaining Mrs House of the Women's Institute at the time. (She actually did call her Mrs Hice!)

"The late Commander Higgs always said the quiet ones are the worst," Mrs Higgs was saying as I went into the lounge. "You never know what nasty little emotions are boiling in their brains." Bob never gave the slightest sign that anything was even simmering in his brain, but it would be interesting to find out.

I suppose I must have spent half an hour thinking before, with Mrs Higgs' permission, I rang Adam. I said I wouldn't mind coming out for a drink. Nothing else, I emphasised. Just a drink.

We met again in the King and Queen. I didn't expect an apology. Adam was never a man to apologise. I thought I might get some sort of explanation, but no. We talked about our studie,; the candidates for election to the Students' Union and, of course, memories of school. Adam had been back to collect a table lamp he had made in woodwork classes and which had been in some sort of exhibition in London.

"I gather Bob Haywood is a mate of yours," I said, over the second pint of the evening.

"Yes. Why do you ask?"

"He saw us together on that morning you drove me to college. I said it wasn't me."

"That's good. He asked me too. I said he must have had a bit too much the night before."

"He's not the only one," I said. Adam looked a bit perplexed. "You didn't have any more than I did," he said.

"I wasn't referring to beer."

"Oh, I see." He grinned. "You can't hold me responsible for my sex appeal," he said.

That idiotic self-satisfied grin did it. Something snapped in my brain. I told him exactly what I thought of him. "You planned the whole thing in advance, didn't you?" I said. "Get Scully pissed and then lure him back to your place for a bit of sex. Just like school. Get Scully interested and then get him in the boiler-house. You know bloody well I want to get into armaments. You know bloody well that I don't stand a chance if they find out I'm gay. "

They're not likely to, are they?" he said.

"With you that's a joke. I imagine you've told all your mates every detail. No doubt they had a good laugh."

"Of course I haven't. Public school ethics and all that. Just not done, old boy. Just not done, besides, I am really fond of you. Always have been."

I said something about a 'funny idea of ethics'. He changed the subject. Not for long and I have an awful feeling that it was me who brought up the subject of Bob Haywood again. We'd had a couple more beers.

"Did Bob get the same treatment as I did?" I asked.

"To some extent. Bob is a very well-equipped young man who is learning to be accommodating. He's not quite ready yet. Give it time."

It must have been the beer. My temper abated and I was ready to listen. It was quite like old times, when we had walked around the sports field at school. According to Adam, Bob was the shy possessor of seven inches of prime uncut cock. He had huge balls and what Adam described as the prettiest arse he'd seen in years.

"Which you intend to penetrate?" I said, crossing my legs under the table. The old fascination had got me again.

"Of course. Bob is due for Burton Clayhanger some time next month."

"Due for what?"

Adam said he had a friend; an elderly man who doted upon him and who lived in the remote Somerset hamlet of Burton Clayhanger. "A pathetic old soul really," he said. "His teenage lover died in the sixties in a motorbike accident. He's a good cook. He's generous and, most important, he's got a spare room with a double bed."

"I didn't know you went for old men," I said.

"Come off it! What do you take me for? Christ, no! Mike Morris doesn't do anything. He's just a nice guy. Period."

"And you're going to lure Bob Haywood down there and...."

"No question of luring. He's as keen as I am. I'm just waiting for him to choose the weekend. He's got his first year exams coming up. Beats me why he's worried about them. They never chuck you out for failing in the first year."

"They do in computer studies."

I was beginning to believe him but there was a way of testing the story.

"I wouldn't mind going down there with you," I said. "I could get bed and breakfast somewhere near."

"That would *not* be a good idea," said Adam firmly.

"I don't see why not. I wouldn't be in your way. I need a break after the assignment just as much as Bob does."

"But Bob doesn't know about you." He frowned at me as if I was some sort of dimwit.

"And yet I know about Bob," I said, feeling as if I really was one.

"But we were at school together," Adam replied. "Can't you see?"

"To be honest, no. Am I being thick or something?"

"Never, never, *never* grass on your school-mates," said Adam. "God! It's the unwritten law in every public school. I would have thought you knew that. I can tell you about Bob but I can't tell Bob about you. It wouldn't be right."

I thought his conceptions of public school life were a bit nineteenth-century, but they were to my advantage. I said I understood how he felt.

We finished our drinks. "Another?" I asked, reaching over for his glass.

"No thanks. Coming back to my place?"

I thought for a moment. "Could do," I said at last. "But only for an hour or two. Not longer."

"That's long enough." He stared fixedly at my lap. "So's that," he said. "Come on."

***

Bob Haywood and I arrived at Doctor Cooper's lecture together on the following morning. Anyone in the know the following morning would have found it amusing to compare the casual way Bob sat down and my own, much more careful approach. The car seat had been uncomfortable enough, but those moulded plastic chairs were not designed to accommodate recently penetrated posteriors.

Doctor Cooper was one of the best lecturers, but I found it difficult to concentrate that morning. I kept glancing at Bob's long legs. In a few week's time Adam's hands would be gliding up those muscular thighs. He had a way of doing it which sent me right over the top. He just touched the hairs at first, moving his fingers slowly up and down and barely touching the skin. I didn't even look at Dr. Cooper's slides. I looked at my mental picture of Bob in the same position as I had been in on the previous night; lying naked with his mouth open and his cock pointing rigidly towards the ceiling as Adam worked him up.

After the lecture I did a bit of research; not for the forthcoming exams and not in the college library, but in the extraordinary building they call The Dome, which houses Brighton's reference library. My source wasn't a computer manual either, but the telephone directories for Somerset. Sure enough, there he was: Morris, Michael, 3, The Old Stables, Burton Clayhanger. So that part of the story was true, but what of the rest? I still had my doubts.

As it happened, some weeks later I got two reports on the same day. I had done as well as my tutors expected, which doesn't tell one much. Bob had also come up to expectations. That is, if one were to believe Adam. I still had my doubts. I'd kept my eye on Bob all that Monday and he didn't look as if he'd been through any sort of traumatic experience to me. In fact, Bob was more than usually talkative that day. He actually asked a question in a lecture. That was a very rare occurrence. I went round to Adam's that evening.

"Well, how did it go?" I asked as I stepped into the hallway.

"How did what go?" That was a giveaway if ever there was one. You take a beautiful young man away for a weekend, intending to shag him. Someone asks you on the day after you get back how it went and you don't know what he's talking about! You can fool some of the people....

"With Bob, of course."

"Tell you later." He reached down and touched the front of my jeans. "Mm. You're keen," he said wrapping his fingers round my swollen cock. If he only knew it, it hadn't been caused by anticipation of anything he was going to do, but by my frantic imaginings of what might have happened at Burton Clayhanger.

In about as much time as it's taking me to write this paragraph I was naked on my knees savouring my favourite object. Certainly by the time it takes you to read to the end of this chapter it was pulsating and thrusting deep in my arse and I was groaning out loud. It's not a time for rational thought, but it did occur to me that he was showing remarkable virility for a man who'd spent the weekend fucking somebody else. He came. I came. The condom went down the toilet and the soggy towel which had been under me went into the linen basket. We showered together, still panting slightly and then, still undressed, went into the lounge.

"So," I said. "Tell all."

"Nothing much to tell, really."

I tried hard not to smile, thinking that those were probably the truest words he'd ever uttered but he continued.

"Friday night was a bit difficult," he said. "He let me suck it but that was all."

All! I'd have given a lot for a chance to get at Bob Haywood's cock.

"But then?" I asked.

"I think Mike had a word with him on Saturday. He was all right Saturday night. I got right up."

The thought of an elderly man persuading an intelligent eighteen-year-old that he ought to let his room-mate screw him was about as credible as a cartoon film, but I let him go on.

"Lovely arse," he said. "He goes swimming a lot. That must have something to do with it. Nice and round and muscular and not too tight. Just right."

"I know. I didn't know he was into swimming, though." When I stopped to think about it, Bob did have the figure of some sort of athlete. I'd only seen him clothed, of course.

"Anyway, I had him twice on Saturday night and again on Sunday morning. Then it was time to leave," said Adam.

"I'd like to meet this Mike," I said. "He sounds quite a character."

"He has his uses. There's no reason why not. We could go down there for a week in the vac."

"I can't manage a week. I have to work," I said.

"Work? What sort of work?"

I explained, leaving out my dad's insistence, that I'd got a job in the vacation and that I would be working at a local pharmaceutical firm to earn a bit of pocket money. I need hardly tell you it wasn't my idea.

"A weekend, then," said Adam. "A weekend in August."

I said that would suit me fine.

"Something's getting you going again," said Adam. "Thoughts of Bob Haywood or a weekend with me?"

It was almost certainly Bob. My cock had started to react again. It hung, rather than stood, away from my groin and dangled over my thigh.

"Can't let you go home in that condition, can I?" said Adam, laughing. He came over and sat next to me on the sofa.

He put one arm right round me and started to play on my nipples with his other hand, a thing he had never done before. "This really gets Bob going," he whispered in my ear. "You too, by the look of things," he added.

It was true. I'd never known my cock leap to attention quite so fast — especially after discharging its load so recently. A sort of shiver ran through me, and that was odd, because Adam's torso was touching mine and our legs were together. His cock was as limp as I had ever seen it.

"Looks like the key to both of you," he said. "I must remember that at Mike's place. Just imagine. Two or even three nights together. God, I'm going to fuck your lovely little arse non- stop."

I wanted to make some sort of witty remark but couldn't speak. I was sweating and panting like a long-distance runner. He pinched both nipples, one after the other, and then did it again, more slowly this time, taking each one between his thumb and the side of his finger and twisting as he did so. I leaned against him. His right leg went over my left leg. He let go of my waist, took his hand away for a second and then took my cock in his fingers. I felt him pulling the foreskin down and all the time the nipple massage continued relentlessly. Suddenly, what I had treated as a fanciful account of his weekend with Bob became real. Less than thirty-six hours before, the same hands which were playing with me had done the same to Bob. I wondered how Bob had reacted and what he had said. Not much; he wasn't a one for conversation. Just: "No

Adam. Don't Adam! Don't do that!" and then Adam's fingers would have found his nipples. "Don't Adam. No, don't. No... Oh yeah! Oh yeah!" I closed my eyes to imagine the scene. Bob lying on the bed with his legs slightly apart. Adam bending over him. Bob's cock springing upwards and his legs kicking open. Bob gasping, "Yeah! Oh yeah!"

I don't think I said anything apart from making a long drawn out sigh. It went everywhere. I put my hand over it but was too late. I'd never come like that before. I was embarrassed but Adam just laughed.

"It really does things to you," he said. "Just wait till I get you down to Mike's place."

***

I really needed that weekend. Humping barrels of ferrous fumarate around is no fun and for the first three weeks I was at Pharma-Giles that's all I did. My workmates were all in their thirties and forties. Nice enough guys; they made me welcome, but their vocabulary got on my nerves a bit. At the behest of Bob Merton, the foreman, I moved fucking drums into the fucking corner so that the fucking fork-lift truck could collect the fuckers and at the end of the day I swept the fucking floor and fucked off home. Then I had a lucky break. Doctor Paget had heard that I knew "something about computers" and I was transferred upstairs to his lab. They gave me a white coat to wear ,instead of a boiler suit, and I sat in a corner recording the results of his analyses, formatting diskettes and generally making myself useful.

Then came the evening of Friday, August 28th. Adam had told me to wait in a lay-by on the A 36 until he came along. My idea. I'm not very good when meeting people for the first time and I didn't want to risk arriving early. In fact ,he was there waiting for me. I didn't have to stop. He pulled out into the road in front of me and I followed him for the rest of the way. It was just as well that I did. It would have taken me ages to find Burton Clayhanger by myself. The last bit of road wasn't even a road, but a track with grass growing between parallel strips of tarmac.

Burton Clayhanger wasn't a village. I doubt if you could have even called it a hamlet. It consisted of a row of small houses — The Old Stables — and a pub about half a mile up the road. Otherwise, nothing. Not even a shop.

Mike was waiting for us, leaning on his gate and smoking a pipe. He was tall, had white hair and was wearing one of those ex-army khaki pullovers with leather patches on the elbows. As the two cars drew to a halt, he opened the gate. Adam got out of his car. I did the same.

"You're earlier than I thought you'd be," said Mike. He shook Adam's hand. I was relieved about that. I'd been a bit worried at the prospect of an over-affectionate greeting. Adam introduced me and we went into the cottage.

Mike was the most amazing man I had ever met. He produced a delicious three-course meal as if by magic. I helped wash up. Adam didn't. He went straight into the tiny lounge. When we'd finished and joined him, I understood why. A pile of magazines was strewn around his feet. 'HUNKS', 'STALLIONS ON HEAT', 'SCOUTING ADVENTURES', 'YOUNG SOLDIERS' — there were loads of them.

"Catching up with your reading?" Mike asked. Adam, deep in contemplation of a young man with the biggest tool I'd ever seen, didn't answer.

"You can look at them later," said Mike. "Right now we're going for a drink." He took the magazine from Adam, gathered up the rest of them and then pulled on the bookshelf on the wall. It opened like a door to reveal a space almost full of magazines and video tapes. He put them away and closed the space up again. Four rows of extremely dull-looking books on English literature and history gave no clue as to what lay behind them.

The walk up to the Red Lion was really pleasant. The smell of cow parsley wafted into my nostrils. The only sounds apart from our voices were the mooing of cows and the low buzzing throb of milking machines in adjacent cowsheds. Mike, it turned out, had been a house-master in a minor public school and, for a man of his age (sixty-six) he was remarkably computer-literate. Adam, obviously bored with our conversation, left us and strode on ahead. By the time we'd got to the pub he was already ensconced in a little niche in the corner. Mike insisted on buying us drinks.

I expected the conversation to turn pretty rapidly to you-know-what. It didn't. I was also slightly fearful of the prospect of a gnarled and ancient hand on my leg. That didn't happen either. We talked about Uni, the cost of running a car, modern farming methods and, of course, about school. Only once did the subject come up. A dazzlingly good-looking young man came in. He had fair hair, a really handsome face and long legs terminating in muddy wellington boots.

"Take a look at that!" said Adam. "I wouldn't mind ploughing his furrow!"

"He's got two illegitimate children he can't pay for," said Mike. "Don't give the poor lad any more worries."

We left the pub at closing time. That is, Adam and I left the pub at closing time. Mike got involved talking to a farmer. He gave Adam the key. "You go ahead," he said. "I might catch you up."

He didn't. We didn't see him again until the next morning. Our bedroom was so small that there was only about a foot between the sides of the bed and the walls. A picture of a dilapidated thatched cottage standing alone in a field of corn hung over the bed. Adam pulled the quilt back on his side.

"You couldn't have a more considerate host," he said. Just under the quilt were two tubes of lubricant, no less than six condom packets, a packet of tissues and four small white towels. There was a note, too. Adam read it, smiled and passed it over to me. "Have fun. Get up when you want to — and arise when you wish for breakfast. Mike."

I was so desperate for a pee that my cock was stiffening in my jeans. I didn't want Adam to think I was too keen so I went into the bathroom first. When I came back he'd undressed, affording me an extremely good view of what I was to enjoy later. Six and a half inches of thick cock; testicles like table tennis balls and, as he left the room, a milk-white behind, beautifully compact and dimpled at the sides. I got into bed. One thought had been uppermost in my mind since about halfway through our time in the pub. Mike hadn't mentioned Bob. Having got to know the man, I didn't expect a detailed discussion of Bob's attributes or his performance, but Mike hadn't even asked about him. "How's Bob Haywood?" or "How is that nice young man you brought down here a few weeks ago?" would have been normal. Once again, I doubted if Bob had ever seen the place and came to the conclusion that the whole pack of lies had been invented to get me down there. Not that I minded. There were many worse ways of spending a weekend.

Many worse! Adam returned. He slipped into bed beside me. I turned to face him and got a whiff of toothpaste.

"So what do you think?" he asked.

"About what?"

"About Burton Clayhanger and Mike and the pub?"

"All very nice," I replied. "Not sure I'd want to live here though."

"Nor me," he replied and I felt his hand on my thigh.

"You'd be in your element," I said. "What about that young farmer?" His hand had started to move up and down, lightly brushing the hairs. My cock responded. I looked down the bed. There was a definite projection in the quilt at the point where his middle lay.

"A bird in the hand is worth two in the bush," he said. His hand moved up and cupped my balls. "Especially two like this and a bush like yours. And as for the bird, I like a good strong cock." His fingers wrapped round it. I reached down, felt his belly, then the hair and finally found it; hard as marble and already slightly damp.

He let go of mine and I released my grip on his. He rolled over onto his side and started again to play with my nipples. I heard myself catch my breath.

"I know someone who wants his arse fucked," he said. So, for that matter, did I, but I said nothing and just lay there breathing heavily whilst he kneaded. He took away his left hand and slid it down my chest and abdomen. For a second or two he twined his fingers in my hair and then moved it further down. My cock, although as stiff and alert as a sentry, let it past. I opened my legs. I didn't mean to. It just happened. His finger curled inwards and I gasped. He stopped. "Get up on your knees," he said.

"What for?" That must rate as one of the daftest questions I have ever asked. He hurled the quilt away. As I turned over and got up onto all fours, I caught a glimpse of his cock. If anything, it looked even bigger and thicker than it had in his flat.

Patiently and gently he arranged me. I remember that the thought crossed my mind that he must have had some experience. I think I moaned slightly as his finger slid in to me. I know I did when the second finger joined it. That hurt. For a moment I thought he would tear me open. He didn't, of course. A wave of pleasure swept through me as his fingers played around in there.

"There!" he said at last. A sudden chill replaced the warmth of his fingers but only for a second. I felt his hands on my hips and, immediately afterwards, his cock head pushing against me. Once again, I thought momentarily of Bob Haywood. Had his arms rested on the same mattress? He'd have had to be further up in the bed. He was so tall that his feet would have been over the edge....

"Aaaagh!" I couldn't help yelling. All of it went in at once. Not rapidly, but inexorably. Inch by inch it pushed into me, expanding me as it went.

"There!" said Adam again and he gave the first thrust. I shuddered. He thrust again and the bed creaked ominously. I deny to this day that I was calling for more when the door downstairs slammed, but Adam was adamant on the subject. I do remember reaching back and touching his legs in an attempt to stop him for a moment. It didn't work. He kept on thrusting away. I heard steps on the stairs. For an awful moment I thought Mike would throw the door open, but he didn't. I was only vaguely conscious of the lavatory cistern being flushed and the sound of his bedroom door closing. I was concentrating on trying to contract my buttocks. I wanted to squeeze out the very last drop of Adam's spunk when it happened. Whether I did or not, I can't say. I certainly tried. He almost fell on top of me, panting and wheezing. I squeezed as hard as I could until I could actually feel the veins.

"Did you come?" he asked at length.

"No."

"Good. Hang on." I felt it slipping out of me. I didn't want it to. At that moment I wanted it inside me all night.

"Okay, lie on your back," he said. With difficulty (my legs felt as if they belonged to somebody else) I did so. He lay alongside me, grinned, leaned over me and took my cock into his mouth. Only just in time, I may say. I just felt the back of his throat when the first load shot. I tried to hold his head but couldn't. The next shot followed and then another. He lifted his head. It streamed out of his mouth, cascading onto my belly.

He licked his lips and then picked up a towel to wipe first his face and then me.

"A spot of shut-eye? He said, throwing it into a corner.

"Just a spot," I said. He retrieved the quilt. We got back into a normal sleeping position and he covered us both.

"I'll have to open your mouth a bit more to get at it," said the dentist, screwing up the gag. I woke up. It wasn't a gag. It was Adam's cock. How he'd managed to do it without waking me, I don't know, but he was laying across me and his cock, erect again, was buried deep in my mouth. Mine took a long time to wake up. By the time I was at boiling point he'd shot and I was gulping hard and trying not to cough. I had to persuade him to bring me off.

"Much better to wait until the morning," he said, but I, foolishly, insisted — with the result that when we woke up in the morning with sun streaming through the window, neither of us was much in the mood and the smell of bacon frying downstairs was much more appetising than sex.

I had a long talk with Mike that morning. He wanted to go for a walk. Adam was engrossed in 'Schoolboy Sadism.' (Authentic un-retouched photos!) Not my cup of tea — and I was a bit surprised that Mike had it. Leaving Adam to 'the whip slashed through the taut skin of his virgin buttocks' we set off, Mike with his stick and his pipe and me with a twig I had pulled off a bush the previous evening.

Mike said I had nothing to worry about. I told him about my career prospects and he knew about my sexual orientation. Even if Adam hadn't told him, he would have heard enough as he went to bed. He never raised that. He said all I had to do was to be careful. "Do what you like," he said. "Fuck or get fucked. Just remember never to cause any harm to anybody else and, whatever you do, don't tell the rest of the world. The rest of the world isn't interested."

I brought up the McAlpine business. "Those guys didn't tell anyone," I said, "but they're all in prison.

"My dear Tim, you can't invite eight soldiers to a Mayfair flat for a sex orgy and expect them all to keep quiet about it. It was the guests who spilled the beans, not the hosts. One talks and the others confirm. 'I was led astray, my lord. They made me drink champagne and I'm not used to it.' Utter bollocks, of course. They knew bloody well why they were there. But you're not the man to do things like that. You should be all right."

Amazingly, to me anyway, Mike had been a teacher and then a house-master for forty years and never so much as touched any of his pupils. "Not that I wasn't tempted," he said. "Some of those sixth formers were beautiful. Some even hinted. I kept my sex life quiet. Do the same and you'll be all right."

A few minutes later, he stopped. "Would you mind if I gave you some confidential advice?" he asked.

"Of course not. I'd be grateful."

"Then drop Adam Saunders as soon as you can. He's lethal."

"I thought you and he were friends," I said.

"Oh we are. I am very fond of Adam and I always will be. Adam talks a lot about the public school ethic. 'We must all stick together' — that sort of thing. The problem is that he sees himself as flypaper and people like you as flies — and you're too nice a man to come to a sticky end."

He was wasting his breath. When we got back to the cottage, we found Adam sprawled face down on a sun-lounger in the garden. I don't know whether he had rolled his boxers up, or if they had just ridden up, but just a glimpse of those long honey-coloured thighs was enough to set me off. I don't know if you are the same as me, but I find partial clothing like that much more erotic than nakedness. I was intimately acquainted with every square (or round) centimetre under those garish shorts, but just imagining it was incredibly exciting. I think Adam must have read my thoughts, or maybe he noticed the effect he was having. Mike said something about going out to see an old water-mill that afternoon. Adam said that he and I had other plans so, after lunch, Mike went off alone.

Adam wasn't the fly paper that afternoon. Adam was more like the fly — or perhaps an exquisitely beautiful butterfly. I certainly pinned him down. There was no trouble with the rubber that afternoon. It went on almost automatically. Adam lay spread-eagled on the bed with his face buried in the pillow. I'd spent some time just playing with his arsehole. I wondered if I'd spent long enough, but just doing that was nearly enough to bring me to the boil. I needn't have worried. I went into him easily enough. He uttered a long drawn-out groan and clenched his fingers into the mattress. His muscle rings seemed to roll up the shaft of my cock in much the same way as the condom had, but there's one hell of a difference between a living arse and a bit of rubber. I relished every millimetre of movement.

Again, I brought him to a climax without even touching his cock. I couldn't have got to it anyway. He was writhing wildly and I was pushing into him so hard that it must have been compressed against the mattress. I came just a few seconds later and lay on him, panting as our sweat mingled.

That night it was my turn. Three turns if you count Adam sucking me off at twenty past two in the morning. He fucked me as soon as we went to bed and he fucked me early in the morning. He was still asleep when I went down to breakfast.

"I'll miss you," said Mike. "Don't forget. Come down here any time and bring whom you wish, but take my advice. Shake off the old school tie and he who wears it."

I had no intention of doing so. That was the problem. I was in, as they say, far too deep to pull out.

CHAPTER FOUR

I went back to do another four weeks at Pharma-Giles and that vacation came to an end. With my bank account looking better than it had for a long time, I went back to Brighton for the new term.

I met Andrew on my first day there. It was a blisteringly hot day and, having no lectures, I was strolling along the sea front at Hove looking down at the people on the beach. Then I stopped. Sitting alone on a breakwater was a young man so stunning that I couldn't believe my eyes. All he was wearing were a pair of cut-off jeans and sandals. He had fair hair. His back was sunburned. I never had been, and I hope I never will be, one of those people who cruise beaches, but in his case I had to have a better look. I retraced my steps for a few yards and went down the steps to the beach. He was so good-looking that he made my heart race. I stopped, undid my shoelace and did it up again. He continued to stare at the beach and the sea. I got a bit nearer. This time it was the turn of the other shoe. He turned round for a moment just as I was about five feet away from him. His face was as sunburned as the rest of him, and as for his chest and torso — he looked like one of those muscle-men in Mike's magazines. I'd never seen pectoral muscles like his.

I was dying to speak to him but couldn't think of anything to say. Further trouble with my shoelaces (both of them) gave me time to fix his image in my mind. It was going to be an early night that night, and Mrs Higgs' bolster was going to get the fucking of all time.

I walked on. Suddenly I was aware of flopping footsteps behind me. I turned round. It was him.

"Excuse me," he said, "Are you a student here?"

"Well, yes. Why do you ask?"

"The first one I've met." He stuck out a hand. "Andrew Forge," he said.

"Hi. Tim Scully." He had a very firm handshake and very soft hands.

"I've only just arrived," he said. "Have you got time to fill me in?"

I resisted the temptation to say something I might regret. Instead, I said I had plenty of time. "There's a café just along the road up top," I said. "Let's have a coffee in there."

"I'd better nip back to my digs and get a tee shirt then. I can't go in there like this."

"It'll be okay if we sit outside," I said. "Where are your digs, anyway?"

"Montpelier Road. Number seventeen. Just along a bit from here."

Things were looking better and better. Montpelier Road wasn't more than a ten-minute walk from Mrs Higgs' place.

Unfortunately, we hadn't been sitting outside the Café Leonardo for more than five minutes when all my aspirations took a nose-dive. He wasn't a student at our place at all, but at Falmer. I'd better explain that there are two universities in Brighton. There's our place, the University of Brighton (once just Brighton Polytechnic) and at Falmer, outside the town, there's the slightly older University of Sussex. That's where Andrew was headed, to read social anthropology and psychology. I was choked. There's not a lot of mixing between the two student bodies, either. He'd end up with other friends and that afternoon was probably the only time in my life that I would see him. I was able to tell him one or two things — the best shops to go to, where to put his name down for the weekly 'What's On' bulletin, that sort of thing. When I wasn't talking I just stared at his chest and took occasional furtive glances downwards. He was sitting with his legs slightly apart. Those cut-offs were so tight that you'd be hard-pressed to get a piece of paper between the denim and his thighs. Just a little bit further up and there it was: a huge, soft-looking lump. It wasn't the prospect of coffee which made my mouth water.

He was a really interesting guy. He'd lived in Dubai for most of his life. His dad ran a firm out there which sold oil-drilling equipment.

"Haven't you got any relations here?" I asked. I was already beginning to think in terms of "Hello Dad. Would you mind if I brought a friend home for the vac?"

"Oh, loads. Aunts and uncles up the ying-yang," he said. (You'll get used to Andrew's vocabulary. It took me some time, too.)

The waitress brought our coffees. We chatted away. I gave him my name, address and telephone number. "Just in case you feel like a drink or a chat some time," I said.

"Thanks a lot. I'll definitely take you up on that," he said. I should have cheered up but didn't. I'd used the identical phrase myself several times without having the slightest intention of accepting the offer.

"Got a girl friend back in Dubai?" I asked.

"Definitely not," he said. "There aren't that many girls out there. What about you?"

Out came the photo of Susan. He said she looked nice. I said she was.

"I'm not interested in girls," he said. My heart missed a beat and then rapidly made up for it.

"What's that supposed to mean?" I asked.

"Just that. I'm not interested. Human beings painting themselves up and displaying themselves in the hope of getting laid. They're worse than animals. Look at this lot coming along the road, for instance."

There were three of them, girls of about fifteen I guess, shrieking with laughter. When they drew abreast of us and spotted Andrew, they giggled. The one in the middle shook her head so that her long hair flopped from one shoulder to the other.

"Ugh!" said Andrew. The Arabs have the right idea. Shut 'em up in harems. Give me the company of my fellow men. They're a lot less complicated."

"True. As a matter of fact, Susan and I are due to split up any minute. It just doesn't seem to have work ed out, with her so far away," I said.

We finished our coffee. I paid the bill. "Hope to see you around sometime," I said.

"You bet you will," he said and I walked back to Mrs Higgs in a state of absolute bliss. Susan's photo went into a rubbish bin in Hove park.

I didn't go to Adam's that week. He rang twice. I said I had a lot of work to catch up with. I jumped every time the phone rang, hoping to hear Mrs Higgs call up the stairs for me.

Twice, or maybe three times, I walked round to Montpelier Road and stood for a moment or two outside the house trying to work out which window was his and imagining what his room looked like. There was so sign of Andrew. I got a couple of books out of the library and mugged up on Dubai — which, apart from the climate, looked a nice enough place. There was a street map in one of them and I wished I'd asked him for his address there so that I could find his road. I did find Dubai College, the school he went to.

Saturday morning came round. I was in the shower and didn't actually hear the phone ring. "Tim! Tim!" Mrs Higgs shouted. I turned off the water and opened the door.

"Call for you, dear," she shouted. "Nicely spoken young man."

I flung a towel round me and padded down the stairs, leaving wet marks on her stair carpet. As usual, despite the state I was in, she hung around.

"This is Andrew," he said. "Have you got anything on today?"

"Clothes or engagements?" I asked. "I've got a towel on. I was in the shower."

"Pity I haven't got a picture phone. What do you say about going somewhere?"

"Sure. Where?"

"Oh anywhere. I leave it to you."

I arranged to pick him up on the corner of Montpelier Road at eleven. Mrs Higgs said he sounded a nice class of person and suggested that I bring him back for tea. For the first time since I had lived there I said I would. Anything to make the day a bit longer.

I spotted him standing on the corner from some way away. It would have been difficult not to. He was wearing a tee shirt of remarkable whiteness and those same cut-off shorts.

"Decided where we're going yet?" I asked, as he climbed into the car. He grinned. "Let's go up on the Downs, miles away from anyone, and have a picnic," he said.

Picnics require food and drink so we drove into Hove and got a bag of filled rolls and a few cans of drink. Andrew paid. "Wagid fuloose at the moment," he said. "Dad sent a cheque last week." For a moment I was baffled, but he didn't actually need to explain that it was Arabic for 'a lot of money'. When he pulled his wallet out of his back pocket I could see for myself. Then I stopped at a chemist to get a prescription. Those words 'miles away from anyone' were still running through my head. I bought one or two other items as well. It was unlikely that they would be needed but it was possible. I shoved the bag into the glove pocket and we drove off. Just having him sitting next to me was exciting. I kept looking down at his extraordinarily long legs and that enticing lump in the middle of his shorts. Andrew had wagid cock as well.

We drove out through Brighton. "That looks like a nice pub," he said at one point.

"Apparently they have a gay night every Tuesday," I said, wondering what sort of reaction that might prompt. I was far from disappointed.

"Really? We ought to go some time," he said.

"Why?"

"It would be interesting." I think it was at that point that I started to congratulate myself. It didn't seem possible that I had managed to hook someone as beautiful as Andrew, but I had.

We left the urban mess. He chatted most interestingly about life in Dubai as we drove onwards. "If you can raise the fare, you'd be welcome to stay with us in the vac," he said. "We could go out into the dunes and spend a night under canvas there. That's great." I had doubts about sex in the sand but said I'd like that very much. He was really enthusiastic. As villages came and went, he'd virtually planned the whole thing. How the family would meet me at the airport. How we'd all go to dinner at the International Hotel. There would be swimming in warm sea and shell-collecting on the beach. His little sister had the best collection of shells he'd ever seen. We could go deep-sea fishing too. A friend of his father's had his own boat and went out after sharks.

"You won't sleep a lot. Not for the first few nights, anyway," he said. "The air conditioners take a bit of getting used to."

"I don't suppose I shall want to sleep a lot," I replied. I caught his reflection in the mirror. He grinned. I grinned back. We were obviously on the same wavelength.

"This looks a good place," he said. "Go down that track." Obediently I turned in and we followed the rough track for some way. It can't have done my suspension much good but to hell with things like that. I was pretty certain what he had in mind. My suspicions were confirmed when we came to a sign marked 'Public footpath'. "We could park here and walk a little way," I suggested.

"Blow that! 'Public' means public."

"Remind me to write that down. A remark as brilliant as that shouldn't be lost," I said. He thumped me lightly on the thigh. "You know what I mean," he said, laughing.

"I think I do," I said. By that time I knew. It was just as well that I didn't have to walk. The condition I was in would have made walking uncomfortable. I drove on. The car lurched and bounced along, throwing us against each other. We both started to giggle. Finally he spoke again. "Here. Let's stop here," he said.

Tall hedges lined the track on both sides but on our left there was a steel gate leading to a field which sloped steeply downwards. The view, if you are into such things, was magnificent. For a moment or two, Andrew blotted it out for me as he clambered out of the car. Not that I minded. I'd rather admire legs than landscape any day.

I locked the car, got the picnic bag out of the back and followed him over the gate. He stood for a moment with his back to the hedge. "It's all so green!" he exclaimed. "Compared to Dubai. I mean. It's amazing!"

"Yet another learned remark by Professor Forge," I said and sat down on the grass. He followed suit. "And not a soul around," he added. For a moment we sat quite still. The distant sound of a tractor drifted up from the valley below us and a bird was singing in a clump of trees. Otherwise he was quite right. It was as if we were in another world.

"Might as well take advantage of the sunshine while we have it," he said at last and peeled off his tee shirt. I said that wasn't a bad idea and did so too, very conscious of my slight build compared to his. We ate the rolls and drank the drinks — which had got unpleasantly warm in the car. He turned over on to his front. I sat there, gazing enraptured at his ass. It was very large, very round and very inviting. For quite a long time, neither of us said anything. A bee buzzed from flower to flower. I got the impression that Andrew was not only awake but thinking; wondering how to say it. I decided to take the lead.

"It's amazing up here," I said. "You could do anything."

"Yeah, I suppose you could," he said.

"I wonder how many couples have been up here for a quick shag," I said.

"Quite a few, I should think," he replied.

"Pity we haven't got a couple of birds with us," I said.

"That's just a sex-urge. Sex doesn't necessarily require opposite sexes. There's enjoyment and procreation. Two different things."

My heart started to thump so loudly that I wondered if he could hear it.

"You ever done it with another bloke?" I asked.

"No. It's never come up."

'It soon will,' I thought, 'and with all the luck in the world, so will I - as soon as I can get those shorts off you.'

"Up being the operative word," I said, with what I hoped sounded like a casual laugh.

"How do you mean? Oh yes. I see. No, my sex life consists of my right hand. That's good enough for me. No emotional attachments."

"I don't think there need be....." Something stopped me. He noticed it too. He raised his head and turned it from side to side like a dog. The sound of the tractor wasn't so distant any more. In fact, it was much nearer.

Andrew cursed. So did I, inwardly. The noise got nearer and nearer. Finally, we caught a glimpse of it through the hedge as it approached. We heard the driver say 'Fuck!' and then call "Anybody there?" I got up and went to the gate. "Us," I said.

"You'll have to move it, mate. I can't get through and I can't back out, not with a harrow on the back. If you keep going the way you came you'll end up on the Eastbourne road."

"Isn't it always the way?" said Andrew when we were in the car again. "That looked like being a really nice afternoon."

"I'm disappointed too," I said. Just how disappointed I didn't say.

***

I'm going to draw a bit of a veil over the rest of that year. The truth is I'm a bit ashamed of myself. I did the most stupid things. We both did. It was the most expensive year of my life ,too. We went drinking almost every night. We brought Christmas presents for each other, standing for hours looking in shop windows trying to find the right thing. Andrew came to tea on numerous occasions. I spent hours in his room watching him pedal his exercise bike but that's as far as it went. If I tried to raise the subject of gay sex he talked about it freely enough but something always held me back from making a move. His landlady came in and went out at irregular times and there was another student there as well; a quiet Japanese girl. We never knew if she was in or out. When she was in, she often tapped lightly on the door and asked if she could borrow something.

We went to that gay pub. Andrew was fascinated. There was nothing like it in Dubai, he said. I was bored sick. The clientele was mostly pretty aged and repulsive. There was one young man. I had my back to the bar — deliberately — but Andrew gave me a running commentary. "The one with the white hair has just bought him a drink. Hello. The other one, the one with the green hat, is with him now. Oh yes. I think he's made contact. I wonder…. Yes. The young man's smiling."

They left together. "Off to the green-hatted man's tawdry dwelling to engage in a bit of sex," said Andrew. "We must come here again. I can get a good essay subject out of this place."

"Just leave my name out of it," I said. "I went to a gay bar with Tim Scully would scupper my career prospects."

I was desperate to get out of the place in case Adam should walk in. He'd told me he often went there, but he didn't appear. In fact, I hardly saw Adam that year. He rang several times and then the calls ceased. I saw him once or twice with a young man in his car. Adam had obviously found someone else. That was just as well, I thought, remembering Mike's advice.

I spent a week of the Easter vacation up at my Gran's, which was enjoyable. She really is the most amazing old lady. She still — even now — goes to the firm's board meetings regularly. They send a car for her now, but during the war she used to go by bike, wending her way through the rubble and lifting it over fire hoses.

My diet supplement was confiscated soon after my arrival. "Good fresh vegetables and a steady diet. That's what you need, my lad!" she said and the outcome of several scientists' research ended up in the waste bin. (I retrieved it secretly later.) I'd only worn that particular pair of trainers for about three months, but they had a similar fate. She bought me a new pair.

But I don't want to give you the wrong impression of Gran. I am really fond of her. I always was. Naturally enough I had to visit the firm. I met Mr Spawling, the new Works Manager, who, like everyone else there, called me "Mr. Tim". He, poor man, got a blasting. Someone had left an inspection lamp of some sort, with the cable neatly coiled, on the floor between two machines. Gran went ballistic - even more so than on the day before when she sent for the manager of Sainsbury's to ask why there were only three check-outs in operation.

I sent daily postcards to Andrew, once making the mistake of writing one on the dining room table. That led to a criticism of ball point pens. I got just one card back from Andrew. "Wish you were here" is usually pretty meaningless, but I read those words over and over again and looked at the picture of Dubai Creek so often that I can still remember every detail.

Term started again. I was round at Andrew's place one afternoon. Suzie Kagasawa was proving particularly frustrating. She'd been in three times; once to ask if Andrew might possibly have a spare bulb for her slide projector He didn't, of course. Then she wanted a bit of fuse wire and finally she came in to ask which shop might have both items. Andrew was perched up on his exercise bike. I was sitting in the armchair trying to read a magazine, but concentrating much more on his long brown legs.

He stopped. "Remember that day when we went out on the Downs?" he asked, wiping his face with a towel.

"Very well."

"It was a nice afternoon — until that bloke came along," said Andrew. "If only we could find a place where we wouldn't be disturbed by other people."

I hadn't given Mike or Burton Clayhanger a thought up to that moment. I suppose I'd sort of sublimated the memory. "There is a place," I said, and went on to paint a rather idyllic picture of Mike, his cottage and the village. "We could pop down there for a weekend," I suggested.

"You sure that this Mike bloke won't mind?"

I said I would ring Mike that evening, which I did. He seemed genuinely pleased to hear from me. He said we'd be welcome. "I take it that Andrew knows what to expect," he said. I laughed. There was no doubt at all in my mind that he did. On the following afternoon I told him that we would have to share a double bed. "There isn't even room for a sleeping bag on the floor," I added, in case that thought had occurred to him.

"I've never shared a bed with anybody," said Andrew. "It could be a bit of a laugh, eh?"

Contented groans were what I had in mind, but I agreed.

Mike was as welcoming as ever and seemed to take to Andrew from the moment we got out of the car. We went to the Red Lion for dinner and drinks. Andrew was as entertaining and interesting as ever on the subject of living in the Gulf. Just as he had when I was there with Adam, Mike gave me the key. He had to stay on after closing time, he said, to talk to the landlord about a forthcoming parish council meeting.

So Andrew and I walked back to the cottage together. The village was eerily silent. Our footsteps echoed back from the walls of the farm buildings we passed.

"Amazing place," said Andrew when we got to Mike's.

"Like it?" I asked as I put the key in the lock.

"It's great!" he replied.

He didn't want anything else to drink and he refused my offer of coffee. That was just as well. My cock was already beginning to show signs of enthusiasm for what was to come. We went upstairs. I showed him where the bathroom was. I had a quick pee and then let him go in. I got the things that would be needed out of the bag, undressed and slipped into bed.

"In bed already?" he asked when he returned.

"There's not enough room for two people to get undressed at the same time," I explained.

"That's so." The bed creaked slightly as he sat on it to take off his shoes and socks. It was going to creak even more in a few minutes, I thought. I wondered if he'd noticed the mound in the middle of the quilt. From my viewpoint, it looked like a volcano. He stood up again. With all the concentration of a cat watching a mouse, I watched him undress. He stood at the window with his back to me. First the tee shirt came off; then his jeans and then, finally those strange shiny white underpants slid down and I had my first view of his breathtakingly beautiful backside. It's at moments like that when you think that if there really is a Great Creator, he has more sense of beauty than any of us. I gazed, absolutely spellbound. Andrew was totally unaware of this. At least I think he was. He stood at the window looking out at the darkened countryside. He put his hands on the window-sill. Dimples formed in the sides of his buttocks. Tight, like that, his bottom became even more enticing.

Finally, he turned round, knelt down and rummaged in his bag. "What are you looking for?" I asked.

"My pyjamas."

"I never wear anything in bed," I said.

"Really?"

"Old-fashioned. That's what they are," I said.

"Dubai's a bit of an old-fashioned place," he replied. "Still, it is a warm evening…"

"Very warm."

"Oh. To hell with them," he said and got into bed. I just had time to take in a luxuriant growth of dark hair and a cock which made Adam's and mine look half grown. It was as huge as I'd thought and so were his balls.

"Feel sleepy?" He asked.

"Not at all. You?"

"Nor me. Let's talk."

"Sure. What about?" The scent of his perspiration was beginning to get to me.

"You haven't mentioned Susan for ages. What happened to her?" he asked.

"Oh, we packed it in."

"Good for you. It's daft getting lumbered with a woman while you're a student. There's a bloke at our place who got married in the Easter vacation and he's only in his first year. Now he's going mad trying to find somewhere in Brighton where they can live. This urge to mate is peculiar."

"Sex," I said. "That's what it's about."

"Of course it is. But I manage pretty well with a hand. It's a bloody sight cheaper and infinitely safer."

"Do you want a laugh?" I asked.

"Sure."

"I use a bolster."

"A what?"

"Sort of like a very long pillow you use on a double bed. The individual pillows lie on top of it."

"And what on earth do you do with it, or is that too much of a personal question?"

I couldn't help blushing as I told him how I lay in bed, conjuring up the image of someone I liked the look of and then, clutching the bolster to me, how I rubbed myself against it till I came.

"I hadn't heard of that technique before," said Andrew. "I just use two fingers and a thumb at first and then go to the thumbs-down method."

"The what?"

"Reverse the hand. You get a better grip on the base and with a bit of practise you can tickle near the head with your little finger. It makes your wrist ache at first."

"I don't see what you mean. Show me."

"Bit difficult in pitch darkness," said Andrew. I expected him to ask me to turn the light on. The switch was on my side. He didn't.

"Do it on me," I said.

There was a very long pause. I could actually hear my heart beating. I guess he could too. Then I felt his hand on my side. It slid up over my abdomen and down through the hair until his fingers touched it.

"Christ! Aren't you hard?" he said.

"Hardly surprising. Even talking about it does that. Go on. Show me."

"Well, you start with the thumb on the top surface and just two fingers underneath. Like this. At first you go very, very gently, just sliding your fingers over the skin. Like this. Feel good?"

I wanted to say something noncommittal — like 'Not bad'. Instead, I heard myself saying "Yeah! Oh yeah!"

"I can't get over how hard yours is," he said. At that point, I could restrain my curiosity no longer. I reached out with my right hand, touched the cool skin of his thigh and then slid my hand upwards. His pubes felt like steel wool. His balls were warm and slightly damp. His cock, when I eventually touched it, was as hard and as thick as a hammer handle and felt almost as long. He gasped slightly.

"Better leave off there or there'll be an accident. Don't want to muck up your mate's bed linen," he said.

I was so breathless when he took his hand away that I could hardly speak. I reached over the side of the bed and extracted two packets of condoms from my shoe. I handed one over to him.

"It's okay. I don't need one," he said.

"Please yourself." I tore the packet open and reached down under the duvet. It went on without any difficulty.

"Okay. Carry on with the lesson, professor," I said.

"In a minute. Mike's just come in," he whispered. I had heard the door too. We lay there and waited. Mike padded up the stairs. We heard him use the bathroom and then his bedroom door closed.

"All clear," I said.

"You're sure he won't come in to say 'Goodnight' or anything?"

"Quite sure. Carry on where you left off."

Once again, I felt his finger tips and his thumb on my cock. I think it had softened slightly during Mike's ascent of the stairs but it very soon recovered. So did Andrew's, when I had it in my hand again.

"You keep doing this until you're nearly ready to come," he whispered as his fingers
slid up and down my rampant shaft.

"And then?" I panted.

"Hang on."

I did. I wouldn't have let go of it for anything. He turned over onto his side to face me. "Thumb and forefinger round the base like this," he said. "That's why I call it the thumbs-down method." I felt his digits in my pubes and the rest of his fingers clasp round my cock. That was all it needed. "Stop there for a minute," I panted. "I'll come otherwise."

"That's the idea," he said. He squeezed the base of my cock and then slid my foreskin back.

"Feel good?" he asked.

"Bloody great!" I said. "Let me try." I turned over to face him. "Like this?" I said, reversing my hand on his cock. It throbbed in my fingers. His pubes were so dense that my thumb and finger were buried in them.

"That's it. Hold it tight. I think I'd better have one of those things on after all."

He let me put it on. I had to switch the bedside light on to do so and had my first good look at it. It stood rigidly upwards from his bush. I'm not exaggerating when I say that it must have been a good eight inches. A very good eight inches. In contrast with most of his body, it was a gleaming, milky white colour and covered with a network of blue veins. I had an urge to lick it and see it gleam as Adam's had done.

From the way he stared at it and flicked the nipple, I suspect he'd never worn a condom before and I wasn't nearly so adept at fitting it as I had been with my own. I think my fingers must have been shaking but I managed it.

I didn't need to say anything. We turned over again to face each other. I clasped his and he clasped mine. We were so close together that our hands kept colliding.

"See who comes first," I breathed.

"That's childish," he said, but he speeded up all the same. So did I. He moved even closer towards me; so close that my hand was moving between my own legs. I felt the old agreeable itching sensation in my ass and was just wondering whether to take my hand away and let nature take over when he came. The flesh in my fingers swelled momentarily. His grip on my cock relaxed for a moment and he let out a long sigh.

"Keep going!" I gasped. It didn't take long. A matter of seconds, I should think. In some ways I felt a bit let down after it was all over. Mike's bed linen was still as clean as it had been when we'd started, but there had be no real need to use rubbers — and a hand, in whichever position, is not so good as a real live and tight arse. But there was still time.

"Better get some sleep. I guess we'll be up early in the morning. What shall I do with this?" Andrew asked.

"Drop it on the floor for now. They can both go down the loo in the morning," I said.

For a few minutes I lay there thinking. "Up early in the morning". They were pleasant words. I fell asleep.

It must have been the Red Lion's famous 3X bitter. It was nine o'clock when I woke up. I reached out a hand. There was nobody there. I found Andrew downstairs having breakfast with Mike.

"Here he is at last," said Mike. "Good morning."

"You were so sound asleep that I didn't want to wake you," said Andrew. I said he should have done. I cursed myself all that day. The weather was warm for early summer and Andrew wore his cut-offs again. A new pair, I think, but just as tight and buttock-hugging as the last ones. If I hadn't had that extra pint, Andrew wouldn't have flashed that sunny smile for Mike's camera as he bounced up and down on a tractor seat or sat astride a fallen tree. His energy was incredible. I thought I was pretty fit, but I was shattered at the end of that day. We went for a drink as usual, but this time, pleading a slightly upset stomach and the fact that I had to drive several hundred miles in the morning, I had just two pints and then went over to soft drinks.

Once again, Mike gave us the key. He had another convenient appointment to keep.

"I don't know about you," said Andrew as we walked home, "but I can't wait to get to bed." It was probably as well that it was such a dark night. If a third party were writing this, he'd describe my expression as 'a lustful grin'.

I grinned again when I was under the duvet and Andrew, naked as he had been on the previous night, opened the window. "Phew!" he said, standing in that beautiful buttock-tightening stance with his hands on the window sill. "No pyjamas tonight. That's for sure."

"Definitely not," I said, feasting my eyes on his broad shoulders, narrow hips and long legs. They all seemed to lead to something I was destined to enjoy to the full. Already sheathed (I had put it on whilst he was in the bathroom) my cock was raring to get between those milky white buns.

He took a deep breath, turned round and got into bed. Once again, his cock was totally limp. For a moment I wondered if he'd had a quick wank in the bathroom, but he hadn't been in there long enough.

"A great day," he said, putting his hands behind his head. "I really like this place. Do you reckon we'll be able to come again?"

"I'm sure we will — in both senses of the word," I added.

"How do you mean?"

"You haven't tried the Scully patent masturbation method yet."

"I'm happy enough with my own," he replied. "Anyway there isn't a bolster or whatever it's called."

"A pillow will do."

"I'll try it when I get back to Brighton. I'm a bit tired, to tell you the truth."

"Nothing like a wank for sending you to sleep," I said. He was obviously waiting for me to warm him up.

"That's true."

"I'll tell you something else which feels good," I said.

"Mm? What's that?"

"Having someone stroke your behind. If it's done right, a person can bring you off without touching your cock."

"Do you reckon?"

"Definitely."

He said nothing for a few minutes. For a moment I thought he'd gone to sleep. Then he spoke again. "Oh, what the hell!" he said. "What do I have to do?"

He didn't want to put a rubber on at first. "I don't think it will have any effect on me. I only come with a hand-job," he said.

"You will. I guarantee it," I replied.

He had to put one on by himself. If I'd done it for him, he would have noticed how prepared I was. He rolled over so that I could put his pillow in the right place and then rolled back again on his front.

"Cock facing forwards?" I asked. He put his hand between himself and the pillow and fumbled around. "It is now," he said.

I reached down and stroked his right thigh. "What are you doing?" he asked in a voice muffled by bed linen.

"Initial stimulation. It's all part of the Scully method," I replied. I slid my hand upward. Hairs gave way to smooth skin. I reached the fold of his buttocks and then pushed down as hard as I could.

"Trying to break my ribs?" he gasped but he got the message. I felt the muscles tighten as he gave the first thrust. "That's it. You've got the idea," I said. After that I said nothing. I didn't know what thoughts were going through his mind. I hoped they were of being fucked by Tim Scully, but you never know. I know that when I was fucking Mrs Higgs' bolster and thinking about someone, a different voice would have thrown me right off.

He gave another thrust and then another and then turned his head away from me to face the window. I took my hand away. I was reluctant to do so. Feeling an ass in action is one of the most delightful experiences I know. However, I had to get ready. I'd secreted the tube under the corner of my pillow. I opened it and squeezed some onto my third finger.

Andrew had started to grunt with every shove. The bed creaked in unison. I put my hand back on his behind, keeping the greased finger up and away from his skin.

"Um! Ah! Um! Ah!" His ass was bobbing up and down like a cork on a rough sea. I reached over so that my hand was right on the cleft. His lunges became more and more violent. I didn't want him to come too soon. Adam had always said that there was nothing so exciting as feeling someone tighten round you as he came and nothing worse than a limp, post ejaculation sphincter. I adjusted the position of my hand and insinuated my finger downwards between his cheeks. I felt a hair and then I was on it; a tight little knot of muscle.

He stopped. Just like that. He lifted his head and turned to face me. "What the fuck?" he said.

"It's okay. Carry on. You'll...."

"You're a fucking queer!" He shouted so loudly that Mike must have heard him. "You were trying to get into my ass!" he said.

"Yes, but...."

"You can fuck off — or rather, I will." He got out of bed and strode to the door.

Those were almost the last words Andrew ever spoke to me. I'm ashamed to tell you that I spent most of that night in tears. I'd made a good few mistakes in my life, but never one that bad.

I hoped Mike hadn't noticed anything amiss, but I think he must have done. Andrew stormed into the bedroom in the very early hours of the morning, picked up his clothes and stormed out again. By the time Mike was up, we were both dressed. Andrew talked to him happily enough but ignored me. On the drive back to Brighton he said absolutely nothing. I said I was sorry but he didn't answer. He was to say only one more word to me.. When I dropped him in Montpelier Avenue, I asked when I would see him again.

"Never!" he said and slammed the car door.

CHAPTER FIVE

What can I tell you about the remainder of my time at university? Nothing, really. I'm not even sure that I want to remember it. They were the most miserable and worrying days of my life. I made a definite resolution that there would be no more sex. Absolutely none. For some weeks even the bolster stayed in its rightful position under the pillow. After all, I reasoned, if Mike could stay off it whilst surrounded by good-looking sixth form boys, so could I. There was no way I was going to let anything compromise my prospects with Nimrod Ltd. I applied to them at the beginning of my third year. I had two interviews and they wrote back to say that, provided I got a good degree, they would be happy to take me on.

And then it happened. Falmer is a long way from our place and, as I have told you, the student bodies don't mix, but I was in the Agadir one morning when two of our students came in. I knew them both by sight, but not their names. I saw them looking over in my direction and laughing. Then one of them called out. "Hi there, ducky," he said. "Fancy a bit tonight, do you?" I frowned and looked away. His mate took up the theme. "Fancy a kiss, love?" he called. Alarmed and worried, I left fast.

Then, two days later, I was with Alec in the King and Queen. "Raped any more Sussex students lately?" he asked. I pretended I hadn't the slightest idea of what he was talking about but knew Alec well enough to pump him for information. What I learned was frightening. Andrew had apparently told just about everyone that he'd been tricked into going to Burton Clayhanger, that I'd inveigled him into a double bed and that I had attempted to rape him. After that, the story got more fanciful. I was supposed to be missing two teeth and to have returned with a black eye.

"You ought to sue him. He could do you a lot of harm," said Alec, after I had satisfactorily proved that I had all my teeth. He, at least, believed me, but several others didn't. Hardly a day went by without some sort of taunt from someone. I took to leaving university as soon as I could and going straight back to Mrs Higgs. Even there I wasn't completely safe. Someone chalked a bottom impaled on a penis on the pavement outside the house. Fortunately I managed to get rid of it before Mrs Higgs spotted it. My name went up on the wall in the King and Queen's toilet too. It's probably still there.

I was horribly worried. I knew that Nimrod or their security consultants were checking on me. I expected at any time to get a letter saying they had withdrawn their offer. But, by some miracle, they never found out. All that staying in to study paid off. I got a first. One of the happiest days of my life was the day when I drove home at last. One final look at my faithful, silent bed companion; goodbye and thanks to Mrs Higgs and I was on the road. I hoped never to see Brighton again.

Nimrod accepted me. I went up there in August, found myself a nice little flat and joined the company at the beginning of September. The job I was given to do could have been tailor-made for me. I was put to work on the computer-guidance system for their new Cobra missile. I liked the people I worked with and I think they liked me. I was invited out so often that I began to look forward to evenings at home. There were pub evenings with the people on the Cobra project, birthday parties and dinners. I was much in demand for daughters' birthday parties. Not so often for sons', but there were some of those too. All in all, I was happier than I had been for a long time. I wonder what my life would have been like if the canteen had been serving an alternative to their notorious shepherd's pie on that Friday. Going to the Taj Mahal had been a sudden whim.

***

"You'll have to excuse Steve. He's not this world's greatest conversationalist," said Adam.

Steve couldn't have spoken even if he'd wanted to. I never saw anyone eat sandwiches like he did. He picked one off the plate and stuffed the whole of it in his mouth using both hands and then sat back on the sofa with bulging cheeks, looking like a cow chewing the cud - save that, as far as I know, cows do it with their mouths closed. Watching him eat deterred me from touching mine and my throat was still burning from the Taj Mahal's curry.

Adam had spent the previous three hours reminiscing about school again. I think I was almost as anxious for Steve to arrive as he was — in my case, just to get off the subject of school.

"Tim and I were at public school and university together," said Adam when he introduced us.

"Oh yeah?"

"Tim and I used to play squash together," said Adam when Steve was ensconced on the sofa with a plate of sandwiches in his hand.

"Oh yeah?" A lump of half-chewed bread dropped out of his mouth and landed on the overalls he was wearing. He brushed it off with his hand and then licked his fingers. I guessed him to be about nineteen or twenty. He was quite good-looking. He had short, dark curly hair. His face was unusual. He had the most expressionless eyes I have ever seen. There wasn't a flicker of interest there. He just sat there chewing with his legs sprawled out in front of him. His feet were enormous. He was wearing those brown, industrial boots. There was a fleck of what looked like yellow paint on the toe-cap of one.

"Are you a painter, Steve?" I asked. He said nothing. He stared at me for a second or two and then went on chewing.

"No. He's a car mechanic," said Adam.

"How did you meet?" I asked, desperately trying to get some sort of conversation going. Again, it was Adam who answered.

"In the garage. I went to collect the car and there were these long legs sticking out from underneath it," he said.

There was another long silence. Another beef sandwich vanished into Steve's champing mouth. My stomach started to rumble alarmingly. I shouldn't have had that curry. Curry does things to me which are best not described.

"I think I'd better go, Adam," I said.

"Why? You said you didn't have to go back to work."

"I don't have to, no, but there are one or two jobs that I ought to finish before the weekend."

"Leave them. You can't go now, besides which you haven't started on your tuck yet."

I hadn't heard that word since my prep-school days. Steve, having polished off his sandwiches, was already staring at my untouched plate. I stood up and handed him the plate.

"Ta," he said. Adam reached over and took it from him. "Afterwards," he said.

"Well, it's been nice meeting you again, and you, Steve," I said.

"Must you?" said Adam. My stomach gave another rumble. I said I had to get back. He came to the door with me.

"You ought to stay," he said, lowering his voice. "He's got the biggest cock you ever saw."

"I'll leave you to enjoy it," I said.

"I thought you might like to."

"No, no. I must be off. See you around some time."

Adam's flat was on the fifth floor of 'The Cloisters'. I was so desperate to get away that I would have gone down the fire-stairs, but he went with me to the lift. "Take my card. Give me a call some time," he said. I took it. The lift arrived. We shook hands. I felt really relieved when the lift door slid to and obliterated him from my sight. I looked at the card on the way down. There were more letters after his name than my doctor has. I recognised his degree in business studies but the others were unknown to me and certainly not awarded by Brighton. It gave both his office and home addresses, but what really got me was the school crest. There it was, in full colour, embossed in the top left-hand corner. He hadn't exactly covered himself with glory there. I thought it the limit of ostentation but then I didn't know Adam as well as I thought.

That day unsettled me in more ways than one. I spent a horrible weekend, mostly in the toilet. I couldn't get Steve out of my head. Not just Steve, but Steve and Adam together. I lay in bed trying not to think about them but the images kept returning. Steve slipping out of his overalls to reveal what hung underneath. Adam taking it into his mouth as he had done with mine. Would Adam have undressed as well? Probably. How had he changed since I had last seen him? Not much, I decided. I reached down under the bedclothes.

"Here we go again," said a little voice in the back of my head. "Here we go again," I repeated.

Sunday was worse. It started with a wank. I had another one whilst sitting on the toilet that afternoon. I just couldn't get them out of my mind. I wondered if Adam treated Steve in the cavalier manner he'd used with me. Maybe he had. Maybe he hadn't. And what did he actually do to Steve? Just sucked it, I thought. That was the only aspect of Steve he'd mentioned, but then I hadn't stayed very long. Maybe he fucked Steve as well. It was possible. How would Steve respond? Not very actively, I thought. He didn't look like the active kind.

Desperate to talk to someone about other things, I called my parents and got the answer-phone. That wasn't surprising. Dad always went riding on Sunday and Mum was probably round at a friend's house. I rang Gran. She was in. I told her about the curry and its effects.

"Got anything to stop it?" she asked. I said I hadn't. She said I ought to get some kaolin and morphine mixture first thing in the morning. "Don't go for any of these new-fangled drugs. There's nothing like kaolin and morphine," she said and then went on to ask about work, referring to Nimrod as 'the opposition'. In fact there was no opposition. Weaver's don't produce missiles.

"How about girlfriends?" she asked, after I had told her about the people I worked with.

"No time," I said.

"That's the answer I expected," she said. "Just stay happy, Tim. That's the main thing."

That made me think. I thought about it for the rest of that day, but Adam and Steve kept intruding. I heated up a pizza for my lunch and wondered if Steve ever stayed overnight at Adam's place and what they did about lunch. I couldn't see Adam cooking somehow. I guessed they went out to eat — probably in some expensive restaurant. But would Adam want to take someone who ate like Steve into a restaurant? Almost certainly not. Adam would do what I was doing. The microwave pinged and brought that chain of thought to an end, but only temporarily. Did Steve help with the washing-up? Did Adam spend Sunday afternoon reading the Sunday paper? Of course he didn't. Adam wasn't like me. Adam had other things to keep him amused. Big things, too. Did people with big feet have big balls too? I thought they would. Adam was probably sucking them and licking them at that very moment. The newspaper didn't help. A naval lieutenant had been dismissed from the service as a result of an alleged incident during a yachting trip with four boys, all of whom were over eighteen. He was appealing the decision.

"Won't do you a bit of good," I muttered. He'd have people like my dad to contend with. I couldn't see how the defence of the realm could possibly be jeopardised by masturbating a nineteen-year-old in the middle of the Solent, but dad would.

I thought about Adam for the rest of that day and I thought about him at work on Monday. It was that school crest on his card that did it, and his extraordinary view of old school ties — by which I mean loyalties — although I was fairly certain that an old school tie of the other sort was hanging in his wardrobe. I'd been wrong about one aspect of Adam. He couldn't have talked about me. He'd had his chances, heaven knows. He must have heard about the Andrew Forge business, but none of my persecutors had ever said that their information came from Adam or that Adam had corroborated Andrew's story. He could have so easily joined the winning side. "Scully? Yes, I was at school with him. We knew all about him there." In fact, I thought, he'd probably say "I was at *public* school with him." I began to wish I'd kept in closer touch with him during those unhappy months. Then I would have known.

The more I thought about it, the more convinced I became that he'd kept silent. "Never, never, *never,* grass on your school-mates." That's what he had said.

By Wednesday, my perspective of the affair had changed entirely. Adam, I decided, had almost certainly defended me. They wouldn't have taken any notice, of course. People involved in witch-hunts didn't. There was that poor sod of a naval lieutenant. It was one lad's word against his. There was no mention of the other three in the paper. They'd probably not even interviewed them.

By Friday morning I'd made up my mind. I rang Adam at his office.

"What are you doing this afternoon?" I asked.

"Oh, the usual. How about meeting at the Taj Mahal again?"

I declined that offer. It was canteen shepherd's pie for me. I had no wish to open the bottle of kaolin and morphine I'd bought.

How about if I came round later in the afternoon?" I asked. Adam chuckled. "Sure," he said.

"I don't want to disturb you if you've got company," I said.

"Steve, you mean? No worry. He's looking forward to seeing you again. You seem to have made a bit of a hit there."

"But I hardly spoke to him and even then he didn't answer."

Adam chuckled again. "Must be your sunny personality. See you later."

Steve liked me. That put me in a good mood for the rest of that day. Even the shepherd's pie went down well. I had a few doubting moments. Adam could have been lying. It was the sort of thing one said. Mr. Thomas, my immediate boss, had told me that Mr. Parsons was pleased with the work I had done and that couldn't possibly be true. Mr. Parsons was the Managing Director and almost certainly unaware of my existence.

At two o'clock I cleared my desk, wished everybody a good weekend and set off. The Cloisters, where Adam lived, was an architectural anachronism. It dwarfed the buildings all around it. I didn't know then that his firm had built it. I parked the car and entered the huge lobby. I pressed the button for the lift and stood reading the list of things residents were urged not to do. Throwing cigarette ends from balconies wasn't permitted. I wondered how they could catch the culprits. By the time one landed on the ground, the person who threw it would have been well into his next cigarette.

The lift door opened. I stepped inside and was just about to press the button when an overall-clad figure came through the entrance doors. Seeing the lift open, he quickened his pace. It was Steve.

"Hi," I said when he was safely inside and we'd started to go up.

"Hi." His face was completely expressionless. There wasn't even a hint of recognition. Crestfallen, I decided that Adam had been lying. I wondered whether to pretend I was going to another floor.

"Remember me?" I said

"Yeah. Tim. Adam's mate."

"And you're Steve." I put out my hand but he didn't seem to notice. There would hardly have been time to shake hands anyway. The Cloisters' lift moves fast.

Steve gave three long rings on the bell; obviously a pre-arranged signal, and Adam opened the door.

"You've come together," he said. "Always a good sign. Come on in."

Steve hadn't waited for the invitation. He was well inside the flat already. He strode straight into the lounge. I followed Adam into the kitchen. "Steve and I met in the lift," I explained. "I wouldn't want you to think I was muscling in on your territory."

"An appropriate phrase," said Adam. "That boy's got muscles in the most unexpected places. Now then, I've done cucumber with prawns, BLT's and chicken. That should be enough."

Adam, I thought, must have a job in a million. It wasn't yet three o'clock on a Friday afternoon, he'd obviously spent a long time making the sandwiches and he was in jeans and a tee-shirt. We both carried the plates into the lounge. Steve started on them almost before the plates touched the table.

"The year book came yesterday," said Adam. "Did you get yours?"

"I never joined the Old Boys," I said.

"Good Lord! Why not?"

"Just not interested. It's expensive, too. Fifty quid a year just to get a glossy magazine and go to a boring dinner in London." Out of the corner of my eye I watched another sandwich go into the human disintegrator.

"It's interesting, though. Remember Mr. Watts?"

"The art teacher? Of course."

"He's died. And remember Ashley Duart-Dyson?"

"Who could forget?" I said, taking a sandwich. Steve had already demolished half a plateful.

"He's working in Dubai."

"Oh yes?" I wondered if Ashley and Andrew would ever meet. Would Ashley tell Andrew what school he'd attended and would Andrew tell Ashley that one of the old boys had tried to rape him? Going to a famous school had serious disadvantages. Adam obviously had a different opinion. For at least half an hour he talked school, sometimes self-consciously dropping bits of school slang into the conversation. He sounded like a Billy Bunter school story. Meanwhile, the real-life glutton was devouring sandwiches at a furious rate, often stuffing one in his mouth before the glutinous remains of its predecessor had been swallowed.

"That's enough for now," said Adam, taking the plate away from him. Steve said nothing. He couldn't. He leaned back on the sofa, still chewing.

"You've certainly got a good appetite, Steve," I said.

Adam laughed. "Not just for food, eh?" he said, patting Steve's thigh. Steve looked at him with a bemused expression as if Adam had spoken in a foreign language. For a moment I wondered if sex with Steve was another flight of Adam's imagination. That thought was rapidly dispelled.

"Show Tim your cock," said Adam.

This time it was me who made a mess of a sandwich. "Jesus Christ, Adam!" I flustered, spraying crumbs everywhere. "There's no need….." but Steve had stood up. He gulped down whatever was left in his mouth and pulled the straps of his overalls off his shoulders. They fell round his ankles. The tee shirt he was wearing underneath them gleamed white where the straps and the top of the overalls had been, but my attention was fixed on his pale blue boxer shorts. Surely, I thought, he wouldn't…. but he did. Seemingly without the slightest embarrassment, he pulled them down.

"Not bad, eh?" said Adam in the proprietary tone one might use to show off a new car. I managed to swallow the remains of my sandwich. "Amazing," I replied.

Seven and three-quarter inches of succulent-looking flesh hung down towards the floor. It was thick, too. The head, blunt rather than tapered, peeped out from his foreskin. I just caught a glimpse of his balls, which were quite as large as I had imagined them.

"Go and have a shower," said Adam, giving him a friendly slap on the behind. "Don't be too long."

Without a word, Steve pulled up his shorts and then his overalls. Clutching the straps in his hands he left the room.

"Don't be too long indeed!" I said. "What the hell's it like when he's got an erection?"

"Pretty good. You'll see. I always make him take a shower first. Otherwise he tastes of motor oil. Incidentally, you didn't tell him your name when you were in the lift together, did you?"

"Tim, yes. Nothing else."

"Just as well. Steve is not exactly the sort of chap who grasses, but in your position it's as well to be careful. If he asks your name tell him it's Dyson or Duarte. Might as well keep the old memories fresh."

That made me feel less embarrassed and much more at ease. I had been worried. Scully is an unusual name, and though I had no intention of telling Steve where I worked, there was always the risk that he might tell someone with connections at Nimrod.

"It's difficult to equate a monster like that with Duarte-Dyson," I said. Showering noises drifted in through the open door.

"Why? Did you ever see Duarte-Dyson's?"

"Well no, but… well I mean…"

"He's got a nice ass," said Adam. "Which end do you want?"

"That's for Steve to decide," I said. I knew what I fancied. I suspect I may have been licking my lips in anticipation.

"My dear man. He's from the working class. Start letting them make decisions and we'd be in real trouble. What do you want?"

"Well, to quote one of your famous remarks, it looks eminently suckable." I could feel my face going red as I said it.

"Did I say that? Well, it is as it happens. Good. That suits me fine. You suck him off and I'll fuck him afterwards. Let's go."

I followed him out of the lounge and into his bedroom. The furniture in his lounge had led me to expect something pretty expensive. I wasn't disappointed. One wall was taken up by built-in cupboards and wardrobes. The bed was huge. A black leather and chrome reclining chair stood in the corner. The only thing I recognised was the alarm clock — the same one he'd had in Brighton.

Adam started to undress. I did the same. Strangely, I didn't feel in the least embarrassed. Not even when my stiffened cock leapt out as my shorts came down. The embarrassment in that direction would come when Steve saw it and compared it to his own. Naked, Adam looked very much as he had when I last saw him in that state. Possibly a bit thicker round the waist, but that was all.

"You haven't changed, have you?" he said. I didn't know if he meant my build or my rapidly reacting tool. His was in the familiar half-hard state I remembered from Brighton days. He put a hand on my ass. That brought back memories too: memories and doubts. Was I doing the sensible thing?

I didn't have time to ponder the question. Steve came into the room. He'd obviously left his clothes in the bathroom. His hair was still wet. He looked first at Adam and then at me but didn't say a word.

"Tim first," said Adam. "Get up on the bed."

Steve sat on the edge of the bed and then shuffled back towards the middle. He took the pillow away and lay back. There wasn't a hint of excitement there. His eyes had the same expressionless look and his cock flopped across his belly with the head slightly to the right of his navel.

I suddenly felt really uncomfortable. "What about you, Adam?" I asked.

"Don't worry about me." He went over to the chair. "God! This leather's cold," he said.

I should have known, of course. Adam had never been known for his sensitivity. He was hardly likely to make himself scarce. I tried to comfort myself by thinking that, in his position, I'd do the same. Watching can be exciting. Being watched isn't. Just let him try to get me out of the room when it was his turn! I wished I had let him go first.

I sat on the edge of the bed and reached out to touch Steve's cock. It felt like putty. I put my hand between his thighs and cupped his balls in my hand. They, at least, felt warm to the touch and were still slightly damp. I ran my hands up and down his thighs, down to his knees and then up again until my fingers were buried in the dense thicket of his pubes. Nothing happened. I slid my hands upwards. I'd never seen arms so strong as Steve's and his pectoral muscles were enormous. Those great pads of muscle were almost the same shape as the bread slices from which his sandwiches had been made but no sandwich was as thick and as appetising as they were and sandwiches don't come crowned with a large, red nipple surrounded by a brown areola. I touched one with the first two fingers of my right hand. He gave a little sigh and his cock moved. I hadn't touched it. My hands were some way away, but out of the corner of my eye I saw it twitch slightly towards his navel. I touched the other breast and it moved again. Putting my thumbs roughly along the line where I thought his breast-bone would be, I played with the yielding flesh with the fingers of both hands. The effect was remarkable. I saw it begin to lift. I kneaded his breasts as hard as I could. Up it came. It was like one of those time-lapse films of an acorn germinating. It got longer and thicker by the second. I took his nipples between my thumb and fingertip and pinched them. He gasped. I did it again. He didn't make a sound that time, but he closed his eyes. The bend in the top straightened out and it stood rigidly upright, jerking slightly in time with his pulse.

I didn't need Adam to tell me he was ready. Even I could tell when a cock is erect and its owner too far gone to do anything else but shoot his load. Steve's massive chest rose and fell as he panted for breath. I shuffled backwards, giving Adam a close up of my ass, upon which he made some comment or other but, like Steve, I wasn't really conscious of anything else. Knowing my preferences as you do, you won't (I hope) be surprised or shocked by the first target of my questing tongue. Obligingly, Steve brought up his knees and opened his legs wider to let me get in there. He wriggled as the tip of my tongue found it and lapped round it — not for long, but long enough to get him really going. Then I turned my attention to his balls, bathing them in as much saliva as I could produce. And then? I licked up and down the shaft. In contrast with his balls, it felt cool and smooth. I knew that if I kept on for too long I was liable to shoot first. Otherwise, I'd have been content to carry on doing that for much longer. I raised my head and lowered it again. I felt his cock head touch my lips. I opened them and took in as much as I could. I remember wishing that the soap in Adam's bathroom was of the non-perfumed variety. For a moment I got a mouthful of some floral taste but that soon went, to be displaced by the unmistakable taste of a worked-up man. I couldn't see what I was doing, but reached forward, letting my hands glide over his body until I had found his nipples. I gave them another tweak. His behind rose from the bed, nearly choking me. Raising my head to accommodate it, I did it again. It was better that time. After that, I gave way to sucking it. I had to. I knew I was going to shoot at any second and I wanted him to come first.

He did, but only by a fraction of a second. He was panting away, raising his bottom off the bed. There was no way I could take all of it into my mouth. I doubt very much if I even had half of it, but that half was enough. He moaned something and then, with a last gigantic heave, he shot. Just how many loads I don't know. I do know that it was dripping from the corners of my mouth on to his belly. I had a momentary panic about making a mess on Adam's bed again. I needn't have worried. Mine landed on Steve's chest and face. I don't think any of it went on the bed. Steve lay there looking as if someone had emptied a bag of pearl buttons all over him.

It was only then that I realised that Adam was talking to me. All I heard was "Move over." He was standing next to the bed.

For a moment I thought my legs wouldn't support me. I got off the bed and had to hold on to the foot-board for a few seconds.

"You're not going to straight away?" I asked.

"Too right I am," Adam replied. "He's just right after he's come."

I sat in the chair and tried not to look, but Steve had got up onto his knees and his rear was pointing straight at me. I saw Adam's greasy finger go into him. Steve whimpered like a puppy dog. I got up, took my handkerchief out of my pocket and wiped my cock. Steve whimpered again.

I don't know what came over me at that moment. I was suddenly desperate to get out. Whether Adam or Steve noticed me getting dressed I can't say. I am sure they must have done. I took a final look round the room. By that time Adam was well inside Steve, with his hands on the young man's shoulders and his ass working feverishly. His loins were slapping against Steve's buttocks.

I was in such a hurry that I was still adjusting my tie when the lift came. It was only when I was home that I felt somehow safer and more in control of myself. I rang Adam to apologise and said I had felt unwell.

"Think nothing of it," he said. "I'll tell you what. What are you doing on Sunday afternoon?"

"Why?" I asked, suspiciously. There was no way I was going back to The Cloisters again.

"I think you'll like my Sunday boy. He's right up your street," said Adam.

I said I was tied up on Sunday. He made a joke about not knowing I was into that sort of thing and I put the phone down.

CHAPTER SIX

I drove home on Saturday morning. I just wanted to be as far away from The Cloisters as possible and home was the only place I could think of to go. Gran's place in Yorkshire is too far away for weekend visits. Mum and Dad made me welcome, of course, and wanted to know about the job and the flat. Mum had got a box of things together which she thought might come in useful. The coffee machine and the toaster certainly would.

I took Ben out for walks and went over to the stables with Dad to get some stuff he needed. On Saturday evening we went out for a meal. All in all, it was the sort of weekend I should have thoroughly enjoyed, but I didn't. I couldn't get Adam out of my head. It was that reference to his 'Sunday boy' which kept coming back to me, not helped by my folks. 'I'd better go to the shops or we won't have enough for Sunday lunch," said my mother. "I'll nip down the road and get the Sunday paper," said my Dad. Adam outdid them all. Adam had a Sunday *boy* and a Friday *boy* and probably a Saturday *boy* too. What did I have? A hand. For the first time, I began to wonder if the job at Nimrod really was the best for me. If I were a property developer like Adam, I wouldn't have to worry. Adam, apparently, had a boy for almost every day of the week. I didn't want that. He wouldn't be a Friday boy or a Saturday boy. I didn't like the word 'boy' anyway. No. Mine would be a friend; a friend for every day. I only needed one; someone I could really relate to. Why, we could even live together. I'd have to tell my folks that we were just sharing a flat.

I left home quite late on Sunday afternoon. The intention was to drive straight to the flat, unpack the box of stuff Mum had given me, put the various food items in the fridge and then have an early night. The nearer I got to our town and The Cloisters, the more guilty I felt about my stupid running away on Friday. Adam didn't seem to have minded when we spoke on the phone, but it was such a crass, stupid thing to do. In fact, the more I thought about it, the more guilty I felt. I needn't have gone at all, but I had. A sensible person would have made a dignified departure the moment Adam said, "Show Tim your cock." Of course he wouldn't have said it if I hadn't been there. It was Adam showing off again — and Steve had to suffer.

The miles went by. I looked at my watch. It was only seven o'clock. I'd be back in the flat in an hour. Who wants to go to bed just after eight o'clock? I pulled into a lay-by, found Adam's card and called him.

"Adam Saunders."

"Hi. It's Tim."

"Hello, old boy. Where have you been? I called you this morning."

"Oh, I nipped home to get some stuff. I'm on the way back now. Do you fancy a drink?"

"Why not come round here?" he said. I wasn't going to fall for that any more.

"You know that big pub, The Gleaners — on the roundabout? We could meet there," I suggested. It was on his side of the town and on my way.

"Oh God, no!" said Adam. I hate that place. There's another, smaller pub just along the road from there — The Fleece. Do you know that one?"

I had seen it a few times. It looked all right. The sort of place that has been there for hundreds of years. We arranged to meet there at eight.

The traffic on the outskirts was lighter than I'd anticipated. I was sitting in The Fleece with a pint in my hand at a quarter to eight. It wasn't a bad pub. The beams in the ceiling were real — unlike those in The Gleaners, which were a pretty good plastic imitation — and the pictures on the wall looked as if they had been there for ever. A large sepia photo on the wall behind where I was sitting showed the Fleece darts team of 1927. One of them was an extremely good-looking young man. An older man, sitting next to him, had his arm round him. Now, I thought, he was almost certainly dead. So much for human life. He'd lived, played darts, maybe the two of them were lovers. Maybe their affair had been the talk of the city. What of it? They were both dead now and it was all forgotten.

"Here he is!" Adam's voice made me jump. I looked up. Adam wasn't alone. "I brought Anthony along to meet you," he said. He introduced us. This time, I noticed, he not only said that we were at public school together but actually gave the name of the school. I cringed.

Anthony looked round the bar. "So this is what the outside world is like," he said.

I was a bit nonplussed. Adam just grinned. "Let me get you another one," he said and went to the bar. Anthony sat down. I can't honestly say that Anthony was good looking but there was something about his smile which I found attractive. I had no idea how old he was then. I subsequently worked out that he must have been about eighteen and a half. He wore glasses and had fairly short, dark curly hair. That was all I could take in before Adam returned with the drinks.

"I'm sorry I had to leave so hurriedly on Friday," I said.

"Think nothing of it, old boy. You did all you wanted to do. That's the main thing."

Fearing embarrassment, I turned to Anthony. "And what do you do?" I said. For a moment I cringed again. It was a badly phrased, question in the circumstances.

"I'm at university," he said — and I breathed a silent sigh of relief.

"Where?" I asked.

"Here."

"I didn't know there was a university here," I said.

"You're not the only one. It started off as a technical college. Then it was the polytechnic and now they've upgraded it again. Basically, it's a technical college."

"You can't beat a real university. That's what I say. Somewhere with traditions. Makes all the difference," said Adam.

I looked at him to make sure I'd heard correctly. Brighton University had started as Brighton Polytechnic. I turned back to Anthony. "What are you studying?" I asked.

He smiled. "It's called English Literature," he said, "but we haven't touched any literature yet."

"Typical of those places," said Adam, learnedly. "They obviously haven't got a syllabus planned yet."

After that, I am ashamed to say, I rather dominated the conversation. Anthony had a computer and was experiencing all sorts of minor difficulties. Ignoring Adam's advice, which was to go out and buy the biggest and fastest set-up on the market at that time, I tried to help. I think I did.

A woman left the crowd she was with and came over to us. "Sorry to disturb you, Anthony," she said. "Can you tell your father that I can't do the flowers this Sunday. Mrs Humphreys will do my turn and I'll do hers when it comes up."

Anthony asked for a piece of paper. Fortunately I had some. He wrote down the message.

"I wonder how many more there'll be. Why couldn't we have gone to the Gleaners, Adam?" he said.

"Chemical beer in plastic glasses? Not on your life," said Adam.

"It's cheaper than in here, though," said Anthony, and then added, "That sounds rather rude. What will you have, Tim?" I asked for an orange juice. He stood up and I noticed his trousers for the first time. They had white stripes and buttons down the outside seams. When he left the table I was still thinking about his computer. By the time he was at the bar, waiting to be served, rather more pleasant thoughts were drifting through my mind. I was wondering if the buttons actually undid and, if so, what on earth they were for. I could think of a use, but I didn't think the makers had that in mind.

Adam seemed able to read my thoughts. "Under those extraordinary pants, there beats an arse of gold," he said.

That annoyed me for some reason. "Don't you ever let up?" I asked.

"Would you, if you fucked that every Sunday? Not that you'll get a chance. Anthony is very much mine and he dare not flaunt his many charms too openly."

"Why's that?" I asked.

"His father's the vicar here. He's a prebendary too, whatever that is."

"Oh, so that business about the flowers….." I wasn't able to finish. Anthony returned with the drinks. Just a half for himself, I noticed. He sat down and Adam became more and more dominating. In hindsight, I suppose I have to admit that I was a bit jealous of his influence over Anthony, but it wasn't just that. "What you ought to do is this." "You'd be a fool to do that. Take my advice and…." The annoying thing was that Anthony sat lapping it all up. He did get visibly annoyed and embarrassed when Adam made not-so-subtle sexual innuendoes. I really felt sorry for the guy. He said that the benches in the Fleece were hard. "Some people like something hard against their arses," Adam replied. Anthony said that beer tasted nicer when it came from a pump. Adam said he knew another liquid that tasted nicer when it was pumped straight into his mouth.

A man came over to us and asked Anthony to tell his father that Nigel wouldn't be able to teach his Sunday School class on the following Sunday. "Don't you get roped in," said Adam. "You've got something else to do on Sunday."

My temper was rising towards boiling pint when the doors to the bar were flung open and three young men and two girls appeared. The quiet, comfortable atmosphere of a pleasant pub (though I agreed with Anthony about the benches) was shattered. With cries of "What'll you have, Fiona? What about you, Nicky?" and "Shall we eat here or go on somewhere else?" they made a beeline for the bar. Then one of them, the oldest by the look of him, spotted Adam.

"Good God! Adam Saunders!" he exclaimed and then, to his friends. "Look who I've found!"

Adam stood up. "Hi, Ralph," he said. "Long time no see and all that. How's things?"

"Not so ducking fusty old boy. Not so ducking fusty. Why don't you join us?"

"Well, actually..." Adam looked first at Anthony and then at me. Simultaneously, but using different words, we said that we wouldn't be in the least offended. He stood up, pulled out his wallet and dropped a ten-pound note on the table. "Get yourselves drinks," he said and left us.

"He's an amazing person, isn't he?" said Anthony as Adam moved away to join his friends.

"Oh, he's all right, is Adam. He'd do anything for a friend," I said, not wishing to show up his idol as clay.

"Or *to* the friend," said Anthony.

I smiled. "If the friend is agreeable," I said.

"You know him pretty well?"

"As he never tires of telling people, we were at school together," I replied.

"*Public* school," said Anthony, smiling. "What sort of place was it?"

"Ancient buildings and even more ancient teachers," I said. "You'd get a much better education at the local comprehensive."

"That's good news. That's where I went. Were you in the same class?"

"Only at the end. He's older than me."

I didn't want to tell him that Adam had failed his A levels, but I suspect he might have guessed. He looked round to make sure that nobody was in hearing range. Even if there had been, our conversation would have been secure. The people Adam was with were making such a racket.

"I suppose you realised I'm gay," said Anthony.

"Adam told me," I said.

"I guessed as much. I wish he'd keep his mouth shut. He could get me in a load of trouble. My Dad's the vicar here."

"So I heard. 'Vicar's son. Scandalous revelations!' That sort of thing?"

"You got it. Dad would have to move for sure."

"So why spend every Sunday with Adam?" I asked. "Why not just break off?" I was one to talk!

"He pays my rent," said Anthony. He went on to explain that his father wanted him to continue living at home whilst he was at university. The vicarage had eight rooms. His dad thought it would be a waste of his money and tax-payers' money to rent accommodation in the circumstances. Anthony, however, wanted to make the break. The money Adam paid him on Sundays was just sufficient for him to maintain a tiny flat near the university.

"And you're happy there?" I asked.

"Oh yes. It was a good thing to do. What about you? What do you do and where do you live?"

I told him the address and said that I worked for Nimrod. Hence I had to be just as careful as he had to be. He nodded understandingly.

I used Adam's money to get drinks. I bought Anthony a pint that time.

"I was thinking about your computer," I said when I had returned. "How would it be if I came round? I may be able to upgrade the memory. I can get the chips from work."

"Would you?"

"Sure. What evenings are you free?"

"Any apart from Wednesday. I have my Latin lesson then."

"Latin? What the hell do want to learn Latin for? It's practically dead in the Public....."

"Public schools?" he said, smiling again. "I know. But there's a fund. Providing they learn Latin, it coughs out a hundred a year to the sons of clergymen while they're in full-time education.

"Hard work, I imagine," I said.

"Harder than spending Sunday afternoons in The Cloisters, and less well-paid, but every little helps," said Anthony. We arranged that I should call at six-thirty on the following Thursday, and talked computers till closing time. Adam left with his friends before us. He didn't even glance at us. Anthony scooped up the change from the round of drinks. "I'll give it to him if he asks for it," he said.

I offered to give him a lift home, but he said he'd rather walk. I got him to scribble his name and address and phone number on a piece of paper and we left. It was just after midnight when I finally got into bed. I had to unpack the stuff mum had given me. Two very bloody pork chops went into the fridge. The box containing the other stuff went onto the table and — you guessed it — a new toothbrush went into the bathroom. I went to sleep with very pleasant thoughts.

At six-thirty on the following Thursday, I stood on the doorstep of The Puffins — an extraordinary name for a house so far from the sea. It was a small, detached bungalow in quite a nice street. I was puzzled as to how anybody could have a flat in a bungalow, but he obviously did. There were two bell pushes, one above the other, and the top one bore his name. I pushed it and heard footsteps on wooden stairs. "Great! he said, as he opened the door. "I wondered whether you'd come."

I followed him up a flight of wooden steps leading up from the tiny hallway. Whoever did the conversion knew what he was doing. Anthony's little flat occupied half of what had once been the attic. Instead of a ceiling, he had rafters. There was a tiny little bathroom at the top of the steps and then the one room in which he lived. A window had been put in, looking down onto the street, and there was a skylight in the roof. A single bed stood along one wall. His bookshelf and his desk occupied another. One ancient-looking armchair and a more modern wardrobe comprised the rest of the furnishings. I guessed that the curtain across one corner hid his cooking facilities.

"Like it?" he asked.

"It's quite cosy," I said. The poster on the wall of a bare-chested and remarkably good-looking young man had caught my eye.

"My latest heart-throb," Anthony explained. "I saw him at the Albert Hall." At that moment I felt almost as old as the Albert Hall. I guessed the guy to be a musician and I'd probably heard of his name but couldn't identify him from his picture. I said I liked him too and hoped Anthony would leave it at that.

His computer wasn't as old as I had thought. They were not bad machines at all for their times. In fact they were much better than a lot of the stuff that was flooding the market. Even if he'd had the money, Anthony would have been mad to take Adam's advice and buy a new one. I suggested that the best thing to do would be to fit the new chips I'd brought with me. Then I could help him with the problems he'd been experiencing.

"Oh, right," he said, in a strangely flat voice, and sat on the bed.

I'd brought all the kit I needed in my new Nimrod leather case. 'Every inch the professional,' I thought. "Just stay that way," said my little voice.

Getting the cover off that thing was a beast. There were screws everywhere and even when I'd got those out, I couldn't work out how the cover came off. I wrenched and pulled in every possible direction. Anthony stayed sitting on the bed. He could, I thought, offer to lend a hand, though there wasn't a lot he could do.

Finally I got it off and fitted my earth strap. Now usually when you put one of those on your wrist, anyone watching will ask what it's for or make some facetious comment.. Not Anthony. He just sat there watching me connect my wrist to a radiator. I set to work.

"You going to be long?" Anthony asked.

"Why? Are you waiting to use it?"

"No, but I might as well take a shower. If I leave it till later there won't be any hot water left."

That annoyed me. I hadn't expected gushing thanks or the act my mother puts on when workmen come to the house: 'You make it look so easy. It must have taken you years to learn how to do it', but I thought he might have shown some interest. If he had called in a firm to do what I was doing, it would have cost him a hell of a lot.

"I won't be that long, Anthony," I said.

"There's only one hot water tank and there are five people downstairs," he said. Once she's started on the washing-up it'll take at least two hours to warm up again. I might as well go now."

Installing the chips took hardly any time. I did that, blew out the dust that had accumulated, cleaned the fan and started putting the thing together again. The sound of water running came through the open door and gurgling noises came from behind the wall — obviously the main water tank occupied the rest of the roof space. I started to re-assemble the computer. I dropped a screw, which rolled under the desk, and that took a long time to find. I was still scrabbling for it when the running water noise stopped. I found the screw and was fitting it when he came back into the room. I didn't look round.

"Finished?" he asked. I didn't answer at first. I would have exploded with anger if I had. I kept doing up screws until my temper had cooled and then said "Nearly."

A drop of water landed on the case. "Hey! Watch out!" I said and turned round to tell him in no uncertain terms that water and computers don't go together. In fact, I said nothing. He was standing stark-naked in the middle of the room, rubbing his hair with a towel. I nearly dropped the screwdriver.

"I haven't got a hair-dryer," he said. I said I had an old one at home he could have. To be honest I was so transfixed that I would have rushed out and bought him one. It had been a long time since I'd seen anything as beautiful as Anthony. He was slender but by no means thin. The arms that wielded the towel so vigorously looked strong. So did his legs. There wasn't a trace of hair on them, but he made up for that by a dense, black escutcheon at his groin from which his cock dangled. It wasn't very large but somehow it looked just right on him. It swayed slightly from side to side as he rubbed his head.

"What are you staring at, may I ask?" he said, grinning.

"A sight like that's enough to distract anyone from his work," I said.

"Then I shall turn round," he said, and all thoughts of chips were replaced by thoughts of cheeks. I hadn't seen a behind like his since schooldays. If I hadn't seen his front view, I'd have said he wasn't more than fifteen years old. Years before, when we were still at school, Adam and I had racked our brains for adjectives to describe attractive arses. 'Chubby', 'cheeky', 'pert' , 'silky' — they all fitted Anthony. His bum was an almost perfect hemisphere, rising from the hollow of his back and sinking again just as steeply into the tops of his thighs. His smooth skin glistened. It didn't look as if he'd dried down there yet.

"Is that better?" he asked.

"Much better," I said.

"You could dry me if you like," he said.

"Let me finish this. There's not much left to do."

He turned round again, came over to me and unclipped my earth strap from the radiator. "I'd say you had quite a lot to do," he said.

"How....?"

He put his hand on the front of my trousers. My cock responded immediately.

"Like this, for instance," he said, feeling it through the material. "Let's get this silly thing off first."

He took the strap off my wrist and then, putting both arms round my neck, he pulled me towards him and kissed me. I was still in a state of shock at first, but as his tongue met mine I came to life again. So did he. I could feel his cock pressing up against my thigh and hardening by the second. He undid my tie first. After that I just stood there as he peeled off my clothes. I'd come straight from work so there were quite a lot of them. My jacket and shirt landed on the floor. I had to bend down and undo my shoe laces. He felt my bum through my boxers. Soon shoes, socks and trousers were on the floor too.

"It feels nice," Anthony breathed, putting his fingers round the mound of cotton at my groin. Then he put both hands on the waistband and slid them down. I stepped out of them. "It looks nice, too," he said. He sat on the bed and, grinning, beckoned me to step towards him. I did so. He looked up into my face, grinned again and then his lips closed over my cock.

He wasn't the best operator I'd come across, but his enthusiasm made up for his lack of skill. There were one or two moments when I feared his teeth might clamp down on it. He only had about a third of it in his mouth, but it was a great feeling all the same. I looked down and watched his cheeks moving in and out as he sucked.

"Not too much," I cautioned. A few more minutes of that treatment would have brought me off and I had other ideas. Adam had said he had an arse of gold. I intended to do a bit of prospecting.

He let it pop out of his mouth, took it in his hand and began to lick up and down the shaft whilst, with his other hand, he played gently with my balls. That felt great but, again, I was getting dangerously near boiling point. I put one hand on his shoulder and gently pushed him to one side. He got the message and let go. I pushed again and he was lying on his side. He looked up at me questioningly. His cock had risen enormously and stood out from its hairy base. Like a spring bud, his foreskin enclosed his cock head, coming to a pursed and tapered end. I would have liked to have got the tip of my tongue in there, but there was no time.

"Got any stuff?" I asked.

"What stuff?"

"KY and rubbers."

"No. Haven't you?"

"No. I've come straight from work."

"I've got some Vaseline. Will that do?"

"I guess so. Where is it?"

"In the cupboard on the wall behind the curtain."

I went over, my cock pointing the way, like one of those hunting dogs. It had a wet nose, too.

The mess behind that curtain was unbelievable. I tried not to look at the coffee cups in the bowl or the condition of the frying pan. The cupboard he mentioned seemed to contain everything except what I was looking for. I moved cans of baked beans and spaghetti, a sauce bottle and a packet of macaroni before I found the jar.

"Couldn't we leave it till next time?" said Anthony. He had got right onto the bed and was lying on his back looking at me.

"No time like the present," I said. He didn't argue the point. He parted his legs and brought his knees up. I sat on the end of the bed, opened the pot and anointed my third finger pretty liberally.

"I think it ...." said Anthony, but he didn't finish the sentence. My finger tip had found it. It felt like a tangled, tightly knotted rubber band. I tickled it. He liked that. He lifted his legs right up and began to wriggle slightly. I pressed against it. Nothing happened. I pressed harder and he groaned. It had to go in — but it just didn't. It was like pressing my finger against leather. There wasn't even a trace of an orifice there. I pressed again, so hard that he cried out.

"Relax, Anthony. Relax," I said. Suddenly he brought both legs down, trapping my hand between his thighs. "It's no good," he said. It won't work. Not here."

"Why?" I was feeling more than somewhat frustrated by this time.

"It's the people downstairs," he said. "They might hear."

If he was that tight, I thought, they probably would.

"Let's just suck each other," he said. "I like that."

It was better than nothing. In fact, I'd go as far as to say that it was infinitely better than nothing. We managed, with a lot of difficulty, to get ourselves into position, me on the bed and Anthony on top of me. With even more shifting around, I managed to get his cock into my mouth. My nose was buried in his pubes, making me want to sneeze. Fortunately I managed to avoid doing so. I felt his tongue on my cock. I sucked his right in. The insides of his cheeks touched my cock as he tried to do the same. I felt it slipping over his tongue until it came to rest at the back of his mouth., He choked, let go of it and then took it again. I put my hands round his waist. It was incredibly narrow. Then I slid them down and clasped his neat little buns. They were still damp and felt beautifully smooth and cool. 'If only,' I thought — and then let myself go.

I'm certain the family downstairs must have heard something. Anthony's bed creaked and rattled like a rusty tandem with us as the riders. First there were regular creaks, as if on level ground. Then the louder, slower sounds of an uphill ascent with the riders stopping every few seconds to take a deep breath. Then, finally, we hit the downhill stretch. Rapid creaks and groans echoed down from the rafters above us — not that the noise worried me. Anthony's responsiveness was sheer delight. If only he had let himself go earlier, I thought. His buttocks tensed and loosened again frantically under my fingers. I tried at one point to separate them in an attempt to insinuate a finger when he was too far gone to resist. It was hopeless. I gave myself up to enjoying the feel and the taste of a delicious young cock and the scent of youthful perspiration. Within seconds I felt myself coming. I wanted to warn him, but couldn't. All I could do was to hold on to his heaving buns for all I was worth as I spurted into his mouth. For a split second, the muscles under my fingers relaxed. He made a gurgling noise and then started up again - if anything with even more vigour. The last feeble outpouring of mine coincided with a powerful buttock-clench and the first gush of warm semen into my mouth. I felt it forcing its way through gaps in my teeth as further spurts followed the first. He gave a little moan and collapsed on top of me. I had to push him upwards and out of my mouth in order to swallow. His last few drops landed on my face. He rolled off me and lay panting for a few minutes. I got off the bed and stood over him. He smiled.

"And from out of the strong there came forth sweetness," he said.

"You what?"

"It's from the Bible. The story of Samson," he said. "It was a lion. Are you a Leo?"

"No. Scorpio."

"I am. Perhaps it's me."

"Sweetness itself," I said, and I bent down to kiss him.

CHAPTER SEVEN

I don't think I have ever slept so well as I did that night. That was peculiar, really. I had thought I would spend the night gloating over my success. I had, after all, had one of Adam's boys and I hadn't had to pay him as Adam did. Most important in my mind was the fact that he had made the running; not me. Tim Scully the frightened school kid and Tim Scully the guy who worried about his sex life conflicting with his job had gone for ever. Goodbye to memories of a disastrous weekend in Somerset. I was Tim Scully, the lover of an intelligent, quite attractive eighteen-year -ld and neither Adam nor Anthony were likely to talk.

Things didn't look quite so good in the morning. For a start, the entire company was in a panic over the Stingray contract. It was beginning to look as if we had big problems with the bloody thing. I spent the entire day with Mr. Harris, the project manager, helping him check the software. That was probably just as well. Nagging doubts were beginning to worry me. In the first place, I had to make some excuse to see Anthony again, and I didn't quite see how that could be accomplished without being direct. Some sort of gut feeling told me that I ought not to do that. If I did, I'd be no different to Adam. He was a bit of a worry, too. If Anthony were to tell him what had happened, he might turn nasty. I couldn't see what he could do, but property developers, I thought, were influential people. One word to one of the Nimrod bosses and Mr. Harris wouldn't be saying, "Thanks Tim. You did a good job there."

I got home late. I shoved a pizza into the microwave and started to put away the things mum had given me for the flat. Among them was a new-looking hairdryer. My own was less than a year old. I sat with both of them in my hands, wondering which one to throw away — and suddenly remembered that Anthony didn't have one. Neither, as far as I could remember, did he have a toaster, and I now had two of those.

I ate the pizza, washed the plate and sat down to watch television. Should I?

I could do. Or would it seem too obvious? Maybe he was round at Adam's anyway. It wasn't Sunday, but you never knew with Adam. His appetite for sex was insatiable. Not like mine. It could wait. Or could it? I picked up the phone and dialled Anthony's number. As I did so, I wondered if there might come a time when I'd be justified in storing the number in the phone's memory. Not yet, certainly, but there might come a time… There was no answer. I put the phone down and almost immediately, it started to ring. I nearly jumped out of my skin. It was bloody Adam — the last person I wanted to talk to at that moment.

"What's this I hear about Stingray? he asked.

"Adam, you know I can't talk about things like that. You're not supposed to know it exists. Who told you? It certainly wasn't me."

"In our game, old boy, it pays to keep your ear to the ground. Quite a lot of your people are our tenants. If you lose this contract, it'll mean job losses and that means problems for us."

My worst fears were confirmed. Adam must have some sort of contact high up in the firm. Most people had no idea that Stingray existed. Even dad never mentioned it at home. I said something about there being one or two minor problems which were well under control. I don't know if he believed me. I tried to sound confident.

"Did you manage to fix Anthony's computer?" he asked.

"Oh yes. It wasn't difficult."

"Nice guy, isn't he?"

"He seems okay, yes. I didn't talk to him much. I just fitted the new chips, cleaned the thing out and left. Nothing else."

"I believe you. You wouldn't stand a chance even if you tried. Very much a one-man boy, is our Anthony, and there's a limit to what even I can do."

"Really? You amaze me."

"He'll be okay once I get him down to Burton Clayhanger for a weekend. At the moment his silk road has been one-way traffic only, and not very pleasant traffic. He'll learn. I'll tell you what…."

"What?"

"We'll have a bash to celebrate. Drinks on me. Anthony's deflowering party. How about that?"

It was a typical Adam idea. No thought to Anthony's feelings. He was to be carted down to the West Country, persuaded to yield, and the whole sordid business was to be celebrated in beer on their return. Yet again, disgust smothered any affection I might have had for Adam. However, I said I looked forward to it very much — which was true, save that my 'it' wasn't what he was thinking of — and hoped it wouldn't be too long in the future.

"Take some time, old boy. He's got this rotten play."

"Play?"

"College dramatic society. They're putting on a play and he's in it. He's an idiot. He spends all his time learning his bloody lines. He even brought his script round here last Sunday and wanted me to help him practice."

"And did you?"

"We got as far as Act one, Scene one, but the scene soon changed — so did the act, if you know what I mean!" He chuckled.

I asked him to give Anthony my best wishes when they next met, he said he would, and the conversation ended. I sat for about an hour watching the film on television, wondering at times whether Anthony might one day become a famous film star. I wouldn't mind helping him to learn his lines. In fact, it was a pleasant prospect — and who could tell? Maybe one day he'd say "I owe my success to Tim Scully". It would be better than having to admit that he'd been fucked by Adam Saunders and that there had been a party to celebrate the event.

Eleven o'clock came round. Still wondering if I was acting wisely, I dialled his number again. He was in. "Oh! Hi, Tim," he said. "I've only just got back from rehearsals."

He told me the name of the play: The Importance of Being Earnest. I'd heard of it. When he came to describe the plot, I wasn't just baffled, I was completely lost. There were people who changed their names, and places and people that didn't exist. He was bubbling with enthusiasm so I let him carry on, interrupting him with an occasional "Mmm" or "I see". I didn't see at all, in actual fact, but while he was talking I was thinking. If he wanted to practise his lines I'd be a much better person to help than Adam. I, at least, had passed English — and I was fairly sure that Adam hadn't.

I managed, after about twenty minutes of Anthony's synopsis ("I forgot to tell you, there is no such person as Mr. Bunbury" and "So you see his name was Ernest, after all."), to tell him that I had a hair dryer and a toaster which might come in useful and got the impression that his head was still so full of the play that the message didn't really sink in. He had rehearsals every week-night, and had no time to collect them as I had hoped he would. Delivering them to him was out of the question, because the people downstairs went to bed early. He suggested that I go to one of their rehearsals and give them to him there. That wasn't on at all. I was keen to see him, but not in the company of a load of amateur actors.

"What do you do on Saturdays?" I asked.

"Learn my lines."

"Well, why don't we meet then? I can help you learn, if you like."

"Would you?"

"Sure. I'm no expert on acting, but I'll help as well as I can."

"That would be great! I asked Adam, but he hasn't got time."

"Where do you learn them? At your place?"

"Well no, actually. I use dad's parish hall. There's a stage there, so I can practise the moving around like Peter says."

The stage of some dingy parish hall was a long way from the cosy and intimate atmosphere I needed, but I'd committed myself. There was nothing else for it. It had to be the parish hall, and all ideas of "That's enough rehearsing for now. Why don't we have a bit of fun?" were going to have to be postponed indefinitely. And yet — and this is the mysterious bit — I wasn't in the least disappointed. Somehow, the idea of the two of us working together eclipsed all other thoughts. I've talked it over with Anthony since then, and with Danny, who was 'waiting in the wings' at that time. In fact, as far as we can make out, that was the day he applied for a transfer down south. It's the only theory we can come up with.

I went to bed perfectly happy. Danny reckons that's because some paranormal powers had told me about his forthcoming transfer. On previous nights I'd wanked myself to sleep over thoughts of Anthony. I didn't, that night. I turned the clock back past Steve; past Andrew Forge and ended up with Ashley Duarte-Dyson; the boy I'd spotted by the school squash courts. The fantasy was almost certainly better than reality. Ashley was more than co-operative and, in keeping with the long-legged, languorous way he walked, I fucked him slowly, pausing several times to enjoy the tightness of his arse, as exemplified by my fingers. I dread to think of the hour when I finally dropped off to sleep

The sense of panic was still permeating the firm when I got in the next morning. Nonetheless, I managed to get out at lunchtime and made my first visit to the public library. Fortunately, the man there knew who had written The

Importance of Being Earnest and was able to find me a copy. I didn't have a moment to look at it, of course. It stayed in the glove pocket of the car until Saturday.

St Mark's church was actually two churches, standing next to each other on a corner. One was an ancient little church, and it was dwarfed by the enormous building which looked to me more like a Japanese temple than a church. I had to ask the way to the vicarage and parish hall. There was no sign of Anthony anywhere, so I rang the vicarage doorbell.

I was only with his dad for a few minutes, but that was long enough for me to wonder if Anthony was quite sane. I mean, I can understand a guy wanting to leave home if his parents are difficult to get along with, or disapproving. Anthony's dad was a really nice guy and not a bit like how I imagined a vicar would be. I found myself telling him about dad's position and Weavers and more about my job at Nimrod than I'd told anyone else. I was even slightly irritated when Anthony arrived and the conversation had to be broken off. Anthony got the keys to the parish hall and we walked over there.

Like the main church, it was a huge building but there were folding screens which could be dragged across to divide it. At first Anthony sat on the edge of the stage and I sat down in the body of the hall with my copy of the play. He was pretty good. We went right through the first act and he only fumbled once or twice. What amazed me was the way the thing seemed to come to life. There's this bit when one character has the other one's cigarette case. He can read the loving inscription from Cecily. The other guy knows it was a present from Cecily, but can't remember the inscription, so he makes out she is his aunt.

"But why does your aunt call you her uncle?" said Anthony and the way he put his head on one side and gave a sort of knowing smile was a real knock-out. This lad was going to be good. Possibly even better with my help. We worked really hard on that first bit. By the end of the morning he had it off pat and was beginning to put in all sorts of expression. What had started off as a boring, Victorian play began to be very funny indeed. He kept a deadpan face, but I couldn't help laughing.

We had lunch with his mum and dad. Only salad, but very nice and the vicar produced a bottle of wine to go with it. His relationship with them was so relaxed and easy and so different from my home that I began to wonder why he'd moved out. Could there be someone else apart from Adam and me? Someone he didn't want them to meet? I didn't think so, but it was just possible. Was all that business about the people downstairs at Puffins an excuse to stop me calling?

"Adam rang this morning, Anthony," said his mum. "Just to make sure you'd go round there tomorrow."

Anthony didn't bat an eyelid. "Yeah. I hadn't forgotten," he said. The family continued to eat as if it was the most normal thing in the world for sons to be sucked off on Sundays.

"I wish you'd stop going there," said the vicar, but then he added, "It's your life I suppose," and I was even more amazed.

"Tim was at school with Adam. Did he tell you that?" Anthony asked.

"No. Were you, Tim?"

I said I was but emphasised the year's difference in our ages.

"I don't trust the man at all, nor his father," said the Vicar. "They're both a couple of fly-by-night adventurers. What kind of property developer asks a university student to spend Sunday afternoons correcting the spelling in his brochures? Begging your pardon, Tim, but it must have been a pretty awful school."

Anthony went into a fit of giggling and coughing — then managed to utter the name of the place.

"No!" Both the vicar and his wife spoke in unison. The vicar wondered how Saunders senior had managed the fees. I didn't know. In my case, the Ministry of Defence had coughed up a fair proportion. I said that, from the car I remembered calling for Adam at the end of term, his dad wasn't short of cash. The vicar said nothing and just sat there calmly dissecting a chicken leg.

I left them at about two o'clock, and drove Anthony back to his place. "I'd ask you in, but the people downstairs might have guests. They often do on Saturdays," he said. I couldn't see what that had to do with it. "Anyway, I've got an essay to finish," he added. "Same time next Saturday?"

"Haven't you forgotten something?" I asked.

"Don't think so. What?"

"A toaster and a hair dryer. They're in the boot."

For a moment he blushed. We got out of the car and I handed them over. "Thanks a million, Tim," he said. "It's really good of you."

I offered to give a hand. With a book under his arm and the toaster and hairdryer in each hand with cables trailing, he looked like he needed one. But he refused, held the garden gate open with a foot whilst gathering the cables together with his right hand, and started towards the front door.

"Have fun correcting the brochures," I called from the car. He turned round and grinned. I caught the words "....a lot of correcting fluid," and that was the last I saw of him till the following Saturday.

I didn't really miss him. Not even on Sunday afternoon. I guess the prevailing chaos at work during the week helped. Something was obviously going on. People arrived for conferences and went away again and Mr. Harris and I continued to check the 'Stingray' software and got nowhere. In the evenings I pored over my copy of the play to see if there were any suggestions I could make. There weren't any. Anthony had pre-empted most of my ideas.

He only popped up once in the night hours, and that was to succeed where I had failed with Andrew Forge. I was the fly on the wall in that particular fantasy, which was nonetheless enjoyable. I must confess, too, that I was envious of Andrew, who lay grinning happily as Anthony's ass jumped up and down looking like a bifurcated, tethered ball.

The following Saturday saw us once again working on the script. He was even better. Four weeks later, feeling happier than I had felt for ages despite a private life better suited to a monk, we ran through the play in its entirety. He was absolutely brilliant. He fluffed his lines just once. I think that was because his dad came in to listen. We roped him in to read some of the other parts and that problem was solved.

The vicar waited till lunch to drop his bombshell. The vicar and his wife would be away for the whole of Friday and the coming Saturday. The wedding, apparently, of some clergyman somewhere. Anthony had agreed to stay over and look after the place. Would I care to keep him company?

I didn't want to agree too hurriedly. I made one or two excuses, dropping Mr. Parsons' name and back-pedalling quickly when the vicar said he knew him well and would call him.

"Go on, Tim," said Anthony, so I agreed.

Whether in fact he did ring Mr. Parsons, I don't know. All I know is that on the following Tuesday, I got a call from Mr. Parsons' secretary. He wanted to see me. I don't mind admitting that I shat bricks on the walk up to his office. All sorts of possibilities passed through my mind. "I've had a call from a chap named Saunders. Says he was at school with you...." "What's this I hear about you knocking about with an eighteen-year-old?" "Mr. Harris tells me that you're useless."

Tim Scully with Peter Gilbert

The secretary said I could go straight in. I knocked on the door and, for the very first time, found myself in the great man's office. Pictures of missiles lined the walls. Models of Cobra and Stingray stood on his desk. He looked up at me over his glasses.

"Ah! Tim," he said, which sounded encouraging. "How are your sea legs?"

"Sorry, sir?" I stammered.

"Do you reckon you could manage five days at sea. I see your father is...."

"I think I'd be all right. I went on several trips when dad had his own command."

"Good. I want you to spend five days on H M S Truro with Jim Harris. Stingray, you know. A few teething problems. Jim feels that seeing it at sea might give us a lead. I don't need to tell you how important it is for the firm. If the Ministry of Defence rejects it, we'll never be able to sell it overseas."

I said I'd be happy to go and asked when. For, to be honest with you, I was beginning to entertain certain ideas about my weekend at the vicarage. He said it would be about a couple of weeks. Arrangements had to be made.

I rang dad that night. He gave me a few tips. Pack warm clothing and seasickness pills. Don't throw your weight around in the wardroom. Don't speak to senior officers until they speak to you. It gave me an idea of what to expect. Plus, as I expected, dad knew the Captain of H M S Truro and would tip him off. When I asked him about the ship, he was extremely reluctant to answer.

So when Friday evening came round, my head was spinning. I'd had several long sessions with Mr. Harris. I'd been out to buy an anorak and seasickness pills (plus one or two other items which I hoped might come in handy for the weekend.) I'd been to the library again to look up H M S Truro, and got all the information that my father had apparently forgotten or never been told.

We did a complete run-through of the play on Friday evening. That was in the lounge, so we were able to use actual furniture. Once again, Anthony was good. I went out to get a Chinese take-away. We ate that and I asked where I would be sleeping. I tried to make it sound pretty casual; the sort of question which one could follow with, "I'll sleep on the floor or the sofa. It's all the same to me."

"In the granny flat," said Anthony.

"The what?"

"It's the mummy flat, really. The previous man here lived with his mum and he had it built on the back. I'll show you."

Once again, I began to wonder. At the back of the house was a complete flat.

Kitchen, tiny lounge, bedroom, bathroom, toilet — the lot. Further, it was approached by going round the house. There was no intercommunicating door of any kind. What student in his right mind refuses to live in a place like that? Only somebody who doesn't want his parents to see the company he keeps. Could it be Adam? No. Adam would certainly have told me, and the vicar and his wife would assume that he'd brought round some brochures to be corrected.

"What about you?" I asked. We were standing in the bedroom at the time. There was just one queen-sized bed.

"Oh, I'm easy. I can kip down just about anywhere."

"There's room in that for both of us," I said. I think I must have sounded as nervous as I felt. Recollections of Somerset and all that.

"That's what I hoped you would say," said Anthony. "There's not a lot on tele this evening...."

"Meaning an early night?"

"Just that. Hang on. I'll go back to the house and lock up. I'll bring your bag with me."

I undressed and sat on the bed. My cock had risen already. "Looks like you're going to be used, old son," I murmured. It nodded in agreement.

From the window I saw the lights in the vicarage lounge go out. Anthony reappeared a few minutes later with my bag.

"You didn't waste any time, I see," he said, putting the bag down.

"No point."

"You're not going to wear pyjamas or anything ghastly like that, are you?"

"No. You?"

"You've got to be kidding." He stood at the end of the bed and started to undress. I put my hands behind my head. I didn't want to sit up. That would have looked too keen — but I wanted the best view possible. There were one or two things I hadn't noticed the first time. A fine line of hair ran down from just under his shoulder blades and along his spine. He seemed much taller, but that was probably the result of watching him from an almost prone position. When he was down to his boxers, he gathered up the discarded clothes and stowed them in the wardrobe in the corner. He bent down and put his shoes away too. Finally, he stood over me. His boxers were stretched out in the middle like a tent. He grinned. "At last!" he said. "I've been waiting for this for ages."

I didn't understand that at all. He had a flat of his own. He could have come round to my place and, to top it all, he had the use of a self-contained flat at the vicarage.

He sat on the bed with his back to me. For a second or two I thought he might be saying his prayers, but then he lifted up his legs and lay down next to me and stared up at the ceiling. I put out my hand. His cock felt as hard as teak under the cotton material. Mine, hidden by the quilt, was in the same state.

"Tell me something," I said, gently stroking the mound.

"Uhuh?"

"There's Adam and there's me. How many others?"

"None. I dare not."

"But you've got your own flat and you've got the use of this place. As for 'waiting for ages', you could have come round to my place."

"Not when I'm rehearsing every night. You don't understand. Nobody does. I'm the vicar's son. You saw what it was like that time we went to the Fleece. Everybody round here knows I'm the vicar's son. Vicar's sons either have to be randy heterosexuals, shagging every bird they can or holy, pious people who think a prick's only use is for pissing. I go to the shops and it's "Oh, Anthony. How is your dear father?" If I go to the pictures somebody will recognise me and tell dad they saw me. Other blokes of my age can do what they like. Not me. That night you came round, for instance. Dad knew about that the day after."

"Not everything," I said. His belly felt hard. I stroked up and down from his naval to the waist band of his shorts.

"Not everything, but Mrs Powell downstairs told dad it was a good thing you came when you did or you would have caught me in the middle of a bath. Honestly, people watch everything I do. It's a real piss-off."

"You'd have been better off to live here," I said.

"That's the whole point," he said. "I want to lead my own life away from the church and the clergy. If I'd got better A levels, I might have been able to go to university in a different place but I didn't. Dad is a trustee of this place and had a few words — so here I am. Still here."

"I see," I said. Truth to tell, he'd made me think about myself. Up till then I'd thought I was badly off.

"But the vicar's away and we can play," he said, and, to my surprise, he rolled over on top of me and planted a very wet kiss on my cheek. My right arm was trapped underneath his considerable weight, but I put the other behind his head and our lips met. Neither of us, I admit, was an experienced kisser. Tongues touched teeth and we seemed to have the same urges at the same time. His tongue pushed into my mouth as I was trying to get into his. I stroked his back. I could feel the fine hairs along his spine, leading, I thought happily, right down under the shorts to his asshole. He rolled over so that he was right on top of me. I brought my right arm into play. There was no sense of feeling in my fingers, but I made up for that with my left hand, burrowing under the elastic to stroke his silky, hard buns.

Holding him tight like that and having his tongue in my mouth was almost unbearably exciting. I think I might have come had it not been for a succession of mighty crashes. They were so loud that they made the windows rattle. He pulled his head away and smiled.

"Christ! What was that?" I asked. Then I knew — church clock sounds like a church clock, but I'd never heard one go off as such close quarters.

"A very good reason for not living at home," said Anthony. "Don't worry. It doesn't ring after midnight."

"So we have to suffer two more times."

"Suffer? You won't even notice it. I think it's time this quilt was taken off. I haven't seen you yet."

He had to get off the bed to do it. He threw the duvet to one side and looked down at me. I put up a hand and touched his cock through the shorts.

"Gorgeous!" he said. I tugged at his shorts and they slid down his thighs to his knees.

"So are you," I said, looking up at least six inches of stiff flesh and a ball-bag like a large, juicy pear.

He shuffled out of his shorts and got back onto the bed. He lowered his head onto my cock. For a few minutes we had what can only be described as a wrestling session. Finally we sorted things out. His mouth was on my cock and I was half-smothered by his groin on my face. Not that I complained. The scent of him was sheer delight. The texture of his scrotum on the tip my tongue was exciting enough, but when I finally managed to get as much of his cock in my mouth as I could take, I was so ecstatic that I don't think I'd have noticed if a battery of artillery had fired. He was making a meal of me, too. I could feel his cheeks against my cock as he sucked on it. He did that for a few minutes and then started licking my balls and kissing them. Then he went back to my cock.

Again, I don't think I would have had the self-control to stop. Anthony suddenly took his head away., leaving my cock feeling damp and cold. "Give it a break," he gasped. "I don't want to come too soon." Reluctantly, I let his shaft slide out of my mouth. He rolled over and lay alongside me, providing a close-up of his cock, his balls and the shiny curly hair that grew around them. For some minutes we lay there, panting. My heart was pounding. So was his. I could actually hear it.

I touched the side of his thigh. I slid my hand upwards and insinuated my fingers underneath him. Feeling had returned to them. His butt felt soft and silky and slightly damp. I couldn't be sure, but I think he lifted himself slightly. He didn't seem to mind what I was doing anyway. I pushed a finger upwards between his cheeks and ran it backwards and forwards. He said nothing. I did it again.

"Are you going to let me?" I whispered.

"Let you what?"

I would have thought my working finger was a pretty good indication of what I had in mind. Apparently not.

"Fuck you," I said.

"No," he replied. Just one word. "No."

"Why not?"

"I don't want you to."

"You're scared."

"Maybe."

I still had hopes that he'd change his mind. I twisted my finger further between his cheeks.

"No!" he said again, and moved away from me.

I didn't know what to say or do. It didn't seem possible that yet another disaster was looming. His cock was still rampant. He was still breathing heavily. Other people succeeded. Why couldn't I? My cock was far from being intimidating. He'd said it was gorgeous. So why not let it find its rightful home?

"I'll be glad when the play's over," he said.

Aha! So that was it. He was nervous. Maybe he thought that being fucked would be so painful that it would affect his performance.

"Stage fright?" I asked.

"Not really, no. Adam and I are going away the weekend after. That'll be good. Some bloke he knows in Somerset. You been there?"

"Twice."

"What's it like?"

"Depends what you mean by 'it'. The village is nice. Mike's a nice bloke."

"You make it sound like there's a hidden snag. What is it?"

I didn't know what to say. Adam had been pretty loyal to me, but not to other people. Should I warn Anthony or keep quiet? It was a difficult decision to make.

"I guess it depends on the company," I said at length. I had a weekend there with Adam. That was okay, I guess. From his point of view anyway. The other one was dreadful."

"In what way?"

"Guess."

"He wouldn't let you fuck him?"

"He wouldn't let me do anything."

"What about Adam? Did you fuck him or did he fuck you?"

"Both, actually."

"I can't imagine Adam being fucked. What's it like?"

"Brilliant. There's nothing like it."

"For the one doing it or the other one?"

"Both."

There was a long pause. I knew he was thinking. I just hoped he was thinking on the same lines as I was. Then he spoke. "Would you let me do it to you?" he asked.

They say life is full of surprises. I stared at his cock. It was twitching very slightly in time with his pulse. It looked manageable. It's probably imagination, but I got the impression that my arse was itching in anticipation.

"Why not?" I said. It wasn't, I confess, the generous gesture he might have thought. One good turn deserves another — and a turn with Anthony could be very good indeed,

All my suspicions vanished as I helped him get ready. He hadn't got a clue. Finally, condom-clad and well greased, he was ready. So, may I say, was I! Handling his cock had really got me going. I turned over onto my front and stuffed a pillow under my middle. I wished I had had more experience. I told him what to do. His finger hurt like hell. Fortunately I managed not to cry out and he couldn't see my face. I hoped he'd think the wet patch was sweat. In fact it was teardrops. It felt like a red-hot skewer at first, but the pain gradually subsided. My muscle ring was clamped firmly against his finger but I could feel the tip of it moving inside me. I tried to relax so that he could get more in. That took some time. Slowly the feeling turned from agony into discomfort and then even that vanished and I started to enjoy it. Those first few minutes had taken me off the boil, too. If they hadn't, I'm sure I would have shot. My balls ached and my heart was still beating hard, but I knew it was going to be some time before I got to an orgasm. In which circumstances, there is only one thing to do, I thought — relax and enjoy it.

Anthony was beginning to pant as if he was running some kind of race. I knew the feeling well. It was time to let him know that fingers are fun, but a cock is better. I don't know what I said — or rather gasped. He got the message. I felt his hands on my shoulders and his breath on the back of my neck. His cock felt like steel against my butt. He muttered something. I reached round to find it, took it in my fingers and guided it down. It touched the spot. His breath on my neck was more pronounced. I winced, anticipating another 'red hot poker' feeling. The first inch or so was a bit painful. I think I might have called out, but after that it went in as though we were made for each other. A perfect fit, you might say.

In retrospect, he wasn't that good at it but he enjoyed it and so did I. He certainly put all he'd got into it. His hard groin slapped against my butt. At one stage he nearly throttled me by putting his arm round my neck. Sweat dropped from his head onto mine and he gasped loudly with every stroke. So, come to that, did I. I couldn't help it. He was right on my button and that made me feel quite faint for a moment or two. I was ready to shoot. I wanted desperately to come at the same time as he did but it wasn't to be. He gave a long sigh and fell on my back. I could feel his cock pulsating in me as his spunk filled the rubber. I put my hands behind me and rubbed his buns. That was all I needed. Three, maybe four spurts soaked the bed beneath me. My hands dropped and I lay there feeling his cock twitch into quiescence inside me as mine did the same below me.

I don't know when that happened. Anthony had been right about the clock. If it struck whilst he was screwing me, I wasn't aware of it. I can, though, tell you when my cock was in him. Six o'clock in the morning. That was the hour when it came back into operation.

It had been quite a night. I had sucked him off. He had done the same to me. We fell asleep in each other's arms, occasionally waking to enjoy a kiss or a fondle. It was still dark when he kissed me first and then said something. I had been in the middle of a peculiar dream about railway trains (of all things!) and had to ask him to repeat it. His hand went down to my cock. There must be something pretty potent about trains. It was steel-hard. He gently pulled the foreskin back and whispered, "I might as well get used to it."

"What?"

"What do you think?"

By that time I was well awake. I knew exactly what he meant. My first instinct was to say 'Are you sure?" I didn't. He'd made up his mind and so had I.

I threw the quilt aside again and grabbed the necessities from my bag at the edge of the bed. A phrase from the firm's first aid manual came to mind. "First put the patient at ease." Anthony was lying on his back but he certainly wasn't at ease. His eyes were wide open. He'd clenched his fists and his body looked almost as stiff as his cock.

First aid came to mind again as I muttered something about not hurting him. I managed to persuade him to bring his knees up. I pushed them apart as gently as I could. He looked at me questioningly and bit his lower lip. I shuffled forward towards him. He leaned back against the headboard and at last I had sight of my target: a tiny pink lump surrounded by smooth, ivory-coloured skin. It takes time between getting sight of the target and firing. I knew I'd have to be patient. I just hoped I could hold out. I managed to get a good dollop of the jelly onto my fingers and with one reassuring hand on his knee, I went to work with the other. I might as well have been tickling a wooden board. I moved forward again and transferred my free hand from his knee to his nipple. He sighed. It felt hard but rubbery; like the eraser on the end of a pencil. I tweaked it and he sighed again. Then, with my right hand still trying to persuade him to open up, I massaged the other nipple. He stopped biting his lip and opened his mouth slightly. I went back to the left nipple. He smiled.

"You like that, don't you?" I said. He didn't answer. "So do I," I said, kneading the pad of soft flesh. "You're gorgeous," I said and, as I said it, something happened. My finger didn't go in but, all of a sudden, stiffness vanished — save, I am glad to say, for his cock. That still stuck outwards and upwards. The hard surface against my probing finger suddenly turned soft. I pushed against it a bit harder. Too hard, as it turned out. He yelled and went to push me away, but he was too late. A fraction of my finger had gone in. He took his arm away. I played with his right nipple for some moments. He sighed. Then, with a slight twisting movement, I gave him a bit more finger. He didn't yell that time. It was more of a sigh than anything. The feeling in my finger was quite extraordinary. When I was a little kid, my mother used to let me dip a finger in warm custard. It was like that: warm and wet and clinging. I am blessed with long, supple fingers —

the result, I guess, of years at the keyboard. All that inadvertent practice paid off that night. I slid a bit more in and then started to play around in there. Strange folds like tiny silk curtains brushed my finger tip. Anthony sighed again. I twisted the finger slightly. He didn't enjoy that much, but when I began to move it backwards and forwards inside him, something happened. He cried out at first and then groaned, interspersing each groan with an intake of breath. It sounded as if he was sobbing, but he wasn't. His mouth hung open and his tongue lay over his lower lip. I gave him a few more moments of 'interior massage' and then, as gently as I could, I withdrew the finger.

"Ready?" I asked. Again, he made no reply, but just sat there staring at me like a man in a trance. I grabbed a condom, slipped it on and then felt round for the tube of lube. I must have been kneeling on it. There was a hell of a mess round it, but there was enough left for me to anoint my cock pretty liberally. Then I lifted his legs — first the left, and then the right — and put them on my shoulders. I shivered slightly. I don't know why. They were warm and felt silky against my ears. I shifted forward again so that the backs of his knees were on my shoulders. A bit more. He raised his behind off the bed. I got my hands under his hips and the tip of my cock touched it. More by luck than judgement, I admit, there was no doubt at all that I was on target. I tried desperately not to push too hard, not wishing to hurt him. I think I must have done, though, because he yelled. I stopped and looked down at his face. He was biting his lip again and his eyes were tightly closed; so tightly that his face was contorted. I waited for a few moments and then pushed in a bit further. He yelled again, but not loudly. A bit more. Another yell. "Just a bit more," I said and at that moment I regret to say that lust took over. I went in much too violently. I almost toppled forward on to him. He yelled and then lay silent. For a terrible moment I thought I'd done him some injury, but he opened his eyes again and gave a watery smile.

"Sorry," I said. "It's all in now."

"It feels enormous," he said — which it certainly isn't.

I gave the first thrust. He twisted slightly. "Ha!" he said. I did it again. "Ha!" Then it was "Ha!.. Ha!... Ha!" He slid down slightly and I think even more of my cock went in. My arms were aching. I remember that. He was no light-weight and I was carrying the lot. He wriggled but I kept on, knowing that it wouldn't be long. I guess I was grunting just as much as he was, but all I was aware of was his weight, my aching arms and the grip on my cock. Anthony was infinitely better than Adam. There was a softness about Anthony that Adam didn't have and Anthony felt much more alive than Adam had felt; so alive that it was difficult to hold him.

"Ha! Ha! Ha!" My thighs were rubbing against the inside of his. "Ha! Ha! Ha!" My cock felt as if it would burst. Then, suddenly, the weight on my arms slackened. He arched upwards and shot. I got most of it on my face. Some of it splattered back on him. My tongue must have been hanging out. I know that at least one drop landed on it, but before I could do anything about it, I came, exactly as the bloody clock struck the first crash of six o'clock. It was like being in an earthquake. Four for the hour and then six successive bangs. Anthony grinned.

"Did the earth move?" he asked.

"Frightened me to death," I said.

"Don't die yet," he said. I waited for a few minutes for my cock to subside and then, very slowly, pulled it out, almost, I may add, losing the condom as I did so. His grip was still fairly tight. His legs fell from my shoulders and I straightened up at last.

"So? Not so bad after all?" I said. I was still trying to get my breath back. So was he. "Nice!" he said. "Very nice. Do you think I ought to go to Somerset with Adam?"

My first instinct was to say 'No'. I didn't. At last I could be one up on Adam. "Why not?" I said. "Just don't tell Adam anything."

"I wouldn't," said Anthony.

CHAPTER EIGHT

I called Dad from Anthony's place. He hadn't yet told the Captain of H M S Truro about me. He couldn't quite understand why I didn't want him to, but he promised not to say a word. I had to wait till Monday to see Mr. Parsons. I went up there three times. He was too busy to see anybody the first two times. I didn't mind in the least. I was on cloud nine that morning. I'd enjoyed the best fuck of all time. I'd sucked the most beautiful cock in the word and, when the Vicar and his wife got back on Saturday night, I'd actually been thanked and taken out to dinner. That was one of the most amusing and enjoyable meals I'd ever had. The Vicar kept saying things which amused Anthony and me. First, it was the decision to keep the buses running to a normal schedule on Sundays. "The godless come fast," he said. Anthony went to the toilet and when he returned to the table he scraped the chair on the floor and almost knocked a wine glass over. "Why can't you be like Agag?" said the Vicar.

"Who's he?"

"'Agag came delicately'. That's what it says in the Bible." I wouldn't personally have described any of the five occasions I'd shot my load that weekend as 'delicate', but the name stuck. In all the time I knew him, Anthony called me Agag.

So, by the time I was shown into the great man's office, I was still a happy lad. I explained that I didn't want the crew of the ship to know anything about my father. Mr Parsons thought that a 'very mature judgement'. As it happened, he had all the papers ready so I got my pass, instructions, and all the rest before Mr. Harris, but he didn't seem to mind. We were due to join the ship on the following Saturday morning. That was a blow. I had hopes of persuading Anthony to do another weekend of 'rehearsals'.

I started to worry slightly on Tuesday morning, and that did perturb Mr. Harris. Instead of thinking about Stingray, my head was full of doubts as to Anthony's ability to keep quiet. I knew he'd been with Adam on the Sunday afternoon. It would have been so easy for him to let something slip. Maybe Adam would notice a difference. You can't expect a guy who's come five times in the last forty-eight hours to shoot with the same vigour, even if he is just eighteen. I know I couldn't.

By Thursday, I was really worried. On Friday afternoon I decided to go round to The Cloisters. I didn't want to go. I knew I might have to apologise. It might turn out to be a row — the perfect reason for chucking Adam once and for all, but there was no way I could spend a week on a ship and not know.

I was late leaving work. There was one of those 'My car or your car?'; Don't forget such-and-such'; 'Make sure you bring....' sessions. By the time I was outside Adam's front door it was well after four.

"Hello, old boy," he said, as he opened the door. "What brings you here. You're just in time for a slice of the action."

I'd forgotten all about Steve. He was sitting in the lounge munching sandwiches. He nodded but didn't stop.

I said I could come back later, but Adam wouldn't hear of it. Before I knew what was happening, I was sitting in the armchair and he was in the kitchen making even more sandwiches. Actually, having missed lunch, I was hungry. When he came back I explained that I wouldn't be around for a few days as I had to go away on a job for the firm. He wanted to know the details but I wasn't going to tell him more than that.

"Your Stingray', I imagine," he said. "Teething problems, my foot. That thing's old enough to have developed wisdom teeth."

Steve laid his half-eaten sandwich on the sofa next to him. "I 'ad them," he said. "I 'ad to 'ave 'em taken out. Bloody painful it was. The dentist 'ad to drill right down inside the gum..."

"Yours were probably worn out by over-eating," said Adam. "Why don't you go and have your shower?"

Steve stood up, scattering crumbs onto the carpet.

"And pay special attention to you-know-what," said Adam. Steve left the room without a word.

Anxious to change the subject, I asked Adam to tell Anthony that I hoped to be back by Saturday for a rehearsal. I had, in fact, told Anthony.

"How is he coming along?" Adam asked.

"I think he's good. It's an old-fashioned play, but it's quite funny in parts. He'd be better off in something modern,"

"He will be soon," said Adam. "I'll be glad when this play's over."

"That's what Anthony said."

"Did he? Good. I like a keen player. His opening night should be quite something. That gorgeous little bum! I can't wait. Burton Clayhanger, here we come. I'll fill his passage. There's nothing like an eighteen-year-old virgin arse. You've never had one, I suppose?"

I said that that pleasure was yet to come.

"You worry me sometimes, old boy. If you're not careful, you're going to grow up into a frustrated old man. Why don't you hang around and get a mouthful of Steve? He's got enough for both of us."

I have to say that I hesitated a bit before replying. Maybe the previous weekend with Anthony had made me randy. I don't know. Certainly if that had been my flat, and Steve had been in my bathroom, I wouldn't have been able to wait as patiently as Adam was waiting. Nonetheless, I declined.

"As you wish. Think of me on Sunday when you're stuck in some dingy hotel room," said Adam. "I'll be conducting a dress rehearsal. An undress rehearsal would be a better way of putting it. Let's see… the play is in two weeks time. I just have this Sunday and next Sunday to get him completely ready. It should be fun."

The bathroom door opened and closed and Steve returned as naked as the day he was born. It was just as well that he hadn't come in earlier. It wasn't the after-taste of Adam's roast beef sandwiches which made my mouth water. Steve's cock had looked appetising the first time I saw it. It hung outwards and invitingly from still-damp hair.

"That's better," said Adam. "Sure you don't fancy a threesome, old boy?"

I made my excuses and left as fast as I could, hoping that neither of them would notice the lump in my trousers. I don't remember much of the short journey home. I couldn't get them out of my mind. First it was Adam and Steve. Then it was Adam and Anthony. Knowing something of the lack of privacy on board a Royal Navy ship, I had the wank of a lifetime that night. I drifted off into a dream in which I enjoyed myself with Steve and Anthony on the sun-lit, warm deck of a tiny boat. Adam, up on the bridge, shouted encouragement. I don't have to tell you that the bed was a mess when I got up in the morning.

It was just as well that I'd agreed to go with Mr. Harris in his car. I fell asleep half-way through the journey. He woke me up when we got to the gates of Portsmouth Dockyard. Getting in there was no problem. Finding HMS Truro was, and getting on board was murder. They searched our bags and scrutinised our passes as if they were expecting saboteurs. Finally, an extremely pleasant lieutenant led us up the gangway and we were on board. There was something familiar about that ship. It clicked as I followed the lieutenant down the companion way to our cabins. The Stingray launch platform had confused me. Otherwise, HMS Truro was identical to dad's last command, HMS Falmouth. I'd been on that twice as a small boy. Even the pattern of rivets in my cabin bulkhead was the same. The same little wash basin. The same wardrobe; the same desk and the same bed. It was like stepping through a time warp, and I knew I'd have to be careful not to reveal my familiarity.

I unpacked and lay on the bed. There was a knock on the door. It was the same young lieutenant.

"Captain's compliments, sir. He'd like to see you both on the bridge in half an hour."

"Sure," I said. "Where is the bridge?"

He said he would come down and collect us. I could have found the bridge without even thinking about it.

The Captain was nice enough. Apparently he was going to take us out into the English channel for us to do our tests. He hoped we'd find the source of the problem as soon as possible. He wasn't the only one.

We set sail (started out, as I put it) that evening with the usual Royal Navy rigmarole. Bugles blared, commands were shouted. Sailors in their best blues lined the rails facing the shore. The merchant navy manages to get their ships out of harbour with one man and a cat on the deck. Not the Royal Navy. The lieutenant took us below (downstairs, to me) and showed us the wardroom (the dining room). We had a drink and a very good dinner there and went to bed. No wank that night. The movement of the ship lulled me to sleep very rapidly.

We started work the next morning. Mr. Harris was always one to work much on his own. I was very much the stooge and there wasn't a lot for me to do. Even less for Artificer Williams, who had been taken off his normal duties to assist us. Mr. Harris sat at the console. I sat next to him watching the screen and Williams stood behind me. It wasn't the ideal arrangement. Mr. Harris couldn't concentrate and neither could I. Artificer Williams was just my type. He was tall. He had straw-coloured hair and whoever it was who had made his uniform trousers knew how to set off a sailor's midriff to perfection. They clung to his butt as though they'd been moulded onto him.

Finally, after an hour and half of mental torture, in which half of my mind was on mathematical figures and the other half on a much more attractive one, Mr. Harris spoke.

"There's not much you can do at this stage, Tim. Why don't the two of you take a break? Come back later."

"That's a relief," I said as I closed the Operations Centre door behind us and followed Artificer Williams' rolling butt up the companion way.

"Yeah," he said. "What do you want to do now? Do you want to go back to the wardroom?"

"Not particularly. What about you?"

"My D.O. says I've got to stay at your disposal. You or your boss, I mean."

There was no sight of land at all. In the far distance one could just about make out a ship of some sort.

"Can we find somewhere to have a chat? Looks like a walk to the shops is out of the question," I said.

I was dying to suggest the forward chain locker. I'd found it when I was about ten. It was the only place where a small boy would not be disturbed by the naval mania to inspect everything. Unfortunately, Artificer Williams seemed unaware of its existence. We couldn't stand on deck, he explained. Someone would note that he had nothing to do. We could go down to his mess, but I wasn't keen. The men who had been on the night watches would be asleep down there.

"So, there's nothing for it but to pretend we're working," I said. "Let's have one of the Stingray junction boxes open and look at wires while we talk."

I didn't need to have been on a ship to know where they were. I could have taken him to one blindfold but I let him lead the way to the biggest, just behind the main mast. It was a heavy-looking steel cabinet. I snipped the wire on the seal and pulled open the door.

"Christ almighty!" said Artificer Williams — with good reason. Salt was everywhere. Quite a lot came away with the door. It didn't register much at the time. Sea water had obviously got in through a gap and slowly evaporated. I poked around aimlessly with my pocket screwdriver and let Artificer Williams do the talking. His name was Andy. He was nineteen years old. He'd been, he said, very lucky to get into the Navy. His school results hadn't been that good. He had two younger brothers and one sister. His father made surgical boots and his mother worked in a hotel in Portsmouth. I tried to be interested in all this, but I have to be honest and tell you that there was something else I found much more interesting. I was crouching down and his waist was level with my eyes. It could easily have been imagination or a handkerchief (though I didn't spot any pockets) but I was certain that something was making that bulge. It wasn't very big, but the more I stared at it, the more real it appeared.

"What about you?" he asked. "How'd you come to get this job?"

I said I had always been interested in computers and armaments. It seemed the right job for me and I was reasonably happy.

"Got any hobbies?" he asked.

"Not to speak of. You? I guess it's a bit difficult to have a hobby on a ship, isn't it?"

"I read a lot," he said.

"Oh yes? What?"

"School stories. They're my favourite. There's a second-hand book-shop in Southsea that's got loads of them. I always stock up when I'm on leave, so I've got enough to keep me going."

"What sort of school stories?"

"Like the one I'm reading now. It's all about this boy who came from a poor family and he gets sent to a public school and gets bullied a lot because he doesn't talk posh and then some other boys get stuck in a quicksand and he rescues them … and that's as far as I've got. It's really good."

"Seems an odd choice for a young man of nineteen," I said, scraping away a piece of salt as big as an Oxo cube.

"They're great!" he said. "Those public schools! They're amazing. In my school you'd be expelled for doing some of the things the boys there do. And our teachers weren't allowed to hit anybody, let alone the prefects. Public schools are really old-fashioned."

"You don't have to tell me," I said. "I went to one."

"No! Which one?" I told him and his mouth dropped open. I might as well have announced that I was the Archangel Gabriel on a short visit to earth.

"That's a famous one. Really old," he said.

"Dead right. The so-called New House was built in 1764. The computer lab is housed in what was the Headmaster's stable and there's a notice on the gate to say that horseless carriages must be driven slowly."

"Wow!" said Andy. "I never thought I'd be talking to someone from there. What was it really like?"

"Bloody grim," I said.

"Did the prefects beat the boys?"

"They may have done in olden times, but not when I was there."

"And did you do things at midnight?" he asked.

"Like what?"

"You know. Have feasts in the dormitory. Go on midnight raids. That sort of thing."

"I think we were all too shattered to think of anything like that. Anyway, we had study-bedrooms, not dormitories. There was one occasion when somebody pinched a bottle of wine and shared it with his room-mates. That's about all."

"What about girlfriends?" he asked.

"You must be joking. The only females at that place were the cooks, the cleaners and the matron."

"So what did you do?"

"For sex you mean? A very quick wank if you were lucky enough to find somewhere private enough to do it."

"A bit like being on a ship," said Andy. "I've got a mate, though. He's got a book and it says in there that the public schools are full of it. The teachers have it off with the older boys and they have it off with the younger boys. "

"We only had one like that and he missed the middle bit. He went straight for the younger ones. Anyway, I don't want to talk about him." I shivered as I spoke and it wasn't that cold.

"What about the other boys?" he persisted. "Surely some of them...."

I was beginning to feel uncomfortable. "If they did, they didn't tell me about it. I think it's time we went back to Mr. Harris." I closed the door as firmly as I could and wrenched the handle hard. Later that day I'd need to get a new seal and put it on. I had plenty in my bag.

Mr. Harris was just packing his things together before going to lunch. He didn't appear to have missed us. He said that the problem looked like sorting itself out at one stage but he was no further forward. And left us to go to his own mess. We had lunch with the Captain and the officers in the wardroom.

Most of that afternoon was spent transcribing data. That needed both of us. Andy kept us supplied with cups of coffee and tea and, under my supervision, put a new seal on the junction box. It was a simple enough job, merely squeezing a lead seal and imprinting the date but it kept him occupied and he had to bend down to do it. Need I say more?

On the following day, the Captain for some reason best known to himself or his masters in Whitehall, elected to conduct speed trials. The sea was pretty rough anyway and Mr. Harris was soon unable to work, and went to his cabin. The sick-berth attendant said it was most unlikely that we should see him at meals. That left Andy and me with nothing to do all day. Neither of us was bothered. I did wonder if I ought perhaps to show some signs of being unwell, but decided against it. I thought I might write a letter to Anthony, but that proved impossible. Waves were lashing the deck so there was no chance of getting a breath of fresh air. I thought of inviting Andy down to my cabin, but I knew enough of naval discipline to know that was out of the question. He went back to his mess and I went below and spent the morning trying to think of something to do and feeling homesick for dry land. You can't even have a quiet wank on a ship. The doors don't lock and they keep sending stewards down to ask if you're feeling okay and if you want anything.

Things improved at about 4 o'clock that afternoon. The roaring and rattling stopped and the ship ceased acting like a dolphin. Dutifully asking every officer I met for permission and for directions, I went off in search of Andy. I found him in a corner of their mess playing cards with some of his mates. I didn't particularly want to disturb their game, but he didn't seem to mind.

"Now you're here I can show you my books," he said. He took me to his tiny little space and opened his locker. This is the one I was telling you about." He brought out a paperback with a picture of a Rugby football game being watched by boys in multi-coloured caps and schoolmasters in gowns and mortar-boards on the cover. Glances at random pages showed that the author had as little idea of public school life as the cover artist. This was Adam's conception of public school life. Nobody 'ratted' on their 'chums'. Most characters had double-barrelled names by which they were addressed, often with 'minor' or 'major' appended, and people went round saying 'Gosh!' and 'Golly!' when they were surprised.

"You can borrow it if you like," said Andy.

"Not if you're reading it." It was the last thing in the world I wanted to read.

"Or we could read it together," he said. Just how two people could possibly read a book together when one had already read most of it, he didn't explain. It was, though, a good excuse for being together.

"Where?" I asked. "Down here is a bit crowded."

"That's a point."

"One of the officers was telling me about a place called the chain locker.

Where's that?" I said.

"Off-limits for me," he replied.

"But not for me. I'm allowed free run of the ship. You're supposed to be at my disposal. We could go in there and look for another junction box."

"Could do." He sounded apprehensive but he got up, shoved the book under his shirt and followed me.

The Royal Navy is amazing. The chain locker on HMS Truro was absolutely identical to the one on Falmouth. The chain on which I had sat to enjoy my frantic small-boy masturbation sessions could have been the same one. It was coiled in the same way. I was much too fast finding the light switch but Andy didn't seem to notice. I clamped the door from the inside and resisted the temptation to say "Alone at last!"

Thanks to the other naval obsession, that of cleaning and polishing everything in sight irrespective of its use, we were able to sit on the chain. It just needed a quick wipe. An 'inspired guess' led me to the locker in the corner. It held exactly the same cleaning wads and cloths which had come in so useful years previously.

Our legs weren't even touching, but Andy's closeness started doing things to me. I hoped he wouldn't notice. He pulled out the book. "You read first and then I'll have a go," he said. Thankful for something to hold over my lap, I began to read. The first chapter, describing Jack Stokes' boyhood in the sums of London, didn't seem of much interest to him. It certainly did nothing for me. He started to fidget. Our knees touched several times, sending little invisible shivers up my spine. Finally, he said, "This bit isn't much good. Go to chapter four. It starts getting good then."

Chapter four found our hero 'shivering with fright'. *"You will clean this study completely and after that you can clean my rugger boots. I want to see my face in them."*

"I'll try, Hilliard-Drake. Honest I will," Jack stammered.

"You know what you'll get if you don't," said Hilliard-Drake. He opened the wardrobe and produced a long bamboo cane. He smiled as he bent it almost double and then brought it down with a loud 'thwack' on a cushion. A cloud of dust rose into the perfumed air. "Look at that!" he shouted. "Dust."

"That's not my fault. It must have been your last fag," said Jack.

"I will judge who's at fault, not you. If there is so much of a speck of dust when I come back, it won't be just the cushion that gets a beating. Do you

understand?"

I had to stop. "Is this meant to be the present day? I asked. "He hasn't gone back in time or anything?"

"No, no. It's now. This is the latest."

"Well, it's rubbish. Sorry to disappoint you and all that but it's utter balls. Fagging was abolished years ago."

"In your school maybe."

I said I couldn't swear to it but I was fairly sure that there wasn't a school in the country which still operated like that. "Anyway," I continued, "there is no way this Hilliard-Drake character could hit anybody. It would be in all the papers pretty fast. And what's this about the 'perfumed air'?"

"He burns joss sticks," said Andy.

"Ha! He'd be out on his ear. They'd think he was trying to cover up the smell of marijuana. If it's meant to be in this day and age, perhaps he was."

"Yeah! Psyching himself up for it," said Andy.

"For what?"

"You know. Okay, it didn't happen at your school but it happens at other places. Sex, of course."

"With the Headmaster, I presume?"

"Course not. With Jack. That's why he chose Jack to be his fag. It's in chapter three. All the new boys had to line up and the prefects chose their fags. He liked the look of Jack, see?"

"You don't think that perhaps Jack might complain or go home and tell his step-father what happened?"

"He couldn't do that. It would be grassing. Same as on a ship."

There was suddenly no doubt in my mind as to what he was leading up to. His leg was pressing hard against mine.

"I didn't think there were any gays in the Royal Navy. Especially after this McAlpine affair," I said.

"There was one on this ship when I joined, but they transferred him."

"I'm amazed they only transferred him."

"Oh he didn't do anything. Not on the ship anyway. He sent me a birthday card. He sent it to my home, but Mum posted it on and I stuck it on the buggery board."

"The what?" I asked.

"The partition between the bunks. It's to stop you rolling over onto the next bloke. Anyway, the Captain spotted it on his rounds and he must have recognised the writing. There was nothing in it, but sending birthday cards to sailors isn't on and they transferred him. He was at a public school too. He said there was loads going on at his place. That's how I know you're wrong."

"Which school was that?"

"He wouldn't say. He just said it was part of the school tradition and it was natural when loads of blokes are cooped up together — just like on a ship."

By this time, my cock was heaving against the inside of my trousers. and the pressure on my leg was making it worse by the minute. I hadn't had a wank that night and that was probably a lot to do with it.

"If there was nothing in it, how do you know he was gay?" I asked.

That had him. He fidgeted slightly and put a hand up to his ear. "Let's just say I do," he said.

"Not going to 'rat on your chums', eh?"

"If you like."

"You did. That's the main thing."

"What?"

"Like it."

"Let's leave that out of it," he said. "Read some more."

I started again but some instinct told me that he wasn't listening. I'd only got through a couple of paragraphs when he said, "There must be something else we can do."

"Like what?"

"Well, anything."

I closed the book and put it on the floor. "Anything?" I said.

"Yeah. I don't mind."

I leaned back, supporting myself with my hands on one of the links. "Neither do I," I said. It took some seconds for my words to have the effect I was hoping for. He shifted his position slightly and, in doing so, put his hand on my thigh. It was the sort of thing somebody would do to support himself but his leg was still pressing hard against mine. His fingers slipped, as if by accident between my thighs and, of course, came into contact with my cock.

"You're hard," he whispered.

"Thinking about you and that officer. What rank was he?"

"Sub-Lieutenant. Still is." His fingers moved very gently up and down.

"Where did you find to do it?"

"He's got a flat in Portsmouth."

"Not on the ship then?"

"No. Too dangerous."

"Fairly safe in here though, isn't it?"

"Should be. Shall I get it out?"

"You might as well. There's likely to be one hell of a mess if you don't."

Digital dexterity was not one of his strong points. He managed to undo my zip without any trouble. After that it was murder! Somehow or other he managed to get a bunch of hair caught in the zip. His fingers fumbled around. At one stage he managed to bend it forwards and that was painful. Anxious not to be too cooperative on what I hoped would be the first of many occasions, I just sat there wincing until, finally, a cool draught against my cock-head told me that he'd managed it at last.

"There!" he said, triumphantly. He wrapped his fingers round it and moved the skin gently up and down. "Do you want to do it to me?" he asked, breathlessly.

"Better not. Not now, anyway." I said it despite myself. It was all too obvious that he had an erection in his trousers that dwarfed mine.

"Okay. Want me to suck it?"

"If you like."

He was kneeling between my outspread legs in a flash. He might not have been very good with his hands, but his tongue work was something else. For a moment, till I ceased to think straight, I wondered what he was doing and then realised that he was flicking the tip of his tongue up and down the individual veins. I'd never experienced anything like it. Then he tugged at the zip, apparently hoping to get at rather more than was on display. That worried me a bit. My eyes were fixed on the two massive clamps that held the door closed. It was just possible that Truro was regulated more thoroughly than Falmouth — and if just one of those clamps were to move a centimetre I should have to leap up, do up my trousers and then think of a convincing reason for being in there. I'd have loved to slip everything down and give him free access, but not then and there. He gave up the struggle and returned to my cock. I felt his tongue in the slit. His lips went to the top of the shaft and slowly moved downwards. His cheeks moved in and out; one minute caressing my cock with their soft warmth and then letting it go. I felt the back of his mouth pressing against the head. I put my hands in his hair and then against his ears, but he needed no help or encouragement from me. Whoever had taught him to suck cock was an expert. Nobody had ever succeeded in making me blow my mind as I did then. If he'd wanted to, or thought of it, he could have torn every scrap of clothing off me and I wouldn't have protested.

I wasn't even aware of the noise I must have been making. All I knew was that I had to shoot my load and there was no point in even trying to delay the moment. It came (I came) all too soon. I remember the gulping noise he made when the first jet cannoned into his mouth. Half faint with sheer exhaustion, I lay back against the bulkhead while the rest spouted. Then a cool feeling enveloped my cock and I realised that it was no longer in his mouth.

He stood up and wiped the sides of his mouth with the back of his hand. "You wanna do me now?" he asked. I wanted desperately to say 'Yes please!' The outline of his cock under the navy blue material of his trousers was so clear that I could spot the point where his foreskin ended. It was enormous; infinitely bigger than mine and, even allowing for the thickness of the material, it was much thicker.

But post-orgasm common sense stepped in. "Reckon you can hold out till tomorrow?" I asked. "I reckon there's something in the tool bag that will seal that door."

"You didn't mind?" he said, as I stuffed my still-damp penis back.

"Mind? You must be joking! You were great."

"How about just giving me a wank?"

I felt guilty but declined. "Make it tomorrow. Try and hold out till then," I said and then, opening the door carefully to make sure there was nobody in sight, we left our little steel love nest and rejoined Mr. Harris.

CHAPTER NINE

The answer to the problem came to me that night as I lay in my bunk. Not the answer to the chain locker security problem, I'd already solved that, but to the Stingray enigma. The main junction box had been filled with salt. I had cleared some of it out and Mr. Harris had said there was a slight improvement. After a day of high-speed trials, it was playing up again. It had to be caused by that salt build-up. I wondered what do — but only for a few moments. I would say nothing. Not yet, anyway. I had one or two things to attend to.

I tackled the first before breakfast. The chain locker was scrubbed out every Tuesday morning and Captain's rounds took place on Thursday mornings. Thus it would be unusable on Tuesday mornings. It was just possible that someone might give it an extra going-over on Wednesday nights, and Thursday mornings it was off-limits until the Old Man and his retinue had been round. I took two big rubber wedges from the tool bags. They are actually designed to stop anything on wheels shifting around on a heaving deck, but we didn't have anything that needed them.

I then bearded the most senior officer at the breakfast table — an appropriate term. He looked like something out of a pirate film. I said I was sorry to trouble him for advice at such a time. He grunted but said he'd be happy to help. I'd already discovered that Naval personnel are as helpful as can be if you admit total ignorance of their customs.

"Your Artificer Williams," I said. "He's been so good and so helpful that I wondered if it would be in order to send him a Thank You card or a letter on our last day."

"I wouldn't, if I were you," he said, putting down his knife and fork. "He's only doing his job. You could drop a line to his Divisional Officer."

"Thanks a lot," I said. "He was going on about some officer sending him a card and getting into trouble. I'm glad I asked you."

"Oh he wouldn't get into trouble. That incident was something else entirely and the officer concerned should have known better. Nobody would think twice about a card or a letter from a civilian. It's just that it might set a precedent."

He started on his scrambled eggs and bacon again. I waited till he had finished and was sipping his coffee before I spoke again. "What actually happened?" I asked.

"Nothing, it seems. Everybody thought the guy was a turd-burglar. The Captain certainly did. But the Special Investigation people came down. No semen in the seaman. Just good friends. McBrine should have known, but he was only a sub, and pretty young — and he'd come from a public school That probably had a lot to do with it. They get a bit sloppy over each other in those places. I should know. I've got a fourteen-year-old son at one and he idolises one of the prefects.

"What happened to O'Brian?" I asked.

"McBrine. Matthew McBrine. He was transferred to a dockyard job. He answers letters from old grannies who want to know if they can come down and wave at their grandsons' ships and that sort of thing. It was all a bit unfortunate. There was nothing in it, but the Captain's got a complex and wanted him off the ship fast — so he went. Talk about much ado about nothing. Incidentally, don't talk about it to the skipper, will you?"

I promised. So… it had been Matt McBrine. I had had a sort of instinct that it might be, when Andy was telling me about it.

Mr. Harris was happy enough to work on his own. In fact I think he was happier. We left him after about an hour and a half of screen-watching. The wedges worked well. I thought they would. You'd have to wrench pretty hard to get just one of those clamps undone and that left plenty of time for dressing before the second one was opened.

"What shall we do?" asked Andy.

"What do you think? You're not the only cat who likes cream."

I started to undress. "Do you reckon it's safe?" he asked.

"Safe as Fort Knox," I said. "I've checked."

"If you say so." He sounded doubtful, but he started to take his clothes off. Naval discipline came to the fore again. I slung my stuff on the locker. He folded each item so carefully that it took him an age, but finally, we were both ready for it. I was, anyway. My cock had jumped out of my boxers as if it was on springs. I wouldn't say that Andy's was completely limp. Limp cocks are never as big and as thick as his but it certainly wasn't hard. Somehow that made it more appealing. I reached out. He moved forward and I took it between my fingers. I must have been subconsciously thinking about cables even then. I remember thinking that his cock felt exactly like one of the cables we use at work. The conductor is very thin and it's insulated by a sort of gel. A short length is stiff but more than six inches droops, just as Andy's cock was hanging. The thickness was about the same, too.

"You need to work me up a bit," he said.

"Like this?" I squeezed it gently and pulled the foreskin back

"Yeah! Talk to me while you do it."

"What about?"

"You know."

"Why don't you talk to me? What about this officer? What did he do?"

"I can't talk about him. "

"I don't see why not. It's not grassing. You're gay. I'm gay. Grassing is telling someone senior or outside the circle. We're boys in the same dormitory." It was just about the weakest piece of logic I'd ever come out with. It made me sound like Adam, but it worked.

"I hadn't thought of it like that," he said. "What do you want to know?"

I moved a bit nearer and played with his cock, lifting it with the palm of my hand. He had huge balls. "How did you know he was gay? It must have been a bit difficult on a ship," I said.

"I didn't even know he was an officer. I was a Junior 'Tif' at HMS. Raleigh. I was home on short leave and went to that bookshop I told you about and he was in there. He bought a book about model-making."

That was Matt. I remembered his room at school. There were model planes and model ships everywhere.

"He saw what I'd bought and he asked me if I liked that sort of thing and I said "Yes", and he said he was at a public school and would I like to go back to his place. I had nothing much else to do, so I did. I knew what he was after, of course. Least, I thought I did. He didn't come across as a dirty old man. He was young and quite good-looking and I'd bought presents for the family, so I was a bit short. So we went back to his place and he started telling me about public schools. That's when he told me what they were really like and how all the boys had it off with each other."

"Oh yes?" It had started to harden at last.

"Then he asked had I ever done anything like that."

"And had you?"

"Only at school. Bit of wanking. That sort of thing."

"Not at HMS. Raleigh?"

"He asked me that. Like I told him, you must be fucking joking! You don't get any time to yourself there. He said Dartmouth is the same. Mind you, there were one or two there…"

It twitched again and I began to feel a pulse which hadn't been noticeable before.

"And then what happened?"

"He started to touch me up through my jeans. I didn't mind that much. Then he said had I tried fucking. I thought he meant him fucking me."

"Didn't he?" I never felt or saw a cock grow like his. What had started off as about six inches of flaccid flesh was a good eight inches long and still stiffening.

"No. He reckoned being fucked was the best feeling in the world, 'specially when the other bloke had a really big cock."

"Looks like he'd struck lucky with you.."

"That's what he reckoned. Anyway, we went in his bedroom and he had all the stuff needed and showed me how to put it on and what to do — so I did."

"Good?" I asked.

"Fucking brilliant. He liked it,too. You could tell. I went round there every afternoon that leave. He was so keen he used to come to the door in his dressing gown. I dunno what it's like on the receiving end, but Christ, it's bloody nice doing it. I'd still be going there if it wasn't for the fact that I got posted to this ship and, sod me, who do I see but Matt. He's a sub on my ship. You could have knocked me down with a feather!"

"Must have pretty frustrating for you," I said. A tiny bead of fluid oozed from the massive end of his cock.

"Only a bit. We had a chat when we could. When there was anyone else around he just sort of looked through me like I wasn't there." By this time his cock had lifted off my hand and was sticking upwards and outwards like the thick butt of a big fishing rod. It was so huge that I think if I'd had the stuff with me, I might have been tempted to try out what Matt had enjoyed. Instead I went down on my knees. The floor felt rough and cold but the moment I started to lick it, I forgot all about that. Andy groaned a bit. He groaned even louder when I opened my mouth as wide as I could and took the first few inches in. I had to get up on my haunches to do it. It tasted really good. There was just a hint of something other than soap. Otherwise it tasted like a cock should taste — of warm, live, human flesh.

I sucked. He moaned. I sucked again and let my tongue play on it. I wasn't as good as he was, which was puzzling for a young man whose only experience lay in wanking other boys at school and buggering a Naval officer. I wondered about that — but only for a second or two. It was pulsating in my mouth. I managed to get a bit more in without choking and put my hands round his backside. That felt good. It was beautifully cool and I could feel the muscles twitching under the skin. He groaned a bit more. I got up even closer and managed to get my third finger in between his ass cheeks. Nowhere near his entrance, unfortunately ,but I could sense that he liked it.

I let his cock go for a few minutes and concentrated on his balls. There was no way I could get even one of them into my mouth. They were huge and as hairy as coconuts, but I enjoyed feeling them against the side of my nose as I licked underneath them. Another drop of fluid got deposited on the side of my face. I went back onto his cock. I was only just in time. Somehow or other I knew the pressure was building up and he wouldn't be able to hold back for much longer. I'd just got as much of it in my mouth as I could possible take when I was dimly aware of him saying something. Then he put his hands on the sides of my head and shot the first load straight into my throat. I swear I didn't taste it. I tasted the others though. It was a bit like being sick, save that being sick leaves a very unpleasant taste. This was almost indescribable. A tang of sharpness, a hint of chlorine and then just sweetness; an almost marzipan-like sweetness. I swallowed as much as I could, but quite a lot ran down my chin.

"Christ! That was good!" he said. I got up with some difficulty. My cock was streaming and my balls were aching.

"Come here. I'll do that for you," he said. We changed places. I stood with my legs outspread and he went down on his knees — more quickly and with considerably more finesse than I had shown. I realised how out of condition I'd grown. His mouth clamped round my shaft. I stared at the locker thinking that it would have been a good idea to get a swab out before we'd started.

It couldn't have taken more than a few seconds. I tried to hold out. I was thinking of cables again, as a matter of fact, but a vision of Matt McBrine as I had last known him kept coming back. Long flowing blond hair. That almost girlishly beautiful face and those big blue eyes. They were obviously not as innocent as I'd thought them to be and — more important — Adam's stories were beginning to ring true. I could have kicked myself. If only I'd believed him at the time, I might have been able to fuck Matt's ass. I'd thought about it often enough, even, would you believe, when we were at prep school. Several of my lone sessions in the chain locker on Falmouth starred Matt, lying prone and naked on a steel school bed.

"What are you going to do to me?"

"Put my thing in your bum."

And I had dismissed them all later as impossible fantasies! Then we found that our respective fathers had signed us both up for the same school. There had been times when I wondered, but Matt had taken up religion and become an altar server. I only went to chapel to look at him. Dressed in his red cassock and white surplice he was the nearest thing to an angel I'd ever seen. . Once or twice he turned round and smiled in my direction during the service and that sent me rushing off to the bog for another frantic wank.

And all the time Adam was..... It didn't bear thinking about. Certainly not at that moment. I came. It was so sudden that I think it might have taken Andy by surprise. Again, he was better than I was. Hardly a drop got spilt and he stood up again, licking the corners of his mouth.

I went over to the locker and took out a swab. I wiped the drops off the floor. It wasn't too soggy so I put it back again, just as I had replaced the ones dampened with my only-just-pubertal emissions on Falmouth.

"Tomorrow?" Andy asked.

"Should be okay tomorrow afternoon. Depends on my boss, of course."

"It's great to have you on board," he said. "I'd have gone barmy I reckon."

"You too," I said. I meant it, but that afternoon I started to have second thoughts. In the first place, I thought I knew what was wrong with Stringray. Mr. Harris was unhappy on board and wanted to get back to his semi-detached and his wife and kids and there was a certain sub-lieutenant I was anxious to meet again. Add all those factors to the dangers of having sex with a seaman in a chain locker and I hope you'll understand why I spoke to Mr. Harris that evening.

"If some of the cabling was caked in salt, would that make a difference?" I asked.

"Almost certainly. That's why it's all ducted so carefully. You'd get an induction-echo off the salt sheath."

I took him to the junction box, snipped the new seal and opened it.

"Bloody hell!" he said. We spent two hours cleaning it out, washing everything in warm water and then spraying it. Then we both went down to the operations room again and 'Stingray' functioned perfectly. We carried out a dummy firing and then another. No problem at all.

The Captain seemed as anxious to unload us as Mr. Harris was to get home. He turned the ship round that night and we were on our way back to Portsmouth. I'd heard some pretty grizzly stories from dad about people who happened to be in chain lockers when the anchor was released. He caught me once when I was a kid. He didn't know what I'd been doing, thank God. I made my apologies to Andy, said I would never forget him and gave him my firm's card. "If you ever get a spot of leave and have nothing to do, ring me at work and I'll come and meet you," I said.

He seemed genuinely sorry to see me go and I felt a bit guilty, but you can't undo what's been done. The following afternoon saw Mr. Harris and I going down the gangplank and on to dry land again. It felt distinctly odd — as if the earth itself was moving. I said that my parents lived not far away and I'd pop in to see them. He offered to give me a lift, but I declined and watched his car dash out of the car park as if the police were on his tail.

Portsmouth dockyard is the most amazing place. The general public swarm all over the place, looking at historical ships and buying souvenirs. Trying to get into the area marked Naval Personnel Only is a different matter. My recently issued pass, allowing me access to HMS. Truro and the freedom to be in any part of the ship, wasn't worth the paper it was written on. The letter from the firm identifying me and confirming that I was on Royal Naval business was looked at and, for a moment, I thought it might work. In the end I had to tell the guy that I was looking for Lieutenant McBrine because we had been at school together. He made a phone call. Then another. Finally, he put down the receiver and said, "Someone's coming over to escort you, er, sir."

My escort was a young Wren officer. "So you were at school with Matt," she said as we walked across an open space criss crossed with railway lines.

I felt as if I was being interrogated. "Yes," I replied.

"Lovely! What school was that?"

I told her. "Lovely!" she said again.

"You're not in the Navy yourself, then?" she asked.

"No. I work for Nimrod. We're armaments contractors to the Navy."

"Lovely! Here we are."

We had stopped outside a rather dilapidated red brick building. She opened the doors and we went in. A long, badly lit and dingy corridor stretched the length of the building. She stopped by the third door on the right, knocked, opened it for me and I was face to face with the man I hadn't seen for years.

Matt hadn't changed much. His hair was shorter. He seemed to have filled out a bit, but his face was the same and so were his eyes. I felt a little tremor of excitement.

"I'm damned! It *is* you. I couldn't believe it when Security rang," he said. He got up from behind his desk and came round to shake my hand. "What the hell are you doing down here?" he asked.

"I've just stepped off your old ship. We've been working on Stingray. I heard that you were stationed here."

He flinched slightly. "So you've heard how I put up a black on board," he said.

"They said something about it. Not sure that I totally understood. Anyway, how are you?"

He opened the door and shouted to someone for two coffees. A Wren brought them. We sat down and chatted about old times. The usual thing: teachers, sports events, the daft things schoolboys do. I was anxious to get down the nitty-gritty. He seemed determined to keep off the subject. He'd met Dad recently, he said. Dad had been down to attend a dinner on board HMS. Victory.

"And your indomitable Gran. How is she?" he asked.

"Very well."

"Still as outspoken as ever?"

"Pretty much so." I'd forgotten than Matt had met her. She used to come to school prizegivings and because both our dads were Royal Navy, the two families inevitably munched strawberries together. I think she criticised Matt on every occasion. There was the time when Matt let his hair grow very long, for instance.

"Going through a sex-change, are you?" said Gran. Then, briefly, he went through the crew- cut stage. "If I need a new lavatory brush I'll know where to come," said Gran.

Strangely, she liked him. I went to stay with her for a week every summer and she always asked about him. Our paths drifted apart, but she still asked.

"Talking about school, I met Adam Saunders recently," I said. "He lives near me. He's doing very well."

Matt scowled. "That's one guy I never want to see again," he said.

"Why not? He seems all right."

Matt put down his coffee cup. "Listen, Tim," he said. "That guy is dangerous. Take it from me. He's like a millstone round your neck. When he goes down, he'll drag you with him. Chuck him."

"How do you mean, 'goes down'? Prison?"

"I'm not saying. Just watch yourself. Have you been back to the schools at all?"

"No. I might do one day. You?"

"Same. How long are you here for?"

"I have to be back at work tomorrow morning. There's bound to be a meeting about the work we've been doing and something is going to have to be re-designed."

"Why don't we go back to my place? More comfortable than this bloody office."

"Don't you have to keep regular hours then?"

"Hardly any point when you've got fuck-all to do. Come on. Let's make a break for it."

The security guards threw up smart salutes as we drove out. "If you don't mind, I'll do some shopping on the way," said Matt. "Henry's due back this evening."

"Who's Henry?"

"The chap I share the flat with."

He stopped outside a little grocery shop and got out, leaving me to think. Finally, after quite a long time, he returned, laden with two carrier bags. He put them in the back of the car, got in and fastened his seat belt.

"Big cock?" I asked.

"Eh?"

"Henry. Has he got a big cock?"

How he missed the bus I shall never know. He pulled out straight in front of it. Brakes screeched. The bus driver shouted. Matt waved a gold-braided arm in apology and we got under way.

"You've obviously heard the full story," he said after some time.

"I met Andy Williams."

"Shit! You have, then. I always hoped he'd keep quiet."

"He didn't just come out with it. I had to draw it out of him. I got something else out of him as well."

"What?"

"Spunk. Nice it was. One of the best."

"You don't mean you're....? I mean you're not... well.... gay?" he asked. He sounded completely incredulous.

"I am."

"So Adam? Adam and you.....?"

"We have done. I wasn't much impressed and, to be honest, I still don't like the guy very much."

"Nor does anyone. This is it. The Broadway, old Portsmouth. This is where I live and breathe and all that."

The living and breathing bit didn't interest me much but 'all that' certainly did. He had the sort of figure that you see in swim-wear catalogues. From occasional glances in the car I'd guessed that he was pretty well provided for in front. As I followed him up the stairs my eyes were on another aspect which was even more pleasant. I hadn't seen a butt like that for a long time; not since we were at school. It didn't seem to have changed since the days when I sat in the bog wanking over thoughts of it. It stuck out from the hollow of his back so sharply that it looked as if you could have laid a pencil on top of his buns.

He opened the door to his flat and we went in. It was a nice place. It wasn't in the least degree opulent, like Adam's, but it looked comfortable.

"I'll just get changed," he said. "Make yourself at home."

'Changed'? Was I about to strike lucky straight away? My cock took an immediate interest in the prospect. I sat down on the sofa. It was almost certainly, I thought, the very same sofa on which Andy had sat and had his cock felt. Andy and how many others? What about the mysterious Henry? I hoped Henry would turn out to be 'just a flat-mate. Nothing more.' and Matt could get rid of him for the evening.

Evidence that at least one of Matt's schoolboy enthusiasms persisted was everywhere. Two beautifully detailed models of ships in glass cases stood on the sideboard. A model of an American bomber was suspended on cotton threads from the ceiling. He hadn't changed and that was a good sign.

"There!" he said, re-entering the room. "That feels better!"

"It looks better too," I said. The uniform had been replaced by tight jeans and a brilliantly white tee- shirt.

"Drink?" he asked.

"Have you got a Jack Daniels and Coke?"

He laughed. "We've got just about everything. Henry drives a lorry for a wholesale drinks firm."

The 'we' didn't sound very promising. Neither did the lorry driver bit. He was probably as strong as an ox and hung like a donkey. I wouldn't get a look-in! Matt went to a cupboard, produced the bottle, went out again, came back with a measuring jug full of ice cubes and poured two drinks.

"Were you gay when we were at school?" he asked.

"Of course. People don't change. At least I don't think they do."

"With Adam?" he asked.

"Correct. In the New House boiler-room. So, according to him, did you. I didn't believe him at the time."

Matt put down his glass and leaned back in his chair. "Did you ever meet his old man?" he asked.

"No. I remember the cars. A different one every time he came to the school."

"That's him. I went to their place for a week in the holidays once. They're both the same. Old man Saunders buys a new car about every month and drives them into the ground. Adam does the same with boys. All they're interested in is having the latest and the best and sod having to look after them."

"Adam's certainly got a good one at the moment," I said and launched into a description of Steve — not Anthony. I told him about the sandwiches. He laughed.

"That's not the only thing he's got an appetite for, apparently," I added. "Adam wanted me to have him as well." I paused for a moment. "I didn't, though," I added.

"Good for you. He only does that so people can admire his choice. A bit like 'Get in. I'll show you what a car can do,' and when he's finished with them they go on display. Just like his dad. 'I drove that one for nearly a year. See that panel, my boy? Pure walnut that is. None of your plastic for me.' God! I can hear him saying it!"

"You're not a bad chooser yourself," I said. "Andy must have been quite a find."

"He was. I was very fond of Andy. I still am. I wish to hell he'd told me he was at Raleigh, though."

"If he had, you wouldn't have had the pleasure."

"True, and I should have known that it would never work out. Sending that card was the daftest thing I've ever done. I never wrote my name but the

Captain knew the handwriting. Did Andy tell you what he had to go through because of that?"

"No."

"They gave him hell. Medical exams and interrogations. He's such a good lad, though. He denied everything. If he hadn't, I'd have been really in the shit."

"He's still very fond of you," I said.

"Is he? That's nice. I missed him badly, I can tell you. The first few months here were hell. He gave me just what I needed to keep going."

"I know what you mean," I said. "He's a well-endowed lad."

"Isn't he just? He knew how to use it, too. He always reckoned that he'd never done it before, but I sometimes wonder. I couldn't get enough of it — till I met Henry."

Those four words dashed all my hopes. I was too late. About ten years too late, from what he'd said.

"So you're a couple then?" I asked, in the vague hope of being told that I had completely misunderstood.

"I suppose we are. He's a great guy. Incidentally, he's late. Traffic jam on the motorway, I guess. It's a terrible job for stress. "

He went on to explain that Henry was the best driver he'd ever known. He drove enormous distances and there was always a risk these days of lorries loaded with spirits being hi-jacked. Henry was also a superb cook, a brilliant model-maker (the two ship models were his) and, I gathered, he kept Matt more than happy at night.

"He's great!" said Matt leaning back in his chair and smiling. I said I hoped to meet him one day.

"But you're staying to dinner?" said Matt. "I got enough for the three of us."

"Only if you're sure," I said.

"Of course I'm sure. And Henry will love to see you. He's never met anyone who knew me in the old days. He's got to be here soon. It might be an idea if I peel the potatoes ready for him. You wouldn't mind?"

Naturally enough, I said I wouldn't. I followed him into the kitchen, where he put on an apron. One or both of them obviously had a huge appetite. The number of potatoes he emptied into the sink would have fed six people. He set to work peeling them. I stood close behind him, hesitated for a moment and then, for the first time in my life, cupped his buns in my hands. They felt delightfully soft. I squeezed them. He didn't pull away from me as I feared he might.

"If you'd done that when we were at school, my life might have been quite different," he said.

"I wish I had."

"I wish you had, too. I used to wank over thoughts of you."

"Really? I lost count of the number of time I did the same thing over you," I replied. I moved my right hand round under the apron and felt it almost immediately. It had the same rubbery feel that I experienced with Andy.

"Go a bit easy," he said but continued to wield the paring knife. I let my fingers slide up and down, tracing its length and shape under the denim.

"I just didn't believe it when Adam told me he was having you," he said. "I thought I knew you pretty well from prep school."

"It wasn't really Adam's fault," I said, delighting in the feel of rising flesh. "He told the truth and we just didn't believe him."

"Of course it was. He could have so easily taken us into the boiler-house together. He did it with Cosford and Walton. I know that. I saw the photo."

"Photo?" I squeezed harder and felt his foreskin sliding back.

"Yes." He was beginning to sound breathless. "Cosford's idea, apparently. You know he had that Polaroid camera?"

"No. I didn't know either of them that well."

"Well he did. He wanted snaps of him and Walton tossing each other off. Adam obliged and kept one for himself. They weren't that good. I knew then that he was telling the truth about them but I still didn't believe it when he said you were one. Controlled truth. That's Adam. Tell 'em just as much as you need to keep them interested. Quite a lot of the time I did it with him just hoping that he might bring you and me together. He never did, of course, so I thought he was telling lies."

"I'm not at all certain that I'd enjoy having my picture taken," I said. "As for you and me together… How much time have we got?"

"None at all, I'm sorry to say. Anyway, it wouldn't work out. I'd feel guilty and Henry would know. He can read my mind. Better leave off."

Reluctantly, I did so. Only just in time, I must say. A few minutes and two potatoes later Henry arrived.

"This is Tim. We were at school together and don't worry, he's one of us," said Matt. Henry grasped my hand. The first shock was his age. I assumed lorry drivers to be men of about forty-five. Henry was twenty-three at most and possibly much younger. He was quite tall and broad-shouldered. His hair was dark and curly and he had a really infectious grin. The sort of person you take to at once.

"Been having old boys' talk?" he asked. That was the second shock. I'd expected what my dad calls 'street language' - every sentence punctuated by expletives. Henry wasn't like that at all.

"A bit," said Matt. He wiped his hands on the apron and planted a kiss on Henry's cheek. "What sort of day have you had?" he asked.

"Don't talk about it. If I have to do Coventry again this week…."

I left them to it and went back into the lounge. The local paper was in a rack, so I read that. I wasn't left entirely alone. One or the other popped in from time to time to make sure I was all right or to ask if I wanted another drink.

Finally, Matt announced that the meal was ready. "You don't mind eating in the kitchen?" he asked.

"Of course not," I followed him. The kitchen table had been immaculately laid out and the meal was out of this world. Henry could have got a job as a chef any time. We went through home-made soup and pork chops decorated with crescents of pineapple, followed by a mousse which not only looked like a work of art but tasted exquisite as well. That was impressive enough, but what got to me as the meal progressed was their relationship. Sometimes they teased each other. At other times they complimented each other. It was almost as though I was eating with two separate aspects of the same person. I'd never got that close to anyone. I began to feel more and more like half a person. With them, if I asked a question, one would answer and the other would add something.

"What do you do at weekends?" I asked.

"Not a lot," said Matt. "Apart from last Saturday afternoon," said Henry, and they both laughed.

"I couldn't control him," said Matt, grinning.

"You couldn't control yourself, you mean," said Henry and, turning to me, he said "He's like a wild thing when he gets going."

"An officer in Her Majesty's Royal Navy is never a wild thing," said Matt. "Cool, collected and always in command. That's us."

And so the evening continued. I really enjoyed it. Matt drove me to the station.

"So, what do you think?" he asked.

"Of Henry? He's a really nice guy."

"Isn't he? Everybody deserves to have a Henry. I'm the one who struck lucky. I got him."

I had a half-hour wait at Portsmouth station. I sat on a bench thinking things over. Next to me was a paper bag. It looked empty. I picked it up, intending to put it in the bin and then realised that it contained two postcards of HMS. Victory and two stamps. I don't know what made me do it, but I used one to write to Gran. I just said that I had been on board a ship doing a job for the firm and that I had met Matt McBrine again. I sent the other one to Anthony.

CHAPTER TEN

It was at this point that my life changed completely. I only wish I'd kept a diary. If I had, I might be able to sort out the various things that happened and give you a more coherent account. I'll try.

Disappointment came first. I think I'd rather hoped that Nimrod would hail me as the saviour of the Stingray project. I didn't imagine Mr. Parsons would put his hand on my shoulder and say "Well done, young Tim. You've saved the firm!" or anything like that, but I thought he could have sent a memo down or possibly got one of his secretaries to ring me to express his appreciation. All I got was "Oh, you're back, are you?"

Mr. Harris had meetings with the people who supplied junction boxes, but I was never asked to be in on them. I did suggest over lunch in the canteen that the junction boxes could be located in chain lockers, where they would be out of the weather. "We did consider that, but it would mean too much re-wiring," he said. That was the end of that. Back to work. After all the excitement of high-speed trials and being at sea, not to mention Andy, sitting at a computer all day seemed a terrific come-down.

I called Anthony on Wednesday night. He'd just got in from rehearsing. I said I'd be free to go through the play with him on Saturday.

"I'm having this weekend off," he said. "We open next weekend and I know the part now and all the moves. There'd be no point."

"So what are you doing instead?" I asked, with visions of a cottage in Somerset in mind.

"Helping dad with the parish magazine on Saturday and going round to see Adam on Sunday," he said.

I asked him if he'd got my card. "Oh, yes. Thanks," he said. "Are you coming to the play?"

"Try and keep me away," I replied. I heard a voice in the background say something about wanting to make a call and he put the phone down. Things were not looking good.

I went home that weekend. At least Mum and Dad were interested, but Dad had to have the last word as always.

"It was absolutely fantastic. There was so much spray that you couldn't see through it. It was like driving at high speed through a thick fog!" I said.

"Oh yes. I knew he was going to do a speed trial. I didn't tell you in case it scared you," said Dad. I told them that it had laid Mr. Harris out but that I had been all right. "So I should hope," he said.

"You could have sent us a card, dear," said Mum.

"They don't sell cards on board ship," I said.

"You sent one to your Gran. That was kind of you. I hope you bought a new toothbrush. Did you bring your dirty clothes with you?"

"No. I put them in the washing machine."

"Oh that's no good. Not if you've got sea water on them. They need to be soaked."

Everything seemed to be a complete let-down. I don't know if the people at work noticed my depression in the next week. I'm sure they must have done. I couldn't seem to concentrate on anything. Everything seemed so mundane. Work, evenings doing housework in the flat, going to the shops… I rang Adam a couple of times. He was out the first time and entertaining the second time. I didn't ask who was being entertained or what sort of entertainment it was. Funnily enough, I didn't feel jealous. I asked if he was going to Anthony's play. He said he hadn't actually got round to buying a ticket.

I got mine the next day. Not without a lot of trouble. I rang the university. They said tickets were being sold by newsagents. The first one I found had never heard of the play. The second one had sold out. The third only had the expensive seats left, so I parted with a fiver, which I thought far too expensive for an amateur, student performance. Having bought the damned thing, I wondered if Anthony might have been able to get me one, so I rang him again. He said I was lucky to have got one. It was a sell-out. I wished him luck. He said "Thanks" — and I spent that evening running the vacuum cleaner over the lounge carpet. I didn't even have enough money on me to go out for a drink.

The theatre at the university is on the ground floor of one of their buildings — and they're spread out all over the town. It took quite a long time to find it, but I got there at last and a volunteer student parking attendant insisted on seeing me into an empty space as if I was piloting Concorde. I could have done it easily without all the arm-waving.

I met up with Anthony's parents in the foyer. Once again, I thought what nice people they were.

"I guess he's nervous," I said.

"A bit. That's inevitable. 'Quietly confident' is what he'd want me to tell you. Thanks a lot for helping him as you have, Tim," said his father.

My place was about four seats away from theirs. I was sandwiched between a woman swathed in furs and a weedy-looking man with little half-moon glasses. Almost certainly a professor or lecturer, I thought, and began to wonder why I had come. I knew the play from beginning to end. There would be no chance of any time alone with Anthony afterwards. He'd probably not even notice that I was there.

I cheered up a bit in the first act. He was good. He was really good. In fact, they all were, but Anthony was outstanding. Not only because of his acting ability. They'd dressed him in a striped blazer and bottom-hugging white trousers. Only some of my attention was on the play at first. I watched his every move.

"He's awfully good, isn't he?" whispered the lady next to me.

"He certainly is," I replied but I wasn't thinking about his acting ability at the time.

By degrees. I began to take more interest in the play than in one of the players. I was in nineteenth-century England and beginning to wonder, even though I knew the answer, how the hell the characters were going to get out of the confusion their lies and deceptions had caused.

Then there was an interval. I followed everybody else into the room at the back that they were using as a bar. We in the expensive seats were at the end of the queue, which was bad planning on somebody's part, I thought. I got a can of beer and a plastic glass and stood in the corner. It appeared that Anthony's parents had decided to stay in their places. I didn't blame them. I felt like a match-stick in an over-full box. It was all I could do to pour my beer and it was impossible to put the empty can down so I stood like an idiot with an empty can in one hand and a full glass in the other. Most of the audience were young — students, obviously — and some of them were rather nice. They drank straight out of the cans and some had been wise enough to buy a couple. I was admiring one of them; a very tall, dark haired, smiling lad, when I was aware of someone pushing through the crowd towards me. It was Mr. Parsons. He was the last person I expected to see.

"Got a moment after the play?" he asked. I felt I should have shaken his hand but I couldn't. It was just my luck to be found by the boss swilling beer out of a plastic glass.

"Er, yes, sure," I said. I'd been hoping that I could meet up with Anthony to congratulate him — and maybe get invited out to a restaurant by his folks. That was obviously a dead duck and typical of my luck.

"Good. See you by the main door," he said. "Enjoying the play?"

"Very much indeed."

"The Prebendary tells me that you've been helping young Anthony. That's good of you. See you later," and he was gone. I slurped the rest of my beer down. The bell rang and we all trooped back to our seats. The thought that the Chairman and Managing Director of Nimrod knew Anthony's folks was a bit disquieting. What if Anthony had let the cat out of the bag? Maybe he had. The Navy had no real evidence against Matt, but he was slung off his ship. The more I thought about it, waiting for the curtain to go up again, the more I thought I was right. It was going to be: "I don't want to bring this up at work. Bad for the firm and bad for you, but I've heard one or two things from Anthony. I think it might be an idea for you to put in your notice. We'll say that you've got a better position elsewhere."

Fortunately, the play grabbed my attention again after a few minutes. I really think that if it hadn't, I might have slipped out, gone home and written out my resignation — all ready to hand in when I was sent for.

The applause when the curtain came down was incredible. The cast took three or four separate bows. I was clapping like crazy; possibly a little too loudly, because Anthony looked down into the audience. He smiled and waved, first to his parents and then to me! I shot from total depression to intense happiness. I might not have been thanked by Nimrod, but who cared about that? Anthony appreciated my efforts. I couldn't have cared less if Mr. Parsons was about to fire me. I could always get a job in the family firm. I'd been dead set against that idea for years, but any port in a storm. Sending that card to Gran might have been a God-sent idea.

"We're taking Anthony out to dinner when he's ready, Tim. Would you like to join us?" It was Anthony's dad. I said I was sorry. I really was. I explained that my boss was there and wanted to see me about work."

"Ah! Alex Parsons! How silly of me. I hadn't clicked that he was your boss.

He's one of my church-wardens."

"Really?" It looked as if I might have been wrong after all.

Mr. Parsons was waiting for me by the door. "Got time for a meal? On the firm, of course," he said.

"Sure. Where?"

"What do you think of the Coq d'Or?

In fact, the words made me think of the zip on Andy's trousers. I'd never been in the restaurant of that name. It's outside my social and financial parameters. I said it would suit me fine. The same student marshalled us out of the car park, paying rather more attention to Mr. Parsons than to me, and I followed his car into the town centre. It looked as if my fears had been unfounded. Pretty obviously, he was going to thank me for spotting the fault on Stingray. Better late than never.

They knew him pretty well in there. He wanted a table in a little alcove. It wasn't laid — there weren't many diners. Waiters dashed about, and in minutes — almost before we'd given our coats up — it was covered with a gleaming tablecloth and cutlery. They'd even put a vase of flowers on it.

"Anything you want," said Mr. Parsons, handing me the enormous menu. "The firm is paying."

I chose a steak. He ordered lobster and a bottle of wine. A waiter brought it. The sommelier, who had what looked like the Legion of Honour round his neck, made a great fuss of opening it, smelling it and pouring it, and then left us.

"I enjoyed my cruise," I said, making it easier for him to launch into his speech.

"I'm glad that went well," he said. "What do you know about MOD ten twenty-eight?"

"Do you want the proper answer? 'I don't know what you're talking about', or the truth," I asked, instinctively lowering my voice.

"The truth."

"Very little. I know it's based up near Newcastle somewhere. I know that it's top secret. That's about all."

That was the truth. You, of course, will be wondering and I wish I could tell you more. At that time, I didn't know any more. Nobody even mentioned Ministry of Defence contract 1028. It was one of those things you didn't talk about. Memos with that number on them were put through the shredder in minutes.

"It's moving down here," said Mr. Parsons. "I wondered how you'd feel about joining them."

"How many of them are there? Where the hell are they going to work? We're tight enough on space as it is," I said.

"You know the Electrochem building?"

"On the other side? Yes."

"They're moving out and we're moving in. There aren't that many of them at the moment. There's plenty of lab room there."

"What would I be doing?" I asked.

"That I can't tell you. Your salary would be considerably increased, of course. MoD ten twenty-eight has its own salary scale. They have their own management structure, too. You'd be responsible to them.

As the meal progressed, I learned a lot more. "What about security clearance?" I asked at last. That was uppermost in my mind.

"That's been done. You've passed all their checks," said Mr. Parsons. I tried not to make the relief I felt apparent. The smile on my face came from thinking what Dad would say if he knew there was a gay working on ten twenty-eight — if, indeed, he'd ever heard of it.

Ever since I'd started with Nimrod I'd had a lurking fear that somewhere in Mr. Parsons' office, or locked away in a secret filing cabinet in Personnel, there was a piece of paper which read: 'Scully, Timothy James. Considerable homosexual activity at school. Possible security risk. Keep under observation.' It obviously didn't exist, and that made me feel more relaxed. Looking back on it, I asked far too many questions which would have been better asked at work. It was, after all, a social occasion and I hardly gave him a chance to enjoy his meal. Mind you, there was a moment when he almost made me choke with surprise. He knew all about Gran and the family connection with Weavers. I hadn't mentioned that to anyone. "No conflict of interests of course," he said. "We supply the hardware for their vehicles. They're a good firm. On the other hand, I wouldn't particularly advise you to tell anyone in the family what you'll be doing."

We left the restaurant at two in the morning! Amazingly, customers were still coming in. What the hell people find to do in our town that keeps them entertained till that time, God knows. I drove home through almost empty streets. For a short time, a car seemed to be following me. It didn't look very official, but one never knew. They were bound to keep a close watch on someone associated with ten twenty - eight. But it turned off at the traffic lights.

Tim Scully with Peter Gilbert

I caught a momentary glimpse in the mirror of a girl in what looked like a leather mini-skirt coming out of the shadows and the car stopping. Wrong again!

I didn't sleep very well at all. Not because of the usual reason for sleeplessness. I didn't touch myself that night. Late-night meals don't agree with me, and I had a lot to think over. A new car or a holiday abroad? Maybe a new car *and* a holiday abroad. What was I going to tell the people at work? They were bound to ask. Even if I said I was working on ten twenty-eight, they'd be bound to ask what it was and you can't say 'I'm sorry. I'm not allowed to tell you", to someone who works in the same firm. It was all right for the people in Newcastle working on the project. They were on their own and didn't have to mix with people on other jobs.

Worries like that always seem to magnify when you're in bed. I don't know why. In fact, I needn't have worried. Mr. Harris said, "I hear you're going over to ten twenty-eight. I'm sorry to lose you," and that was that. One of the girls asked when I'd be moving up north. I said I had no idea. Mr. Parsons threw another surprise. I went over to Electrochem with him and another man whom I'd never seen before. Electrochem was a tiny subsidiary company which made sea-water reactive batteries for one of our products. At least, that's what I and everybody else thought. In fact, they had been making something else as well — connected, as you will have guessed, with ten twenty-eight.

"I thought Scully could go in here," said the stranger, opening a door. I might as well have been a piece of furniture. "He'll be sufficiently near the people he'll be working with," he added. There were three girls in there. They all looked up from their computer monitors. One of them waved. I half raised a hand and then decided I'd better not.

"All right with you, Tim?" asked Mr. Parsons who, up to then, had hardly spoken to me.

"I don't mind," I said. "Who will I be in here with?"

"Nobody. It'll be your office."

I was staggered. Hardly anybody at Nimrod had his or her own office. The main building was open-plan. People had made pathetic attempts to screen off spaces with potted plants and room dividers brought in from home. It was even bigger than Dad's office at the Ministry of Defence.

If you'd been at Nimrod a few weeks later you would have seen me doing the oddest things. Several times I stood on the back of a lorry supporting stacks of office furniture as it trundled round the old perimeter track. On another occasion

I was in the sales office, begging for a model missile for my desk. They kindly dug out an old Cobra but eight inches of phallic shaped plastic put me off my work and it went home, to be replaced by a picture of my 'girlfriend' — alias my cousin.

After all that, there was nothing to do. I just hung around for days. Painters moved in. I was so bored that I cleaned up after them. Mrs. Robertson in the personnel office was dealing with the travel plans and accommodation for the staff coming down. The list was quite frightening. Doctor Adamson, Doctor Page, Doctor Hamilton, Doctor Varsjani — and so it went on. There were just six misters at the bottom of the sheet. It looked like I should be amongst the small fry, despite the size of my office.

Summer broke suddenly that year. It seemed that we were wrapped up well one day and going round in shirtsleeves the next. I doubt if it was actually that sudden, but that's what it felt like.

Mr. Parsons came over one day. "They won't be here for another two weeks, Tim," he said. "Why don't you take a holiday?"

I didn't like to say that holidays on my present salary were a luxury I couldn't afford. What with my rent and keeping the car on the road, I had very little spare cash. On the other hand, it seemed a sensible thing to do. I think I should have gone mad doing nothing for another two weeks. I thought about it carefully. I couldn't afford a hotel or anything like that. Neither did I like the idea of being on my own. I rang Anthony.

"How did the weekend in Somerset go, or shouldn't I ask?" I said.

"We didn't go. Haven't you heard?"

"Heard what?"

"About Adam."

"No… I've been too busy at work — or, to be more honest, too preoccupied."

"His firm's gone bust and he and his dad have done a runner," said Anthony.

"No!"

"It's true. You want to go round there to have a look. The tenants are all under notice to quit or buy their flats. Dad always said he was a dodgy character."

For some minutes we discussed various hiding places. My money would have been on Burton Clayhanger, but if his father was on the run too, I guessed they'd probably fled the country. I felt an extraordinary sense of relief. I'd never had the courage to break with him as I knew I should. Now he had done it for me. I almost forgot the reason for my call. I didn't think Anthony would be able to take time off, but it was worth asking. No chance. He had his studies. I was on my own.

I didn't want to go to my folks. I saw them regularly enough anyway. On the other hand, I hadn't seen Gran for a long time and I wanted to get the news across to her that I had been moved to another division of Nimrod before she found out about it on her private intelligence network and started making enquiries. I rang her and she seemed enthusiastic, so on Saturday I was speeding up the motorway with the obligatory bunch of flowers in the back of the car. 'Speeding' is not quite the word I want. Don't get me wrong. I'm very fond of Gran and the thought of being pampered for a few days was pleasant enough, but I'd rather have been going somewhere a bit more exotic with someone nice; Anthony or Matt maybe. Not Adam, though.

The first few days were much as I thought they would be. Gran hadn't changed. She was interested to hear about Matt. I just told her that he was a sub-lieutenant and he worked in Portsmouth Dockyard and, as far as I knew, he had a flat somewhere in the area.

"He'll go a long way, will that lad," she said. "All he needs is someone behind him to give him a push." I nearly choked over my cornflakes!

I had to tour the firm, where everybody addressed me as 'Mr. Tim'. They were working on a big order for Saudi Arabia — tracked vehicles to carry our Mamba so that part was interesting. What got me down — it always did — was the procession of people who called at the house to be introduced to the only grandson. I sat in the lounge, drinking coffee in the mornings and tea in the afternoons, being told how much I had grown up and asked if I remembered doing all sorts of extraordinary things when I was a boy. I think most of them had their wires crossed — at their age, I guess you have to expect it. I never was the sort of person to swing on trees pretending to be Tarzan. I loathe football, so it was unlikely that I kicked a ball through some old biddy's bathroom window.

The only place I could be alone, it seemed, was my room. It was the room I always slept in, at the top of the stairs next to the bathroom. That was handy.

Thursday morning. Gran had been up for hours, as usual. I was enjoying a delightfully slow wank. The stars of that particular one were Anthony and Matt. They'd never met in real life, but imagination is a wonderful thing. I'd got Matt kneeling on the floor and Anthony leaning over him. He'd just got the first inch or so in and Matt was groaning softly, but loving it. Anthony put his hands on Matt's shoulders — and then the doorbell rang. I stopped. I heard Gran walking to the front door. "Now who can that be?" I heard her say. It had happened so often that I could visualise her drying her hands on her apron as she walked to the door.

"Oh, it's you," she said. "Yes, he's in. He's still in bed. Why don't you go up? He's awake. I could hear him moving around."

I put up with them in the lounge, but to have some old lady barging into the bedroom, especially at that moment, was too much. I pulled the quilt over me and grabbed for the nearest book from the bedside cabinet — Russet Leaves, a romance by Valentine Lovemore. Someone came up the stairs. There was a knock on the door. "Come in," I said, making my voice sound as weak as I could. I knew I was sweating. She was bound to notice that and tell Gran. The Doctor would be sent for. I was furious.

"Hi! I'm Barry Freeman." This was no old lady. This was a boy. My first impression was of cut-off jeans with very frayed edges and thighs as thick as tree trunks. I looked up from the book. The little steel-framed glasses didn't do much for him, but the thick-lipped smile, blue eyes and fair, close-cropped hair were enough to start my cock rising again. I didn't think he would notice. The quilt was quite thick, but I turned on my side to face him.

"What are you reading?" he asked. I showed him the cover. He wrinkled up his nose. That made him look even more attractive. "Not my scene at all," he said.

"Nor mine."

"I came to see if you'd like to come round to our place and then we could possibly go for a picnic or something. The forecast says it's going to be a warm day."

"Anything to escape from Russet Leaves and rusticated old ladies," I said. "When?" I was beginning to wonder if he was some sort of hallucination. He was almost too beautiful. From my sideways position I could make out tiny little golden hairs on his thighs and I had no doubt about the ridge which ran down the front of his shorts under the fly.

"I'll wait for you if you like," he said.

"Sure. I won't be long."

In fact, I must have been quite a long time. For a start, I had a fully loaded gun to discharge. By the time I got downstairs, showered and shaved, Barry was nowhere to be seen.

"Barry decided to wait in his car," said Gran. One look at the open album on the table was enough to tell me why. "Our First Grandchild'. It had come out of the drawer a good many times that week.

Gran, of course, insisted that I have breakfast. I swallowed orange juice and cereal as quickly as I could.

"Such a nice boy, that Barry," she said. "I told his mother that you were coming and might like a bit of young company."

"How old is he?" I asked.

"Barry? Younger than you, of course. I think he must be about eighteen. His father was Mayor three times. A very nice man. In fact, they all are. Mrs Freeman is a leading light in my Dorcas Society. We make woolly toys for refugee children."

"Has he got a girlfriend?"

"Lord knows. Young men don't seem to have girlfriends any more. Just hordes of painted trollops to jive with."

Once Gran starts on a topic like that, she'll go on for hours if you let her. Leaving her to do the washing-up, I left the house.

"You took your time," said Barry, as I climbed into his car.

"Breakfast is compulsory. So is looking at that bloody album. Sorry about that."

"No worry. I've seen more attractive photos, though."

"Me on the leopard skin and the lock of hair are all banned subjects," I said. He laughed.

Their house was enormous and set a long way back from the road. I think the style is called Stockbroker Gothic. It was all eaves and wooden beams set in white plaster. From the outside it looked like a picture in a history book. Inside it was startlingly modern. I liked his mother a lot. She wanted to make quite sure that I had had breakfast. She hoped that Barry hadn't called at an inconvenient time. That made me feel slightly guilty. She asked me to get my 'dear Grandmother' to ring her that evening about the sale of work. When we managed to get away, I followed Barry up the wide staircase to his room. Two rooms, actually. The first was a surprisingly neat study. There was a desk, upon which sat a very good computer. A rowing machine stood in the corner and there was a long, low bookshelf with various trophies arranged on top.

"More comfortable in the bedroom," said Barry, and we went in there. He closed the door. It was pretty obvious that he spent much more time in there than in the study. I don't think I've ever been in a more untidy room. Shoes littered the floor. The bed was one of those queen sized things - much bigger than the one in my tiny flat. It looked like it hadn't been made for days. A pile of discarded clothes lay on the only chair. He gathered them up in his arms, dumped them on the floor and sat down. I sat on the corner of the bed.

"Sorry about the mess," he said. "I don't let Mum or the cleaner come in here." Untruthfully, I said that my flat was always untidy.

"It was interesting seeing those photos of you," he said.

"Banned subject," I replied. Five of them were in Gran's album and I knew my folks had some more. The one thing to be thankful for was that Dad's mania for photography waned when I was about six. Up to that time, he'd caught me grinning toothlessly on a tiger skin, in the bath with a yellow plastic duck, bouncing up and down on Mum's knee and several times on a beach somewhere.

"I guess it must be a bit embarrassing if the person who sees them knows you," he said.

"You've got it in one. One day I swear I'll get hold of that bloody album and burn it. She shows it to everybody. There can't be many people in this town who haven't seen me naked."

Barry laughed. "You've changed since then," he said.

"So I should hope. Anyway, let's change the subject. What do you want to do?"

"Oh, I don't mind. Like I said, we can go for a picnic."

"Sure." Neither of us said anything for a moment or two. I felt awkward, feeling that I should take the lead in some sort of interesting conversation. I wanted to find out more about him, of course, but it didn't seem the right moment to ask questions.

"Do you like reading?" he asked, suddenly.

"Yeah. Sometimes. Providing the book isn't bloody Russet Leaves by Valentine Lovemore."

He stood up and went to the wardrobe. He opened the door and then pulled out a drawer and reached under a pile of shirts to produce an extremely large book. It wasn't thick — just very large. It was the sort of book you expect to be about Chinese enamel-ware or orchids.

"What do you reckon to that?" he asked, passing it to me. I looked at the cover. 'States of Nature. Volume one. Alabama'. Barry sat down again. I opened it at random and got quite a shock at a full-page colour photo of a totally naked, very good looking, young black man. His cock was enormous; considerably thicker than the handle of the pitchfork he was carrying.

"Good, eh?" said Barry. I turned back to the preface. The Hutchins family of Alabama, I read, were farmers and all were dedicated naturists. There were three of them: Ma Hutchins, Pa Hutchins and son Robert, who was twenty - one.

I turned the pages one by one. Pa Hutchins might have been good-looking when he was younger, but years of farm work had taken their toll. His skin was wrinkled and his pubes were grey. As for Ma Hutchins, the memory of those dreadful floppy tits haunts me still. But Robert was something else!

Barry got up and stood by my side as I turned the pages. It soon became clear that Robert Hutchins was either a great self-publicist or that the publishers had a very specific market in mind. Like you, I suspect the latter. We saw Robert lying on his back under a tractor with his knees bent and his legs apart. You could see everything he had. There was Robert energetically stirring a pot, making his cock sway to one side to expose his equally large balls. Meanwhile, Ma Hutchins was taking the Thanksgiving turkey out of the oven. As Barry pointed out, she was slightly out of focus whereas every detail of Robert was so clear that you could pick out individual pubes. Then came Robert with one foot on a stool, polishing a harness. I swear that his backside gleamed brighter than the strap over his knee. Then Robert again, shovelling a huge pile of straw.

"You'd think his dad would give him a hand," said Barry.

"I'd give him a hand any day," I said, thankful that the book on my lap covered the excitement I was beginning to feel.

"Alabama's a long way away," he said — which could have meant anything.

Robert on a tractor; Robert on a horse; Robert tightening a nut on a plough. Finally, on the last page, we were treated to shot of Robert on his bed, once again with his legs apart and that huge cock dangling between them. 'The end of a hard day,' said the caption - which again could be taken several ways.

"I'll just nip down and get the picnic ready," said Barry. I went to return the book. "I'll put it back before we go out," he said, and left me alone. I thumbed through the pages again, thinking. Why would a person have a book like that? Why would he show it to me? It looked as if he was trying to tell me something but, if he was, he wouldn't have left me and gone downstairs. His mother and the cleaner didn't come into the room. There was a key in the lock. Surely he would have done something or said something. I came to the conclusion that I'd got the wrong impression. Thank God I'd kept my self-control. I could have so easily tried to touch him up as he stood there, and there would have been all hell to pay. He would have told his mother. She would have told Gran. The consequences were too awful to contemplate. I picked up a magazine from the bedside cabinet. It was about rowing. Lots of huge young men in baggy shorts holding vast oars and grinning. Not as nice as 'States of Nature' but it had the desired effect. My cock soon went to sleep again.

"Ready when you are," he said when he returned. I handed him the book.

"Good, eh?" he said as he slid it under the shirts again and closed the drawer.

"Very interesting," I said.

The drive was interesting too. Not for the scenery, though that was pretty breathtaking to a southerner used to fields and hedges. I learned a lot. Barry had just finished school; a Catholic boarding school for boys run by monks and 'brothers'. It made my school sound quite modern. His account would have confirmed all Andy's prejudices. Nudity was absolutely forbidden. The boys slept in curtained cubicles. They showered in curtained cubicles and had to wear pyjama trousers when they washed in the morning. If a boy accidentally 'exposed himself' he got the 'cuts' with a cane on his naked backside — which seemed to contradict the rule. I began to see the reason for Barry's fascination with the book. To get to the age of eighteen without so much as a glimpse of another cock was weird. I would have gone barmy if it hadn't been for the constant procession of teenage male nudity at our place. That row of wiggling arse cheeks in front of the wash basins as the owners brushed their teeth used to set me up for the day.

He was hoping to get into a University famous for rowing, that being his favourite sport. I looked down at his honey-coloured legs and imagined them straining against a board. I soon had to look up again. Other thoughts had started to intrude. He didn't have a girlfriend. That was understandable. Even at our school, to be seen with a girl in the town meant an interview with a housemaster.

He drove off the road. We bumped along a stony track, past a small wood and came to the most extraordinary pool. From the stone sides, I guessed it had once been a quarry. Moving shadows of the trees which shaded it flitted across the surface of the water and the grass which surrounded it. It was so peculiarly quiet that I instinctively closed the car door carefully. It was like being in a huge church. There was just one bird singing somewhere in the distance.

"They call it Silent Pool, said Barry.

"I can see why," I replied in a whisper.

We lugged the picnic box out of the boot. Barry dragged a blanket out, affording me a delightful view of a very tight but plump backside. He spread it on the grass and we sat down to eat. It was apparent that Barry was one of the do-it-yourself brigade when it came to packing a picnic lunch. There was plenty there; a cold chicken; a lettuce, tomatoes, salad dressing in a plastic container, plenty of bread rolls and a pack of butter (which had started to melt) together with six cans of beer. Fortunately there was a knife. We cut off chunks of what we wanted and ate them. I had two beers, Barry just one. Finally, we cleared up and lay back. The sun was in my eyes, so I closed them. The sight of him bending over the car boot to put the box back in the boot had done things to me. The middle seam of his cut-offs had vanished into the cleft of his bum. Another glimpse of that could have been dangerous.

Again, there was a long period of silence. I thought he might have gone to sleep, but suddenly he spoke.

"When you come to think of it, there's a lot to be said for it," he said.

"Yeah. It's a nice place. Sort of relaxing," I replied.

"I was thinking about the book."

"How do you mean?"

"Well, here we are on a hot day with nobody around for miles. There's me in these things and you in jeans. Why don't we do it?"

"Do what?" My eyes were still closed.

"Strip off."

"And swim you mean?"

"No. It's too dangerous. Just strip off and sunbathe."

"Well, I...." As far as one side of me was concerned it was a brilliant idea but I knew what was likely to happen and Barry wasn't one to fall for "Beer always gives me a hard-on."

"I'm going to, anyway," he said. I kept my eyes closed but was aware of his shadow on my face as he stood up. Something rattled as his shorts landed on the ground. I wondered whether to turn over. That would have hidden it from sight.

"That's better!" he said.

"Might as well," I said. I just got a glimpse of his naked body as I stood up. A flash of bronze pubes; a limp but thick cock and the whiteness of his midriff in contrast to the rest of him. Then I stared fixedly at a tree trunk as I undressed. By that time he was lying on his front. He'd put his glasses on the blanket beside him. Trying desperately not to look too closely at that gorgeous butt, I lay beside him — also face down.

"Nice, eh?" he said.

"Very nice," I replied. I was thinking about the whiteness of his backside. Virginal white. The thought made me tremble slightly. I don't think he noticed.

"Do you think the Hutchins family really live like that?" he asked.

"I guess so. There's no way of knowing. They're sun-tanned all over."

"I wish I was."

"Too much sun is bad for you," I said. "Anyway, you've got a better tan than I have. I sit in an office all day."

"Yes, but not all over."

"Nobody sees that," I said.

"You can."

I didn't know if he had ability or permission in mind. I chose the latter, opened my eyes and turned my head towards him. Fortunately he couldn't see what was happening beneath me. My cock was sliding over the blanket as it enlarged.

"I'd like to go there for a holiday," he said.

"Just America or Alabama?" I was quite relieved to have got off the subject of the Hutchins family. The relief didn't last long.

"No. To the Hutchins farm."

"It didn't look like the sort of place which has a spare room."

"I could sleep in Robert's room."

"You'd have to share his bed then. There's no room for a sleeping bag."

"I wouldn't mind that."

"You might give him ideas. If Robert got a hard-on, that thing would force you out of bed."

He laughed. "He doesn't look like he's that way," he said.

"Appearances can be deceptive. He's probably the stallion of Alabama. A nice white boy in bed with him is probably what he dreams about."

Some sort of almost electric messages were getting to me. My cock was so hard that it was painful to lie on it. Unless the subject was changed rapidly, the outcome was inevitable.

"How did you find this place?" I asked.

"Years ago. Dad used to come here fishing. He never caught anything, though."

"You could. You could catch this one easily enough," said a strange inner voice.

"Have you ever been to a Sea Life Centre?" I asked.

"No."

"They're fantastic. You walk through a sort of plastic tunnel and the fish are all round you. They've got sharks and rays. Just about everything." I launched into a description of the one at Brighton. He'd never been there. I described the Pavilion and the Marina and would have gone on happily enough, but he snored. I stopped. He snored again. One beer and he was fast asleep. It was just as well. Memories of Brighton were not doing anything to lessen my discomfort. I turned round and sat up. My cock pointed towards the tree tops on the other side of the lake. Carefully, I removed a piece of hair from the blanket which had got trapped under my foreskin. That felt slightly better but I was desperate for a wank. If I could do that, everything would be all right. Unfortunately it was out of the question. If Barry were to wake up and catch me at it.. 'Guess what. You know Mrs. Weaver's grandson, Tim? We went to Silent Pool and he wanked right out in the open!'

I tried to concentrate on the water instead and wondered what sort of fish were gliding around under that dark green, dappled surface. Suddenly I was aware of a loud buzzing; much louder than Barry's soft snores. I turned round. It stopped. One of the largest insects I had ever seen had landed on his right buttock. It was a shiny brown colour. It had a long, dangerously pointed body and large wings. If it had wanted to emphasise its presence, it couldn't have done better than to land on that smooth white skin. I reached over and flicked at it with my finger-nail and it flew off. Unfortunately I had touched his skin as well. He woke up.

"What was that?" he asked.

"An insect of some sort landed on your behind."

"The bloody thing stung me!"

"I don't think so." There was no mark on his skin and I was looking pretty closely.

"It did. Put your finger on the place where it landed."

I did so. It was at the place where the gentle gradient of a thickening thigh turns into the soft, almost vertical lower edge of a buttock.

"That's it," he said. "That's where it hurts."

"I'm sure it didn't. There'd be a mark if it did."

"There must be. Maybe it'll swell up in a minute. Is there any butter left?"

"Plenty."

"Rub some of that on it. That might do the trick."

"I'm quite sure...." I said and then all self-control left me. *"Go on! Do what he says."* said the inner voice. I went over to the car, my cock pointing the way, and retrieved the dripping butter pack from the cold box.

"You're right!" I said, kneeling beside him. "There is a sting of some sort there." There was nothing of the sort. There wasn't a blemish of any sort on that milk-white surface.

"I told you so."

"Wouldn't you rather do it yourself?" I asked.

"No. You do it. You can see it."

I dipped a finger into the butter and applied it gently to his skin.

"Feels nice and cool," he said.

I ran my greasy finger across and under his buttock and then slightly upwards. It was like stroking velvet.

"I guess there's lots of insects in Alabama," he said.

"Almost certainly. If you went there Robert would be doing this to you every day."

"Mm. Talk like you are Robert."

"How do you mean?" My finger was describing little nervous circles. By stretching my thumb downwards I could feel the little hairs on the top of his thigh.

"Like I'm staying on your farm and you're Robert."

I was a bit lost, to be honest. I don't mind helping beautiful boys learn their words but acting has never been my 'thing'.

"Lark this yo mean?" I said in the worst imitation of an American southern drawl ever heard.

"That's it. Put some more butter on."

"Ain't nuthin' ah like better than plenty of butter on ma buns," I said. I slapped at least twenty-five grams onto his buttocks. Little yellow rivulets ran down his thighs and some, I noticed with still rising excitement, vanished into his cleft. I rubbed vigorously. His ass cheeks wobbled like blancmanges and felt just as soft and as cool.

"Ah been out ridin' today," I said. "Ain't nuthin' like ridin' a hoss to make a man think o' ridin' somethin' else when he gets home."

"Like what?"

"Like ridin' a good lookin' white boy. That's what."

I kept rubbing, waiting for him to answer. I didn't have to wait long.

"I don't mind," he said.

"That's what ah hoped you'd say 'cos ah'm goin' to ride you whether you like it or not." With greasy fingers and thumbs, I parted his ass cheeks.

"Anyone ever ridden you before, white boy?" I asked. It didn't seem possible. That tiny little pink orifice didn't look as if it would take a drinking straw.

"Only once — sort of." he said.

"What you mean,sort of?" I asked.

"Bloke at school. He couldn't get it in."

"Well now. Ain't that just dandy? Ah'm goin' to have to break you in and when you got Robert's tool in you, you're goin' to buck just like a bronco. "

Yet more butter. This time I pushed the melting chunk right down between his cheeks. He gasped.

"Just get a finger in there first," I said in my normal voice.

"Robert! Robert!" he gasped. I could feel the butter melting round my finger tip. I pushed. He flung his legs apart. Trying not to get too much melted butter on the lenses, I moved his glasses and went back to work on him.

It took a long time. It seemed like an eternity and my balls were aching badly by the time my finger tip managed to penetrate. He groaned so loudly that a faint echo came back from the rock face on the other side of the pool. That scared me for a moment.

"Ain't no need to be afraid," I said. "More the hoss resists, the more it hurts."

In fact there wasn't that much resistance. After my finger nail had gone in, he took the rest easily.

"Rob...ert!" he gasped and the last syllable coincided with the last centimetre.

The play-acting had some advantages. Somehow it made me see the whole process dispassionately. Certainly I wanted to fuck him. I knew I would. When I'd been rehearsing with Anthony I'd had several times to say 'Slow down. Let the audience enjoy the joke.' The same technique worked with Barry. I kept up my appalling imitation of Robert Hutchins. He enjoyed it. Before long he was wriggling around on two of my fingers like an insect on a pin.

"You sure are goin' to be one good fuck," I said.

"Yeah! Yeah!"

"Bet you're glad you came to our li'l ole farm?"

"Oh yeah!"

"And you knows what you're a-goin' to get, eh?"

"Yeah! Do it!"

"You're going to get the biggest dong in all Alabama right up your sweet little asshole." That was a laugh. Robert's was worth three of mine, but dramatic licence and all that.

"Yeah! Yeah!"

I slid my fingers out — not without a certain difficulty. He seemed to want to keep them there. I wiped my hands on the grass, fumbled in my jacket pocket for my wallet, found what I was looking for and pulled it on.

I knelt between his outspread legs and leaned over him. "Ready, white boy?" I whispered.

"Yeah! Oh, do it. Do it!" He was panting hard. I lowered myself as gently as I could. I had to fumble around a bit to find the spot and then I drove into him. I never, up to that time, experienced anything like it. Whether Barry was a natural or whether it was the butter or whether the prolonged fingering had done the trick I didn't know. I was just aware of a tight, silky grip that seemed to ripple up the shaft of my cock until my balls were touching his. He gave another long groan which, again, echoed back to us, and I gave the first thrust.

I put my hands under his heaving torso and found his nipples. I played with them and gave another push. Then I let my fingers play down his chest to his belly. I found his navel, put a finger in that and shoved again. Then down even further. The bristly hair felt slightly damp. Even further down, pushing my cock further and further into him. His was pretty easy to find. It was almost as if it leapt into my fingers. Obligingly and delightfully, he lifted himself off the ground slightly so that I could get my fingers round it. It was as hard as steel and already weeping sticky fluid. I squeezed it and his juice oozed between my fingers.

He grasped two tussocks of grass and forced himself back against me, almost throwing me off balance. It was pretty clear what he wanted me to do. I couldn't see what I was doing but I could feel it well enough. I slid his foreskin back, paused and then lunged into him. I let go. Paused and gave another lunge. He went crazy. It's the only word I can use to describe that frantic wriggling, gasping and groaning.

Unfortunately — just my luck — he came before I did. Not long before - but I had hopes of being able to withdraw, let him go off the boil slightly and then drink his spunk. Not a hope. It splattered so far in front of him that I saw the drops land on the grass - and, incidentally, on his glasses.

In not more than a couple of rapid stabs into his soft, yielding ass, I came. I could feel the rubber swell slightly inside him. My stomach was pressed against the small of his back and we slithered together on our mutual sweat as he shot yet again.

"Like that, did you, white boy?" I whispered.

"Christ, yes!" he gasped.

It took a long time to clean up. We dipped bunches of grass into the water. "Am I still Robert?" I asked as I washed butter from his buttocks.

"Only when we're having sex," he said. He picked up my wallet and, as he did so, credit cards dropped out, together with a newspaper cutting. He apologised. I picked up the cards.

"A play?" he asked, opening the cutting.

"A friend of mine. He's the one in the striped blazer," I replied.

"Phew! He's nice. He's very nice. Does he…."

"As a matter of fact, he does but his dad's a vicar so he has to be careful."

"My dad was mayor, come to that."

We got into the car. On the journey home I asked the question which had been nagging at me all day.

"How did you know?" I asked.

"Know what?"

"About me?"

"I don't know. I knew the moment I went into your room when you reading that book."

"That was a cover. I'd been having a wank."

"I sort of sensed that. How about me? How did you know?"

"Again a matter of books," I said.

"Volume two is coming out soon. 'Alaska'. That should be good."

"If you think I'm going to fuck you in the snow, forget it," I said.

"Oh, we'll think of something. I'll tell you what could be fun…"

"What?"

"Why don't you bring your friend up here? The one in the play? We could make a trio. That could be fun. I fancy him."

"As a character in a book or a play — like me trying to be Robert?"

"Why not?" said Barry.

CHAPTER ELEVEN

I don't need to tell you that Gran's friends didn't have much of a chance after that to admire the only grandson. I drove over to Barry's place immediately after breakfast and didn't usually get back to Gran's until just after Mr. Freeman had got back from work. Gran didn't seem to mind. She thought it was a good thing that I'd 'teamed up with such a nice lad'. Gran was holding court one evening when I got back. "I can't think what they find to do round there. Tim gets back so tired sometimes that he falls asleep in his chair," I heard her say. If she had known....

I learned a lot in those days — not so much *from* Barry as *with* Barry. I learned how to get the tip of a cock right down in my gullet, which he enjoyed a lot. I wasn't so keen. I wanted the taste of it. I learned how to hit his button every time I fucked him, sending him into a squirming ecstasy. I got my addiction to licking out an ass from Barry too. Providing it's spotless, that's a great way to spend an hour or two. The Freeman's had an attachment on their shower which was just right for washing it out, so we spent an enjoyable half an hour in the bathroom with Barry first kneeling in the tub and then sitting on the loo to let the water run out. After that it was a quick, dripping walk to his bedroom, where my face was soon between his cheeks — and stayed there till he couldn't hold back any longer. A quick change of positions and I got several mouthfuls of his spunk.

There was always the imagination business with Barry, and that did put me off a bit. I always had to be someone else. The real Tim Scully, it appeared, was not much of a turn-on for Barry. I had to be Robert Hutchins or a cowboy who had found this English youth on my ranch. He invented a new persona for me almost every day. He kept on and on about Anthony. I lost count of the number of times he read the cutting and admired Anthony's picture.

"Just imagine what it would be like with the three of us," he said one afternoon when we sat, naked and semen-soaked, on the edge of his bed. "You'd have two of us to fuck, one after the other — and the one not being done could watch. It'd be great!"

I didn't like to tell him that just one fuck with him resulted in my missing several hours of television in the evening. "You'll have to bring him up here next time," he said. "I can't wait to meet him."

It was, I thought, out of the question. I tried to explain. Bringing someone younger than I with me would certainly make Gran suspicious. She was no fool. Anyway, I doubted if it would work out. Two's company and all that. Barry got round that problem in a couple of days. His parents would be glad to have Anthony staying with them, he said. I wasn't keen on that idea either. Barry and Anthony would be at it all day and all night, and I'd be stuck with Gran's friends. A non-starter — or so I thought.

I drove back in a much happier mood than I had been in on the journey up. The car seemed to gobble up the miles and, as the odometer figures climbed, I tried to work out how many times I'd gobbled Barry. Not as many as my final mileage, certainly, but quite a few times.

The first few days at work were chaotic. The ten twenty-eight people had arrived together with all their equipment. They were an amazing bunch. Everybody — and I mean everybody — called everybody else by his or her first name. After working with Mr. Harris, this was a shock. Dr Adamson was Brian. Dr. Hamilton was Tom. Dr. Varsjani was Rajesh. It should all have been smooth enough. The trouble was, the unknown man who'd done the planning hadn't taken all the considerations into account. Brian Adamson, being the boss, had to have an office. He had that, but he also wanted a lab of his own next to the office and with a communicating door. That moved one lot and room had to be found for them. It was like a peculiar sort of musical chairs and I knew damn well what was going to happen to my newly decorated office. I lost it in days and ended up in a much smaller room. That was bad enough, but one has to put up with these things. Meanwhile, all sorts of structural alterations went on. An ordinary shredder wasn't secure enough for ten twenty-eight waste paper, so an incinerator had to be built behind the building. That was one of the very few jobs done by outside contractors. It wasn't in the least unusual to arrive in the morning and find three or four men with doctorates galore wielding electric drills. Rajesh Varsjani plumbed the sink into what had been my office himself.

Gradually we settled down to work and that is all I can say on that topic. The real blow came after I'd been back for about a fortnight. Tom Hamilton shouted for me. I went out to see what he wanted. He was sitting on a desk in the corridor. "You've got company," he said. "Give us a hand in with this, will you?"

So much for solitude! It had been really nice to be on my own. I got much more work done. Anthony and Barry could phone me in the office and I had some pretty steamy conversations, especially with Barry.

The desk acquired a computer. A calendar appeared on the wall next to it, but there was no sign of the new occupant until the following day. Wow! Danny Taylor was twenty-three years old. He was very tall; much taller than I am. He had the build of a sportsman. You could see that despite the dark suit.

He was very dark-skinned. He had big brown eyes with long lashes and he wore glasses. My heart started thumping the moment I saw him.

He had a lot of work to catch up on, so I didn't speak to him properly until the afternoon. I got him coffee and showed him where the personnel people were; that sort of thing. When he was sipping his first cup of Nimrod afternoon tea, I asked him where he was living.

"Lewis Street," he said. "Number thirty-four. A bed-sit."

"Lewis Street! What the hell are you doing in that tip? I thought you were all being put up in hotels until you found somewhere."

"The others are, but hotels drive me nuts. It's all I could find in a hurry. I'll keep looking."

Lewis Street is a standing joke at Nimrod. If anyone wants anything, they get advised to go to Lewis Street, where just what they are looking for can be arranged to fall off the back of a lorry. Nobody actually went to Lewis Street. Hostile mobs of very large young men hung around menacingly and strange cars attracted their attention fast. It was said that someone had driven through there once; had stopped at the traffic lights for not more than two minutes and had driven away without his hub caps, his windscreen wiper and the raincoat he kept in the boot.

The idea of someone who worked for ten twenty-eight living in digs in Lewis Street haunted me for the rest of that afternoon and evening. I was a bit sorry I'd given that stuff to Anthony. Danny could have made better use of it. As the evening went on, I thought about it more and more. I got out of bed in the middle of the night and prowled round the flat. It could work, I thought. It wouldn't be for very long. A person could find a flat in about three weeks. Providing he didn't mind sleeping on the sofa, his clothes could go into my wardrobe. We'd have to work out a roster for using the bathroom. Meals would be a problem. Who was going to cook? Who would buy the stuff? I went back to bed determined not to rush into it. I'd find out a bit more about the guy first.

The photo on his desk was the first blow. "Your fiancée?" I asked.

"Girlfriend, at the moment. We hope to get engaged at Christmas."

"Great! What's her name?"

That opened the floodgate. Her name was Wendy. She lived near Newcastle. She worked for a cosmetic firm as a demonstrator. There was no one, and never would be anyone, so kind-hearted, beautiful or as interesting to talk to as Wendy.

I went back to my own desk to work. It could all be a blind, I thought. Susan smiled up at me from her photo. If anyone were to tell John, her current boyfriend, that I was claiming her for my own, I'd get a black eye pretty rapidly.

That afternoon I invited him out for a drink. He accepted enthusiastically so, with considerable trepidation, I drove into Lewis Street that evening. All the house numbers had vanished from the front doors years before. Empty fast-food containers and drink cans rolled around in the evening breeze. A young man very much the worse for wear and carrying a bottle lurched off the pavement right in front of the car. I managed to pull up in time. He got back onto the pavement and I drove off, just in time to avoid the bottle, which crashed and shattered onto the road behind me.

I found the house by deduction. Number sixteen was the only house with a number, so I counted along from that. What had once been a little front garden contained a broken sink, a rusty bike without wheels and what might once have been either a baby-buggy or one of those shopping trolleys. There was a bell push but it didn't work. There was no knocker so I rattled the flap of the letter box.

"Who is it?" a female voice shouted.

"Visitor for Mr. Taylor!" I shouted back.

"Danny! Danny!" she screamed. I heard him answer.

"Someone for you. Come down and open the fucking door. I'm feeding the baby!"

The front door opened. I was swamped by the smell of cooking cabbage and the awful sickly sweet odour of baby shit. Danny stepped out and closed it again. Not before time.

"Phew. That's better!" he said. In jeans and a red top he looked even more attractive than he looked at work.

Miraculously, the car hadn't been touched, though a crowd was gathering on the opposite side of the road. We got in and I drove off.

I took him to the George. It's outside the town but it's next to the river and reasonably quiet. He liked it. We sat outside until it got too chilly and watched the anglers and the swans. I liked him more and more as the evening progressed. He was so delightfully unassuming and honest that I wondered how on earth he'd got through his interview with Nimrod. He was very keen on football; not so much on watching it on television (thank God!), but he liked playing it, although he wasn't very good and was known as 'Own Goal Taylor' by his ex team-mates. He was into body-building only, according to him, because something needed to be done to a body like his. (I kept my ideas to myself.) He thought marriage to Wendy would be the best thing that could happen to him. Wendy was so good at everything. Wendy could cope with car repairs. She was brilliant when it came to saving money. Their joint savings account increased every month and they should have enough to put down the deposit on a cheap little house when they were married. They'd been living together for six months in a flat. He hadn't wanted to come south but the opportunity was too good to be turned down.

That gave me the opportunity to mention the flat. I said it was very small and it would be a question of sleeping on the sofa, but if he wanted somewhere while he looked for a flat of his own he was welcome.

"Anything is better than Mrs Anstey's," he said. "Are you sure?"

"Totally. It will be nice to have some company."

"I know what you mean. It's completely different, of course, but I got really depressed if Wendy had to go away. The firm she works for does lots of seminars and things like that, about new products."

It was still reasonably early when we left the George. I was anxious for him to see the flat before making up his mind. He said that wasn't necessary, but I persuaded him.

"It's really nice!" he said, the moment he was inside the front door. My tiny kitchen impressed him. "I like that double draining board," he said, "and it's a great idea to have the fridge at eye level like that." It was up there because there was nowhere else to put it. I showed him how the sofa opened up to form a reasonable-sized bed and I showed him the bathroom.

"It's really great!" he said. "If you're still sure, I could move in tomorrow after work. All I've got with me at the moment is two suitcases of stuff."

And so he did and the flat became more of a home from that time onwards.

Instead of watching television, I spent that evening helping him put his things away. His clothes went into my wardrobe easily enough. I needed, as he pointed out, a cupboard of some sort in the lounge. His dad, apparently, ran some sort of furniture business and he reckoned he could get one to match the dining table and chairs and the TV/video cabinet. His large collection of various toiletries just about went into the bathroom cabinet. All except one, I noticed, were made by the same firm in Newcastle. I still had a lingering hope that his relationship with Wendy was about as real as mine with Susan, but it was dwindling fast and two days later it had gone. She telephoned him. I sat with the television at the lowest possible volume listening to sickening endearments and, when they had finished, he told me all that Wendy had done that day.

He went up to see her at the weekend. Strangely, I didn't feel lonely. Just having his things there was nice somehow. I rang Anthony on Saturday morning to see how he was fixed for the weekend. He had two essays to write and had to go shopping.

"We could meet for a drink in the evening," he said.

"Or you could come round here," I suggested. He wasn't keen.

"How about tomorrow? You haven't got Adam to worry about any more. I reckon I could be a pretty good substitute," I said.

"Could do. Let's talk about it tonight," he said — which was not the enthusiastic response I'd been hoping for.

We met in The Gleaners, which was his favourite pub. Mostly, I think, because it was unlikely that any of the clientele there would recognise him and ask him to relay messages back to his dad. It's not a bad place. Adam had exaggerated when he'd referred to the food there and the plastic glasses. The glasses were made of glass and the service was slick and efficient.

"Typical of Adam to run the place down," said Anthony. "Anyway, he's gone. We shan't see him again."

I touched the wooden table instinctively. I'd thought the same at one time. I was convinced that we would.

Anthony was on a 'downer' that evening. The play had ended in a triumph for him. He'd been contemplating leaving university and going to a drama school, but his parents insisted that he should get his degree first. Work was piling up. He didn't think he'd make it. The others were all that much brighter than he was. Having been through the same depression myself, I tried to cheer him up. I think I succeeded (or maybe it was the beer). He was distinctly happier by the end of the evening.

"I met someone who wants to meet you when I was up at my Gran's," I said.

"Meet me?"

"Sure. A guy called Barry Freeman." I lowered my voice, though in the din that surrounded us, nobody could have heard a thing. "Eighteen and as randy as a rock rabbit," I said.

"Did you tell him about me then?" His face flushed.

"Only a bit."

"I wish you hadn't. Adam was bad enough. You know what it's like for me."

"He's hundreds of miles away and I didn't come out with it like that. He found the cutting with your picture and wanted to know who you were."

"Cutting?"

"This one. It fell out my wallet." I produced it again. It was getting a bit worse for wear.

He smiled again. "Not the best possible shot of me," he said. "The footlight has obscured my nice white shoes."

"I don't think he was that interested in your shoes."

"What did you say his name was?"

"Barry. Barry Freeman."

"Barry Freeman. My first fan," he said. "Tell me all. You've told him about me. The least you can do is to tell me about him."

I told him about the book and about the events at Silent Pool. He fell about laughing at my accent.

"It's awful!" he said. "Have you ever seen Tennessee Williams acted properly?"

I didn't know if Tennessee Willliams was a man or a play. "Go and see something by him before you go up there again, for God's sake," said Tim. He might believe in it, but if I'm there I'll be in hysterics."

"Do you want to go up there?"

"I wouldn't mind. It would make a break from this place. Anyway, we've got tomorrow afternoon to think about first. I haven't had it for far too long."

We went to the Cloisters before going home. Everything he said was true. Very few windows were lit up. The huge atrium was deserted and dark and just one lift was working. Pinned to Adam's front door was a long, official-looking envelope stamped 'Deemed to have been served'.

"Dad says we won't see him again," said Anthony.

"I hope you're right," I replied. "You'll miss your Sunday pocket money, though."

"You could hardly call it that. I never had a pocket at the time I earned it."

"I only wish I could afford to…." He never gave me time to finish but put his arms round my neck and kissed me. If it hadn't been for the sound of the lift coming up, we'd have stayed like that for much longer. I was a happy man as I drove home.

In fact, that Sunday wasn't as good as it might have been. By the time Anthony arrived at four o'clock, I was in a state of nerves. Danny had said he would come back 'on Sunday'. Common sense said that if he was coming from Newcastle, he would be pretty late. On the other hand he could have left early in the morning. I wished I had asked him. I didn't even have a number for his portable phone.

"Sorry I'm a bit late," said Anthony as he stepped into the flat. I double locked the front door behind him.

We sat together on the sofa. My heart was thumping in my chest. He seemed quite unmoved.

"Tell me more about Barry," he said. "Does he speak Yorkshire? Ee bah goom! and all that?"

"Far from it. He went to a Catholic boarding school. He hasn't got a trace of an accent."

"Coming from you, that's funny."

"I don't have an accent."

"Didn't you realise that I was copying your speaking voice for Algy in the play?"

"No."

"Well I was. It's just as well that you didn't see the review in the other paper. It said I captured the languid tones of the idle upper classes perfectly."

"Then it must be Adam you were copying. I'm a worker."

"As witness the expensive leather coat hanging on the hall stand. That's new."

"It belongs to the guy staying here at the moment."

"Ho, ho. Tell me all."

"Don't give him another thought. He works in my office. He's hundred per cent hetero and at this moment he's either in Newcastle still fucking his bird or he's just left off to drive home.

"He doesn't know what's good for him," said Anthony.

"But you and I know better," I said, glancing down at the ridge in the front of his jeans. "We'll go in the bedroom. If he does come home early, which I doubt, he won't disturb us in there."

I wished he hadn't spotted Danny's coat and I certainly wished I hadn't mentioned the possibility of his early return. Anthony was back to his old worried self. There was no chance whatever of getting him into the bathroom. Anyway, I doubted if my old-fashioned shower attachment would be as effective. We undressed and, once again, I marvelled at his slim waist and slender figure. I had just a side view at first. Apart from his cock, straight and standing outward at about forty five degrees, he was all delightful curves. There was the inward curve of his back and the sudden transition to round, jutting buttocks. There were the muscles of his lower legs and the very slight inward slope under his pectorals. He turned round to face me.

"Ready when you are, but don't you dare try out any American accents," he said.

I didn't. There was very little opportunity. Sucking balls one after the other takes a deal of concentration and when you've got a cock like his in your mouth it's impossible to do anything more than grunt. I managed the trick I had accomplished with Barry. Not, I am happy to say, for too long. As soon as he started to gasp and rear I left off, leaving him panting on the bed with his feet still on the floor. My cock dribbled onto the carpet as I went across the room to get the necessaries. I switched the computer on as I returned, thinking that even if Danny did come back, the sound of the hard disc drive going would be enough to convince him that we were working or playing on the computer.

In retrospect I don't think he would have been fooled.

"There!" That was me. "Get your legs up. Right up. A bit more. That's it."

"What ...." Small wonder that he was puzzled. He was practically standing on his head and both legs were splayed over my shoulders.

Sucking, liquid sounds interspersed with groans from Anthony. Then, some five minutes afterwards, "Christ! I thought.... kiss my.... ass was... an expression of abuse!"

"Ready?"

"You bet. Phew! That's better! Mmm. That feels good. That's really good. Go in a bit more. Mmmm. Oh gee. That's great. Do it like you did it before. Oh yeah! Yeah! Try another finger. Yeah! Ow! Oh yeah!"

A soft 'plop'. Would Danny have heard that? If you could hear the disc drive whirring, maybe he could.

"They say …. you never know what you've missed ….. until you get it the second time," he panted.

"Mmm. It feels hard. Down a bit. Bit more. That's it. Aaaaah!"

"Ooh!" (The best way I can put the sound of my first thrust into a word.)

"Ow!

"Ooh!"

"Ow!"

Bed springs creaking. Both of us gasping. Liquid, slippery sounds of a well-oiled cock sliding into a saliva-lubricated, incredibly tight but soft passage. Anthony's loud, guttural groan as (more by luck than skill) my cock brushed against his hard prostate.

Danny might have heard it, had he been at the door, better than I. I had two silky legs clamped against my ears. I looked down at Anthony's face. It was very red. That wasn't surprising in view of the position he was in. His mouth was open. It was difficult to assess whether he was smiling or grimacing. Not that I cared at that moment. I could have told his dad a few things about heaven from that experience. Heaven is fucking a slim young man and feeling every part of him reacting in sheer delight.

I came first that time. His mouth opened wider as if he was going to scream. Instead he gave a low groan and continued to writhe around so energetically that it was difficult to hold him. I felt my cock swell and then subside in twitches as successive jets of spunk shot into the rubber.

"I'm…. I'm….." Anthony panted, and that time I got the full load right in my face and on my neck and shoulders. When we came to clean up, there wasn't so much as a drop on the bed or the floor, which made a change from the last time his juice-fountain had operated. I got some of it into my mouth and relished his taste. It was completely different from Barry's. I won't say nicer. That would be like comparing different brands of caviar. (Not that I had ever eaten the stuff, but Dad and people at school had always said there was a terrific difference, depending on where the sturgeon was caught.) I wouldn't like to be rated as an expert on the taste of spunk, but I would say that young men from Yorkshire are slightly more sour than sweet and that southern England semen is predominantly sugary with a tinge of saltiness. Both are delicious.

We went downstairs. I made a couple of cups of coffee. We watched a bit of television.

"When are we going up to see Barry?" Anthony asked. We were watching a programme on the Yorkshire Moors at the time, so it wasn't an unexpected question.

"I don't know. When are you free?"

"The vac starts in three weeks. We could go then."

"That's a bit too close. Gran will wonder what's up if I turn up on her doorstep so soon after seeing her. I'll work something out, okay?"

"Make it soon. I need something worked in," said Anthony.

CHAPTER TWELVE

Back to work again and we were busy. What, for want of a better word, I'll call the 'prototype' had been to the firing range in Australia and they sent the report back. I never read it. I know that it was more like a book than a file. I caught glimpses of it on Brian Adamson's desk from time to time and little excerpts were given to me and to Danny to work on. That's all I can say about that. Being busy had advantages, because Danny was driving me mad. Don't get me wrong. He was the nicest, most thoughtful person anyone could possibly live with. He didn't mind vacuum cleaning and he did it better than I did. Danny moved the furniture around to get behind it. He was amazingly strong and very good with his hands. Not that they ever touched me. (I'm sorry to say.) The cupboard he had asked his parents for arrived as separate pieces to be put together. He did that in less than an hour, only stopping once to read the instructions. As he had said, it matched the other stuff perfectly. The lounge looked a bit less like an indoor car boot sale.

My frustration had nothing to do with any shortcomings on his part. Quite the opposite. There was the night when he decided to take a bath. I was watching television at the time and, hearing the water running, thought I'd have a quick pee first. I came across him standing naked in front of the airing cupboard.

"Oh sorry. I didn't think to ask if you wanted to use the bathroom," he said. "You haven't seen my yellow towel by any chance?"

I stood transfixed at the sight of the most beautiful backside I'd ever seen. It was as brown as the rest of him. It was broad and smooth and, as he reached up to the next shelf, delightful dimples formed.

"Er.. top shelf I think."

"Ah yes! Ta," and he turned round. It was enormous! Four inches of broomstick-thick soft flesh crowned with a straight-topped thick bush of black hair. From what I could see of his balls, they looked pretty well developed too.

"You go and have your pee. I'll hang on here," he said. He made no attempt to cover himself up with the towel. He just stood there. Having a pee in those circumstances took some time. My cock had started to react. I managed it — but only just. He was still naked when I came out. I deliberately averted my eyes and went back to the television to recover my composure.

Wendy rang. Wendy had a real talent for calling at awkward times. Danny had to get out of the bath and this time he stood at the phone with the towel round his waist. By the time he'd finished talking, the wet footprints he'd left on the carpet had dried. It was all 'Yes, darling,' 'No, darling,' and 'That's a great idea, love!' — not that I was concentrating much on the conversation. I'd had to turn the sound down anyway, so I couldn't help hearing him. I gave up trying to watch the programme and concentrated on that long, dripping back. The towel was tight enough on his backside to show the exact contours of each buttock. Once again, my cock started to rise. There had to be a reason, I thought, for that beautiful brown colour. Where the hell did a person go to get a suntan like that? An all-over suntan, too. The skin under that towel was just as brown as the rest of him.

I found out the answer to that question without having to ask. I was telling him about Gran. Not about Weavers — just Gran and her house and the charity work.

"I never knew my grandmother," said Danny. "She died in India when I was a little kid."

"What was she doing in India?" I asked.

"She was Indian. My Grandad was English. Funnily enough, you wouldn't know that my Mum wasn't one hundred per cent British. I'm the only one in the family who gets mistaken for an immigrant."

"Oh, you're not as brown as all that," I said. "It looks quite good." I would have liked to say 'gorgeous' or even 'mouth-watering'. He was almost the same shiny colour as the buns Gran baked. That night I had a great session thinking of licking brown buns — and filling them with cream. I hoped Danny had gone to sleep. If he hadn't, he must have heard the bed creaking.

He joined a health club. The firm had an arrangement by which employees got in without paying the joining fee. That made things worse, because he took his track suit off when he came home and sat around in little skimpy white satin shorts. If he was sitting on the sofa and I was in the armchair, I could see right up his thigh. Sometimes I could actually see the tip of his cock. It seemed to be peeping at me like a little purple-nosed ferret in its burrow.

I missed him at weekends. Anthony's visits compensated, but, if I am to be truthful, there were times when I closed my eyes and imagined that it was Danny I was sucking or fucking. I don't think I was the only one imagining another partner. He kept on and on about going to see Barry.

I wouldn't describe myself as the world's greatest psychologist, but it became apparent after some weeks that all was not well in Newcastle. The usual pattern on Sunday evenings was for me to flurry round getting rid of the slightest traces of Anthony's visit. Sheets in the laundry basket; condoms carefully wrapped in old newspaper and put into the dustbin; cream tube back in its hiding place; a double check all over the flat to make sure there were no traces and then I'd settle down in front of the TV and wait for Danny. His normal arrival time was about eleven o'clock, which was just about bed-time — but there was no chance of that happening. I had to sit and listen to an account of all the wonderful things that Wendy had done in the previous week. Invariably, she had given him a little present to bring home and I had to admire that. He rarely asked what I had done — which was just as well.

Then,one Sunday evening he arrived rather more noisily than usual. I heard the car door slam, which was most unusual for a considerate person like Danny.

"Hi! How's Wendy?" I asked as he came in.

"All right. Fancy a coffee?"

"I'll do it," I said, standing up.

"No you won't. I will." I sat down again.

"Good weekend?" I asked later.

"Not bad. I think I'll turn in if you don't mind."

"Sure." I went to my room and left him in the lounge. I heard him open up the sofa. Again, he did it more noisily than usual.

He seemed all right again at work, but on Tuesday morning announced that he wouldn't be going to Newcastle that weekend.

"Why not?" I asked.

"I thought I'd stay down here. The car needs to go in for a service and I can do that on Saturday."

"Why don't you invite Wendy down here for the weekend?" I said. "I was going to take a long weekend sometime to go up and see Gran anyway. I could go this weekend."

He thought for a moment. "Sure you wouldn't mind?" he said. Spending the weekend without Anthony's visit and having Danny drifting round the place in his usual half-undressed state would have been too much of a strain. I said I didn't mind at all. Things had worked out perfectly.

"Let's hope," he said. That was the first real clue as to what was worrying him. I wish I had realised at the time.

Getting a long weekend at Nimrod was usually a question of getting a form from Mrs Robertson, filling it in, sending it up the line to Mr. Parsons and waiting for it to come back with his signature. Not so with ten twenty-eight. Brian Adamson was in the corridor.

"Brian, can I have this Friday and next Monday off?" I asked.

"Sure. Do you reckon you can finish (and he told me what it was) before you go?"

"I think so."

"Don't panic if you can't, but I'd be grateful," and that was that. I finished the job on Thursday morning.

Anthony was delighted and so was Barry. "It'll be great with three of us," he said.

"That's in the daytime. I'll have to sleep at Gran's," I said.

"I don't see why. There's plenty of room here."

It was an appealing thought. "Too risky," I said. "She'd find out that I'd been there. Your mother would almost certainly say something."

"No she wouldn't. Not if I tell her not to. Didn't you say you had a mate from Newcastle?"

"Yes."

"Then it's easy. You stay here and, just in case she has found out or seen your car, you pop in and see her on the last day and say you've just come from visiting this guy in Newcastle and you're on the way home."

It sounded horribly deceitful, but it was an answer. Funnily enough, I wasn't in the least concerned about the two of them bonking each other twenty four hours a day. It was just that I didn't fancy the idea of sitting talking to Gran's friends in her lounge while they were doing it. Barry rang on Thursday afternoon to say that he'd arranged it. His mum quite understood and wouldn't say a word. His dad was away, so my car could go into their garage and not be taken out until it was time for me to drive home. On Friday morning I said Goodbye to Danny before he left for work and an hour and a half later I was driving up the motorway with Anthony in the passenger seat. I really was going as fast as possible that time. Anthony couldn't get there fast enough. He was looking forward to meeting Barry. That was understandable enough, but until we'd gone at least a hundred miles he was frightened of being recognised. It was a real neurosis. There was nothing in the least odd or sinister about the two of us driving north. The chances of someone he knew spotting him were just about nil and even if they did… But he wouldn't have it. I was busting to stop for a coffee but he didn't want to. We were north of Birmingham when he finally relaxed and I was able to pull in to a service area.

By the look and sound of things, he was as desperate for a pee as I was. He didn't want anything to eat. "I can't wait to get there," he said, for at least the tenth time. I drank my much- needed coffee as quickly as possible and we were on our way again.

***

My first and only attempt at match-making was a resounding success. Literally. Those two made so much noise that I am still amazed that Mrs. Freeman didn't come in to find out what was going on. I won't say that it was love at first sight. Lust at first sight is probably nearer the mark. The way they held on to each other after shaking hands was a pretty good indication of what they were thinking. At first things didn't go entirely to plan. Mrs Freeman had put me in a room by myself and installed a single bed in Barry's 'study' for Anthony. Using the excuse that we would be talking well into the early hours, Barry tried to get two single beds in his room, but there was no way that could be done. So one went in there for Anthony and I used the one in the study. I didn't mind that. Barry had already said that he was looking forward to 'threesomes' during the daytime and many of the scenarios (as I learned later) were planned in the night hours when they'd finished.

I enjoyed lying in solitude, listening to them and playing with my cock as I imagined what was going on. I knew both of them well enough to distinguish voices and, more often than not, I was able to envisage what was happening to the 'speaker' at that time. 'Speaker' is not the most accurate word to use. Most of the sounds that came through the closed door were animal-like grunts. I recognised the extraordinary series of grunts indicating that a cock was working its way into Anthony. At such times he sounded much like a man with acute constipation sitting on the loo. Barry was much more vociferous, and yelled loudly — which surprised me. Anthony was a well-developed lad, but by no means huge.

It didn't need a lot of imagination to guess what was happening when one of them was silent and the other moaning happily. Occasionally my guess was borne out by liquid sounds. There were one or two fleshy slaps, too, and odd commands: "Open up!" "Yes you can." "Get a load of this!"

I was up and about first. They were enjoying another session when I climbed out of bed, disposed of the tissues I'd used and went into the bathroom. I had breakfast with Mrs Freeman, who then decided to give me a tour of the grounds. She had the idea (from Gran I shouldn't wonder) that I would benefit from having a few plants around in the flat. When the jobbing gardener came in, later that day, she said she would instruct him to take a few cuttings and pot them for me. I didn't like to mention Danny's possible reaction, but his stay was really only temporary — a thought which I found oddly depressing.

By the time the other two were up and had breakfasted, I was beginning to wonder if we would ever get away. Eventually, we did — in Barry's car. I sat in the back and was surprised when, instead of driving out into the countryside, he took the road into the city.

"Got to do a bit of shopping first," he explained. I was annoyed at first, thinking that anyone with a grain of sense would have done his shopping before we got there. He parked the car and we walked though a series of little alleys (known, apparently, as 'ginnels' up there) to a rather shabby street not far from the station.

"This is it," he announced suddenly. "They've got everything!"

The shop was called OMO: apparently, though I didn't know it at the time, from the initials of the owner, Mr. Osmar Mohammed Osmar. Nobody was ever given such appropriate initials. We pushed our way through the beaded curtain which hung over the entrance and found ourselves in a treasure store. Barry hadn't exaggerated. Mr. Osmar stocked everything from gigantic latex penises to strange balls on strings. Lurid magazines lined the walls, each with a well-endowed and smiling model on the cover. All three of us wandered round gaping. We had a tiny spot of trouble. Mr. Osmar came out of his little room at the back and wanted proof of Anthony's age. He said he didn't have any. I knew that was untrue. He had his students' union card with him. However, we both vouched for the fact that he was over eighteen and Mr. Osmar shuffled back into his hidey-hole, leaving us to gaze at his stock. Barry bought three tubes of special lubricant. Anthony was taken by a packet of the most peculiar-looking condoms. They looked a bit like those rubber things cashiers put on their fingers to count bank notes. I wasn't a bit keen, and selected some ordinary ones.

Anthony wanted to buy a whip (of all things!) and a leather helmet. I am glad to say that both were far too expensive.

With our prospective purchases still in our hands, we were looking at the magazines on display when the wind got up. It was one of those sudden gusts which you get on a hot day — the sort that makes little whirlwinds of dust on the pavements. The curtain blew inwards suddenly, waved around for a bit and then gradually settled down again. The condoms fell from my hand onto the floor.

"What's up with you?" Barry asked.

"Gran!" I said. "She's standing outside."

"Never!"

"Well, if it wasn't, she's got a double." I had spotted the silver-topped cane she carried whenever she went out.

Cautiously, Barry approached the curtain and peered out. "She's not there now," he said. "You must have been dreaming."

I guess Mr. Osmar must have had a closed-circuit TV. He was out of his little back room like a flash.

"First you pay. Then you go out," he said. Barry tried to explain that he had merely been looking for someone in the street. I don't think Mr. Osmar believed him. We left the shop and went back to the car. I had to have been mistaken. There was absolutely no trace of Gran and she couldn't walk that fast.

A strange thing happened on the way to Silent Pool. For some reason my cock started to harden in the car. There was no reason for it to do so. I was admiring the countryside. The other two were talking about acting. It had not happened like this since I was about twelve and on a particularly bumpy bus ride. The ride in Barry's car was smooth enough and yet it happened and, somehow, I knew that the other two were similarly affected. The conversation continued. Neither said anything about it, but somehow I knew.

I was right. When they climbed out of the car the saveloy-sized lumps in their jeans were very apparent. I caught Barry stealing a glance in my direction. He smiled. Silent Pool hadn't changed a bit - which is not really surprising. The eerie silence made it feel like being in some sort of time warp - an illusion made even stronger by the same water bird following exactly the same trajectory over the water as it had the last time I was there.

"Lunch first, after or during?" Barry asked.

"Oh, during or after," said Anthony. I'm not too hungry at the moment."

"You will be," said Barry. "I'll just get the things out of the car."

He came back with three plastic beakers. Each contained two dice.

"What's this for?" I asked.

"All sorts of things," said Anthony with a sort of Mona Lisa smile. "First we undress. The person who throws the lowest number takes something off."

As it happened, he was the first. There was some discussion as to whether it should be a shoe or both shoes. Impatience, I think, made Barry and I decide that the plural was intended. Slowly — far too slowly in my view — a pile of clothes formed on the grass until Barry was naked and sporting that magnificent erection I'd only felt on the first occasion at Silent Pool. Anthony was down to a rather garish pair of boxers, pushed out in front as if he had a spring in them. I still had my shirt and my boxers. Anthony threw a seven. I threw a seven. Anthony threw a nine. I followed with a nine.

"There's a jinx on it," said Barry. "Come on, for Christ's sake!"

Anthony achieved another seven. I rattled the cup vigorously and threw the dice out. Six. Off came the shirt. Anthony picked up the cup, shook it and emptied the dice onto the back of his hand. "Seven again," he announced. I was dying to strip off. My prick was pressing hard against the cotton material. Fortune smiled. One dice came up with a one. The other with a two. I stood up and let them slide down.

"That's a sight for sore eyes," said Anthony. He threw again and then stood up. It sprang out and pointed at the tree tops. My mouth started to water. First Anthony and then Barry — or should I do it the other way round? Maybe there would be time for the first one to come again. You never knew — and they were both young.

"And now?" I said

"A slave auction," said Barry. We worked it out last night. The person who throws the lowest number is the slave. We crouched down and picked up the cups again. Anthony got nine. Barry got seven. Me? Three!

"I forgot to bring the rope," said Barry, which was a relief. "You'll just have to stand still and not mind what we do, all right?"

"Providing you don't mind what I do," I replied.

"Ah. You're just a slave. You're not allowed to do anything."

My inward voice said, "Oh yes? You must be kidding!" but I smiled my assent.

They made me stand in the shadow of a tree and walked away from me, still carrying their dice-cups. Then they turned round and came towards me.

Gran always complained that in any exhibition of military hardware, people always noticed a missile rather than the bright and shiny Weaver truck that carried it. I knew then how she felt. I was only dimly aware of the contrast between their nipples. Barry's were bright red and stood out on pads of muscle. Anthony's were larger but paler. All my attention was on things lower down. Two very large, very stiff cocks pointing upwards and outwards and looking as if they might shoot at any moment. The heads of both had protruded from the enveloping skin. Again, Barry's was brighter and shinier and slightly larger.

"Looks like a good one," he said as they came up to me. He put a cool hand on my belly.

"Very good," said Anthony. "I like them best in their mid-twenties. They know what's expected of them."

"All that hair on his legs, though," Barry replied and ran the hand down, over my cock to my thighs.

"Nothing wrong with that. It shows he's ripe — ike a tomato," said Anthony.

"Berk! They didn't have tomatoes in those days!" Barry's hand slid up and down my thigh and came to rest on my right buttock.

"Okay. An apple, then — except that apples and tomatoes go soft when they're ripe, and he's hard."

"Not here he isn't. Feel this." Anthony's hand went on my other cheek and for a moment the two hands moved in different directions. "Total lack of exercise," said Barry. "Soft as butter. You'd never get a behind like that in a rowing club."

"Unfit for the galleys, you mean?"

"Totally useless. A lovely fuck, though. Let's see how much I can afford. Best of three?"

"That's what we agreed." The hands were removed. Barry shook his cup and emptied the dice onto the palm of his hand. "Seven," he said. Anthony shook his cup much more vigorously, smiled at me in that peculiar way he had and then threw the dice. "Nine. Your go."

Barry's turn again. "Come on, come on!" he exhorted the rattling dice before he emptied the cup.

"Beat that! Twelve!" he cried.

I don't know if I should write 'Unfortunately' or 'As luck would have it'. Anthony came off worst with a total score of sixteen. Barry got nineteen, and I had a pretty good idea of what I was in for. His cock didn't look like a gut-splitter. It was thick but quite straight. If he was careful…. My cock twitched enthusiastically at the thought. It had been a long time.

"How are you going to have him?" asked Anthony.

"I know just the place. See between those two trees over there?"

"Yeah."

"There's one that was blown down a couple of years ago. Make an ideal fucking couch."

Ideal it might have been, but it was certainly not like a couch. It was enormous — fully four feet in diameter and the roots, still with clods of earth clinging to them, stood up out of the ground like old, gnarled fingers. "Lie on it and let your legs hang down either side," Barry commanded.

"Bit like riding a horse you mean?" I said as I climbed up the rough surface.

"A bit, but it's my turn to do the riding. Can you bring the stuff, Ant?"

Anthony ran off and returned with the plastic bag with the discreet OMO logo in the corner. The tree was horribly uncomfortable and I was a bit scared of insects finding my cock. I have to admit that it was just right for size. My ass was on a level with his waist.

"Hold him open for me," said Barry, pulling a tube out of the bag and opening it. I felt Anthony's soft hands pulling my cheeks apart.

"That's it. Nice little hole, that is." I jumped a bit. The gel was cold. His finger scratched around for a bit and then pressed hard against me. I willed myself to open up, but that was more easily said than done. Lack of practice, I guess. He didn't notice. "Easy as that. Amazing!" he said, and something that felt a bit like a barge pole pushed inside me.

"I can't suck him in that position," said Anthony. "I like doing that."

"Course you can. I'm only using the tree-trunk for this."

"Oh! Like last night?"

"You got it."

"I hope he's a bit more comfortable than I was. That bloody chair of yours is all sharp corners."

"I'm not," I gasped and got a slap on my behind. "Slaves aren't supposed to talk," said Barry. "Shut your mouth and open your ass!"

The first I could manage — just about. His manipulations to achieve the latter caused the occasional moan. He wasn't, as I now know, very good at it. Once or twice a pang of pain made me clench my cheeks. He didn't say anything but he was breathing hard and I think he dribbled. Something wet landed on the small of my back. I turned my head to look at Anthony, who stood, very red-faced, nearby. He was still holding the plastic bag but his other hand was busy, fondling his cock. When I caught his eye he stopped. I stuck my left thumb in my mouth and smiled. He dropped the plastic bag and did the same thing.

"Nearly ready," said Barry. I think, but I'm not sure, that he had two fingers in me by then. It felt like his fist, but the discomfort was subsiding.

I climbed down. Gel ran down the insides of my thighs.

"What now?" Anthony asked. He was standing behind us.

"I'm not sure if this will work," said Barry, "but if you sit on the ground so that you can get his cock in your mouth, he can bend over your head. Let's have a go."

I stand to be corrected, but I learned that afternoon that threesomes might be appealing as a concept but in practice they are difficult. Anthony sat on the grass. I moved up to him and felt his tongue lapping on my balls. The two halves of a condom packet fluttered down and landed next to him. Then Barry put his hands on my shoulders and pushed me down over Anthony. I could feel Anthony's hair on my abdomen but nothing else. He'd lost contact.

"Hang on a sec," he said, speaking from somewhere between my legs. His fingers touched my cock and then it touched his lips.

"Okay now?" Barry asked — and, of course, the moment Anthony said 'Yes', he lost it again. Finally, impatience got the better of all of us. I managed to steer my cock towards Anthony's mouth. It went right in that time — to the extent of making him choke. Barry's cock travelled up the cleft of my ass and touched the right spot. I was about to say 'Okay. Go ahead,' but didn't need to. He gave a thrust so powerful that I almost toppled over Anthony. It went in all right but God, it was painful! It felt like a red-hot poker. Anthony kept gobbling away underneath me but I could feel my cock subsiding. I must have yelled because Barry said 'Sorry'. He stopped. Anthony carried on and I kept as still as I could, bent over Anthony's head to such an extent that I couldn't see any of him. All I had in front of my eyes was grass, and the pain was so intense that even that was out of focus.

I decided then and there that it was the very last time I'd ever go in for athletics of that sort. Almost every part of me was aching. I tried to think about Danny and what he was doing at that moment. The thought of that polished nut-brown ass rising and falling, even though Wendy was getting the benefit of his cock, helped a lot. My cock started to rise again. Anthony's hands slid up and down my thighs and Barry gave another, much more careful, thrust forward.

That felt better. He gave another; not so much a thrust as a little nudge, and I felt his cock inside me inch forwards, tentatively feeling its way. That was a glorious feeling. I started to come alive again. The grass came into focus. Anthony's oral manipulations felt less like a surgical procedure. I managed to get the palms of my hands onto the back of his shoulders and the texture of his smooth skin made everything even better. Barry pushed in even further and his thighs touched mine. Another push, and I felt his pubes against my skin. I had all of it! For a moment or two I tried to visualise it. I'd seen it often enough. I'd handled it. I'd watched it spurt. Now it was deep inside me. How far? I couldn't tell. It felt huge and I could sense his pulse, racing much faster than mine.

There's something very odd about pain. You know when you're suffering and you know when it's gone. The actual moment when it leaves you never registers. At least, it doesn't with me. I don't know if it was a gradual process or whether the ecstasy that flooded over me came suddenly. All I know is that I wanted as much as possible of that stiff organ and I wanted Anthony to suck and to swallow as hard as he could. I think I must have said something to that effect. Barry's hand went down to may waist. His flesh slapped against mine. Anthony, still invisible, gobbled and gulped. His cheeks pressed rhythmically against the shaft of my cock and I could feel the hardness at the back of his mouth.

Why can't ecstasy last? I came first. I didn't even try to hold back. It wouldn't have worked. I never even gave Anthony a warning. I couldn't, even though I could feel the pressure building up. It just cascaded out of me into his hungry mouth. I heard him choke and gurgle and felt his lips slacken but Barry was hammering his meat into my asshole as if he wanted it to stay there forever. Some hopes! It swelled up inside me for a second and then slowly subsided. I felt his mouth on my shoulder. He bit into the skin and then sloppily kissed the spot. It cooled under his panting breath.

Anthony disengaged himself and lay face up on the ground between my legs. There was semen all over his chin. He grinned and licked round his mouth. His hands went to his own penis. Up to then it had been neglected. He must have come in a matter of seconds. He gasped just as Barry started to pull out, and I felt his spunk spatter on my legs.

Cleaning up after a session like that took ages. I was all for getting into the water but Barry said it was dangerous. Coils of barbed wire, relics of the war, lay just under the surface. So we made do with various leaves, which we soaked in the lake first.

Tim Scully with Peter Gilbert

"I'll bring some towels next time," said Barry. That's something else I'd like someone to explain to me. I wasn't keen. A feeling of total 'flatness' and depression came over me and lasted for the rest of that day. Not even the second volume in the 'States of Nature' series could shake me out of it. It had apparently just arrived. We had dinner. We watched a bit of television. Barry told his mother that we were going upstairs to play computer games and then go to bed. Bed appealed to me more than playing with a computer! We went into his bedroom and he produced the book, still in its cardboard box.

It was Anthony who suggested that we should all strip off and read it naked. I had nothing against that, but again that strange feeling of lassitude came over me as I undressed. At any other time, being in the same room watching two extremely beautiful teenagers stripping would have brought me near boiling point. This time it didn't. They both had semi-erections, almost from the moment the book came out of its box. We sat on the edge of Barry's bed. Me, Barry and then Anthony. Barry opened it. This one concerned two single-parent families who had moved to Alaska. Lou McGraw and Rob Hewitt both had two sons. Like the Hutchins family in Volume One, they were ardent naturists and, I may say, considerably braver than the Hutchins family. The boys loved wrestling naked in the snow and young Billy McGraw was a very well-built lad, as you could see in the picture of him reaching up to hang a gutted salmon on the line to dry.

"Just imagine getting fucked by him!" said Anthony. "What do you reckon, Agag?"

I said I'd had enough for one day. I had, in more ways than one. Barry laughed and turned the page.

"Uncle Rob and me get on real well. We're buddies and do most things together," he read. "I'll bet they do," he added.

"Yeah! Just imagine. It gets dark pretty early up there," said Anthony and he started to stroke his cock. Inevitably, it hardened.

"I'll do that. You do mine," said Barry, and Anthony slid a hand underneath the book. From that moment on, there was no chance of reading the text. It was difficult enough to concentrate on the wobbling pictures, so I left them to it. Neither seemed in the least concerned and that annoyed me slightly.

I didn't even have a wank that night. My backside felt sore. My legs ached. I lay for some time listening to the sounds coming from the next room: whispering; bed-springs squeaking; boys groaning. Twice during that night their yells woke me up and they were still at it in the morning. Sun streamed through my window. I'd forgotten to close the curtains.

"That's great! Oh yeah! Make it slow. Oh yeah!" That was Anthony's voice. Barry — in fact both of them — had more energy than I had, that was for sure.

I had breakfast with Mrs Freeman. The gardener had produced no less than six plants. She told me their names but they didn't register. There was one with red and green leaves that I liked. We've still got that one. I wondered how the hell I was going to get them all in the car.

That problem was solved when the two lads appeared. "Agag, would you be offended if I didn't come back with you?" Anthony asked.

Explain this if you can. I wasn't in the least offended and said so. The fact of the matter is that I felt relieved. The depression left me at that moment and I suddenly felt happy again. Danny says that it was telepathy. In view of the events of that afternoon, I would disagree.

Predictably, both Barry and Anthony were shattered. We went to Silent Pool again. Anthony fell asleep almost as soon as he was in the car.

"Give it a rest this afternoon, I think," said Barry. "Just do a bit of sunbathing and have a picnic. How does that suit you?"

I said, truthfully, that it suited me fine. In fact, to be quite honest, I was beginning to think of excuses to get away that night.

"I brought wine instead of beer," he said when we got there. "Beer makes me sleepy and I'm tired enough already."

We woke Anthony. Barry draped two huge tartan rugs over the grass. Anthony brought out the cold box. Once again, we all undressed. This time all three cocks were limp. We sat down and started on our Barry Freeman patent picnic, tearing bits of meat off the two roast chickens. We had to break the rolls and spread the butter on them with Anthony's front door key. Barry had forgotten to pack the cutlery. At least he'd remembered a corkscrew and three plastic beakers. I opened the wine. It was good stuff. Barry said his father was in a wine club. Anthony said he wasn't keen on wine. Barry didn't want too much either, as he was driving. That didn't worry me in the least. I'm very fond of the stuff — especially wine of that quality.

We finished — or at least they did. The remains of the meal went into the pool. I half-expected a giant pike to snatch the chicken carcasses. Instead, they floated for a few minutes and then disappeared under the green surface of the water. I stood there for some minutes watching to see if any living creature would appear and dispose of the bread. The moorhen or whatever it was came over and nibbled it and then swam back.

I turned round. Both Barry and Anthony were lying on their fronts. I was about to say something like 'They don't appreciate good food!' when I realised that they were both fast asleep. Barry's head rested on his crooked elbow. Anthony was using both hands as a pillow. I went back to my rug, poured another glass of wine and sat there, still watching the moorhen.

The extraordinary silence of the place started to get to me. It was the sort of silence which gives you the urge to shout at the top of your voice. There wasn't even a faint traffic sound. It was Sunday afternoon and I guess that's why.

"Fine company you two are," I muttered. They lay on either side of me. Four long legs; two with dark hair and two covered with blond fuzz. Two extremely attractive backsides. Two bodies and two sleeping heads. I poured myself another glass of wine and then had an idea. Not — you might be surprised to learn — an erotic idea. It started off as an innocent joke. Very carefully, I poured a drop of the wine on Anthony's back — just at the point where it is most concave. I expected him to wake up. He didn't even stir. I shifted a bit nearer and added another drop or two. It formed a little pool but still he made no move.

"This is bloody ridiculous!" I murmured and added even more. This time it started to run across his back and down his sides. He moved slightly and grunted. I wondered if Barry might be a better bet, so poured some on him. His back had a more pronounced inward curve. I poured quite a pool in there before it started to run. He did react. He shook his head slightly, grunted and apparently went to sleep again. I poured a bit more wine and then refilled the beaker. Half of it went down my throat and then I tried again. The hot sun had evaporated most of what remained on Anthony. Carefully, drop by drop, I increased the size of the puddle. Again, there was no reaction, so I turned my attention to Barry; but not, this time, onto his back. There is, after all, a much more sensitive place.

I think my hand must have been shaking. Far too much spilled from the beaker on to his backside. Some of it ran down and joined the rest in the small of his back, but some vanished between the cheeks of his arse and that gave me something to think about. I had to open the second bottle to refill the beaker and, as I twisted the corkscrew down into the cork, my cock started to stiffen. 'Corkscrews - screws - pushing downwards - twisting - the soft resistance of the cork ….The squeak of the cork turning was an almost human sound; the sound a boy would make… By the time the cork was out I was back on form.

I am quite certain that Barry was awake, though he's always denied it. I didn't bother with the beaker. I laid the neck of the bottle along his cleft and gently tilted it. He groaned slightly. More to the point, he opened his legs. I watched the wine run down. I couldn't see much but I imagined it seeping into his arsehole and dripping down onto the back of his balls. I put a finger in the pool on his back and licked it. It was warm and distinctly salty; not very pleasant at all. On the other hand, or rather 'elsewhere', it would taste much nicer. Wine, after all, is supposed to be stored in a dark, cool place. Carefully, I put the bottle aside and knelt down. I couldn't get between his legs, so had to lean over him. I ran my tongue along between his cheeks. That tasted much nicer. I lowered my head so that my lips were pressed against his soft skin and pushed my tongue down as far as I could. I can't say it tasted much like wine but that musty aroma did something to it which turned it into nectar as far as I was concerned. I had to get deeper in there and there was only one way to do that. Somehow or other, I managed to kneel between his feet. I would say that he must have opened his legs further but I was too far gone to notice. I put my hands on either side of him and lowered my face between his thighs. I waggled my tongue from side to side. That time he definitely parted his legs wider. He denies it. Maybe it was instinctive. I know that I was able to lick his balls. I also know that my tongue found the spot and that, thanks to earlier sessions with him, I managed to curl it and push it into him. Wine tastes much better than water from a shower and a tartan rug spread over hard ground makes a much better 'plate' for a good meal than a soft, yielding bed.

He began to squirm a bit. I pushed my tongue in as far as I could. The cheeks of his arse were pressing against my face. He squirmed a bit more and, in so doing, must have thrown out his arm and woken Anthony. It was just as well that my ears were 'above surface' or I might not have heard.

"Don't forget me," said Anthony.

Two of them! One after the other? No. Professional wine-tasters go from one to the other and then back again. Which would be better; the eighteen-year-old blond wine from the north or the slightly older, darker one from southern England? There was only one way to find out.

I stood up and crossed over to Anthony. A real professional would have washed his mouth out first. There was no time for that and I certainly didn't want to lose any of Barry's flavour. I knelt between Anthony's thighs with the bottle in my hand and looked over to Barry. He was still wriggling around, obviously trying to bring himself off against the rug. I'd have to work fast and that was a shame.

With Anthony now wide awake, I was able to part his cheeks and actually watch as the wine poured down onto his balls. In my haste, I tipped the bottle too steeply, so I put a hand under him to catch the spillage and prevent it from soaking the rug. His cock was as hard as steel. For a second or two I held it, pulsating in the palm of my hand. I put the bottle down. He reared up so that his buttocks pressed against my face. With one hand on his cock and the other somewhere near his nipples I pushed my tongue down into him. He tasted quite different; as different as salmon from trout. Both squirmed like hooked fish; both were beautiful but that's where the similarity ended.

Anthony's opening closed up at the moment the tip of my tongue touched it. If I hadn't had the pleasure of fucking him, I might have given up. I didn't, of course. I knew him and it too well. Slowly, hesitantly, it opened again and then seemed to clamp on my tongue and draw it in. It seemed almost to curl as it went. I massaged his cock gently and he began to breathe heavily. It was time to move back to Barry.

I struggled to my knees. Barry slid across the rug and lay, panting, with his left leg touching Anthony's right leg. He put an arm over and around Anthony's shoulders and Anthony did the same to him. The intention was obviously to enable me to move from one to the other without difficulty. It didn't quite work out like that. Kneeling with two legs between my knees was a bit uncomfortable and I couldn't get in as far as I would have liked. Down I went, first into Barry's wide-open cleavage. He gasped and wriggled, loving every moment. Then to the left to keep Anthony equally happy. Back to Barry and so it went on — for how long, I couldn't say. They held each other tight; so tight that their heads were touching.

At moments like that, rational thought is impossible. It is with me, anyway, and it certainly was for them. Their backsides heaved and dimpled as, desperate to bring themselves off, they hugged each other and rubbed their cocks against the rug. I'd learned enough by that time to know that when a boy is in that state, there's only one thing which will fulfil his deepest longing. Mine was more than ready to oblige. It was already oozing enough to oil its own way in — but into which one? The male human body is endowed with two of just about everything else but only one penis. I'd read a story in which a guy fucked two boys one immediately after the other. He might have been able to, but I knew I couldn't. It would have to be one or the other. Which one? That was the problem.

Not having planned in advance, my one and only condom was in my wallet and that was in my jeans which lay underneath all my other clothes. Unsteadily, and with my heart beating as if it might burst, I got to my feet and went over to the pile, still thinking and still wondering what (or rather 'who') do to.

It wasn't just the sight of them lying there that was exciting me. Thoughts — odd, unrelated thoughts — kept coming into my head. Why hadn't Barry used his tongue on my arse the previous day, instead of fingers that felt like fire-tongs. He knew it was a turn-on as far as he was concerned. I pictured myself splayed over the tree trunk with Barry lying with his head buried deep in my wide open buttocks. His tongue, long enough to lick round his mouth, would have been so much better. He was young, of course. That probably had a lot to do with it. He needed, ideally, to be older. They both did. Not too old, of course. Just a bit older and wiser. The next image that flashed into my mind was totally ludicrous. He, at that moment, was probably screwing Wendy on my couch. On the other hand, the thought of screwing Danny or of Danny screwing me was so potent that my hands couldn't open the packet. I'd found it by then, and clothing lay scattered around where I had thrown it in my frantic search.

I tried to tell myself to calm down. I tried to think scientifically. It was, after all, just a question of physiology. Stimulating their anal erogenous zones had caused all three of our penises to harden. There was nothing strange about that. I was about to push mine past a sphincter accustomed to traffic in the opposite direction and into an anal canal. Some inches inside that, it would brush against the prostate gland and that would bring the boy to orgasm. The movements of my foreskin as I thrust in would do the same to me. "What's so odd about that?" (I have a feeling that I actually uttered those words.)

I stood, looking down at them over the tip of my cock. It was almost as if it was some sort of indicator, pointing first to one and then to the other. I'd got myself sufficiently under control (or so I thought) to slip the condom on when the time came. They were both lying still by that time, each with an arm around the other. Protecting each other? No. I dismissed that thought. They both wanted it. They were both waiting for it. The physiological bit was all very well, but which sphincter? Which anal canal? Which prostrate was going to get a cock massage?

Very gently, I raised my right foot and touched Anthony's left buttock with my toes. It tensed instinctively and felt hard and cool. Of the two of them I liked

Anthony best. I liked his sense of humour. I even enjoyed his hang-up about being found out. Now that Adam was out of the way, he was mine. Barry too. I put my left foot back on the grass and touched Barry's soft mounds with my right. Barry was nice, too and, until I had introduced him to Anthony, mine was the only cock which had managed to penetrate him. Visions of the Alabama book. I had broken him in; tamed him. He was mine too.

I knelt down again and ran my fingers over Barry's buttocks. Once again he groaned slightly and began to wriggle. I put the condom packet on the grass and did the same to Anthony with my other hand. In a matter of minutes I'd got them going again. Anthony spoke. "Oh yeah! Fuck me!" he gasped. Barry just groaned but the message was the same. I knew that.

"Which one? Which…. " Suddenly I felt quite faint. Surely not. I couldn't be….

I was and I did. I never, in all my life, shot so hard or so far. I'd say that a drop or two actually landed in the water, but that's impossible. It must have been a small fish that made those ripples.

Successive spurts spattered over Barry and Anthony. From the backs of their knees to their heads, they were covered in flecks of semen which shone bright in the sunlight.

Barry let go of Anthony. "I thought you were going to…"

"So did I," said Anthony. He took his arm from Barry and brushed his back. "That wasn't very Agag-ish," he said. "There are better places to sow the seeds. Why didn't you fuck us?"

"No. It wouldn't have been right. I see you two as a couple now," I said. My strange little inner voice must have prompted the words. They certainly didn't represent my thoughts.

"Well, something's got to be done," said Anthony, dreamily. "What about it, Barry?"

Barry said nothing. He didn't actually get to his feet. Neither of them did, so how they managed to end up clasping each other's buttocks and each with the other's cock in his mouth I don't know, but they did.

I wiped my still-dripping cock on a dock leaf and sat down to watch. Barry's fingers slid up and down Anthony's ass cheeks. Anthony was rougher. Anthony kneaded Barry's flesh. There was already a slight scratch there, but I don't think Barry was aware of anything other than Anthony's mouth and Anthony's tongue, sucking and massaging his member — coaxing it to deliver Barry's warm juices. It would be an exchange, I thought. South to north and north to south.

Suddenly Barry's ass tensed up and he stopped moving. I watched Anthony's throat carefully. Sure enough, he swallowed and then swallowed again. There was a pause. Then Barry stroked Anthony's backside again as Anthony were some sort of prized pet. I guess he was, really. It didn't take long. Barry's cock flopped out of Anthony's mouth. Anthony gave a long contented groan and that time it was Barry who did the swallowing - or tried to. He lost a lot. Anthony tensed up at the vital moment. Barry got the first one or two spurts. The remainder splashed onto my lags. Not that I minded.

"That was nice what you said," Anthony said, after a couple of dock plants had been defoliated to assist in the cleaning process.

"What was that? Hang on. There's a bit on your shoulder."

"About us being a couple. Do you really think so?"

"Well, yes."

"But what about you? There's Barry and me but you and who else?"

"Don't worry about that," I said. "My Gran always says there are plenty more fish in the sea."

"And you don't mind going back by yourself?"

"Course not."

"We'll keep in touch though?" said Barry, who was rubbing his thighs energetically with the remains of a leaf and leaving green stains on his skin as he did so.

"Of course we will," I said.

CHAPTER THIRTEEN

I left the Freeman's straight after breakfast on Monday morning. Believe it or not, Anthony and Barry had kept me awake half the night. They were at it until two in the morning and again when I woke up.

With the car boot full of potted plants and with my bag and one plant on the back seat I drove round to Gran's. She said I looked tired, which wasn't surprising. I explained that I'd spent the weekend with a friend in Newcastle.

"You must have started before dawn," she said. "That's not a good idea, Tim. Young people need their sleep. What was the point, anyway? You won't be at work today."

I said that I had a lot to do at home. I would have liked to get away there and then, but she wouldn't have that. I had to have breakfast. She came out with me to wave goodbye. "Oh! A poinsettia," she said, spotting the plant. "A nice one."

I said my friends in Newcastle had given it to me. "Don't over-water it. That's the main thing," she said. "Your car looks bright and shiny."

"I put it through the car wash once a week," I explained and then drove off. She stood outside the house and was still waving when I turned the corner. A nice old lady, I thought. Everybody up there was nice. Barry was nice and I was glad I'd introduced him to Anthony. I felt guilty about the silly thoughts of the previous day. It was strange how lust can overcome common sense. Barry and Anthony were about the same age and obviously meant for each other. As for me; well, maybe there really were more fish in the sea. Maybe I'd catch one but even if I didn't - what the hell did it matter? Sex wasn't everything.

By the time I got home, I was quite cheerful. Danny was at work so I arranged the plants. The one with the big green leaves that Mrs Freeman said liked humid conditions went into the bathroom. I put the others round the flat. They did make a difference. The place looked altogether brighter and more like 'home'.

Danny had obviously been as careful over obliterating traces of Wendy's stay as I was when Anthony came round on Sundays. A couple of fast-food containers were in the dustbin, but nothing else as far as I could see. (I had to open it to throw away the paper from the flower pots.) I could, of course, have opened the sofa to check the bed linen but that would have been going too far and, besides, he could come home at any time.

In fact he was quite late. It must have been just after six when he came in. I know I was watching the news at the time.

"Have a good weekend?" I asked.

"Okay. You?"

"Not bad."

"How's your Gran?"

"Fine. The plants are from her."

"Oh yeah?" By this time he was in the kitchen and conversation was impossible. He returned with a pizza on a tray and sat down. Neither of us spoke for some time. I hate having to talk when I'm eating and I guessed he did as well.

"So how's Wendy?" I asked when he had finished.

"Okay as far as I know."

"Did you go out anywhere?"

"No." That, I thought, was hardly surprising. They'd probably seen nothing more than the four walls of that room.

"What did she think about the glorious south, then? Has she got any plans to move down here?"

"If you must know, she didn't come," said Danny. He stood up to take the tray back to the kitchen.

"Why not?"

"I don't know, do I? She's entitled to make up her own mind about things."

"Of course she is. I just thought...." but further conversation was impossible. He'd closed the kitchen door behind him.

I didn't bring the subject up again. Something had obviously gone very wrong. Just how wrong I didn't realise until Thursday morning. He'd been surprisingly quiet both at home and at work on Tuesday and Wednesday and one or two strange little things had happened. He reorganised the fridge for instance, separating all his stuff from mine. I went to have a shower on Tuesday evening and he went out and stood in the road.

He was still in bed when I left for work on Thursday. I didn't think much of it at the time. He often did that. By ten o'clock he still wasn't in and I wondered if

I ought to ring home and wake him up. Brian Adamson came in. I didn't know whether to say nothing or make up a story about Danny having a cold.

"Danny's not coming in today. He's going up north," he said.

"Oh yes? Why's that?"

"He's got something to sort out up there. He'll be back on Monday," he said, leaving me speechless. I was pretty certain that what he had to sort out was personal and not connected with the project. It wasn't so much his going that angered me, though I felt he could have said something. I'd thought we were friends. Obviously we weren't. There was the silly fridge business. He could, though, have told me what was worrying him. I wouldn't have fussed over him or anything like that, but I would have made a good listener. It was time he moved out.

On that day and the next I worked as hard as I could. It seemed the only thing to do. The weekend came round. I managed to fill Saturday morning with shopping and Saturday afternoon with housework. I did the most stupid little jobs. I scrubbed the kitchen shelves. That gave me an idea. The bathroom cabinet had never been touched. At least Danny hadn't thrown the toiletries Wendy gave him away. I cleaned the cabinet and put them all back again and then spent the evening watching TV. I went to bed early. That was a mistake. I made sure the tissues were ready to hand, stripped off completely and slid under the quilt looking forward to a really good, slow wank. Danny's absence had one advantage. I didn't have to worry about making too much noise.

Then came the process of selecting my imaginary partner. Barry? No. Anthony kept intruding and when I thought of Anthony, Barry did the same. Steve? I wondered what had happened to him now that Adam had gone. Adam himself? No thank you. He was best forgotten. Matt McBrine was okay. Nice round arrse; long legs and a beautiful face — not that I would see much of his face. That would be buried in a pillow. At last my cock began to rise and take notice. I kept thinking. It was the moon which inspired the subject for that night. I could just see a glimpse of one side of it through the gap in the curtains. A white semicircle. The last time I was conscious of the night sky and a window had been at Burton Clayhanger with Andrew Forge....

Andrew Forge. The boy from Dubai. My great disaster. I remembered how I'd admired his butt from the bed as he stood looking out of the window. It had looked just as silvery white and the roundness of his arse matched the curve of the moon exactly.

What had failed miserably in real life was successful that night. Where would we be without the occasional bit of fantasy? I was able to simulate just the right degree of sphincter tightness — after knocking him around a bit until he was pleading with me to fuck him. By moving my hand to and fro I had him writhing; gasping for more; begging me to do it harder.

I woke on Sunday morning feeling quite refreshed and more like my old self — until the silence of the flat got to me. By eleven o'clock I was feeling angry and lonely. I didn't think he would have returned but I rang Anthony's number. No answer. I rang Adam. Line disconnected. It was possible, I thought, that Anthony would be with his folks, so I called that number. No answer, which wasn't surprising. Vicars are busy on Sunday mornings. I finally got through to his father at lunch time.

"He's staying with a college friend in Yorkshire," said the Prebendary. "I don't know for how long. Neither his mother nor I have heard from him."

That wasn't surprising, I thought bitterly. Anthony was busy keeping Barry busy. Meanwhile I — who had introduced them — was on my own. 'College friend' indeed!

I had lunch — a microwaved meat pie — and then went out to get a paper. I didn't go to my usual newsagents, so the idea must have been in my mind. From a tiny little Asian-run place on a corner not far from Lewis Street, I bought a Sunday Telegraph and, from the topmost shelf, a magazine: Call-Boy. It wasn't much of a turn-on. There was one reasonably good story illustrated with carelessly chosen photographs. Chuck, the hero, was described in the story as having long hair the colour of ripening wheat. In the photos, his hair was dark brown — if not black. He had a nice behind, though. The sort of backside which would open up slowly like a clam if you worked on him the right way.

The rest of it was advertisements. That, I thought, might be an idea for the rest of my life. I had no idea what those boys charged and none of the ads gave a clue. There would be no real 'involvement' with a boy like that. I'd just call up the one I wanted and arrange to meet him somewhere. There were one or two small hotels in the area which would be suitable. I wouldn't want him coming to the flat.

Pierre (23) looked attractive. I liked the way he was posed across a bed with one leg hanging over the edge. Toni (19) had a lovely looking arse but nineteen? I'd had my fill, in more ways than one, of teenagers.

Suddenly a car door pulled up outside. I knew the sound of Danny's car well enough to know whose it was. I slung the magazine between the pages of the Telegraph and laid it on the floor. The car door slammed. Our front door slammed - and Danny appeared. Thanking God and all the angels that Anthony was still in Yorkshire I looked up.

"You're early," I said. He grunted.

"Everything okay?" I asked. He didn't answer but went into the kitchen, again slamming the door behind him. Why he went in there I don't know. He was out again in a matter of seconds.

"I'm going to have a shower? Do you want to use the bathroom?" he asked.

"No. You go ahead." He vanished again and I heard the shower running. That gave me a chance to rescue the magazine and lock it away in my desk. Danny, I thought, when I was sitting down again, was in too bad a mood to receive his marching orders that night. I'd do it in the morning. I hate scenes.

He was ages in the bathroom. In fact I was beginning to wonder of he was all right. You hear about people cutting their wrists in bathrooms. Eventually, he reappeared. He'd changed his shirt and hadn't been to the wardrobe. I guessed he must have had it in his bag.

"Tom said you'd gone to sort something out," I said. "It's none of my business of course but..."

"I'd rather not talk about it," he said.

"Please yourself." I picked up the paper. He turned the TV on. For an hour I sat staring at various pages of the paper without taking anything in. I was fairly sure, too, that he wasn't concentrating on the programme. Finally, I could stand it no longer.

"We," I said, emphasising the word, "are going for a drink."

"You can. I'm not," he said.

"Yes you bloody are. You need one and so do I. Come on."

It wasn't as easy as that. It took half an hour to persuade him that both he and I would go crazy if we stayed in.

We went to the George. I bought the first round. He bought the second round. They weren't consumed in total silence but conversation was difficult to say the least. I mentioned the condition of his car. We'd driven to the George in mine but I couldn't help noticing that his was unusually muddy. Apparently the motorway from Newcastle was under repair. The significance of that didn't hit me at the time. I got the next round. He wanted a Scotch. I got him a double and a Coke for myself.

I waited for him to get most of the whisky down and then said, "I'm sorry. I really am." Just that.

I'd never seen a person of our age cry before. Tears formed. He blinked and then they streamed down his face. Fortunately we were in an alcove and nobody could have seen. They couldn't have heard either. In a soft voice, breaking at times like a teenager's, he told me the whole story. Things had started to go wrong with Wendy when they were living together. He thought that coming down south for a time might improve things and it had seemed to work. Their weekends together up there had been pretty good. Unfortunately, Danny wasn't the only male in Wendy's net. The bed his parents had provided for them had accommodated quite a few others - and, on Thursday night, he'd arrived to find Wendy using it to entertain a Pakistani lad. Both she and he had been more than a little surprised at Danny's intrusion.

"At least I gave him a black eye," he said, smiling for the first time since he'd arrived home. "You can't really blame Wendy."

I had my own ideas about that but said nothing. "You having another one?" he asked, getting unsteadily to his feet.

"Not me. I'm driving. You go ahead though."

"Yeah. I bloody need it," he said. I watched him weaving his way through the crowd. He came back with another Coke and the biggest Scotch I'd ever seen.

"A triple," he explained. "Cheers!"

I had to support him on the way to the car. He wasn't completely drunk but it had had an effect. His speech was slurred. His left arm was round my shoulder and I clutched his hand to stop him from sliding off. With some difficulty I managed to get him into the car and clicked the belt round his middle. Getting him out again at the flat was even more difficult and I hope none of the neighbours saw us. I had to let go of his hand to get my key out. He flopped against the door-post and I was only just in time to catch him and prevent him from falling. I guided him to a chair and set about opening the sofa for him. That having been done I would have left him but the awful possibility of vomit occurred. There was a plastic bucket in the kitchen so I brought that out.

"Better have a pee," said Danny. He tried to stand up, fell back in the chair and began to open his fly. I don't think I have ever moved so fast in my life. I had his cock dangling into the bucket in a split second and watched as its enormous brown length spewed urine down the yellow plastic.

" 's better," he said, and sank back again with it still hanging out of his jeans.

"I think we'd better get you undressed and into bed," I said. "Come on."

I opened up the sofa. Like a small child, he clutched my hand and allowed me to pull him off the chair. He collapsed onto the sofa and lay on his back. I took off his shoes and socks. Then I tackled his shirt. I'd been right about that. It was new. I could tell that from the stiffness of the material — which didn't make it any easier to unbutton it, but I managed it. He sat up slightly and let me pull it out of his jeans and over his shoulders.

"Now don't get carried away," said my little inner voice. I wasn't likely to. If he were to throw up at that moment, the bucket was about eight feet away.

"You all right?" I asked.

"No," he replied.

"You're not going to be sick or anything?"

"No. I'm okay."

I undid his belt and the top button. His cock was still dangling out. I tried as hard as I could not to let any part of me touch it. I grabbed his jeans just below the knees. "Up a bit," I said. He lifted himself up and I pulled as hard as I could — and off they came. Only his boxers were left. Grey ones with red streaks. Once again he lifted himself. They were off and he lay there naked. I put the boxers on the floor.

"You sure you're going to be okay?" I asked.

"I guessh …. I guess sho."

I emptied the bucket in the loo and brought it back. "Sleep well. See you in the morning," I said and was about to leave the room when he said, "Don't go. Shtay a bit."

It wasn't that late. "If you want," I said.

"Wanna say something."

"Oh yes?" I sat on the edge of the sofa, wishing I'd thought to cover him up. He was lying on the quilt.

"It's not really Wendy'sh fault," he murmured.

"So you said."

There was a long pause; so long that I thought for a moment he'd fallen asleep but his eyes were still open and — once again — he was crying.

"It's you," he said.

"Danny, don't be a berk. I've never even met the girl."

"I don't mean that. I mean you and me. I think I like you better. I think…. Oh, forget it. I'm pissed."

"Nothing like drink for opening the flood-gates," I said, with unpleasant memories of the bucket in mind. "Tell me now."

"Impossible, of course," said the inner voice. *"You've got quite the wrong idea."*

"I think I'm gay and I think I'm in love with you," said Danny. So much for inner voices!

Then he told me the whole story. Poor old Danny. Twelve years at school, three years at university, two years with Nimrod and, all the time, trying to convince himself that he wasn't 'one of them'. Eighteen months of a living lie with Wendy. Then coming down south and finding himself in an office with me. That was, and still is, the bit that I didn't understand. Why me? If Brian Adamson hadn't wanted an office and a lab, Danny would probably have ended up with David Elgar. (One could do worse. David Elgar was about the same age as me, and very attractive indeed.)

"I can't help it," he sobbed. "I've tried. I really have. I don't know why...."

"Danny," I said, but he carried on.

"I mean nobody got at me when I was young or anything like that. My brother's normal. So's everybody else in the family. It's just me. You won't tell them at work, will you? What with security and all that. I'd never get a job as good as this one.

"Danny....."

"I don't know what to do. You feel so sort-of dirty and isolated. People like you don't understand what it's like."

"Danny. I'm that way too."

"I mean; I have to... What did you say?"

"I said I'm that way too."

"But what about Susan?"

"My cousin. Currently going out with a very nice Canadian dentist. A cover story."

"So me and you? We're both gay?"

"Looks like it — and I happen to think the world of you. If you knew the number of times I've lain awake in my room wanking over you. That day when you were looking for a towel, for instance."

He smiled. Then he brushed the tears off his face and laughed.

"And I had a wank in the bathroom about you," he said.

"Daft bugger! You only had to ask," I said — and we both laughed.

He sat up and put a hand on my shoulder.

"Can I?" he asked.

"I'm all yours," I replied. He put his other arm up and our lips touched; then our tongues. He held me tight. I did the same to him and we both fell backwards. It was the most incredible experience. I could have done without the taste of whisky but I guess he felt the same about beer and Coca Cola. I don't need to tell you that my cock was rock-hard and pressing against some part of him. We lay there for some time, kissing lips, cheeks, ears. He had one of my ears between his lips when I felt a hand slide down my side, move inwards and very gently touch my cock.

"Mmm," he murmured. I said nothing.

"Mmm," he said again and, very gently, he moved the foreskin back. I ran a hand down his front. First to his navel, then further down to the mass of hair I'd admired in the past, never thinking for an instant that my fingers would be playing there. His cock was as soft as a piece of putty: the effect of the drink. His balls were as huge and heavy as I thought they would be. They were warm, too. He began to play with my cock — so softly and so gently that his fingers might have been the paws of some tiny animal.

"Better … stop…." I gasped. "I'll come if you keep on like that."

He let go immediately. "Sorry," he said.

"Don't get me wrong. I've nothing against coming but not alone."

"Oh."

I kissed him again. We lay awake for ages that night. Mostly, believe it or not, just talking. Sometimes one of us would reach out a hand and stroke the other. I know I did. Probably just to convince myself that it wasn't all a dream. I could hear his heart beating and feel the warmth of his body. I told him just about everything. I told him about Adam and Steve and Anthony and Barry. I even told him about Andrew Forge and he laughed. "You won't get any refusals from me," he whispered. And then he told me about himself. How he'd had a crush on a boy at school and hung around bus stops just to get a sight of him. He'd had a rough time at University too. Like me, he knew he wanted to work in the armaments industry, so he spent three years being aggressively 'normal' - even going so far as to share digs with a twenty-five-year-old rugby player with a broken nose.

"He was so repulsive you wouldn't believe it," said Danny. "It was like living with an animal. He used to drink milk. Pints of it — and he left the empty bottles just about everywhere. You'd go to sit down and find a stinking milk bottle shoved down the side of the chair. Having a bath was a long job. I had to clean the bath first."

"I don't think I'm as bad as that," I said.

"You're just perfect," he said. There was a pause. Then he spoke again.

"Can I...."

"Sure. Like I said, I'm all yours."

"You don't know what I was going to say."

"Just carry on," I said.

He sat up. I lay back and closed my eyes. The sofa wobbled a bit and then I felt his tongue in my navel. I put out my hands and touched his hair. I stroked it gently. His mouth went further down. He was dribbling. I could feel it. Some hairs caught between his lips and tightened as he took his mouth away. Then he found it. He licked up and down its length; long, very wet licks. I opened my legs as wide as I could. His fingers played with my balls and his lips touched the tip of my cock.

That was the first time in my life that I did absolutely nothing. I let go of his head and just lay there while he sucked and licked just about everywhere. His tongue lapped my balls and then he turned his attention to my cock again. I just hoped it would last for hours. It didn' of course. I started sweating. My balls started to ache.

"Going - to - come!" I gasped. I wish I hadn't. He took his mouth away and, in a split second, it happened. Not, I am sorry to say, in mighty spurts. I guess the beer had a lot to do with it. It just streamed out and ran down the shaft of my cock onto my balls and into my pubes.

Danny did much better. That was about six o'clock in the morning. Our neighbour had just started his car, and when I had at least half of Danny's gigantic cock in my mouth. The 'Scotch effect' had worn off by that time. I had been drowning in a canal and a man with a broken nose was pushing me under the water with an empty milk bottle. I woke up to find something like eight inches of solid flesh pushing against me. It didn't take long to snuggle further down the bed and take it into my mouth.

His impatience didn't help. He kept pushing upwards, choking me. Then he put his hands on my head and tried to force me down onto it. I managed to grab his wrists and he got the message. Finally I got the tip of it in my throat and started work. He loved that. So did I. The scent of him was a turn-on. The feel of that massive, throbbing cock in my mouth did the rest — and not a drop was spilt. He groaned and said something, but I was too far gone to make out what it was. His cock pulsated even more strongly. He gave a sort of strangled moan, arched up and I could feel it filling my gullet in powerful spurts and then seeping back into my mouth. Salty, sweet, warm and sticky. I knelt there for some minutes savouring it. He smiled. I smiled back.

"Glad you went out for a drink after all?" I said, when I'd swallowed the last drops.

"You bet," said Danny. "Sorry. I didn't know you were meant to swallow it."

"There may be lots of things you don't know yet," I replied, "but there's time to learn."

***

I never knew time go so fast as it did in the next few months. So many things happened that I don't really know where to start. We'd drive to work in our respective cars. We thought it might look better if we did that. More often than not, I'd look up from my computer and Danny would do the same and we'd smile at each other. I kept Susan's photo on my desk and I don't think anyone had the slightest suspicion of how we spent the evenings and most of the nights. A quick dash home — a pizza or something from the microwave. We could easily have relinquished the television licence. Danny drew the curtains tight. I opened the sofa bed, and then came the indescribable pleasure of undressing each other. Just the sight of that superb, brown body was almost enough to make me come. The feel of him in my arms was even more potent. Time and time again we'd have to break off and simmer down.

He soon got used to my preferences. I loved kneading the soft flesh of his buttocks before getting my tongue as far into him as I could and then turning him over to start work on his already dribbling cock.

And Danny? Well, the first time he fucked me, it hurt. It hurt so much that I had to ask him to take it out and my arse was so sore that I went to the local chemists, asked to see the pharmacist and explained that I had an inexplicable soreness there. He put it down to constipation and had just the thing. I never used the laxative tablets. I think they are still in the bathroom cabinet. The cream worked wonders. It contained an anaesthetic of some kind. A dab of that, followed by a generous dollop of lubricant and I was ready and more than willing. Danny liked me lying on my front, propped up in the middle by a pillow. The sensation of that monster sliding inexorably into my slippery arse was enough to make me pass out with sheer pleasure. It still is. Feeling Danny's breath on the back of my neck and imagining his beautiful arse rising and falling as he drove into me made me tingle all over and the long, lingering kissing session that followed was the most perfect bliss I'd ever experienced. If we kept on long enough, as we were able to do at weekends, we were both ready for another session.

Until the break-up of the Wendy business, he'd been a non-playing member of the Rangers. Now he was able to play for them on Saturday afternoons, which he enjoyed. I went to watch once or twice, but football has never been a great interest of mine. It was far more sensible to spend that time doing the shopping for the following week. I got the food, the magazines, the household goods and then the most important items; condoms and 'lube tubes'. Danny would come home, give an account of the match, have a long bath and then we were ready for bed — often not troubling to get up till mid afternoon on Sunday. Then we did the house-work, went for a quick drink at the Gleaners or the George and then came back for more bed and not too much sleep.

It was an ideal life, but there were dangers. There was the time when someone hammered on the door at about eleven o'clock on Saturday morning. Danny, at the time, was wriggling happily as the tip of my tongue explored his inner self. I didn't hear it at first. Big, brown, silky arse cheeks pressing against your ears make very effective silencers and a squirming arsehole as tasty and alive as Danny's demands a lot of concentration. When, finally, the sound got through to me, I wanted to ignore it but Danny said the repeated knockings denoted something important, so I had to leave off. I dashed into the bathroom, stuck my head under a tap, wrapped a towel round my middle and went to the door.

It was a young man from his football team wanting to see Danny. "He's still in bed at the moment," I said, and added that I was in the bathroom and hence hadn't heard him knocking at first. He still wanted to see Danny, so there was nothing to do but to let him in. Apparently the time of the match that afternoon had been changed and the bus would leave earlier than planned. It was only when he had gone that we realised that door to my bedroom was wide open, revealing a bed which had not been slept in for months. It was covered with computer magazines and books.

"We ought to find somewhere else; somewhere bigger," said Danny, and that started the hunt for a flat. With an enormous amount of difficulty, he got the money which had gone into the joint account with Wendy back — or most of it. I had a bit saved. We were both on good salaries and so we decided to buy rather than rent.

The pattern of life changed slightly. We must have seen thirty flats. Some were awful; some were nice but too expensive and then, one day, we were in the estate agents again.

"What about the Cloisters?? Have you thought of that?" said the girl. "There are still a few flats left there." The property company which owned the building had gone broke, she explained. The flats were being sold by the receiver's office. She reckoned that if we made an offer, it would be snapped up, so we did and, to my amazement, it was accepted. Daniel Taylor and Timothy Scully became the leaseholders, for the next nine hundred years, of Flat Number 754, situated in the property known as The Cloisters.

Danny had our solicitor draw up a document which enabled either one of us to buy the other out. Neither of us could envisage a break-up of the partnership, but it seemed a sensible thing to do. The flat was perfect for us. The lounge was spacious. The kitchen was ideal. The bathroom had a shower and a bath and it had two bedrooms.

We moved in on a wet, miserable day in January. For the first and only time, sex was abandoned in favour of shifting furniture around. We shared the bedroom on the front side of the building. Officially, it was to be known as my room and the other — which we furnished properly with help from Danny's parents — was his room. His clothes and his other stuff went in there and we still keep up the pretence by keeping it clean and laundering his bed linen. We threw a little party. The ten twenty-eight team and their wives came, plus some ofDanny's mates from the Rangers.

We'd just about got settled in when Gran came on a visit. Sitting in the back of the firm's car, she looked very old and frail, but soon proved that she was anything but. She approved of the flat and the furniture. She also approved of Danny. You could see that. Stepping straight into territory which other people carefully avoided she said, "You didn't get that sun tan in England. Where are you from?" and he explained. She went round tapping the plant pots. Two of them needed water, she said. One had been over-watered. She wandered round the kitchen, nodding at times and flinching at others. The cooker, brand new and hardly used, she said was in need of a thorough cleaning. It was almost an hour before I could persuade her to sit down and have tea.

I asked her about Barry. She said she very rarely saw him. He was at a drama school. Anthony's influence, obviously, I thought. The conversation turned to family matters and Danny was amazed when she spoke of Weavers. When she'd gone — on her way to spend a few days with my folks — and he was playing gently with the front of my jeans, he said "Do you mean to say that she owns Weavers?"

"That's right. But I don't want anyone else to know, so keep it to yourself."

"Sure. You going to keep this to yourself?" He stroked along the length of my cock.

"No. It's all yours," I said.

CHAPTER FOURTEEN

"It's all yours," or "I'm all yours," became our bywords for the next year. In fact, you could chart the progress of our relationship through the use of pronouns. The food in the fridge was ours. The flat was ours. The furniture was ours. The Rangers football team was his and, because Danny wasn't that keen on plants, they became mine. Most important; he relinquished all that beautiful body to me and I was only too happy to let him do what he wanted to what had been mine alone. There were innumerable occasions when I would sit up after we'd finished just to look at him and wonder at my good luck.

We had little arguments. I wouldn't want you to think that it was honey and roses all the way. There was the time when I forgot to pass on a message that football training had been cancelled. That annoyed him, and I have good reason for remembering that incident. He drove about fifteen miles for nothing and arrived home in a rage.

"If you were younger, I'd smack your arse," he said.

"You can try," I said. That was the time when I realised just how strong he was. The room swung round me and I was over his knees. He delivered a couple of not very painful slaps and then said, "Actually, of course, you should have your pants down."

"Suits me," I said and stood up.

"Or, even better, everything off," said Danny.

"What about you?" I said, pulling my tee-shirt over my head.

"I'm the punisher. You're the one on the receiving end."

Never having been much interested in the SM scene, my cock didn't rise as it usually did when I was undressing in front of him. I was surprised when I lay over his knees again to feel his. It felt like a pick-axe handle in his track suit bottoms. I was about to mention it when he landed the first slap. It hurt. The next one stung badly.

"You won't forget messages again," he said and landed another one on the other buttock. It was painful but I didn't yell. I flinched in anticipation of another one but, instead, his hand landed gently on my still-stinging right buttock and stroked the skin.

"Lovely arse," he murmured, and then, "I've got an idea. Stand up for a minute."

I was glad to oblige. He stood up and went into the bedroom. I was about to follow him, with a good idea of what he had in mind, but he came out again, with the cream tube in his hand. Just seeing that was enough to send my blood racing. As rapidly as the second hand of a clock, my cock went from half past to about five to the hour. Danny smiled, put the tube on the arm of the chair and pulled off his track suit and then his shorts. He sat down. His cock pointed up to my face as if accusing me:'That's the one. The one who forgets messages.'

"Right," he said. "Let's have you back in position, shall we?"

"No more smacking," I said.

"No. No more smacking. I've got a much better idea."

So, once again, I went down over his knees. His cock pressed against the side of my left buttock like one of those stakes they use to prevent logs toppling over. There was an interval of a few seconds and then he put the cream tube on the small of my back and I felt his greasy fingers moving up inside the top of my thighs. I flinched when he touched my anus and the cream tube rolled off me and on to the floor. I pushed my right leg outwards as the pressure of his finger-tip increased. It went in easily enough. One of the oddest sensations (I presume you've experienced it as well) is hearing something well greased moving around inside you and feeling it at the same time. The sound is slight enough; just a slippery, squelching noise, but you seem to hear it with your whole body and not just your ears. It invariably coincides with a gasp or a moan you make yourself. The feeling is out of this world, especially if the person concerned has fingers as long and as tactile as Danny's. Considering he'd never done anything like it until we met, he'd learned an awful lot in a very short time. He certainly knew where my hot spots were. I was squirming around on his lap in minutes and totally oblivious of the indignity of my position. All that mattered to me at that moment was the thought that one part of Danny was getting me ready for another part; the best part — the triumphal entry.

The finger came out. The muscle closed again, but not before a tiny soundless fart escaped.

"Stand up again," said Danny. I did so — a bit unsteadily — and looked down.

Two glittering, viscous trails ran down the sides of Danny's cock. Lovely stuff! My favourite apéritif for what was to follow shortly. If I hadn't been convinced that it was about to be used for its proper purpose, I'd have gone down on him and licked it off.

He lowered the back of the chair as far as he could and then lay back on it. He slipped a rubber over his cock and then wrapped his fingers round the base of it. "Sit on it," he said.

"How do you mean?"

"Get your arsehole right over it and then lower yourself."

This was something completely new to me — it must have been a Wendy/Danny invention. It just didn't work. I stood, facing the curtains, lowered myself gingerly downwards. I could feel him manoeuvring his cock into the right position. I wanted it badly enough and the first centimetre or so went in. After that it was agonising. I had to stand up again. Danny said I wasn't trying and that annoyed me. There was nothing I wanted more than to take every centimetre of its greasy, blue-veined length. I tried again and he made it worse by rearing up as I moved down. It felt like a red-hot poker. Neither of us could understand why. Time and time again I had lain on my front and he'd got in easily enough. Once or twice he had fucked me in a kneeling position (which I didn't enjoy so much,) yet there we were in the same relative position and it wasn't working.

I really don't remember which one of us suggested that I should turn round and face him. It was probably a mutual agreement brought on by frustration. I put my hands on his shoulders and, flinching at the thought of what might happen, lowered myself very, very gently. I was too far forward at first. It pressed against the hard skin just behind my balls. Danny groaned. I shifted backwards a little, made sure I was in the right position and then sat on it. Danny groaned again. I guess my weight on the end of a cock must have hurt him a bit, but then, to my astonishment, my sphincter gave way. Danny's long drawn out "Ye …ah!" lasted just as long as it took for the whole of his gorgeous member to glide up into me, like a well-oiled piston. I opened my eyes, put my hands behind his neck and kissed him.

That time it wasn't a question of him surrendering to me or me to him. That was a mistake. I suppose we should have come to some agreement before we started, but you don't, in circumstances like that. I lifted myself and let myself down again, and that got him going. He shoved upwards just as I was coming down and that hurt. It was good, though. I'd never actually seen his face when he was fucking me and certainly not in close-up like that. His mouth opened and his eyelids drooped. I felt his breath on my face. I lifted myself up again. Danny's cock has a very prominent ridge and I swear I could feel it sliding back towards my anus and then, as I sank down again, it plunged further in. He reared upwards, lifting me until my mouth was level with the top of his nose. Then I sank slowly down again. I kissed his chin, then his forehead.

The pain ceased (or seemed to) when his fingers went round my cock. That was all that was needed. The moment I felt them I knew I wouldn't be able to last long. There were just three or four convulsive heaves, and I don't even remember if they were instigated by me or by him. It spurted all over his belly and chest. He gave another upward shove and the pain returned. I'm pretty sure I yelled. He did it again and I felt the rubber expanding momentarily inside me.

"Christ!" he exclaimed and then leaned forward to kiss my dropping head.

Getting off it was a problem. We had to wait until it was completely limp and, even then, it was painful. By that evening it hurt so much that I had to lie face down on the sofa to watch TV. Danny went out to find the duty chemists to get some of that amethocaine cream for me. He was back fairly soon with the cream. I lay there with my jeans round my ankles as he applied it. It felt better almost at once. "I wish you'd said it was hurting," he said — so maybe I didn't cry out after all.

"There," he said, putting the cap back on the tube. "I'm sorry. We won't do that again." I was about to say that I wouldn't mind trying it again some time. There had to be a way of doing it painlessly. He spoke again.

"You know that guy you spoke about? The one whose dad owns this building? Lived on the fifth floor?"

"Adam Saunders, you mean?"

"Yeah. There's a light on in his flat."

"Probably someone moving his stuff out or their stuff in," I said.

"I wouldn't have thought so. Not in the evening."

Danny let me sleep that night. In the morning, the pain had almost gone but I took the day off. Danny was even more apologetic and was so concerned about me that I was almost glad to watch his car leave the car park on the way to work. I spent the morning reading. Then I took a few steps round the lounge. That didn't hurt. It was a fairly pleasant day so I decided to go for a stroll and pick up a few groceries whilst I was out.

Walking made it feel better. By the time I got back to the Cloisters I felt normal again. I stood with a plastic bag of shopping in my hand waiting for the lift and thinking pleasant thoughts of what I would do when Danny came home. Suddenly, a hand landed on my shoulder.

"I thought it must be you!" Adam Saunders! I'd known all along that I hadn't escaped. He was like a cat playing with a mouse, and I was the mouse.

"Hi, Adam," I said. "I didn't expect to see you. Somebody said you'd gone abroad." There were three other people waiting for the lift, so I didn't want to embarrass him.

"That's right, old boy. Dubai, actually. Got time for a coffee?"

"Could do."

Why did I agree? I was curious and, for some reason, I didn't feel the same nervousness which I had felt before. Maybe it was because I was a resident there. It might have been the knowledge that he was hundreds of thousands of pounds in debt. As we travelled up in the lift, I looked at him closely. He hadn't changed a lot. He was still immaculately dressed, even to the point of having a carefully folded, spotless handkerchief in his top pocket. Outwardly the successful business man. Inwardly — If only the other people in the lift knew.

He wasn't in the least embarrassed or repentant. In the familiar surroundings of his flat he told me all about it. It was all a 'minor matter of liquidity' and, according to him, all they had to do was to pay a small percentage of the money owed to their creditors and everything would be all right.

"Not allowed to go into business here until it's been sorted out," he said, "so we've moved over to Dubai."

"Property again?" I asked.

"Good Lord, no, old boy. The pater's started a school."

"The what?"

"The pater. You know. My dad.. He's started a school and I'm a partner."

"But you're not a teacher. Nor is he, is he?"

"You don't have to be a teacher, old boy. We just sit back and take the fees. Proper teachers do the teaching. That's why I'm over here. Got to recruit the staff.

He got up and went into the kitchen, returning with two cups of coffee and a plate of expensive-looking biscuits.

"Tell me, who's the Indian idol living with you? I've spotted him once or twice since I've been back," he said.

In a building like the Cloisters that had to mean that he'd been snooping. Danny and I didn't even know the people who lived on our floor, let alone the people on other floors.

"He's British, actually. His grandmother was Indian," I said. "He works with me. That's all. Danny is a hundred per cent hetero, so forget it."

As I said it my arse started to ache again. They say all lies get punished.

"But living together…" he said.

"Purely on financial grounds. Thanks to you, the flats were going cheap and we snapped one up."

"It's him you ought to snap up. Not the flats. Christ! When I first saw him in the lift! Bit on the old side for me, but I'll bet he's got a lovely cock!"

"I wouldn't know," I said — and had another twinge.

"Typical of you. If I lived with him, I'd have it. They don't hold out for long when I'm around."

"Do you still see your lads? Steve and Anthony and whoever else?" I asked.

"No. Steve's moved and Anthony's still filming as far as I know."

"Filming? I asked, with a pleasant vision of Anthony, oiled and glistening, delighting one of the well-known and well-hung stars of the few videos I'd seen.

"Yes. They discovered him, apparently. He's only an extra at the moment, but he reckons it will lead to greater things. I gather that he's the third soldier on the right if you look quickly. That sort of thing. I've got an absolute cherub at the moment. You'll have to come up and watch him in action. Martin. Works in Harris's. Got a beautiful cock and delivers the cream like one of those espresso machines. Mind you, English boys don't measure up to Arabs, if you know what I mean. Circumcised and eminently suckable. They fuck pretty well, too."

"Is that the reason for the school?" I asked.

"Good Lord, no, old boy! Not when the pater's around, anyway. When he comes back I might have a few proprietor's perks. No, the school is strictly legit. We're founding it on English lines, of course. The have to wear shorts with their blazers over there. Not that I mind that. Plenty of good old rugby football and school houses; all that sort of thing."

"You're building a boiler-house I presume?" I said, and took another biscuit.

"No need out there, old boy. It's all air-conditioning, but I guess they won't be long in finding somewhere to get up each other's arsees. I'll find out where, too. Might be an idea to put a video camera in there."

He went on to describe his various plans. From the sound of things, the

Saunders School in Dubai was, if anything, a bit more mediaeval than the place we went to. He wanted me to come back to hear more, but I made the excuse that the shopping ought to go into the fridge and that I had a lot of work to do. I left him, made myself a quick lunch and then settled down with a book for the afternoon.

Danny got back reasonably early. I didn't waste any time warning him. I knew damn well that Adam would pay us a visit and that I wouldn't put it past him to be watching the car park. It seems I was right. We had just finished dinner and were washing up when the doorbell rang. Not the outer door bell, but the internal one. Danny rushed into his room — by which I mean the spare room. I opened the door.

"Sorry to bother you, old boy. You don't happen to have a couple of first-class stamps on you by any chance?"

As it happened, I did. I got them out of my wallet and gave them to him. He fished around in his pockets for the money. I said it didn't matter. He said he had to pay. He didn't want to be in debt — especially to a chap he'd been at school with. That, I thought, was a laugh.

"Your mate back yet, is he?" he asked, as he handed over the last two pence coin.

"Danny? Yes. He's in his room, I think. I don't think he went out. Did you want to meet him?"

"Naturally, old boy." He lowered his voice. "Might as well give the goods a once-over, even if they aren't for sale," he said.

I knocked on Danny's door. "Yes?" he said.

"Someone wants to meet you," I said and he came out.

"Adam Saunders. We were at school together," I said. "Adam. This is Danny Taylor."

They shook hands. Danny asked if Adam would like a drink. Adam said he'd love one and I, anxious as hell to get rid of the man, was furious. But I had to hand it to Danny. He went on and on and on about football and the Rangers. He hardly gave Adam time to say anything except the occasional 'Oh yes?' He wanted Adam to join as a non-playing member - possibly even become a sponsor. Adam said he couldn't, because he was based in Dubai. I watched him wait for an interested reaction. He didn't get it. Danny wondered if he'd ever been to Newcastle or seen Newcastle United play. Adam said he was a rugby man — which was a lie. His only association with rugby at school had been our walks round the sports field. Danny produced a book about Newcastle United. You could see Adam desperately trying to finish his drink. When he had, he remembered the letters he had to post and left us.

"What a nasty, slimy piece of work! Is it southern England or public schools or a mixture of the two?" Danny asked. "He's a caricature. That's what he is. And you had sex with him?"

"I didn't know you at the time," I said. "He wouldn't have had a chance if you'd been there."

"He wouldn't have had a chance if he'd gone to my school. Someone would have kicked his arse," said Danny. "Speaking of which, how's yours?"

"Oh, better," I said. He smiled. "In that case, how about an early night?" he asked - and I was happy to agree and to oblige.

***

Some four weeks passed. They were very happy weeks. We seemed to complement each other, both at home and at work. Danny hated shopping, whereas I didn't mind it. He was much better than I was at running the household accounts. He did all the heavy housework. I looked after the washing machine and the kitchen. At work there were aspects of his job which I understood better than he did and he helped me out with some of the trickier parts of my job. More than that, you understand, I can't say.

We spotted Martin, Adam's new boy friend, one Sunday afternoon. I was standing on a chair hooking up the curtains which I'd just put through the washing machine and Danny was handing up the hooks.

"That's nice," he said.

"What is?" I was trying to insert a hook.

"Down in the car park. Just parked his motor bike and taken his helmet off. Look."

I wouldn't have troubled, except that Danny very rarely commented on people. I did. David Elgar, at work, for example. After a visit from David Elgar I'd say something like, "Grrr! What wouldn't I do to him if I had a chance!" and Danny would look up and tell me I was being coarse or that I hadn't a chance. I let go of the curtain for a moment and looked down. He was right! The boy's advantages were apparent even from a fifth-floor window, He had fair hair, a very slim figure and long legs. "Must be a new resident or the son of one," said Danny. The boy looked at his watch and crossed the car park.

"I shouldn't think so. We haven't seen a removal van for weeks," I said. "I rather think he might be Adam's latest. He was telling me all about him when I met him that day I was off work."

"And Adam lives on the fifth floor, right?" said Danny.

"Right."

"Hang on here for a minute. I won't be long" — and he left me standing on a chair, trying to retrieve several yards of dangling curtain and reach down for the hooks at the same time. I gave up and sat on the chair. The boy had vanished from sight. All I could do was sit and look at the motor bike. I hadn't seen him get off it, but there was only one in the car park - one of those which has a front mudguard about six inches above the wheel. From the little I'd seen of his bottom, he didn't need a lot of springs on the bike.

Danny was ages. I was beginning to wonder what was happening when he came back.

"You're right," he said.

"How do you know?"

"Simple. I grabbed the lift before he did. He got out at the fifth floor so I did too. I got out of sight when Adam opened the door to him. His name's Mark."

"Martin," I said.

"Maybe. I didn't hear that well. Adam said something about expecting him half an hour ago. Just fancy that, eh?"

"You obviously do. Now, shall we get back to curtain hanging?"

I don't know if you have ever tried to do a job with a person who's thinking of something else entirely. It isn't easy. When we started, we'd got into a routine. Danny handed me the hook, I put it in the pleat and then latched it onto the rail. He'd already got the next hook ready. It was dead easy. After his little excursion in the lift it was murder.

"What does he actually do?" he asked.

"Adam? Just about everything. Can I have another hook?"

"What?"

"A hook, Danny. A hook."

"Oh sorry. Here. He must have a preference, though."

"He likes sucking."

"Lucky sod. Sucking that one must be great. Looks like he's got quite package under all that shiny leather."

"Plastic. Another hook please."

"Same difference. Here. Does Adam fuck as well?"

"You bet."

"I wonder what he's doing right now."

"Well, whatever it is, we weren't invited. Another hook please."

"He'd be a lovely fuck. You should have seen his legs and his arse."

"Danny! A hook please. We'll never get the job done today at this rate."

He handed me the hook. "Some people have all the luck," he said. "How does a slimy toad like Adam manage to pick up someone so good-looking as that?"

"Money. He pays them," I said. "He did with Anthony, anyway. He provides the petrol money for the bike. It wouldn't surprise me to find that he's paid for the bike too."

"He's worth more than a measly motorbike. A car. That's what he deserves. Something really fast. Not too flashy. A Mini Cooper or something like that."

"He didn't look old enough for a car."

"He's old enough," said Danny. "Old enough for something else too. You fancied him too. You might as well admit it."

"I didn't see as much of him as you did — or at least I didn't see him close up," I said.

"I'd give a lot to see more and, given half a chance, I'd get so close to him that you wouldn't be able to put a bit of paper between us," he replied.

For the rest of that day I suffered Martin. Danny only gave up when we went out for a drink and then only because I said I'd had enough. I'd never known him like that. It was completely uncharacteristic. He would certainly have continued talking like that in the pub if I hadn't stopped him. Danny! The man who told me to keep my voice down if I so much as mentioned anything to do with sex. He was obsessed.

I pointed out, forcibly (but untruthfully), that Adam would be furious if he knew that Danny was lusting after one of his boys. In fact, of course, Adam would have been delighted. They'd have sat for hours comparing notes on Martin's performance. I also told him — and this I knew to be true — that Adam would tell as many people as he could that there was another gay man in the Cloisters — and that news would spread.

"He didn't tell anyone about you, though. You said that yourself," said Danny.

"Only because he's got this weird notion about grassing up people he was at school with. Honestly, Danny. He's dangerous. Leave off and forget it."

It didn't do a bit of good. That night we both agreed that it might be a bit premature to let him fuck me, though I felt perfectly all right. I lay there with my legs open, feeling his tongue move up the insides of my thighs. By the time he'd actually got it in his mouth he couldn't say anything of course but I was fairly sure that, if he'd been able to, it would be "Martin!" not "Tim!" that he gasped.

I worked on him in the usual way afterwards but there was no wriggling around this time. He came. He came very copiously but I missed the usual wild excitement. That worried me and the worry continued for the next three weeks. He'd stopped talking about Martin but every Sunday afternoon he stood at the window, waiting and watching. "Martin's late," he'd say and then "Ah! Here he is," and then, in the evening. "Martin's just leaving. That's three hours and forty minutes. I'd give a lot to know what they've been doing. Three hours and forty minutes!"

He was okay when Adam called one Saturday morning. As it happened, he was packing his football bag in the lounge. Adam came to say he was going back to Dubai and would be away for a few weeks. He didn't know exactly how long. He wanted to know if either of us wanted anything from there. Electrical goods were cheaper there and so were CDs. Neither of us could think of anything from Dubai but I was terrified that Danny might ask for something nearer home. He didn't. Instead he gave Adam another lecture on football.

On the following Sunday afternoon I went out to post a letter. There is no point in posting letters on Sundays in our town. There's no collection, but Danny wanted to watch a football match on TV and I felt like a breath of fresh air. The post box is only round the corner, so I posted the letter and came back to the Cloisters only to find Martin waiting for the lift. At first I thought Adam's departure for Dubai must be one of his tall stories. We travelled up together and I have to admit that Danny was right about his good looks. He leaned against the back of the lift with his feet slightly apart — almost as if he was inviting me. Naturally I did nothing. I didn't even speak. I regretted that as I got out of the lift. I could easily have asked if Adam was still at home.

"Either Adam's not gone or he's forgotten to tell Martin," I said when I got back to the flat - and instead of the usual, "Tell me later. I want to watch this." Danny leapt out of the chair.

"How do you know?" he asked.

"Just ridden up in the lift with him," I said.

"Well I'm damned!" Danny was at the window like a shot. The football match was totally forgotten — but only for about ten minutes. "Adam can't have told him," he said. "There he goes now, putting on his helmet, getting on the bike… Christ, just look at that bouncy little behind! … He's starting the bike now ….and away he goes. I wonder where he lives."

"No idea," I replied.

"You'd have thought Adam would have told him he was going away. He told us."

"I've long stopped wondering about the things Adam does," I said. Danny hadn't, though. Once or twice in the ensuing week he brought the subject up — usually wondering what and which part of Adam Martin had actually missed. When I told him, in answer to his question, that Martin's cock was not particularly noticeable under the plastic motorcycling trousers when I'd seen him, he decided that he couldn't have been looking forward to being sucked. "Adam fucks him. That's what," he said. "The lucky sod!"

I wouldn't have gone home that weekend, but Mum rang to say that Gran was coming down for the weekend.

"You ought to go home more often than you do," said Danny.

"What about you?" I asked.

"My folks are too far away for weekends. Yours aren't."

I asked if he wanted to come with me. Gran, I felt sure, would have liked to see him again.

"No… I'll be all right. Anyway, there's a match on Saturday. You go."

So I did. Gran, good old soul as she is, said nice things to Mum and Dad about Danny. She obviously hadn't caught on and I was glad about that. The picture she presented was of two young men with hugely disparate interests who, because of football and Danny's practice sessions, hardly ever saw each other. I think Mum might have been slightly suspicious. She asked who did the cooking. I said I did.

"I wouldn't have said you were a master-chef," she said.

"Whose fault is that, child?" said Gran. "Any ordinary family would have kept him at home and not sent him to some silly boarding school. He could have learned how to cook if he'd stayed at home."

"It seems odd to me," Mum continued. "I hope this Danny person does his share. I wouldn't like to think of you waiting on him hand and foot."

"Good God, woman!" said Gran. "What does it matter who does what? Danny's a nice lad. The flat is immaculate. There's nothing unusual in sharing a flat. They were very lucky to get it."

That seemed to calm Mum down. She started rummaging for things which might come in useful. Gran went through the selection afterwards and halved it. "Cut-glass grapefruit dishes! A toasting fork! A silver-plated cake stand! They're a couple of young businessmen who share a flat — not a honeymoon couple!" said Gran. I ended up with a spice rack, another toaster, some mugs and a bread bin — but I didn't keep that for long. Just before I left, Gran pressed a folded ten-pound note into my hand. "Bin that bloody bread bin as soon as you can," she whispered, "and use this to buy a modern one."

I got back early on Sunday evening. Danny was out but the washing machine was working. That was unusual. Washing, as I have explained, was my job. I guessed at first that his football gear must have got into a state. It had rained a lot. I peered inside to see something white revolving in there. That was a bit alarming. Something white washed with a red football jersey would come out a delicate shade of pink. I was attempting to stop the cycle when Danny came back. He'd been over the road to get some bacon, having forgotten to put it on the shopping list.

"I thought I'd do the laundry. Save you a job," Danny explained.

That was decent of him. I usually did it some time in the weekend. It was a really thoughtful gesture, I thought — until I went into the spare room to sling the stuff Mum had given me in the bottom of the wardrobe in there. The bed, which had never been slept in, had been stripped. I stared at it and all the pieces of the jigsaw fitted together. Danny's anxiety to get me away for the weekend. Martin not knowing that Adam had gone away and now this. I could almost see and hear the events of that day.

"This will have to be our secret. I don't want my flat-mate or Adam to find out. Understand?"

"Okay by me, Danny."

In the remote hope of finding a button from motor cycling leathers or even a slight smell of oil, I got down on my hands and knees. I had to have some evidence. There wasn't any — apart from the sheets, but they were enough. I went back into the lounge. He was sitting there reading the paper.

"Good weekend?" he asked, without looking up.

"Okay. You?" I was so angry that my voice changed.

"So-so. We lost."

"How about today?" I asked.

"Nothing to tell."

"Or nothing to tell me."

"What's that supposed to mean?"

"Keep it a secret from my flat-mate and Adam," I said. Danny put down the paper.

"What are you on about?" he asked.

"I wasn't born yesterday. You've had Martin up here. You've had Martin on the bed in the spare room. Why else wash the fucking sheets?"

Having used the word once, I'll spare you a verbatim report of the argument, largely because I'm ashamed of using such language. What made it worse was that Danny kept his cool throughout. He said that anyone who felt those sheets would know that they were new and had never been used. I wondered who he had in mind. He couldn't think of anyone but said it was a risk we couldn't afford to take. Coming from someone who had lured somebody else's boyfriend up to the flat, that was rich!

I remember shouting something about going to the solicitor in the morning to get our agreement cancelled. Strangely enough I don't remember leaving the flat and I don't remember getting into the car. I know I felt I had to get away. But where? By the time I got my thoughts and emotions back in control I was on the motorway. God knows how I missed having an accident. A sign came up. 'SERVICES 1 MILE'. I could have done with a stiff drink but that was out of the question. I had no wish to end up in a pile of twisted metal or in a police cell. But a cup of coffee and chance to sit and think was just what I needed. There was a lot to think about. Parting with Danny. Getting another flat. Changing jobs too, probably, unless he did the right thing and took himself back to Newcastle where he belonged. I turned off and passed under the sign 'WELCOME TO THE TOLL BOOTH. OPEN 24 HOURS.'

The 'Toll Booth'.. the 'Toll Booth'? I'd heard the name before. I'd certainly never been there, but it was familiar.. and then I remembered. Brian Adamson and Rajesh Varsanji were both keen hobby-archaeologists and spent most of their weekends helping to dig out some mediaeval building. They'd been talking to Dave Elgar one day in the corridor, persuading him to come along.

"It's in a field next to the 'Toll Booth' motorway service station," Brian had said. "We could meet there."

David had laughed and said he wasn't that kind of lad and had gone on to explain that the 'Toll Booth' was notorious as a gay pick-up spot.

"It's disgusting at night," he said. "Their pimps take them there in mini-buses. You can't move for gay rent boys."

Dave is known for his capacity to exaggerate (including, according to Janet Perkins in Despatch, the size of his tool but that's another story.) There were just three young men there, all playing the fruit machines. I got my coffee and sat down. The job situation was my greatest worry. I couldn't stand the idea of working in the same office as Danny any longer. I wondered if Brian Adamson would smell a rat if I asked for a change. I could come off ten twenty-eight entirely and go back to Mr. Harris. That would be the best solution. Otherwise I was fairly sure that Gran could get me into Weavers. She'd been trying for long enough. Like the boy in the corner playing a fruit machine. I watched as coin after coin went into it. Nothing came out. A bit like my life. I'd put a lot into our relationship and what had I got out of it? Sod all! As far as Danny was concerned, I was just a fruit machine. Sooner or later he was bound to get fed up with me and move over to another one.

The boy did just that. He wasn't bad-looking, I thought. He had dark, curly hair and quite a nice face. He could have taken a bit more trouble finding jeans that fitted him a bit more tightly and the jacket he wore had seen better days. Out of work, I guessed and probably hoping to augment his unemployment money by a win on the machines or... I got up and went over to him.

"Complicated?" I asked.

"Not really. It's a question of patience mostly." He put in another coin and pressed buttons in rapid succession. Nothing happened.

"Looks like tonight is not your lucky night," I said.

"So far... I dunno though. I wouldn't mind a game with you."

"Sure." I reached into my pocket for a pound coin.

"You won't get a lot for that," he said. "I wasn't talking about machines."

The penny dropped - at the same time, coincidentally, as a few tokens spilt out of the machine. He scooped them up.

"I wouldn't mind," I said. "How much?" It would be worth anything, I thought, to get even with Danny. *"For your information I've been out having sex and it was bloody great. That's how it's going to be from now on."*

"Depends on what you want and you pay for the room," he said.

"Room?"

"Here. In the motel part. It's okay. They don't charge you the full rate if you don't have breakfast."

The sleepy-eyed, surly receptionist hardly looked up. She just handed me a key and took an imprint of my credit card. I signed the slip and she went back to her magazine. I wouldn't have had a clue how to find room 17 but the boy knew the place like the back of his hand.

His name, he said, was Tom Mason. Hoping he hadn't seen my credit card, I said I was Timothy Weaver. He wanted to know what I did. I said I dealt in coffee beans in London. He said it sounded a boring job and I agreed. His last job, he said, was selling sweets in Woolworths but he got the sack for sampling the produce.

"I like to have something in my mouth," he said, with a leer. Nothing like sucking a Mars bar if there's nothing else around. "You got a rubber on you or shall I get one? There's a machine down the corridor."

"No. I've got one. Where else do you like to have something?" I started to undress. He followed suit. My cock had been rising ever since we first met. His, I noticed, was beginning to do the same.

"I'm easy," he said. "Anything you want. Twenty quid for a fuck. Ten for a suck."

"Suits me," I said, laying my jeans on the suitcase stand. In fact, I wished he hadn't mentioned money. I suffered a momentary loss of interest. It didn't last long. He slipped his boxers off and his cock sprang out. It was quite an appetising-looking one, too. Not huge, but reasonably fleshy looking and I got a kick out of its hardness. After all, he probably did it several times a night. For all I knew, he might already have shot his load several times that day. I knew I couldn't get a hard-on in those circumstances. I must have passed muster. Most of his clients were probably middle-aged men with paunches. A person still in his twenties would be a pleasant change for him.

"You've got a good one," he said. He sat on the bed, put out a hand and held it.

"So have you," I replied. There was no way, I decided, that I would suck it without a rubber — and that was a pity. On the other hand, one never knew what germs those middle-aged business men might have had in their mouths. Fucking him didn't worry me. I always used one for that — even with Danny. For a moment I felt a bit remorseful and wondered what Danny was doing at that moment.

"What do you want to do?" he asked. "You going to fuck me?"

"Why not? I haven't brought any cream with me, though. Does the machine sell that too?"

"You won't need it with me," he said - and I suffered another momentary loss of interest. His arse had probably been screwed so often that it was wide open. All those businessmen.....

"Spit," he said. "Best lubricant in the world. Better than any of these things people buy in the chemists. It's natural too, see? Organic and all that."

"Is it?" My mind went back to Danny, lying with his legs open and my tongue pushing into him. I'd always used a lubricant as well when I came to fucking him, and he always did when it was my turn to be on the receiving end. Maybe we'd been wasting money.

"Christ, yes. If you honk up some of the real sticky stuff from the back of your throat and use that. Bloody marvellous, that is. Go and put a rubber on it and I'll show you."

I found it with some difficulty. My jacket was on the other side of the room. I rolled it on and went back to the bed. He put his hand up to his mouth and for a second, I thought he was going to be sick. It sounded like it. "There," he said. "Come a bit closer." I did — and he smeared it liberally all over my tool. It felt cool and, I have to say, very pleasant. "Now a bit more," he said. His hands went round my buttocks and he drew me forward. I felt his lips brush along the length of my cock. His tongue lapped it. He withdrew slightly, made that dreadful noise again and my cock was bathed in warm liquid.

"That's enough of that, he said. He let go of me and (rather reluctantly) I took it out of his mouth. It streamed a trail of saliva down onto the floor.

"It'll go in a treat," he said. "How do you want me? Doggy, missionary or a bit of the fancy stuff?"

"Just lying on your front with your legs spread out," I said, not having much idea of what he was talking about.

"Suits me. Some of the others have more imagination," he said. Again, I wished he could have kept his mouth shut. The image of those businessmen returned.

He didn't have much of an arse. In fact he was probably the flattest person I have ever seen. He was also deathly pale — almost pure white. At that moment I longed for something darker, more exotic and more rounded but he had gone out of my life — or nearly so. I'd have to learn to put up with second-best. Knowing me as you do by now, you'll know what I wanted to do before getting right over him, but the businessmen, or the thought of them, ruled that out of the question.

Tom raised his head from the pillow. "Okay, stick it in," he said. "Don't let it get too dry." That finished me. If he hadn't said that, I might have done it. I was already getting into position.

"It's no good," I said, clambering back. "I can't."

"What do you mean, you can't. Go on. It'll work. It always does."

"It's not that, Tom. It's something else. I'm not in the mood. Sorry."

"You're a right one. You'll have to pay something. I'm not going this far for nothing."

I said that was no problem. My cock shrunk as I spoke. I went to wash it in the bathroom and then decided I might as well take a shower as I was paying for the room. I suspect that he had a wank whilst I was in there. I certainly heard some strange noises. When I came out, he was dressed again. I paid him the full fifty pounds and that pleased him. I think he might have been anticipating a row. It didn't please me very much. I drove home with a single fiver in my pocket and the tank was showing 'empty' when I pulled up at the Cloisters.

Danny's car was there but he didn't seem to be in the flat. He wasn't in bed and he wasn't in the lounge, so I slept alone that night. I woke up to find the spare bedroom door open and the usual sound of him having a shower.

"Where did you get to last night?" he asked.

"Went out to see a friend," I said.

"You never even took your phone with you. I was trying to get you."

"Oh yes. What for? To tell me you'd been shagging Martin?"

He said no more then. He left for work before I did that day, but the moment I got into the office, he went to the door, opened it, looked along the corridor, shut the door again and then locked it. He picked up the phone on his desk. "No calls until I tell you, Jean," he said. "That goes for both of us." He turned to me.

"A relationship like ours depends on honesty and trust. Would you agree?" he asked.

"You know bloody well I agree."

"So where did you go last night?"

"It's sod-all to do with you. Anyway, you can't talk. 'Honesty and trust'! That's a laugh coming from you."

"Tim, I swear absolutely that Martin was never in the flat. I have never spoken to Martin, let alone anything else. Sure, I think he's attractive, but I would never do anything that you didn't know about."

"So why launder the sheets?"

"You went to see your Gran, right? If you recall, she inspected nearly everything the last time she was here. She's bound to come and see us again. The chances are that she'll want to see where I sleep. So, I thought I'd get some of the starch and the creases out of those sheets. For all I knew, you could have brought her back with you."

"And you really never did anything with Martin?"

"Definitely and absolutely not. I swear it."

Again I'm going to draw a veil over the next three quarters of an hour. It got a bit sloppy. I told Danny about my disastrous evening with Tom. He laughed — especially when I described how Tom had looked spread out on that cheap motel bedspread.

"Never again," I said — after he'd let go of me and I had picked up the chair I'd knocked over.

We talked about it at home too, fantasising like crazy and laughing. I never thought I'd do that.

"Quite nice, but nothing compared to Martin," Danny would say after he'd climbed off me.

"Give me someone with a white skin any day," I'd reply.

"You wouldn't see where you'd shot," said Danny.

Apart from the levity, we did make one resolution. Neither of us would ever have anyone else. If anyone else ever turned up, it would be both of us or neither of us.

"I can't see that happening," I said.

"Neither can I," Danny replied. "Now then, let's see if you fuck as well as Martin."

CHAPTER FIFTEEN

Any lingering doubts I might have had about Martin (and I didn't have any) were cleared up when Adam returned. Martin was in Dubai, working for Adam and his father as a general office boy. On that day we'd seen him, he'd come to the flat to collect any mail that might have accumulated. He flew to Dubai that night.

"No doubt he has certain other duties not connected with the office?" I said. Once again I had been trapped in the lift and invited to see the new school brochure.

"You bet, old boy. You bet! He's bloody good, but there's this Arab boy. Mohammed, his name is. Christ what a little goer! You need to get out there. They're all hot for a cock in their arsees. Don't see any girls, see? Perfect environment and all that."

"So you'll be flying back there soon?" I asked.

"In a bit. Got one or two problems to sort out here first. The school's up and running. We've got a top-hole headmaster, good staff and some jolly fine prefects. It's amazing how quickly they learn how a public school runs."

I managed to escape after about an hour. The prospectus was an almost exact copy of the one at our school. A list of the staff with all their qualifications. Pictures of the science lab and the language lab. A few (very attractive) boys standing on a patch of grass chatting with a gowned schoolmaster. All it did to me was bring back memories I wanted to forget. Adam seemed determined to perpetuate them.

And so life continued. Adam had other young guests. We both watched them from the window. We noted their arrival and departures and, in bed, we both fantasised about what they had been doing. I could have found out easily enough. We both met Adam often enough in the lift. I never asked and neither did Danny.

And then, one day — it must have been about six months after the Motel incident, we were both sitting in the lounge.

"Seen this?" Danny asked.

"No."

The Advertiser must be one of the most boring newspapers ever produced. Danny has bought it ever since he joined the Rangers. I was obviously going to be treated to another reading of his outstanding success on the previous Saturday afternoon. Certainly the Rangers' prospects seemed to have improved since he started playing for them, but I wished he would let me read about it for myself.

"German boy, eighteen," he read. "Wishes accommodation in your area for six weeks in the summer for improving English. Any reasonable amount paid. Schweiger. And then there's the address."

"So?" I said.

"So why not us? 'Any reasonable amount paid' sounds good. We could do with the extra money."

"We're not that hard-up," I replied.

"Every little helps. And just imagine. A nice German eighteen-year-old. You never know.."

"Some chance," I said. "We couldn't even contemplate it. Where the hell would he sleep?"

"In my room. It's never used."

"Out of the question. As soon as he found out we sleep together, he'd be off home like a shot."

"Of course he wouldn't. We'd tell him that we moved in together to give him a room of his own. Simple."

Danny is nothing if not persistent. He worked on me when I was most vulnerable.

"I wonder what a German boy would taste like," he said that night, licking the remnants of my spunk away from the corners of his mouth.

"Rotten cabbage, probably," I replied.

"I'll bet a German boy would be a lovely fuck," he said on the following night.

"Meaning that I'm not?" I asked dreamily. His cock was still deep inside me.

"Certainly not, but it would be good for you to have a change. I wouldn't mind, either. And we did agree. If we word the reply carefully, he'll get the message. Eighteen-year-olds are pretty astute."

And so we composed the letter. For eighty pounds a week, two young men who shared a flat would be pleased to accommodate the Schweiger person. I got the translation people at work to do a German version and sent both off.

To our surprise, a letter arrived the following week. It was easy to see why Michael Schweiger was keen to improve his English, but we managed to make out that our terms were acceptable and that his parents thought it would be better for him to live with two young people. 'The other peoples what reply to my ad all are old and I like to be under young peoples' he wrote, to our great amusement. I hope the girl in the translation department didn't notice our disappointment when she explained that it was a direct translation from German.

On July thirtieth we were both in the arrivals hall at London airport watching the passengers from the Lufthansa flight come through the controls. I had one or two near heart attacks.

"I'll bet that's him," I said as a bearded youth came through with a rucksack almost as big as he was. Fortunately, it wasn't.

"How about this one?" said Danny as an extremely good-looking youth wearing an immaculate suit appeared.

"One can but hope," I said. Again I was wrong.

We'd almost given up hope when he appeared. I was sure it was him by the way he put his suitcase down on the floor and scanned the waiting crowd. I waved. So did Danny. "Ber - loody hell!" he said — with good reason. Michael Schweiger was a stunner. He was tall; I'd say about five foot ten. He wasn't so much thin as lean, if you know what I mean. Even in jeans and a jacket you could see that. An athlete's figure. He had close-cropped hair and there was something about his face which was attractive, even though he was frowning when we first saw him.

"Could still be wrong," said Danny, but then Michael noticed us and smiled. My heart missed a beat. That smile would have melted steel.

"Excuse me. You are Danny and Tim?" he asked.

We shook hands. He had a remarkably firm grip. I took his suitcase and Danny led the way out of the terminal to the car park. Michael didn't say much on the journey. He was too busy looking out of the window and flinching at the concept of a nation that drove on the left hand side of the road.

"Is this your first visit to England, Michael?" Danny asked.

"Oh yes. For many years I want to come but my parents they say I must be eighteen. Until now I stay the holidays with my uncle."

"Your folks were probably afraid you'd fall into wicked hands," I said.

"Excuse me?"

"Oh, nothing."

That afternoon we showed him the sights of the town; namely our appalling dirty concrete shopping mall which looks like it was made by a giant playing with his Lego set. Danny stocked up on hamburgers, pizzas and German sausage. In the evening we took Michael out to the George for a meal and a drink. He didn't think much of English beer, but knocked back two pints. It was a nice evening so we sat out in the garden. The swans were out on the river. The anglers were telling each other stories.

"Is this better than staying with your uncle, Michael?" I asked.

"Oh. I like my uncle. It is my parents who say I cannot go to him."

"How will you go about improving your English, Michael?" Danny asked.

"Excuse me?"

"How will you make your English better?" I added.

"Oh this is very easy. On Monday I shall get for me a job and with the colleagues in the working place I will talk English."

We tried to explain that it wasn't as easy as that. There were about three million Brits all looking for work at that time. Michael seemed undaunted. An angler hooked something and he went over to watch it being landed.

"You could see Mr. Parsons about him," said Danny, staring at Michael's back.

"In what way?"

"To get him a job."

There were times, as I told him, when Danny talked utter rubbish. Getting an eighteen- year-old unknown foreign national into a firm making top-secret missiles was the daftest notion I'd ever heard. True I was in Mr. Parsons' good books, but I was sure it would never work.

"What about all that grass by the old perimeter track? That needs cutting. It would look much better from the road. And he wouldn't need to go near anywhere sensitive..."

Michael returned. "That man has catched five trouts," he said. "Also many small that he to the water returned." It was pretty obvious that more than a bit of grass-cutting was needed to improve his English.

We explained that he would be sleeping in Danny's room and that, during his visit, Danny would be in my room. He accepted this without query. I expected raised eyebrows or some sort of polite argument on the lines of 'I can sleep on the couch in the lounge'.

On the following day, a Sunday, Michael said he wanted to 'go at' London. I thought it was a grammatical mistake. It wasn't. He really did go at the place. We saw Buckingham Palace, Westminster Abbey, the Houses of Parliament and then Madame Tussauds. That place bores me. I was taken round there so many times as a kid. Danny took Michael into the chamber of horrors. I waited for them in the restaurant. They were in there for ages. Then we went to the Tower. I bought him a guide book in German and he went off on his own. Danny and I were both shattered. We'd been awake a long time the previous night talking about him.

We sat on a bench. "I wonder," said Danny, as we gazed at his departing bottom.

"Not a chance," I said. "He probably wanks every night to thoughts of some busty German maiden."

"Do you reckon?"

"That he wanks? Of course. Everybody does."

"I'll bet he's got a nice tool," said Danny. "It's selfish to keep it to himself."

On the following morning I got up at about seven. I always do. I make a pot of tea for us both and get back into bed. I nipped into the bathroom and had just come out when Michael appeared — totally naked. I averted my eyes, but not so fast that I missed a glimpse of a beautifully slim waist and a very nice cock set in a thicket of bronze-coloured hair.

"Oh. Are you with the bath ready?" he asked.

"Yes, sure. Go in."

"I stand always early up." he said, making no attempt to move or to cover himself up.

"Do you? In English it's 'get up'. I always get up early." I said, addressing his navel.

"Thank you. When the people correct my English I learn fast to speak it good."

I would have liked to stay and correct that sentence too but if I'd have spent any longer looking at his cock my interest might have become apparent. He went into the bathroom. From the kitchen I heard the toilet flush and the bath water running in.

"With reference to our conversation in the Tower of London yesterday, you're right," I said when Danny had woken up and I was in bed beside him again.

"About what?"

"Michael's cock. I just had a conversation with him. He went into the bathroom without a stitch on."

"Good God! Is he still in there?"

"Yes."

"The tea can wait," said Danny, clambering out of bed. "I have an urgent need to use the bathroom. I'll wait outside until he comes out."

I lay in bed listening intently and trying to visualise what Michael was doing. I heard the bath water gurgling away. 'Drying himself,' I thought. More water noises. Good lad, he was cleaning the bath. I took a sip of tea and then the bathroom door opened.

"Oh! I am sorry. I think you are still sleeping," said Michael.

"Just got up to have a pee," Danny explained.

"Excuse me? Oh. Yes. I understand. You should come in. I do not mind. In Germany we shame us not for the nudity."

"So I see," said Danny.

"I ... er... like to get up early."

"Me too," said Danny. "Get up as soon as the opportunity presents itself. That's my motto."

"Me also. But I must not keep you talking. You wish to use the W C quickly."

"Bloody hell! What a little beauty!" said Danny when he returned.

"Not so little from what I saw of it," I replied. "I'll bet yours made his eyes pop out of his head too."

"Not sure he even looked, to be honest. I was too busy checking him out. I like them when they taper like that. 'This way to my feet' if you know what I mean. I'd love to see it when it's saying 'This way to Danny's mouth'. Did you see his arse?"

"No, I missed that."

"You certainly did. You'd go into raptures. Do see Mr. Parsons tomorrow. In this weather Michael would be working in shorts. Just imagine looking out of the office window and seeing that."

To my surprise, Mr. Parsons agreed. He made lots of conditions, of course. Michael couldn't enter this building or that building and particularly our building. He had to stay well clear of the scanning antennae but there was a motor mower and the old man who used to do odd jobs had retired. The security people issued a temporary pass with most departments blanked out and

Michael started work the following day. He was good, too. He got the mower started without help and waved to Danny and me as we watched him steer it through the undergrowth.

Danny was right about the weather. On the next day, jeans and sweatshirt had been superseded by shorts. Just shorts. Not a lot of work was done in our office that day.

Even better, the pre-ablution chats outside the bathroom continued. Michael was totally uninhibited. He'd stand there with his legs slightly apart and talk about the weather or work or what Mrs Robertson in the personnel office had told him. Danny and I stared at him like starving kids looking in a confectioner's window. By the time a week had gone by, I was able to sketch his cock, his balls and his bottom from memory. The office shredder worked overtime.

Saturday came round. Both Danny and I got up late. I couldn't have gone out to the bathroom even I'd wanted to. You don't when you've got a cock like Danny's pumping it into you. By the time we were up and dressed, Michael was already up, dressed and watching the morning show on the television.

"What shall we do today?" he asked.

"Not a lot actually, Michael. Shopping this morning. Danny's playing football this afternoon."

"Oh good."

"Why? Would you like to come and see the game?" Danny asked.

"Not really. I make the shopping with you and then I write to my Uncle Otto."

So we saw Danny off and wished him all the best, and then did the shopping. We had lunch and Michael settled down to write his letter. For want of anything better to do, I settled down with a book. Suddenly he spoke.

"A friend of me in Germany lives also in a block like this. He does the sunbathing on the roof. Can you do that?"

"I've never thought about it," I said. "There is a key to the roof. In case the place catches fire and we all have to be rescued by helicopter."

He folded his letter and put it in an envelope. "Can we look?" he asked.

"Why not?" I took the key and we went out to the lift. I'd never been as far as the top floor before. We found the door marked ROOF ONLY. I opened it and we stepped out. A huge air conditioning plant buzzed in one corner. Another small building was marked MAINTENANCE STAFF ONLY and from the intermittent machinery noises coming from it, I guessed it to house the lift mechanism. Apart from that, and an array of aerials, it was one vast empty space. I wasn't too happy about the tiny wall round the edges and didn't go near it. Michael did and leaned over to look down at the street below.

"This is a good place," he said, and began to peel off his clothes.

"You need something to lie on," I said. He was undoing his jeans. They slid down. If I stayed much longer there was a severe danger of something embarrassing happening. "Hang on. I'll go and get a towel. A couple of towels," I said.

"No. I go. I am younger," he said.

"Not like that you won't," I replied. "You'd frighten the old ladies." His boxers gaped open in the front to reveal a tantalising glimpse of white skin and dark hair. In truth it wasn't so much the old ladies I was concerned about. On Saturday afternoons Adam was often at home and if he was to encounter Michael in the lift, Michael would be invited in for cucumber sandwiches, cakes and I don't know what else.

Michael laughed. "They were expensive but still they show too much," he said. He went to twist them to one side and it popped out as if to sample the English air.

"Looks like you've got too much to restrain," I said, trying in vain not to stare at it.

"For the sunbathing I take them off. It is better so." said Michael.

With a thumping heart I went down to the flat and rummaged in the airing cupboard to find two bath towels which were not too new. As always on a Saturday afternoon, I had to wait a long time for the lift. When I got back onto the roof, Michael was sitting, naked, on the low parapet.

"Here we are," I said, spreading the towels out. He stood up. I couldn't help laughing. Some sticky black substance from the wall had transferred to his behind. A broad black stripe ran across his buttocks and thighs.

"It makes nothing," he said when I told him about it. "In the bath it will come off." He lay down on his front. I took off my shirt and lay next to him.

"You are not wishing to get the overall brown?" he asked, turning his head to look at me.

"English modesty," I explained. The real reason was already pressing against my jeans. For a moment we lay silent. Then he spoke.

"Later I must post my letter," he said.

"No point. There's no collection until Monday morning."

"Oh."

"You must be very fond of your uncle to write so much so soon," I said.

"My parents say to me I cannot visit him or write," said Michael ruefully.

"Why?"

"You will not tell my parents?"

"I don't even know them, so I can't."

"It start when I am ten. Maybe eleven. I drive to my uncle for the school holiday.. He is the brother of the husband of my cousin. When I am there I break the window in his special glass house where he grow the tomatoes. He take me inside the house and he take off all my closes and then he smack me."

"Oh yes," I said. I was getting interested despite myself.

"But he give me twenty Marks."

"Not counting the marks on your backside," I said.

"Excuse me?"

"Oh, nothing. Go on."

"I think maybe you think I am dirty."

"I don't see why. You did something daft and got whacked for it. There's nothing dirty in that."

His face reddened. I deliberately turned away. "There is more," he said.

"Like what?"

"Every year I go to my uncle. He make it every day. In the daytime we go out in his car and when we come back he ask me to take off my closes. First he smack me on my bottom and then...."

"And then what?" I was thankful to be lying on my front.

"I think you will think I am dirty and send me home."

"There's no question of that, Michael. It'd probably do you good to get this off your chest."

"I am sorry?"

"I mean it is often better to talk about these things."

"He plays with my bottom. He says I am a very beautiful boy. This I like very much. I was very young and do not know it is wrong and dirty. He send me much letters."

"*Many* letters actually,"

"Thank you. He send these letters. He says I am a good boy and he likes me very much and the days are very long till the time I come to him again. And he say not to forget that if I do the wrong things he will hit me. My parents read the letters and they also say I am a good boy and Uncle Otto is a good man. So every year I go to Uncle Otto and ever day he smack me and play with my bottom and says I am a beautiful boy. Then, last year.....""

"What happened?" I was more than just curious.

"Last year we go to the beach and he take much photos — many photos — of me with no closes. Then he writes to me a letter. I did not show this letter to my parents but my father finds it and...."

"Went spare," I said, imagining what would have happened if someone had a written a letter like that to me and my father had found it.

"He is very angry on me. He say no more Uncle Otto. He say I go to England and meet young people. No more old men."

"I see. You know, Michael, you really ought to turn over. Your back's quite red."

"My behind will make the towel dirty."

"Don't worry about that. It'll wash. Sunburn won't."

"In a moment."

I knew what the problem was, of course. Thinking about his uncle had turned him on. I changed the subject and asked him what he wanted to do on Sunday. After a few moments, he turned over. I was right. It had grown from the four inches of flaccid flesh I was used to seeing to something like six inches. It lay across his thigh, twitching slightly. An erection such as he could achieve would be worth seeing... I didn't really need to get him talking. Just remembering would probably do the trick.

"What was in the letter?" I asked.

"Oh, nothing,"

"Parents don't get upset over nothing. What was in it?"

"Oh, he say I am a very beautiful boy and when we go to bed together in the summer he will show me how much he love me,. Also he sends two of the photos of me with no closes."

"Did he tell you exactly what he had in mind to prove that he loves you? Did he say?"

"Yes. He say it every time I visit."

His face had gone even redder. Not that I was concentrating on his face. Inexorably, his cock was rising.

"Tell me," I said.

"I think you will laugh at me and think I am a dirty boy."

"Certainly not. Tell me."

"Every time I see him I must take off my closes and he make me hard. And he take me into the bathroom and makes the you know with my.... What is this in English?"

"What?"

"This." He reached down and touched it.

"Proper English is penis. Most people say cock."

"He play with my cock and say it is very beautiful but most beautiful is my behind and he want me to go to bed with him so he can... I don't know the word... in my behind."

"And you were looking forward to it?"

"You think I am dirty?"

"Of course I don't."

"It feels so good when Uncle Otto do the you-know to me," he said. "When I think about it, it makes my cock hard."

"So I see." I looked at my watch. "We'd better go down to the flat," I said. "Danny takes ages in the bathroom when he comes back from football and we've got to get that mark off your behind."

There was no way he could have got his jeans on, even if I had wanted him to. The tar or whatever it was would have ruined them anyway. He draped himself in both towels. Fortunately, nobody got into the lift between the top floor and our floor but I was still relieved when the front door closed behind us. It had gone down slightly but not much.

I followed him to the bathroom. "It is okay. I can do it myself," he said.

"The man isn't yet born who can see his own behind," I said.

He took off the towels and stood over the toilet to pee. Predictably, it took an awful long time before I heard water. I rummaged in the cupboard. He flushed the toilet.

"Right, let's see what we can do," I said. "This isn't going to be easy. I think it's tar or bitumen or something like that."

"Maybe it is easier if I do what I do for Uncle Otto," he said. My heart leapt. "He make me get over the side of the bath," Michael explained. "Like this."

He took a towel from the rail, folded it, placed it on the side of the bath and leaned over, supporting himself with his hands on the other side.

Uncle Otto certainly knew a few things about showing off a boy to his best advantage. Not even the sticky black stripe across his buttocks detracted from the sheer beauty of his body. I took in the line of his vertebrae running down from his neck and vanishing at the slightly parted cleft of his arse and his long legs. The tendons at the back of his knees stood out prominently.

I said something about it being an ideal position. "I'd better get my things off, I think," I said. "That stuff is going to make a mess." I was down to my boxers within seconds. Michael stood up until I was ready. Whether he noticed the state I was in I don't know. I'm sure he must have done but he didn't say anything. He got back into position. I covered my hands with the industrial soap I got form work and, for the first time, touched him. The silky feel of his buttocks was an instant turn-on — not that I needed one.

"Comes it off?" asked Michael.

"I'm afraid not." I rubbed harder.

"That feels good," said Michael. "That is how uncle Otto does it,"

"Oh yes?" I added some after-shave lotion to the soap. I was a bit scared that it might burn him. All he said was that it smelt nice. That had the desired effect. The suds in my hands went grey; then black. I washed them, loaded up again with the same mixture and started again; kneading the flesh like putty. Soon; all too soon, the stripe had gone and his arse cheeks were the same uniform creamy white.

"There!" I said. "Keep still. There may be just a bit more in here." I parted the cheeks. There wasn't a trace of tar to be seen. "Ah yes," I said. "Just a bit here." I soaped my hands thoroughly. Not, that time, with the industrial stuff. Danny's ex-girlfriend worked in a cosmetic factory. She used to give him samples. An arse as attractive as Michael's deserved the best. I treated him to 'Cream of Lavender', which, according to the tube, 'cleanses and softens the skin'. Danny puts it on his feet! I was lucky, too. There was just one condom in the cabinet. One of my old ones, I guess.

"That smells nice," said Michael as I parted the cheeks again with the thumb and forefinger of my left hand and pushed the lavender-laden second finger of my right hand between them.

"Wait!" said Michael suddenly and he stood up. For a moment my heart sank — until he turned round and I saw his tool. It wasn't just erect. It was rampant and pointed to a spot just forward of his chin. At least seven inches of solid cock. Danny and I had both agreed that it was beautiful when limp. Erect it was superb.

"Oh, you also are hard," he said, looking down at the projection in the front of my boxers.

"Inevitable," I replied.

"Excuse me?"

"I couldn't help it," I said. He smiled.

"I help it for you," he said. He reached forward and pulled my shorts down. It sprang up.

"It is good," he said and curled his fingers round it. I did the same to him and he grinned.

"You wish me to do the you-know?" he asked.

"I've got a better idea," I said. My voice sounded strangely husky. "How about if I do what Uncle Otto had in mind?"

He looked doubtful. "You were looking forward to him doing it. You said so," I continued.

"Uncle Otto said it is only right when the man loves the boy very much. I think you love Danny."

So he had realised. We'd both wondered. There had been times when one or the other of us had made too much noise in the middle of the night.

"It's a different kind of love," I explained, which was true. I loved everything about Danny. I had also come to love Michael's smile and his fractured English. At that moment I was madly in love with a very pretty, neat little butt and a cock which was desperate to fire its load.

"Danny is very big," he said, squeezing mine. It wasn't, perhaps, the most tactful thing to say but I had to agree.

"I like it very much if Danny loves me," he said. "One day I think he does. We are talking and his cock start to go hard."

"I'm not surprised," I said and, still holding his cock, I stroked his backside with my left hand. "Both Danny and I are very fond of you."

"Wishes he to do it in my behind also?"

"Does he want to fuck my arse?" I corrected. "The answer is yes. We both do."

"Fuck my arse. Fuck my arse. Fuck my arse. I like that. It sounds good."

"It feels even better," I said. An idea came into my head. "It would be more sensible to let me do it first. Then you'd be able to take Danny's more easily."

I felt a drop of sticky liquid on the side of my finger. There wasn't a lot of time for further discussion.

"I like it very much if we three love each other," he said.

"No problem."

"Shall you tell Danny?"

"Do you want me to?"

"Of course. Then we are all very happy together. But first you fuck my arse." He released his hold on my cock and took a step towards the bath. I let him go. He picked up the towel which had dropped to the floor, folded it, placed it on the side of the bath and leaned over again. He spread his legs. The packet was opened and its contents on me within seconds.

"I am ready," he said.

I had his bedroom or ours in mind, but it was a superb position. His long legs formed a broad 'V' and I could actually see his little pink arsehole. More 'Cream of Lavender'. Much more. He winced as I touched it. I said something about trying to relax. Stupid really. In that position his whole body was tense. I pushed a finger against it. He winced again. I pushed a bit harder. He made some sort of movement and, suddenly, I was in him.

"Ow!" he yelped. The sound echoed back from the empty bath-tub. His legs jerked even further apart and my questing finger went even further in. He felt warm and, not surprisingly, very tight.

Slowly, the muscles loosened up; first clenching, then gripping and then just holding my finger. I wiggled it around. He liked that. I did it again. He wriggled. I pulled it out, added yet more of the cream and then pushed two fingers against it. It opened. Not easily but it opened for them. He groaned.

"All right?" I asked.

"Ja!"

I parted my fingers and felt his silky lining stretch. He muttered something in German. My cock was weeping. I managed somehow to empty the tube and anointed it with the rest of the lavender. Slowly, I pulled my fingers out and leaned forward, putting my hands next to his on the opposite side of the bath tub. I remember noticing that his knuckles were white.

Full marks again to Uncle Otto. My cock head found the right place immediately. Michael tensed up for a moment. I licked the back of his neck. He relaxed again and I pushed in.

"Ooooh! Ja! Ja!" he gasped as I slid up into him. "Oh! Ja!" as I thrust a bit harder. I slid my hands round under his armpits and felt his nipples. He wriggled. That felt good. His arse felt slightly less tight.

"Oh! Mach es. Mach es!" he groaned. I didn't know what it meant but it sounded encouraging. His arse cheeks felt cool against my balls and incredibly smooth. Trying desperately to keep myself under control — which I am not good at, as Danny will testify — I fucked him, seeming to move further in with every stroke. His gasps were amplified by the bath.

"Ah! Harter! Ja! Ah! Oh ja!"

I was desperate to make it last as long as possible. Unfortunately, I couldn't. My balls ached. My legs ached. Perspiration was dripping off me onto his long back. I gave one final thrust.

"Ooooh! Ja! Ja!" he grunted as I pumped it into him. "Oh! Ja!" He wriggled again. I clutched his nipples. I never saw him come. He made a sort of gasping noise. There was a soft splashing noise and he was still.

"Good?" I asked, when my heart had stopped thumping.

"Oh yes. Very good. I like it." Gently I withdrew and stood up. The bathroom seemed full of the scent of lavender.

"I make it in the bath," he said. "Look."

Spots of his spunk were spattered on the side and the bottom of the bath and glittered in the light. He turned the water on.

"Now I shall have a bath," he said. "I make it very much."

So had I. I slung one very full condom into the lavatory and washed my hands and cock at the wash basin whilst the water was running in. I watched him climb in. He seemed to do it much more gracefully than I. I slipped on my boxers.

"Make the door open," he said, as I left him. "Then we can talk."

Still finding it difficult to believe my luck, I settled down in the lounge with my library book, listening to the splashing noises which emanated from the bathroom.

"Can I stay with you next year also?" he called.

"I'm sure you can."

"When comes Danny back?"

"Pretty soon."

"If I come next year, can I also work in the same job?"

Resignedly, I put my book down. "I'll have to ask. Probably."

"Oh good."

Silence. Just as I picked up the book again, I heard the key in the front door. Danny appeared.

"Good game?" I asked.

"Terrific! I scored. What have you been doing? Teaching young Michael

English?"

"Actually, believe it or not, but I scored too," I said.

"How do you mean?"

"Tim," Michael called from the bathroom.

"Yes?"

"When Danny comes back, will you tell him he can fuck my arse?"

Danny looked as if he'd been struck by a thunderbolt.

"He's here now," I said. "You can tell him yourself."

"Fuck my arse?" said Danny. "You really have been teaching him English, haven't you?"

"You're due to give the next lesson," I said.

CHAPTER SIXTEEN

"I can't believe it," said Danny that night when we were in bed. I looked up from my book. We rarely have sex on a Saturday if Danny has been playing football. Sunday morning is a different matter, but I'll come to that.

"It's perfectly true," I said.

"Oh I know. I heard him say it and you forgot to flush the loo. The evidence stuck to the side of the bowl."

"Sorry. So… when are you going to take him up on his kind offer?"

"I'll have to see. It seems wrong somehow. I think I'd feel guilty."

"I can't see why. He's eighteen. He's almost certainly gay. He likes it and he's invited you to do it. Besides which, we have an agreement. What else do you want?"

"I'll think about it. Ready for lights out?"

"Sure. I put my book down. He kissed me. I kissed him and we were both asleep within minutes.

Now, every Sunday morning in our household is the same, I am happy to say. Danny wakes me up in his own special way. In fact I'm usually well-roused by the time his tongue is in my navel, but I don't let on. I wait until he's got it in his mouth before I do my sleepy "What time is it?" act. He turns me over and strokes my arse while he makes the necessary preparations and then gives me my weekend treat. After that I nip into the bathroom for a shower and then go into the kitchen to make the tea. We sit in bed talking for a bit and then we get up.

On that Sunday morning I was able to wait for longer than usual. The result, I suppose, of having shagged Michael on the previous day. Danny was licking my balls when I uttered my line. He didn't answer, of course, and he never wears a watch in bed anyway. I let him continue for a bit. When you have a lover with lips and a tongue like Danny has, you don't feel inclined to stop him. I don't, anyway. But all pots boil eventually and I was getting pretty near. I pushed him away and rolled over voluntarily.

"Not today," he said.

"But...."

"Remember when you came to see us play against Merton?"

"No. What's that got to do with it?"

"And there was that player of theirs who scored both their goals?"

"Vaguely. The bloke who came off the pitch holding his hands in the air?"

"That's it. You said he needed a good fucking to bring him down to size."

"Did I?" I was feeling really frustrated by this time. I can cope with Danny's football in the week but Sunday morning in bed was a bit too much.

"I scored three times yesterday."

"I know.... Oh! I see!"

"Come on then. Bring me down to size."

"Bring you up is more like it," I said — and did. When I was well into him, I put my hands underneath him. Feeling his cock and stroking it as I fucked him made me amazed that a thing as big as that can feel so good when it's in my arse. I could feel the veins throbbing. He shot into my hands, which was messy, but I knew it was going to happen. Danny has a way of waggling his arse for a few seconds. Then there's that sudden clenching on the base of my cock. I felt his hands on my arse cheeks, pulling me even further in, and then I shot my load.

"Time for tea," he said after I'd withdrawn.

"You're not supposed to give the orders. You're the underdog. Remember?" I said but climbed out of bed willingly enough. I had my shower, went into the kitchen and made the tea. It was when I was carrying the tray to the bedroom that something suddenly clicked.

"Did you get out for a pee in the middle of the night?" I asked, handing the cup over.

"No. Why?"

"The bedroom door was open."

"It couldn't have been."

"It was."

We'd made a special point of closing it during Michael's stay. We both tend to make a bit of a noise. In Danny's case it's long groans. I'm told that I grunt and have been known to call his name. 'Oh! Oh! Oh! Dan .... eeh!' That's what he says. I've never been aware of doing so.

"Maybe we didn't shut it properly and it opened itself," he said. "So.. what's the topic for this morning?"

"I should have thought that was obvious. When's it going to be?"

"What?"

"You and Michael, of course. The football story wasn't one of your best. You're saving it for Michael."

"Oh... I don't know. We've had all this out before. A third person always causes complications. I don't want to hurt you again."

"How do you think I'll feel if I've had him and you haven't? He's invited you to do it for Christ's sake. What else do you want?"

"You're sure?"

"Of course I'm sure."

"Not tonight," he said. "It's work tomorrow."

"That's never put you off before," I said.

"With you it's different."

I couldn't see why. "What about this afternoon?" I said. "Tesco's is open all day and there are one or two things I forgot yesterday. I can go there."

"You're quite certain you don't mind?"

"Let's not go through that again. I go out. You go in. No more arguments."

So it was arranged. Or, at least, I thought it was. Danny and Michael were washing up the lunch dishes in the kitchen. I'd done the cooking so I was sitting in the lounge with bits of the Sunday Times scattered round my feet.

"Oh, no!" I heard Michael say. I pricked up my ears. Danny said something. I couldn't hear what it was.

"I think it is better when we all go to the Tesco," said Michael and Danny said something else, to which Michael replied "Fuck off!". I couldn't believe my ears at first, but Danny came storming into the lounge, picked his paper up from his chair and slung it onto the floor. He slumped into the chair.

"Selfish little sod!" he said.

"Did I hear what I think I heard?" I said.

"You did. I said you were going to Tesco's and we could have a good time whilst you were out and I got told to fuck off."

"Well, we're not having that are we?" I called out "Michael!"

"Yes?"

"Come in here for a minute, would you?"

He appeared with a fork in one hand and a tea-towel in the other.

"Did you just tell Danny to fuck off?"

"Yes."

"Why?"

For a moment or two he looked really angry. Then he stared at Danny and stared at me. Then he spoke.

"He say to me you go to the Tesco and when you are gone we do the you-know."

"So? You said you wanted to."

He sat down. "My English is not good enough proper to explain," he said. "It is like I said to you yesterday in the bathroom. You love Danny and Danny loves you and I love the both. It is like.. what is a dry eck in English?"

"No idea."

"It is in mathematic. It have three sides."

"Oh! A triangle."

"Yes. A triangle. I think we three should be a triangle. There is me and there is Danny and there is you."

"That's a nice thought, actually," said Danny.

"I do not think it is right if one side of the triangle is not there," Michael continued. "There was yesterday when Danny played football. And there was...." He stopped.

"There was what?" Danny asked.

"I went in your room this morning to see if you are getting up and you were…"

"So it was you! I knew I hadn't left the door open," I said.

"I am sorry."

Danny laughed. "Well, he was getting up," he said.

"I think when I am here we do the you-know together," said Michael. "Then we are the triangle."

"I've nothing against that. What about you, Danny?" I said. It was a silly question. I can read Danny's mind like a book and he can read mine.

"Sure," he said.

"Good!" said Michael. "Now I finish to dry the plates."

"Not so fast," I said. "There's the little question of telling Danny to fuck off."

"Is this a very bad thing to say?"

"Yes it is, and I'm not having you tell a friend of mine to fuck off. Triangles or no triangles."

"I am sorry. I am really sorry. Mr Burley at work say it very often. I know it is bad because Mrs Robertson tell me, but I didn't know it was very bad. Mrs Robertson she laughed when I say it."

I think we both looked at him open-mouthed. I know I did.

"Mrs Robertson the personnel manager? You told Mrs Robertson to fuck off?" said Danny.

"Only once. She laughed. She said only it is not good to say it to a woman."

Danny and I laughed all the way to Tesco's. Michael sat strangely quiet in the back seat. Once, during a pause in the merriment he said "I'm sorry, Danny. I'm really sorry."

We both told him not to worry and continued to laugh. If you knew Mrs Robertson, you'd see the funny side of it too. She's tall and walks very upright; every inch a lady. As Danny said, it was surprising she even knew the word.

I got the various items I'd forgotten; batteries for my Walkman, razor blades and shampoo. Danny picked one or two items from the same shelves and put them into the basket. "Let's hope he doesn't change his mind," he whispered.

"He won't," I replied but, all the same, looked at the expiry date on the packet. They'd still be usable years after Michael had gone home.

The journey home, I have to say, was not an example of Danny's driving at its best. At one point I leaned forward to tap the speedometer. He got the message and slowed down.

"It's now a question of who does what and to whom and where," he said when we were finally in the flat again.

"Not in here. That's for sure," I said. Our three-piece suite, a present from Danny's folks, was brand new and I had memories of a spunk-strewn bath-tub.

Michael had sat down and was thumbing through the comic section of my Sunday Times. He looked up. "We make the you-know now?" he said. Substitute 'sandwiches' for 'the you-know' and you'll get some idea of his tone. Danny and I were almost drooling at the prospect.

"No time like the present," said Danny.

Michael put down the paper and stood up. "Okay," he said.

The boy was amazing. My cock was swelling fast. I imagine that Danny's was in the same state. To look at Michael, standing there in a sea of newspaper and with his feet slightly apart you'd never know that he even had a cock, let alone the substantial member I'd had my hands on.

"I take off my closes in my room and then come in," he announced. Danny put out a hand. Whether to have a preliminary feel or to restrain him I don't know. He was too late anyway. Michael was in his room and the door closed behind him.

"I wouldn't have said no to taking his clothes off for him," said Danny when we were both in our room, taking off our shoes and socks.

"He'll learn. He hasn't had a lot of experience," I replied. I stood up and started to undress. Danny did the same.

"I was going to ask you about that. What does he like?"

"You'd have to ask his Uncle Otto."

"Who's Uncle Otto?"

I realised then that, in all the excitement of telling him, on the previous evening, that our stunning German guest was gay and giving him a detailed account of events in the bathroom, I hadn't given Uncle Otto a single mention. I told him. He stepped out of his shorts and sat on the edge of the bed. His cock pointed rigidly to the ceiling.

"That's weird," he said.

"Not so weird as some things I've heard about."

"Maybe not but smacking little kids' arses..... that's way out. Wait till he's old enough and then suck him or fuck him but that.... You sure he wasn't having you on?"

"Fairly sure, yes. Here he comes." There was a light tap on the door and Michael entered. Once again I was struck by his slim build. He didn't look as if there was an ounce of fat on him. Michael was all muscle from his broad shoulders and powerful arms to his long, muscular legs. From experience of it on the previous day I'd say that his cock was just beginning to react. It hung down between his legs; long and fleshy and tapering to a little knot of foreskin at the end.

I saw him glance at Danny's midriff and the expression on his face was enough to tell me what was in his mind. He didn't need to put it in words..

"You will use very much lavendel please?" he said, anxiously.

"The what?" said Danny, staring at him as hard as I was.

"I used some of that lavender cream you got from Wendy. There was nothing else to hand," I said.

"Don't worry. We've got some marvellous stuff here," said Danny. He opened the drawer of the bedside cabinet and brought out one of the tubes I'd bought. "You won't feel a thing," he added.

Michael continued to stare at his rampant cock. It was already showing signs of augmenting anything that came out of a tube.

I suddenly remembered Tom in the motel. "Let's use that as a last resort," I said. Without knowing it, he'd described the great disadvantage of amethocaine hydrochloride. When your partner has got a superb cock like Danny's, it's nice to feel it going in.

"It is very big," said Michael dubiously. "Maybe we do something else."

"Rubbish!" I said, inadvertently taking control. "You'll love it. It's just a question of patience and lubrication."

"Please?"

"I'll show you. Now, if Danny can lie on the bed — as far up as possible, Danny."

Danny did so. I got him to move even further up so that he was sitting with his back to the head-board.

His cock was as rigid as I'd ever seen it.

"Now then, Michael. What do you think of it now?" I said.

"I am thinking still it is very big," said Michael.

"The biggest things go in if they're wet and slippery. Now get down on top of him and lick it. Make it really wet and slippery. Try to get some of that thick stuff out of the back of your throat. That's really good."

"And what about you?" Danny asked.

"Need you ask? Michael oils the piston. I oil the cylinder," I replied.

Getting them started took some time. There was a confused flurry of arms and legs for a few minutes. Michael obviously hadn't understood a word I'd said. I guess he was too scared to concentrate but, once he was lying between Danny's outstretched legs and had his mouth on Danny's cock, he got the message. In retrospect, I guess he thought he'd been let off the hook - not that eight inches of stiff flesh was anything like a hook.

"Make it really wet. Danny will tell you when to stop," I said — and then I got to work. I was very glad that we'd decided not to fit the board at the bottom of the bed when it arrived. I wouldn't have been able to reach his arse if it had been. I had to open his legs. For a moment he let Danny's cock out of his mouth and looked round questioningly. In doing so he gave me a quick flash of his cock, which had hardened. That was an encouraging sign. Then I leaned over him and got to work. He was surprisingly tight-arsed at first, which surprised me after the events of the previous day. I had to open his cheeks with my hands to get my tongue down there. Slowly, he got the message. The flesh pressing on either side of my chin softened. He kicked his legs wider apart and the tip of my tongue touched it.

That lad was as clean as a whistle. You honestly wouldn't gave known that tiny, puckered orifice had a second function. If anything - and this may well be my imagination - there was a faint tinge of lavender down there. I could have done without that, but when you've got a boy as beautiful as that with his arse twitching in anticipation you're not fussy. I wasn't, anyway. I lifted my head to take a deep breath. Danny was sitting there with his eyes half closed. Michael's head was moving up and down as he licked up and down Danny's enormous and already glistening member. For a second or two I watched Michael's shoulder blades moving up and down. Then with a hand on each cool, silky buttock, I parted them again and went back to work. The transition from the skin just inside his cleft to the rubbery feel of his anus was a revelation. From his spine to that point it felt as if I was licking smooth porcelain. Then, suddenly, my tongue found it. There wasn't a hair or a bristle of any sort there and that increased the pleasure. I could feel my cock throbbing.

I went down a bit further and licked his balls. He gave a convulsive jerk and opened his legs even wider. I licked upwards again, lingering for a time when I found that little knot of muscle. Then downwards. This time I stopped, curled my tongue and pushed. That did it. He gave a little wriggle and then a more pronounced one. I pushed against it again and this time it yielded. Not much, but it certainly wasn't so resistant as it had been. Another deep breath and I went in as far as I possible could. I don't know what he did then. I was nearly thrown off balance. He didn't kneel exactly. I think he must have drawn his legs up and tried to. His arse rose in the air, pushing me upwards and backwards. Then he stopped — and I resumed. He waggled his backside invitingly — which made what I had in mind rather more difficult but, by holding on to his cheeks I managed it. Just the tip of my tongue went in but that was enough to send him wild. I tried to get more in but it didn't work. He was moving frantically. It's difficult to dribble when you're in that position, but I got some into him. I was about to have another go when Danny spoke.

"That's enough Michael. I don't want to come just yet." Michael kept moving.

"Enough," said Danny. I raised my head and let go of his arse-cheeks and was just in time to see Danny with his hands over Michael's ears trying to curb the lad's understandable enthusiasm. Conscious that I hadn't done nearly so good a job on Michael's arse as he had done to Danny's cock, I parted his cheeks yet again and dribbled as much as I could down there. Some went in, I think. A tiny bubble formed over his anus and then burst. He was as ready as I could make him. I stood up and grinned at Danny who smiled back.

Call it curiosity, voyeurism or just plain lust. Call it what you will. I just had to have a close- up view. I shifted the pile of clothes from the armchair in the corner. (We put it in the bedroom when the new suite was delivered) and sat down as close to the bed as I could. Positions were changed. Michael lay on his front with his legs apart. When Danny got off the bed, I reached for the rather crumpled pillow he'd used to support himself. Michael lifted himself for a moment so that I could slip it under his midriff. In doing so, I couldn't help touching his cock. It left a trace of sticky fluid on the back of my hand.

Danny knelt on the bed between Michael's outspread legs and then, placing his hands just in front of Michael's shoulders, he lowered himself downwards. I'd felt it many times before but never watched. That afternoon was a revelation. I saw Danny reach out for the rubber. The packet lay on the bed slightly out of his reach. I stood up and handed it to him. He tore the packet open and slipped it on. He did that so rapidly that it was almost impossible to follow his movements. He held his cock between his finger and thumb and guided it in between Michael's raised arse-cheeks. I watched, fascinated as it slowly vanished from view. Michael gave a long groan. Danny stopped for a second or two. Then, almost imperceptibly, his arse moved downwards again. Michael's face was turned towards me. I don't know how to describe the expression on his face. It was a mixture of grin and grimace. His teeth were showing but his eyes were tightly closed. He groaned again. If I hadn't been watching so closely, I'd have said that Danny made no movement at all, but he did. One moment there was about three inches of wet cock shaft between him and Michael. Then there was less - and then even less. Michael gave a long drawn out "Aaaah!" and their bodies joined. It seemed incredible that anything so long and so thick could be inside someone so slim.

Danny started. I stared, amazed, and realised what an inept idiot I was. This was no humping, up and down movement. The only indication that anything was happening were the dimples in the side of Danny's arse. They deepened, filled in and then deepened again. This was screwing, rather than fucking. Indeed, Danny's arse began to make slight rotatory movements; hardly noticeable unless you were, as I was, transfixed by the spectacle.

Then Michael opened his eyes and stuck out his left hand in my direction. At first I didn't understand. He made a beckoning movement. I thought perhaps he wanted me to hold him. He beckoned again. I stood up and took a step forward. He crooked his finger again and I took another step. My legs were actually touching the bed. His hand reached out again, touched the top of my thigh and then his fingers clenched round my cock.

That was the clumsiest, most inexpert wank I've ever had. Several times he was forced to let go of it and clutch the side of the bed for support as Danny drove deeper and deeper into his wriggling arse. It worked, though. I think the sights and the sounds in that room alone would have brought me off. He just gave the finishing touches. There wasn't a lot of Michael to be seen. Just his head and the lower parts of his legs. Danny was straddling the rest of him. Both their tongues were hanging out. Michael grunted and groaned rhythmically. Danny was just breathing heavily but the squelching sound of his cock driving into Michael's tight arse was incredibly exciting.

I think all three of us came at about the same time. Mine splattered over Danny's back. Danny's was safely contained but when Michael eventually staggered off the bed there was a dinner-plate-sized wet mark on the duvet. It's still there, as a matter of fact. No amount of laundering seems able to remove it. It's a souvenir of a sort.

After that afternoon, we all three slept together and, surprisingly, we did get some sleep. Having a teenage cock in your mouth is a good soporific. I recommend it.

We still get letters from Michael. I would describe his letters as 'scorchers'. We take them into work and shred them there after reading them, so I can't quote any. Our letters back (mindful of his father's curiosity) are more circumspect. Every letter he writes is signed above a triangle, the points of which are always labelled 'M', 'D' and 'T' in varying order.

Mrs Robertson confirmed that Nimrod would be glad to take him on again. That interview was quite amusing.

We might be able to give him more to do," she said. "I'll have to talk to the security people. The trouble with continental boys is that they are no naïve. They don't have the discretion a British boy has. He could so easily open his mouth and let something slip out."

"He won't, Mrs Robertson. I'm quite sure he won't," I said, and left her office smiling at the memory of our 'naïve' guest's last night with us. He hadn't said anything then. He couldn't. He was sucking on Danny's cock for all he was worth. Nothing had slipped out either. Slipping in was a different matter but that was me; not Michael.

CHAPTER SEVENTEEN

"Leave off. There'll be an accident if you don't watch out," said Danny. The road was straight. There wasn't a lot of traffic and Danny was a good driver, so he wasn't thinking of a pile-up, and I didn't want to stop what I was doing — which was far from accidental.

I don't usually like being driven by somebody else for a long distance, but in the case of that journey it made sense for Danny to take his car. We were on our way to his college reunion and I had something to play with; an eight-inch slab of man-meat. When we started the journey it had been difficult to locate and felt like a bit of sponge through Danny's denims. Twenty miles out, it began to react. It was longer, thicker and very much alive. I could feel it pulsating under the cloth. Obligingly, Danny moved a leg. I turned to look at his face. It wouldn't be long, I thought, before he was at the point of no return. He would have to pull off the road and let me enjoy another mouthful. Probably only one mouthful. He'd come twice in the night. My arse still ached slightly. I pulled down the zip. Danny pushed my hand away.

"Stop there, Tim," he said.

I was furious with myself. I'd got to know Danny's physiology pretty well. If I had spent just a few more seconds marseaging it through his jeans, he wouldn't have been able to deny me access.

"We could stop somewhere. Look, there's a turn-off coming up," I suggested.

"No, I'd rather get there as soon as possible, especially as we're stopping off at your Gran's place." That had been my idea. I really didn't want to meet Danny's university friends. From all I'd heard, they were a pretty boring lot who spent their spare time playing football and drinking the local brown ale. But I did want to see Gran again and, according to Mum, she was anxious to see both of us.

"There won't be a chance there or at your parents' place," I said.

"I don't see why not."

"Oh, come off it. 'Hello, Mum and Dad. This is my partner Tim and we screw.'
I can just imagine it."

"They know," said Danny.

"They what?"

"They know. I've told them."

I was shattered. When Dad had made those very occasional nudge, wink
remarks about me having a good time, I was quite sure he wasn't envisaging
his son in bed with a gorgeous male hunk called Danny.

"When?" I asked when I'd got my breath back.

"Oh ages ago. That's why I wanted you to come; so that you could meet
them."

There really was a difference between northerners and southerners I
thought, as we drove further and further north. Adam never made any secret
about his sex life to his contemporaries but not even Adam would have dreamed
of telling his parents.

I felt frustrated and annoyed. I resented being driven up to the north to be
inspected. I dreaded his folks' reaction. I could easily have said I couldn't go
with him and driven up to see Gran alone. Danny switched on the car radio.

"I don't believe it!" said Danny. "She's haunting us,"

Mary Maudlin's latest hit, 'The Boy I Love' had been top of the charts for
some weeks. We both agreed that it was silly and banal. It didn't even have a
good tune. We made retching, vomiting noises every time we heard it.

"Ugh!" I said, "Pass me the sick-bag." Danny laughed and that, somehow,
made me feel a bit happier.

> 'The boy I love is always near me,
>
> He stays with me through thick and thin,
>
> In the good times. In the bad times,
>
> When we're happy and in the sad times,
>
> He loves me and I love him.'

Mary Maudlin crooned.

"Thank Christ we're nearly there. They're bound to play it again," said Danny.
He switched channels.

Gran was working in the front garden when we got there. She wiped her
hands on her apron and shook hands. "You're later than I thought you would
be," she said. "Come inside. Tea's ready."

I don't think either of us will forget that meal in a hurry. It started off well enough. Danny made me sound like some sort of saint. I wish he wouldn't do that. It's him, not me, who is the expert housekeeper. Gran listened intently and then said "Do you think you'll still be together in ten years time?"

"I don't know really," I said. "It's a purely business arrangement, see, Gran. Neither of us knows what will happen when the present project is finished."

She smiled. "In normal circumstances, I'd ask Danny to leave before I said what I'm about to say but I won't," she said. "You, dearly beloved Grandson, haven't fooled me for the last fifteen years and if Danny is living with you without realising that you're gay, he must be the most naïve soul on this earth."

I didn't exactly choke but a slice of cucumber landed on the table cloth.

"I've known about you since you started making eyes at that nice McBrine boy," she said. "School sports day. You'd have been about eleven. Remember?"

I didn't. I looked at Danny for some sort of support. He just sat there rigid and staring at the window.

"What I want to know," said Gran, "is whether this is a Barry Freeman-type fling or are you really in love with each other."

Danny spoke. "Yes we are, Mrs Weaver," he said. Just five words, but enough to ruin me and the family.

"Thank God for an honest young man," said Gran. "Now then, I have a proposition to make. Stay together for ten years and I'll leave you my holding in Weaver's.

I couldn't believe my ears. I was already rolling up my serviette, convinced that we were about to be shown the door and told never to come back.

"Sorry Gran. What did you say?" I asked.

"What I said. There's nobody else. You're the only grandson. If you and Danny can make a go of living together for ten years, you'll jointly inherit Weaver's. I'm likely to pop my clogs before that, but I'll see the solicitors and have it all drawn up properly."

"But you don't know me, Mrs Weaver," Danny protested.

"True, but Tim's in love with you and that's enough for me. He's a devious little bugger at times, but you'll sort him out."

I protested. Gran smiled. "Picnics at Silent Lake — and I saw you in that seedy shop," she said. "And you're the young man who drove from Newcastle on a motorway that was covered with mud and arrived here with a car that looked like you'd just bought it. I was born seventy three years ago, dear — not yesterday."

"So you knew about Barry?"

"Of course I did. That's why I got him round here. You needed company."

We left her house in a daze. "Do Mum and Dad know? About me, I mean?" I asked as I got into the car.

"Your mother probably does, Tim. Not from me, but mothers generally do. As for your father, I'd say certainly not. That man wouldn't see a brick wall in front of him if he didn't want it to be there or it wasn't mentioned in some Naval manual or chart. Now, off you go. Have a good time, Danny. Come up and stay whenever you can."

"We will," I said and we drove off.

***

The first sight of Newcastle made my heart sink. True, there is a magnificent bridge and some of the buildings looked really modern. The centre might be quite nice, but Danny wanted to take a short cut. We drove through streets lined with seedy shops — 'Ali's Video Parlour', 'Take-away Fish'n'Chips', 'Immediate Cash Loans' — and I yearned for the good old south. Danny would have been far better off without me.

Then we broke out of the urban sprawl. Suddenly we were in countryside again. There was even the occasional farmhouse. Danny turned off the road and we were in an estate of really big houses. Each one was different. Some had green roofs, some were red. All of them had at least a double garage and lay back from the road, separated from it by a wide bank of neatly mown grass.

"Here we are," said Danny. He swung into the drive of one of the biggest houses in the road. It was an enormous place: much larger than my folks' house. The Taylor family were obviously rich, a fact which made me feel even more nervous. If they were as I had imagined or wished them to be, I would have felt a bit more confident. Mrs Taylor with her hair in curlers and her legs in wrinkled stockings and Mr Taylor in a cloth cap might have taken more easily to a foppish southerner who screwed their son.

'Ah well, love,' Mr. Taylor would say. 'We sent our lad to university. It were a struggle but we did it and it's not for us to complain if he gets a job down south and falls in with their funny ways.'

The real life Mr and Mrs Taylor were going to be very different. I was obviously going to be the evil influence who had corrupted their son.

'Different' was the right word. Mrs Taylor was charm itself. She came to the door as soon as Danny had put his key into the lock. She kissed him, shook hands with me and said how much she'd been looking forward to meeting me. Within minutes, we were sitting in the comfortable lounge sipping coffee and eating slices of a delicious cake she'd made and addressing her as Pat: something one just didn't do in the environment I'd grown up in.

"Tell me about this flat of yours. Is there anything else in the way of furniture that you need? Danny's always so vague about such things," she said.

I thanked her and, prompted by Danny, told her about the flat and as much as I could about the job.

"My husband and Paul won't be back for an hour or so," she said. "I've put you in the guest room. I hope that's okay."

Imagining that she was talking to me alone I said it was very kind of her. I was more than somewhat bowled over when I was in the room with Danny and realised that the double bed in the guest room was intended for us both.

She left us to unpack. I wondered if Danny was in the mood. He was, but he wanted to drive down to see his Dad at work. I went too.

That was the second huge shock. Taylor's Furnishings wasn't the shop I imagined it to be and if your conception of a warehouse is the same as mine, it wasn't a warehouse, either. It is vast; easily as big as any of the many factories we'd seen. 'Bedrooms', 'Kitchens' 'Lounges' and 'Office Furniture' each have a whole floor devoted to them. It's quite a way out of the town on the side of a major road. The car park was full of cars and they have a fleet of self-drive vans for people to take stuff home.

The third surprise was the way the staff addressed Danny. I'd expect, in a place of that size, for them to whisper about 'young Mr. Taylor'. Not a bit of it. "Hi, Danny? How's it going then?" a young man in the carpet section on the ground floor shouted.

"Not so bad. You?" Danny called back.

"Oh, okay I guess. Up for the weekend?"

"Yeah. Back to work on Monday."

"Poor sod. I've got Monday off. It's my long weekend." Then he turned away to serve a customer.

A girl on the 'Kitchens' floor called him 'Lover-boy' and blew a kiss. I'd been a bit scared that word might have got round about us. Mr. Taylor could easily have told some senior employee that his son had moved in with a queer and the word would have got round the place pretty fast. Apparently not. Danny introduced me to several people and they were as cordial as could be.

As it happened, Danny's older brother Paul was with his Dad when we were shown into the office. I knew that Paul was twenty-eight. I wasn't prepared for the good looks. Strictly between you and me, I wouldn't have said 'No'. In many ways he looked like Danny. He was a bit slimmer and a bit taller and he had a nice smile.

Mr Taylor ('Geoff to you') was a really nice, down-to-earth sort of man. He teased Danny unmercifully — and Danny did the same to him.

"I read modern history at Cambridge and then sort of drifted into this business," he explained.

"His whole life has been one long drift," said Danny. "Not a parent to be proud of. A very poor example to his hard-working sons."

"Ha! I work harder than you two layabouts put together," said Mr Taylor.

"Since when?" Paul asked.

"You must have changed a lot since I last saw you," said Danny.

It was obvious that Danny wanted to talk to his Dad alone. I wondered if it might be about me. Wrong again. Danny told me later that it was about money. Geoff suggested that Paul show me round the place. That had its moments. He made me lie next to him on a water bed to show me how comfortable it was. For a moment or two I wondered about him, but I was wrong. He knew about us though. His mother had told him. "You don't mind?" I asked as we toured the Office Furniture floor.

"Why should I? It's Danny's life. If he's happy, that's the main thing," he said.

All three of us left the building together, or I should say in our respective cars. First was Mr. Taylor in his big BMW; then Paul in his smaller one. Danny and I followed in Danny's car.

That evening at their house was a revelation. I suppose all families relax a bit over dinner but I wouldn't have dreamed of teasing my dad like Paul and Danny. They called their dad a 'silly old fool' to which he quickly struck back by referring to them as a couple of ignorant layabouts.

The mood continued after the meal. I usually hate washing-up but was glad to help. We laughed so much that it's a miracle nothing was broken.

We watched television. At ten o'clock Danny looked at his watch and raised an eyebrow. I nodded. I wondered whether someone would make some sort of remark. Nobody did. We said goodnight and went upstairs. I'd rarely been in a happier mood than I was that night.

"Shower?" he asked, as he peeled off his shirt in the bedroom.

"What about the family?" I asked. As always, anticipation had made my cock leap to attention. It was quite a struggle to get my jeans off.

"They won't come up for ages," said Danny. He pulled down his jeans and shorts together. It sprang up to greet me. Danny grinned.

"Let's not get too carried away this time," I said as I followed him into the bathroom.

"Why not? We don't have to get up early tomorrow." He closed the bathroom door behind us.

I put my hand on his behind. "You'll see," I said.

Fortunately, the Taylors' shower cubicle was bigger than ours and, in case you're puzzled over that word 'fortunately', I'd better explain...

Showering with Danny is one of the most erotic experiences I know. Soaping the bristly hairs on his head and his neck first is enough to get me going. Then, starting with his ankles and feeling his soapy fingers caressing my arse cheeks as I do so, I work slowly up his legs. Short, downy hairs give way to longer ones and then my fingers are buried deep in his bush. By that time he's well away and his cock is all mine. The problem at home is that when we are standing facing each other at least one cock ends up between the other's thighs. More often than not, it's both and then we can't stop ourselves. By the time we've wiped the spunk off the plastic curtain and the walls we're both tired and fall asleep the moment we're in bed.

The Taylors' shower was much better. I had to put an arm round his middle to draw him close enough. He did the same to me.

"Happy?" he whispered.

"Very," I replied and set to work. The water splashed down on my back as I explored his thighs, running my fingers up and down the smooth skin. His cock waggled from side to side slapping the side of my head.

"Take it if you want to," he said in a husky voice. I did want to, but there was something else I wanted even more. Obediently, he turned round. His behind shone white. I soaped his cheeks. Little rivulets of foam ran down his legs. I kept on, kneading and massaging, working the soap deep into his furrow. He grunted. I stopped. He turned round and clasped my cock in his foam-covered hand. He grinned.

"Hard as iron," he said. I put my arms round his waist and let my hands drop down onto his bottom. "Soft as butter," I replied. "Just like it should be."

"You going to fuck me?" he asked.

"Too right I am, but not in the shower. Come on. Let's go.

He turned the water pressure up. The last remnants of soap ran away. We stepped out.

"Want me to dry you?" he asked.

"If you like."

It was quite an experience. He'd never done it before. He rubbed my head and my upper part briskly, pausing for a moment to play with my nipples. I had to tell him to stop. Then he moved down. The drying became more gentle. He crouched down and played with my cock and my balls. I would have thought it hardly possible but his cock seemed to be stiffening even more as he did so.

"Going to do it nice and slowly?" he asked, sliding my foreskin back and tickling the head with the corner of the towel.

"I'll try," I said. "Come on. Let's get a move on."

He made a cursory attempt to dry himself. More of a show, really. I love the feel of his skin when he's slightly damp and, by the time we've finished, he's dry again — at least on the outside!

Once we were in the bedroom, he flung himself face down onto the bed. He turned his head to watch me fumbling in my bag for the cream.

"Not too much," he said.

"Okay." I found the tube. He spread his legs wide open. I held the tube in both hands for a few moments to warm it. I parted his buns and squeezed out a few drops; then a few more. The one or two wispy hairs growing round it gleamed.

"Just a bit more," I said, squeezing the bottle again. A bubble formed and then vanished. He sighed as I pushed against it with my finger. Slowly, his resistance lessened. I pushed slightly harder and my finger slid down into him. He sighed again, more loudly. I wiggled my finger. This time he moaned; a signal, with Danny, that he was ready for something rather more substantial though, as always, he gripped my finger hard as I pulled it out.

I poured oil onto the palm of my hand, transferred it to my cock and climbed up onto the bed.

"Slowly," he said. His voice was muffled by the pillow.

I tried. I certainly went into him slowly. He gave a long drawn-out sigh. A soft warmth enveloped my cock. His muscles gripped it, rippling along the shaft as it went in. He jerked as it touched his button, lifting his behind several inches into the air. His soft buns quivered against my groin. He lifted his arms as if he was going to fly and then put his hands on my backside, pressing me even further into him. All thoughts of doing it slowly evaporated. I thrust as hard as I could.

"Oh! Ah! Oh! Ah!" he gasped.

I tried hard to hold back. I always do, but by the time I shot into him, he was writhing wildly, lifting himself up against me and moaning. He carried on for some time. I desperately wanted my cock to stay hard for his orgasm. It did. Probably, I think, because it was clenched so hard. I slid my hands underneath him and felt his nipples, his belly and then his cock. It was hard, warm and wet.

"Oh yeah! Oh yeah! Yeah!" he panted and sank down on to the bed again. His weight pressed against my arms and my fingers caught the full warm, viscous flood.

"Jesus, that was good!" he said.

"Sure was," I replied. I kissed the back of his neck.

You probably know more about psychology than I do. You couldn't possibly know less. I often wondered why that time was the best. Was it because it was in a strange bedroom? Was it because of his family's acceptance? I don't know, but we both talk of it as 'a night to remember'.

We didn't sleep much. We just lay there hugging each other and feeling each other like it was the first time.

The following morning and most of the afternoon was taken up with visiting his various relations. They are nice people. I loved his grandfather. He was a dear old man and had me in fits with his stories. Danny had heard them all before, but he laughed as well.

Then came time to dress for the reunion; an opportunity for a quick feel and for me to relish the prospect of having it inside me when the festivities were over.

They were held in the 'aula'; a word I'd never heard before. It was a vast hall on the university campus.

"You won't mind if I mix a bit?" said Danny.

"Of course not. You go ahead."

He did. I watched him dance first with one girl, then another and another. They smiled and laughed. Once or twice, during the slower numbers, he whispered into their ears and they looked over at me and smiled. Were they welcoming me or laughing at me? I didn't know. What had he said?

'See that guy sitting over there by the bar? He's terrific. I work with him,' or

'See that guy sitting over there by the bar? He's a queer.'

I had a beer. The band played a tune I could dance to, so I found myself a partner; a really nice girl as it turned out, and from my part of the world. She was a medical student. The next was equally as nice. I bought her a drink and things started to go wrong. Working with missiles designed to kill people was, in her view, the worst thing anyone could do. She was studying animal husbandry and thought nothing of keeping animals in conditions worse than in any concentration camp. I was glad when another guy came up and took her off my hands.

Then there was the one who was doing research on shrimps' eyes. Something to do with keeping them in exactly the right depth of water in fish farms before boiling them alive. She considered me brutal and unfeeling too.

All the time I kept looking over at Danny. It was difficult to believe that he was the guy I'd spent the night with; the guy who I'd been kissing and cuddling and who had done the same to me. Watching him making up to the girls didn't make me angry. I was just puzzled. Things got worse when the dinner was served. I thought he'd sit with me and found a table in the corner. I waved him over but he shook his head and escorted a rather pretty blonde to a table on the other side of the hall. He smiled at her. She smiled back and put her hand on his wrist.

"Is this free?" I looked up. The speaker was an attractive dark-haired girl.

"Sure," I said and made a clumsy attempt to get up so that I could help her into the chair.

"Don't bother," she said. "You're Tim, Danny's friend aren't you? I've heard a lot about you."

For a moment I wondered if she was Wendy, Danny's ex-girlfriend who had given him such a difficult time.

"I'm Claire," she said. "I was in Danny's tutor group."

"Oh yes?"

"He's a great guy, isn't he?" she said. I looked over towards the great guy who, at that moment, was nibbling his companion's fingers.

"I don't really know him that well," I said. It was true. The Danny I was watching was totally different to the one I lived with.

"You can be honest," said Claire. "He tells me everything. He thinks the world of you."

I nearly said that he had a funny way of showing it. Instead I said something about my undetected faults, which made her laugh.

A waiter filled our wine glasses. Another brought the soup.

"I just wish he'd come out," said Claire, sipping her wine delicately.

"He has at home," I said.

"I know. That took a load of courage. I really admire him for doing that. Do the people you work with know?"

I nearly choked. It's just as well I didn't. Claire's beautiful pale blue dress would have been spattered with asparagus soup.

"He couldn't — we couldn't — even if we wanted to," I said and tried to explain that people working on secret defence contracts just didn't admit to that sort of thing.

"I don't see why not," she said.

"It's a question of blackmail risks, really," I said. "If some foreign government were to find out, they'd have a sort of lever to use against you. 'Tell us all you know or we'll spill the beans.' That sort of thing."

"But if the firm knew about it already, it wouldn't matter, would it?"

It was a thought I'd never considered before.

"I think the real reason is your southern reserve," said Claire. "What about your parents? Do they know?"

"There doesn't seem to be any reason to tell them," I said. "It would only upset them."

She smiled. "I rest my case," she said.

She was a really nice girl. We talked about all sorts of things — including Wendy.

"She isn't here by any chance, is she?" I asked. I was beginning to wonder if she was the girl whose company Danny was so obviously enjoying and whether, at the end of the evening, Danny was going to announce that they were together again.

"Wendy? Good God, no! You obviously don't know Wendy."

"I never had the pleasure," I replied.

"You must be one of the few that haven't," said Claire. She went on to tell me that Wendy had been 'engaged' twice since Danny and she split up.

"Those are the official ones," she continued. "God knows how many manly members she's had apart from them. She's quite a connoisseur of manly members, is our Wendy. The area membership secretary, so to speak."

"I can see what she saw in Danny then," I said, without thinking. I blushed. Claire laughed.

"There you are," she said. "Now you're beginning to open up. That's how you should be all the time. Don't bottle it up."

I don't think I've enjoyed a meal more than I enjoyed that one. I found myself telling Claire about things I hadn't told Danny. My school adventures; the dreadful time I'd had at university after Andrew Forge told everyone I'd tried to rape him and my more recent adventures. It all came out.

"Are you..." I asked

"No. Depressingly hetero. That's me. We have one thing in common, Tim. We both fancy men, speaking of which, he's got a nice bottom don't you think?"

"Danny?"

"No, the lad going out to the toilet."

I turned round to look. "It's okay, I suppose," I said. In fact he had one of the nicest behinds I'd seen for a long time.

"You're not being honest again," said Claire. "Now tell me what you really think."

"It's very nice. Very nice indeed. I wonder what he's hung like."

"That's it. Say what you really think. You could always follow him and have a peep."

"Definitely not my scene," I said. "I hope I never sink to that level."

"I don't think you ever will," said Claire. "Not while you've got Danny."

After the meal we danced a few times. Then Claire left me. I sat at the bar and watched. She danced with Danny a few times. I couldn't see his dinner companion but the hall was very crowded. The whole scene reminded me of my college days — the most miserable time of my life. The beer was stronger than the stuff I am used to drinking and it was probably that which set a train of melancholy thoughts going. Maybe I would end up in public urinals, peering at penises. I wanted desperately to talk to Claire again to tell her how I really felt but she was sitting in a corner talking to Danny. She seemed to be making a point with some vehemence. I saw her tap his kneecap with her finger. He nodded and stood up and walked right through the swirling couples on the dance floor.

"Seen some other bird he fancies," I muttered.

"Beg pardon?" said the barman.

"Oh. Nothing."

I was wrong. Danny waited until the band had finished playing and then went up on stage and spoke to the band-leader who nodded. Danny climbed down and walked over to me.

"What's up?" I asked.

He took the glass out of my hand and placed it carefully on the bar. Then he smiled and grasped my hand and nodded to the band-leader. I recognised the tune straight away. Danny put his arm round my waist and started to sing softly.

"The boy I love is always near me," he crooned. I felt him trying to swing me round.

"He stays with me through thick and thin," he continued. Somehow, my feet seemed to follow his. Someone clapped. As we turned I saw who it was. Claire. She smiled.

"In the good times..." Danny sang.

"And the bad times," I added.

"When we're happy and in the sad times," we both sang. More people were clapping. I felt light-headed; as if I might faint at any moment. The applause was coming from all round us, getting louder and louder every second. Danny's chin was resting on my shoulder. I lay my head on his arm and took a deep breath. I wanted them all to hear.

"He loves me and I love him," I sang — and Danny kissed me.

Other books in the PROWLER BOOKS collection:

Fiction:
Diary of a Hustler
• ISBN 0-9524647-64
Slaves
• ISBN 0-9524647-99
Young Cruisers
• ISBN 0-9524647-72
Corporal in Charge
• ISBN 0-95246478-0
Hard
• ISBN 0-902644-01-8
Active Service
• ISBN 0-902644-06-9
the Young and the Hung
• ISBN 0-902644-07-7
Aroused
• ISBN 0-902644-08-5
Brad
• ISBN 0-902644-09-3
Summer Sweat
• ISBN 0-902644-10-7
Campus Confessions
• ISBN 0-902644-11-5
Going Down
• ISBN 0-902644-12-3

Photographic:
Planet Boys
• ISBN 0-9524647-13
Kama Sutra of Gay Sex
• ISBN 0-9524647-05

Travel:
New York Scene Guide
• ISBN 1-90264400-X
Paris Scene Guide
• ISBN 1-902644-02-6